MUCK

DROR BURSTEIN

TRANSLATED FROM THE HEBREW BY
GABRIEL LEVIN

FARRAR, STRAUS AND GIROUX

NEW YORK

Farrar, Straus and Giroux
175 Varick Street, New York 10014

Library of Congress Cataloging-in-Publication Data
Names: Burshtain, Deror, author. | Levin, Gabriel, 1948– translator.
Title: Muck / Dror Burstein ; translated from the Hebrew by Gabriel Levin.
Other titles: Ṭiṭ. English
Description: First American edition. | New York : Farrar, Straus and
    Giroux, 2018.
Identifiers: LCCN 2018017730 | ISBN 9780374215835 (hardcover)
Classification: LCC PJ5055.17.U7 T5713 2018 | DDC 892.43/7—dc23
LC record available at https://lccn.loc.gov/2018017730

Designed by Abby Kagan

1   3   5   7   9   10   8   6   4   2

Published by arrangement with the Institute for the Translation
of Hebrew Literature

CONTENTS

PART ONE

JEHOIAKIM

1

BROCH, THE AGING CRITIC, scheduled all his appointments for twelve o'clock sharp, as he liked to say, and woe betide anyone who was late: at 12:01 he would secure his door with three bolts—the large, the very large, and the huge—lower his weighty drapes, and affect the expression of revulsion he reserved for just such moments of deep disappointment in our national poets and writers. The writers could pound on his door till midnight—to no avail; the poets could drum their fingertips all they liked on the stuccoed walls of this citadel of the beleaguered art of literary criticism in the Jerusalem neighborhood of Beit Hakerem. But: An author who fails to arrive precisely on time to an appointment is bound to be equally imprecise in writing a sentence, and I have nothing to offer or advise anyone who isn't going to be precise in writing a sentence. You arranged to meet me at twelve o'clock sharp? So come at twelve o'clock sharp. Not at five past twelve, no, or at twenty to one, nor at four-forty-five! Come at twelve o'clock sharp or don't come at all.

Broch: As for his first name, no one had a clue. All sorts of possibilities were flung into the empty air, but no one knew for sure, and in the end people started believing that he didn't actually have one. There was a story going around that at the age of eighteen he went to the Ministry of the Interior, applied for a change of name, then blotted out his forename in the civil registry and made a break for it; the clerk, who'd been waiting for the applicant to enter in his new preference, was astonished to discover that the person who'd been sitting opposite him had vanished, and in this way Broch's birth name was expunged and no new one ever took its place, and there was nothing anyone could do about it. His published articles all carried his handwritten signature, *Broch*, plain and simple: the *B* invariably emphasized and just as invariably followed by a brutal little *o* swinging from galley proofs like a hangman's noose, the sort of noose that slips around your neck only when you're already yearning for the sweet release of death, your head cocked and keen as—in your life's final delirium—you regret ever having published that ridiculous book of yours . . . but no, no, by now it's too late.

Broch the critic would dole out his critiques gratis to penniless writers by virtue of his own sense of prestige and public-spiritedness, nailing authors to their places once and for all on the map of Hebrew literature for generations to come, and with a perseverance arousing both admiration and sorrow. And Jeremiah, who'd written what he'd written, and published what he'd published (one book of poems, one novel), and had been forgotten as he'd been forgotten—conclusively, and at the age of twenty—approached the door hesitantly, rang the bell as he'd been instructed, precisely at noon—synchronized with the first warning notes of the twelve o'clock news—so as to avoid finding the gate locked, so as to avoid his own shamefaced expulsion, to say nothing of possibly provoking the dog, the critic's legendary canine, Sargon, since not infrequently Broch would blow his top and set Sargon on tardy young poets and writers, or even on those who just couldn't answer a few simple questions correctly. Have you visited the poetess Zelda's grave this year? He liked to surprise his visitors with questions that were bound to trip them up. No, no one visited, they all forgot. And what are you reading of Gnessin's these days? Nothing, no, they hadn't read him. And that was the end of them. Jeremiah rang the bell, which was—it was no myth, he was seeing it now with his very own eyes—molded to resemble the face of an editor of a book series devoted to innovative nonfiction and much despised by the house's occupant. On the critic's door was plainly written: BROCH. The voice of the newscaster erupted from within the house, merging with Sargon's barking: the dog had tensed up, sensing an intruder outside.

The door opened. Eyes in which flared just a trace of courteous loathing greeted Jeremiah. A white, dry hand limply clasped his own before Jeremiah found himself seated in a high wooden chair, a touch higher than usual, while Broch sank into the depths of his enormous armchair—all the tall tales about the critic's furnishings being proved right before the poet's eyes. It was said that even Broch's furniture penned reviews, late at night; that Broch's bookshelf had trashed more than one novel in the weekly literary supplement; that his rocking chair ran a regular poetry column. Take off your sandals, Broch suggested, I'll wash your feet; I've already prepared a bowl of warm water and soap, and I bought a towel just for you. Jeremiah froze in fear but did as he was told. Broch's colossal private library stood before him like the rampart of a fortress, its height and breadth greater than the National Library's own collection, indeed containing several volumes that the National Library did not. National Library librarians and the king's own librarians would arrive every now and then and abase themselves before the critic so that he might lend them a rare title, while he, they said, prepared them individual library cards, which he then stamped with a violet seal that included each book's allotted lending time, measured not in days but in quarter hours. All my books are available for limited loan periods only, he ruled. People would sit in his backyard and thumb through book after book, leaning against the dumpster and the huge gas canisters, copying down in haste whatever they were looking for.

I must say, the critic began, as he rubbed Jeremiah's feet dry with the towel, I was very impressed by your last collection of poems, and even more so . . . by the novel. What a novel. It's a magnum opus. You've written the book of Job for our times, he told Jeremiah, who strapped his sandals back on, aghast, while Broch set a pot of coffee on to boil, which he scrupulously served with sweet pastries. Jeremiah stared suspiciously at Broch's rocking chair, took a sip from his cup, and nearly seared his tongue. The thick layer of foam topping the coffee had been whipped to perfection, clotted and rich, and what it lacked in sweetness was made up for by the delicious sweet pastry, a recipe bequeathed to the critic by the late Mrs. Broch (1899–1969, also the author of a doctoral dissertation on the poetess Bat-Miriam). Allow me to clip your toenails, said Broch; a poet must be careful to clip his nails evenly. I fear black lint from your socks has wedged itself under your nails; permit me to poke around in there with a toothpick, and then I'll begin our talk with a few fundamental principles concerning the masterful formation of the character of Frederick in your first novel, *Spite*, Broch said. And Jeremiah— blood drained from his face, and he started to sweat profusely, and his toenails shook like false teeth in the cold, since he'd never written a novel called *Spite*, nor had he ever dreamed of conjuring up a character like Frederick. Death had blown in and gotten all tangled up in his hair like a raven, and it—the raven, that is—was struggling in vain to free itself. His heart stopped beating. He stood up shakily and set his bitter coffee and the crumbs of his pastry aside. Sir, will you forgive me, he stuttered, there must have been a mistake. I didn't write . . . and Frederick? But no . . . The critic rose to his feet and stood there at his full, enormous height, leaning against his similarly enormous armchair, his head striking the ceiling, his arms spreading out and nearly reaching the huge windows. No? How so? Are you not the author Ernesto Bograshov, born in Buenos Aires, 1940? Jeremiah, who'd never heard of said Bograshov and was fifty years younger than the señor, muttered that, no, he feared not, that it didn't seem to him that—that no. The critic was stunned for a moment. I don't understand; surely you're pulling my leg, my dear Ernesto, making fun of an old critic of Hebrew literature in his dotage, but why . . . ? Why the mockery? Stand and unfold yourself! *Nu*, Buenos Aires . . . After all, we walked arm in arm on the promenade running the length of the Assado . . . And then Broch stopped, convulsed with laughter. Certainly, certainly not Ernesto Bograshov, rest assured, *there is no such author*, ha-ha. Ernesto Bograshov—what a fine name he'd concocted. He was only jerking Jeremiah's chain, putting him to the test, just a bit of drollery, he chortled, as he wiped his tears and wept from laughter. Sit down, Jeremiah, sit down, the old man gurgled out of his only lung, you needn't be so upset. We have ahead of us a lecture of four to five hours. I've been applying myself to your writing for a month and a half, but there's no harm in opening with a bit of banter; we'll have plenty of time to be serious. Forgive me my little flight of fancy . . . It can be dry as dust in here, with all the boring literature that your friends produce . . . A bit of humor now and then . . . And Broch sank back into the armchair and gathered the last shreds of his belly laugh like a heap of quivering petals. But before we start with your book of poems, did you bring what I asked you? For an instant Jeremiah didn't understand, but soon remembered, of course, and bent over, removed the keyboard of his home computer from his shoulder bag, wrapped in a wrinkled plastic bag from the supermarket, and handed it over. The 12:30 p.m. *Breaking News* announced Egypt's unconditional surrender to Babylon, and Broch aimed his house slipper at the radio and silenced the newscaster. Sargon barked at the radio, and Broch removed his other slipper and cut the dog short as well.

The critic gripped the black keyboard, out of whose side dangled a black cord like a rodent's long tail, got to his feet, and strode up to the north window, where he inspected the letters in the soft light. Jeremiah began to munch noisily at another crumbly pastry. How interesting, the letter *H* and the letter *P* are completely worn down on the keyboard. Also, the *S* is beginning to fade, like a decaying milk tooth. Excuse me, yes? But your *H* is completely erased, and the *R* looks like a sickly *P*. Haven't you thought of having the poor letters retouched? Eh? Jeremiah didn't answer—he kept on munching as he thumbed through some early reviews by Broch in an old issue of *Horologe* in which the old man had sentenced to death an entire *pléiade*—and Broch waited in vain for an answer and continued: Or is it that the letters *H* and *P* are maybe—how shall I put it?—are so insignificant in your eyes that you feel you needn't bother taking your keyboard in for repairs? Eh? Please, can you speak up! Stop mumbling as though you're standing at the door of a house of ill repute, Mr. Righteous, he said in a friendly tone. Jeremiah raised his eyes from the issue he was perusing and said: Uh, what's that? To tell you the truth, I type blindly, I don't look at the keyboard, so it doesn't really matter; in my view, all the letters might as well be rubbed out.

A dead silence hung over the room, as though an enormous plague-blanket had been flung over a city already under siege and numb with cold. Sargon sneaked under the round tabletop. It doesn't really matter, the critic repeated in a tone flat as an echo, and for the first time Jeremiah thought he detected a certain frostiness in Broch's voice. It doesn't matter, he said to himself again. It doesn't matter, he said, and turned to Sargon. We wash his feet and risk catching who knows what, but it doesn't matter to him. Broch turned over the black rat and tapped its back, and all sorts of tiny bits of grit and orphaned staples fell from the interstices between the keys. You know, Broch pondered as he looked from the fallout to the table, what the problem is with your generation? Come to think of it, with the entire new wave of Hebrew literature, not counting a few well-known exceptions? Let me tell you. Come on and learn a thing or two. Up to now you've been gushing on like an unstoppable sprinkler; up to now you've hosed me down both inside and out, like at a car wash. You've flushed down the engine for me and waxed the body against my will. Thanks a lot, but now let the old man get in a word edgewise. May I? And all of a sudden he roared, Will you put down that miserable *Horologe*? Glued to *Horologe* like a starving woodworm, enough is enough!

Jeremiah shut the literary journal and pushed it aside, and Broch whispered, Thank you, and sat down. So, as to your question, here's the problem: You all—how did you put it?—type blindly. You said it, to me. Blindly. The letters of the alphabet merely provide a service, as far as you're concerned. Have you heard of the *Book of Creation*? In thirty-two wondrous paths of wisdom YH YHWH of the Hosts carved His world—does that sentence mean anything to you? And Jeremiah said, Of course, it . . . But the critic cut in: If so, then *why*—well, go ahead, explain to the senile Terah who brought upon himself this catastrophe called literary criticism—why won't you show some mercy toward your faded letters, to the erased *H*, to *R*? Don't you realize what you're doing? No, you don't have a clue. And why? Because, in your view, if *you* know what letter is there, everything is okay; you, after all—how did you put it?—*type blindly*! But the letters, who's going to defend the letters that you're wearing down and erasing and destroying with your sweaty fingertips day after day? Who will defend *their* integrity? And Jeremiah assumed that Broch was kidding again, and at once relaxed, and started to chuckle. Broch, astounded by the poet-writer's crass laughter, stood up, the black keyboard clasped in both hands. He approached Jeremiah in measured strides and in one fell stroke struck Jeremiah's head with the peripheral. Jeremiah was transfixed from the shock. Blood gushed and trickled down toward his right eyebrow. Broch then pounded the stricken keyboard against the edge of the table, again and again. Keys flew out, and Broch made sure to smash the remaining ones to bits before proceeding to place the keyboard on the floor and setting the heel of his shoe down on the numeric pad at one end—whatever was left of it—while reaching down to twist the other end out of shape with his bare hands. The bowl of soapy foot-water spilled on the carpet, and Sargon barked angrily at its incontinence. Jeremiah tried to staunch his bleeding with one hand while using the other to rummage for something, a piece of paper, with which he could improvise a bandage, but Broch, perceiving this, flung the crooked keyboard in the direction of the poet and again struck him in the face; Jeremiah slumped over and fell from the wooden chair, and Broch stooped over him and fixed a nifty-looking noose out of the keyboard cord and started to strangle him. Don't think you can debase the alphabet in my home, he whispered into his ear. You'll write literature only after honoring each and every letter. I won't let you fuck over the *S* like you fucked over the *H* and the *R*. There's an *R* in my name; I'm extra sensitive about honoring the *R*. You want my advice, here's my advice: a novel is made of sentences, and sentences of words, and words—of letters. But maybe words aren't made out of letters now?! he screamed into Jeremiah's ears—Jeremiah, who couldn't breathe because of the keyboard cord. Perhaps books are made out of Google, perhaps words are made out of the Internet, out of Facebook, out of all those screens of yours, all you writers inundating me in this inferno of pulp fiction? Why aren't you writing with a pencil in a notebook? Why type all the time? And why keep dashing every day to be published? Reams dispatched to the printers, *but none of it deserves to be printed*, Broch screamed into Jeremiah's bleeding face as the poet struggled to thrust his fingers between the electrical cord and his skin, turning blue, *none* of it deserves to be printed; that's why you really, really, really don't need your keyboard, which I've shattered; you'll thank me yet for having destroyed your keyboard, because *this keyboard is your delusion*, the delusion that what you write is ready to see print—and it isn't, it *doesn't deserve* to be printed, those printed letters are blinding you, you're blind, *you're typing blindly*, as you yourself told me, you confessed to your own guilt and handed over to me the contemning word, you and your entire generation, blind writers typing blindly. Agnon stood upright day after day and wrote by hand until he lost all feeling in his lower back; Gnessin toiled in a printer's workshop, the lead gnawed under his nails and into his heart, with his ailing heart he breathed in the lead of the letters, and the lead smothered his heart, but he didn't think for a moment *to type blindly*, no. Letter after letter, he arranged! Letter after letter! Letter after letter!

BARELY MANAGING TO FREE HIMSELF from Broch's garrote, Jeremiah crawled away over the carpet. Sargon and the critic both—and both were now, for some reason, on all fours—glared at him as though he were an intruding cat. The critic's eyes were flecked with capillaries. Shock and blood blurred Jeremiah's vision. He grabbed his shoulder bag, stood up unsteadily, and started to look for the door while groping along the length of the walls and knocking over his cup of coffee. He couldn't find the way out—the room was lined with books, every inch of the walls with books and more books, and he understood that even the door must be blocked by bookshelves—nor could he locate a window. Mr. Broch, please . . . he muttered. I've got to leave now. And the critic said, Are you nuts? We haven't said a thing about your collection of poems yet, or about your novel; you didn't make an appointment with me just to eat some pastries. But I'm hurt, Jeremiah said, and Broch answered, Well, I've also been hurt, time and time again, there isn't a day when I don't get hurt, okay? As if you poets didn't love making me bleed! Undoubtedly, you know that the ever-so-courteous Fogel, Fogel the suave novice, once slashed at my stomach with a penknife . . . that Brenner once shot at me with a Turkish pistol . . . Whoever writes literature, all the more so whoever writes criticism, let him count on being badly wounded! These are the front lines; this is the true field of battle. So I caressed you on the head with a keyboard— that's what you call a wound? Well, well, aren't you sensitive . . . Okay, I hurt you, but I'll bandage your wound. That's my duty as a critic; sit down while I shave your head and disinfect and bandage your wound, and then we'll finally get to the heart of my literary analysis of your work. He opened a drawer and took out an electric sheep-shearing razor and a first-aid kit and placed them on the stack of comments he'd prepared. Jeremiah objected, but the critic brandished the keyboard again threateningly. Believe me, you've gotten off lightly, Broch told him. But I'm obliged to stitch you up. And he picked up and shook the bottle of disinfectant.

2

HEAD SHAVED, bandaged, and with a broken keyboard, Jeremiah rode the light rail to his parents' home. Only six months ago, he'd rented an apartment on Ha-Yarmukh Street, and he still hadn't moved all his books and belongings into his new place. In order not to have to answer the likely questions about his bruises, he crawled through the window. He sat at his desk and thought of writing something, but he couldn't write without the keyboard. He'd just about forgotten how to write by hand and was ashamed of his handwriting, which seemed to him like the scrawl of a nursery-school child. He sat there in front of the desk, mortified by the anguish Broch had caused him. Outside, he could see through the window the new, fierce star that glowed in the bright midday light. Several days ago, its light had become visible even at noon. They said that its diameter during its lifespan was 440 times the size of the sun, and that if it had been positioned at the center of the solar system its outer fringes would have licked the dust between Mars and Jupiter. Now, having exploded at the end of its days, it shone almost like a bright full moon. After the initial excitement, no one took any notice anymore—how long, after all, can one go on applauding a ruined star?

He peered for a long time at the dead red giant. And he dozed off upright in his chair in his parents' home in the ancient village of Anatot, just north of Jerusalem, at four o'clock in the afternoon. He didn't know whether his parents were home. Silence reigned in every room, or might his ears have been closed to their voices and movements? And the silence was as long as the night. But the following morning he woke to the sound of a voice at dawn. The star was still there, a strong and steady and distant light, and Jeremiah didn't think it strange that the star hadn't budged from its place, even though, after all, it was supposed to have set by now, off to shed its light on others. Not until several hours later, when he'd have taken out his notepad and jotted down from memory what he'd been told in the early-morning hours, would he somehow succeed in understanding what had been said, its meaning and purpose, where the voice was leading, and what it was demanding of him. When the voice spoke, the words seemed transparent, verging on music, like a song in a foreign tongue that you marvel at but must translate in order to grasp fully. Before I formed you in the belly I knew you, and before you came forth out of the womb I sanctified you, the voice said, I have appointed you a prophet to the nations. And Jeremiah didn't understand what was said to him, and what was happening. Mutely, his body shouted: What? What?

It was a little less than an hour after the voice had addressed him before he opened his mouth to answer. I was very late in answering, he would think later. He figured he'd speak to the open window, since he didn't know where else to reply. The rolling hills between Anatot and the length of Wadi Qelt loomed out of the dark beneath the star as though in evening prayer. For a moment Jeremiah felt like giggling and switching on the light in order to have done with all this, but he sensed that the matter was serious, even if it wasn't the first time he'd heard such a voice. Some ten years ago, in the middle of summer camp—or, to be more precise, in the middle of a youth science club at summer camp—when he was thirteen, he'd ignored the voice, he'd shut his eyes and covered his ears with the palms of his hands, closed his mouth tight, and not answered, and the voice had finally desisted.

Jeremiah recalled what he'd said, back then, with his mouth closed, in the summer camp: Ah, Lord, behold I cannot speak, for I am a child. And since he had nothing else to say, he said it now as well, aloud. But now he was twenty-two. And right away, from behind him, an answer was heard. Do not say: I am a child, said the voice. And Jeremiah answered, But I'm scared. He meant to say that he was scared of whomever he was talking to; that he was afraid of turning his head and seeing who was speaking, and most of all afraid of the possibility that he wouldn't see anyone there. But the voice pretended not to understand what exactly was frightening Jeremiah, and said, Do not be afraid of them, for I am with you to rescue you. And Jeremiah recoiled in fear—to rescue you? He opened his mouth to answer and shut his eyes. The torn star rose in the darkness of his closed eyes, and in the darkness that descended on him he felt a coarse hand touching his mouth, like Grandpa had touched his mouth a long time ago, when he worked as a steelworker, and the voice said—this time emanating from within the hand itself—Now I have put my words in your mouth. See today I appoint you—the voice began, and Jeremiah continued, in his own voice, as though he were reciting a portion of the Bible he'd learned back in elementary school—over nations and over kingdoms. To root out and to pull down. To destroy and to overthrow. To build and to plant.

Then: silence, as though everything had already been said, and it was possible to start walking on the trail the words had blazed and would continue to blaze. Jeremiah hadn't noticed it yet, but his voice changed at that very moment; his voice would be from now on the voice of him who'd spoken to him, as if he'd been trying to mimic the voice and his voice had gotten stuck that way.

The sun's outer rim edged over Anatot, and light from the new star faded. When Jeremiah opened his eyes, he found himself in the botanical gardens on Mount Scopus, overlooking his parents' home from on high. He didn't remember going up there and told himself, I must have been transported by some other means. He gazed at a branch without flower or fruit or leaf, directly in front of him. Am I still dreaming? Jeremiah asked, and the voice shot back, What do you see, Jeremiah? And Jeremiah said, I see the branch of an almond tree. And the voice said, You have seen well. And after some time—during which the bough grew three meters high and branched out and put forth serrated leaves and white flowers and a green fruit and roots of its own, and swarms of bees alighted on the flowers and flew off and returned, and sweet, irrigating waters streamed by in rivulets, and fish swam in the waters, and insects kicked at their reflections in the water, and all of nature reeled around him and around the tree—the voice went on to explain: For I am watching over my word to perform it. The almond tree faded away and shortly reappeared and grew transparent inside Jeremiah's body and blossomed inside his head. When he opened his mouth to say something, a bitter almond stuck to his tongue. He had a locket with a snapshot of a girl he'd loved a long time ago; they were photographed together over there, in the bookstore above the lake. He'd dreamed once that he was walking beside her in an almond grove, and everything was white, even the mountain that towered beside them. And once he dreamed that there was someone else in the dream, someone chasing them both. Jeremiah placed the almond from his tongue inside the locket and snapped the lid shut. He didn't even think it strange that the locket was the exact shape and size of the new almond, as though it had been given to him by the girl he'd once loved with the certainty that a day would come. A Piper plane flew overhead and skywrote a message in dreadful pink. But the message was in Akkadian, and Jeremiah was unable to decipher the cuneiform contrail.

He turned to stare at the new neighborhoods of North Jerusalem and beheld above the homes a hovering circle of stainless steel. At first he thought it was the new star, but, no, it was a pot, similar to the old saucepans his mother used. And it was obvious that the gigantic pot was seething even though it was empty. The pot had no handles and was ashen, like the setting sun. Indeed, the sun, the star, and the pot all shone in the sky, a blazing trio. Flames approached the pot and singed its silvery metal. Its bottom was pointing north, as if a fire there were bringing its formless contents to a boil. Crows cawed under Jeremiah's feet. The pot glared at him, and though the pot had no eyes or mouth or nose, it was clear that it was gaping at the city, too. From within the locket, from within the almond, the voice burst out, now speaking into Jeremiah's chest. It asked, the way someone shut in a cave might ask whoever is outside: What do you see, Jeremiah? And Jeremiah answered, I see a seething pot, tilted away from the north. And in a split second he understood and explained to himself, and the words in his mouth were as red as a burn: Out of the north calamity shall break out on all the inhabitants of the land. He looked north and east. He didn't see a thing there, only the village where he was born, Anatot, and deserted Ramallah. A wind swept through the botanical garden, causing all the branches and leaves to sway for several moments at precisely the same angle, in unison. Jeremiah covered his eyes to protect them from the whirling cloud of dust.

A BEARDED SOLDIER with a gas mask strapped to his face sat next to him, reading a book on the train from Ammunition Hill to the center of town. Jeremiah fell asleep, and the soldier, who was in the window seat, shook him awake. He wanted to get off, and told Jeremiah, moments before they arrived at the Shimon

Ha-Tzaddik stop, as if striking up a casual conversation: But you gird up your loins, stand up and tell them everything that I command you. Don't break down before them, or I will break you before them. Jeremiah didn't catch the sudden, insinuated threat in the soldier's words—in fact, none of it made much sense to him. He wanted to reach out and touch the soldier, but something kept them apart. The car reeled from side to side, and Jeremiah heard: And I for my part have made you today a fortified city, an iron pillar, and a bronze wall, against the whole land. They will fight against you, but they shall not prevail against you, for I am with you to save you. To save? Jeremiah wanted to ask. Save how, and from what? He opened his eyes in the empty car, and the conductor stood impatiently before him, holding a bottle of water, intending to empty its contents on him to wake him up; and Jeremiah slumped for a moment on top of the book the soldier had forgotten when he left the train car, murmured an apology, crossed the tracks, and entered another train, which was traveling in the opposite direction, just as it slid into the Mount Herzl stop, arriving from Ein Karem and grinding to a halt, its doors whooshing open, seemingly just for him. Someone said, Get in. And someone else grumbled in the crush of commuters.

A new prophet, whom Jeremiah hadn't noticed before, was standing and prophesying there on the light rail from Mount Herzl to the center of town. The prophet was very young, maybe twelve years old. Prophets seemed to be getting younger and younger lately. As the strength of the Babylonians rose in their distant land, according to rumor, so, too, did the strength of the prophets in Judah. Who would have believed that the walls of the everlasting Assyrian Empire would one day crack? Prophets came and went, prophesying the ruin of its capital, Nineveh, but Nineveh stood like an elephant with a hundred legs, and everyone took for granted that it would remain standing, more or less, in perpetuity. The prophets shouted till they were hoarse, but the walls of Nineveh only grew thicker, and while the prophets foamed at the mouth, the Assyrian army only added more legions, and more kingdoms knelt at their feet and bowed to and fro seven times, as was the custom. Nineveh was a large city, a three-day walk—that is to say, it took three days to circumnavigate its walls on foot, but no one ever crossed Nineveh on foot, since it had a nonstop express subway that made the rounds in ten minutes flat and operated day and night. It was said that it never paused in its journey.

We need lots of money, of course, the twelve-year-old prophet said, as the light rail headed east. Without money, how are we going to stand against the Babylonians, also called the Chaldeans, that most bitter of nations? Ladies and gentlemen, it was revealed to me, and I beheld in the skies cuneiform inscriptions, and they soared above the skies of Jerusalem in shades of pinkish red, and they seemed to me like sticks, and they seemed like pins, and I interpret them now as swords thrust into the flesh of a captive. Between the two rivers they write on clay and they bake the writing in fire, and the writing isn't destroyed but, rather, hardens. It isn't like Egyptian papyrus, the prophet sneered, where all it takes is one match to burn down an entire library. They might use the same old form of writing the Assyrians used, but their words will be sharp and new, like razors on our necks. With the Babylonians, the prophet called out, the wilder the fire, the firmer the writing; every conflagration preserves their writings for another hundred years. In other words, prepare yourselves for fire, prepare yourselves for a sweeping conflagration. It won't be long before you'll be pining for the Assyrians. It's an enduring nation, the Babylonians, it's an ancient nation, a nation whose tongue you know not, nor will you understand what they say; their quiver is an open grave, the prophet rejoiced, they are all mighty men. Shemayah, we'll buy them off, shouted someone in a black suit, who'd recognized the prophet, or we'll shut ourselves up in our fortresses. And the prophet—whose name was indeed Shemayah, nicknamed Shemayahu the Phantasmer, after the dreams that assailed him—answered, Bah, shyster, they don't need your gold, they're just passing through here on their way to Egypt; they crave Egypt's gold and all its produce; they'll run over you like a race car squishing two dung beetles on a highway. In this parable, the prophet hastened to explain, you're the beetles *and* you're the dung. Jeremiah closed his eyes and leaned his brow against the windowpane of the car as it came to a halt at the central station. No one got out, no one boarded. He could see, in the darkness of his tightly shut eyes, both his parents marching in a long procession northeast, and then he stood and moved toward the exit door without opening his eyes. The young prophet noticed him and roared while pointing in his direction, Ho-ho, a false prophet riding the light rail, or, better yet, the *blight* rail—what better for a false prophet with maggots crawling in his rotting carcass—a blight on this false prophet and all his gibberish! The doors slid closed, and Jeremiah, who hadn't had time to slip out, sat back down. The prophet's words frightened him, and he gasped, short of breath. The little prophet grabbed a Coke can from the car's vending machine and flung it at Jeremiah; the can hit the bandage Broch had wound around his head, and a nauseating pain shot through the wound. As the light rail continued on its way, the prophet stretched his hand out, and, as if by magic, the Coke can shot back to him again. A miracle, a miracle, the passengers shouted in the car. Amazing, did you see how he charmed the can? In order to purchase something, of course, we must pay for it—the boy prophet approached Jeremiah from behind and placed his hands on his shoulders—we buy, and, having bought, need more money, he explained reasonably; it's like Economics 101. It seemed to Jeremiah that the prophet had sprouted into a young man in his twenties as he continued: One needs money in order to cover one's expenses, and, incidentally, that's why it's always worth having more of it. Money goes to money, money begets money, money sticks to money, and also the glue that glues money to money is made of money. I'm speaking the truth, hear ye and hearken, he said. When I say money I mean *cash* money and not silver, even though silver also has a fixed value. But what's the value of silver today? Twenty dollars an ounce—that's trash, that's trash, that's *traaash*, he shouted. I sold a ton of zinc for seventeen hundred dollars, the prophet said, and he ground his teeth in rage. I bought zinc stocks, and the zinc zonked me. I've been zinczonked, zinczonked with bitter herbs and tears. Oh, light rail! he suddenly exclaimed, Don't call yourself light but blighted, blighted gold on the way to the Holy Temple, empty your pockets of gold and of precious polished stones into the prophet's hat!

Purses were drawn, and cash and coins and rings and earrings were flung in the direction of the hat as it made its rounds the length and breadth of the car. The hat fluttered back and forth in the car like a caged dove, and Jeremiah was taken aback. He was on the verge of throwing up. Hunched over, all he saw was a thicket of legs, and his head ached under the bandage, and he felt as though a dentist were filling one of his teeth without anesthetic. A one-hundred-shekel bill suddenly dropped in front of him, and without thinking twice he grabbed it and stuck it in one of his socks. Give me one hundred thousand today, and tomorrow you'll receive sixty million in return, Mister! the prophet cried out. How are you going to fight against Babylonia without big budgets? Weapons aren't free, weapons aren't even cheap, iron chariots are expensive, Egyptian bows aren't bought for a song, a Philistine pike costs a mint, and you're not going to buy nuclear submarines in exchange for three black goats. What, you think you can get a free ride in this world?! he roared. No such thing as a free ride, several passengers answered in alarm, and someone said, Amazing, the rhetorical skill of this guy— you'd think his tongue was coated in honey. Show me the exchange rate and I'll prophesy for you on the sword and on death. We've got to believe in money, for what else do we have left? We've got to believe that money will bring us enormous benefits, that he who doesn't invest won't see any gains, that he who doesn't give his money a chance will be frowned upon by fortune! Happy are those who give their money free rein, the prophet proclaimed. We must give our money the chance to burn if we want interest to rise from its ashes. The market's unstable, he said, you've got to know how to read the market. Prices skyrocketed on the spot; passengers placed their shopping bags filled with vegetables at the prophet's feet, amazed by the soaring expenses; someone who looked like a beggar in a headscarf stuck a sesame-seed bun in the prophet's hand, and he miraculously turned it into a savory stuffed pastry and ate it on the spot. The light rail reeled as it passed the Jaffa–King George intersection, and the electronic board announced in Arabic—although ages had passed since anybody had heard this tongue spoken in Jerusalem, they hadn't succeeded in reprogramming the recording—*Jaffa Center*, and Jeremiah had just enough time to catch sight of the billows approaching and crashing against the doors and windows, and clouds covered the skies above Jaffa Road, clouds as one finds in the heart of the seas, when lightning strikes and a mighty torrent pours down on deck and on the coiled hawsers, and your sails are nearly torn to shreds in the astonishing winds. Jeremiah turned ashen and opened his mouth to puke, but nothing came up save the scent of almond, which wafted around him, and he clasped his locket as though he were drowning and clinging to the anchor chain for dear life, and remembered Jonah the prophet, who was a distant cousin on his mother's side: Take me up and cast me forth into the sea, so shall the sea be calm unto you, for I know that for my sake this great tempest is upon you. And the young prophet yowled, And it shall be unto you a sign, my words have shaken the foundations, and your cursed light rail is reeling toward the sea. Nine hundred billion yen, he thundered, four thousand ounces of gold. Gems! the prophet shouted. Idiots! We've got to conquer everything right up to the Tigris, he proclaimed. You'll rule over the Euphrates, he promised an old man, we'll abolish that ugly cuneiform of theirs, we'll impose our own script. And now the prophet's head was within sniffing distance of Jeremiah's, close up, low, practically on the floor, and the veins on the prophet's temples were red and swollen, and someone smashed a window with the little red fire-hammer, because it had gotten so stuffy in the car, and salt water came crashing in and struck both their heads, and the prophet told Jeremiah in a whisper, as water streamed like a river through the car and over the entire light-rail system, barely containing his hatred: What do you propose for them? As for death, death, right? And as for the sword, the sword? This they're already familiar with, this they've *already been told* a hundred thousand times over, better leap into the river and get out of my face or I'll cut you up bad. The prophet stood up and shook himself. Prophesying seemed to add to his years. All at once he was old. The veins at his temples bulged and turned gray and pounded like pistons. Stooped over with years and rage, he waded in the water above the baskets of vegetables, grabbed an oversize carrot, and, crushed between the passengers holding on to the handles and bars, swam vigorously against the current back to Jeremiah and thwacked him on the head with the carrot, again and again, as if it were a truncheon. Jeremiah's bandage fell, the brine ate at his open wound, and for a moment he lost consciousness. The prophet noticed Jeremiah's dangling locket and, with an ear-rending scream, tried to seize it and tear it away from Jeremiah's neck, but Jeremiah steadied himself and scrambled on top of the vending machine and slipped his locket back under his shirt, though in doing so he once more left his head undefended, and the prophet wasted no time before landing another blow. Jeremiah fell into the streaming water and tried to extricate himself, but the now old man kicked him in the shins, and when Jeremiah doubled over, he kneed him in the face, after which Jeremiah again fell back into the river coursing through the entire length of the commuter train, and he went under for a split second and then bobbed back up. The passengers looked on avidly from their seats. They were approaching the City Hall stop. Barely a day went by without some squabble or other between prophets on the light rail—they were basically hoodlums; they liked to smash up idol-worship conclaves just for the hell of it—and the transit officials were all fed up: Go ahead, see if you can tell the difference between a false prophet and a true one, a burly inspector told his colleague, leaning against a ticket validation machine. Jeremiah tried to flee, but the car was jam-packed. His clothes were soaked in brine, the river was a salty seawater river, and so, too, were the old prophet's hair and garments soaked through. And the still-aging prophet would have struck Jeremiah yet again with his shaking white hand if the doors hadn't finally slid open, and Jeremiah hadn't forded the river, which had turned as shallow as trickling sewage. And he was shoved and jostled as he strode out, drenched, toward the City Hall Plaza, where he stood in the sun, bewildered, and dripping wet. The Phantasmer kept on beating feebly with his carrot at the train car's window, until the same burly inspector strode up to him and socked him in the face with his inspector's brass knuckles, sheathed in fake leather and stamped with the company seal, and the prophet collapsed on the spot like an inflatable mattress slashed by a razor. Passengers were boarding and disembarking, and after several moments all that was left of the mattress were a few plastic shreds sticking to soles and heels, dispersed all along the aisle of the mud-splattered train car, which would be hosed down in the evening; later, the shreds would scatter even farther afield, over sidewalks and lanes, and onto doormats at the entrances to Jerusalem homes.

3

His mother plunged a wooden spoon into a pot when he entered and sat down. She hadn't expected him. His head was swollen from the blows he'd received from Broch and the old prophet. He went up to the freezer, removed an ice cube, and pressed it against his head. His mother didn't pay attention, didn't ask questions. She said, I read that there's now an organized tour to Nineveh, with attractions; you travel in a red double-decker to the inner city, get to visit the important sites, circle the walls, Nergal Gate, Addad Gate, Shebanbi Gate . . . He remembered his mother standing in the butcher shop when he was just a child, facing a sheep's head that stared back at her, its eyes gleaming on the verge of tears, and she told the butcher, That's enough, I can't be part of any of this anymore; my daughter died; please understand, I'm sorry. And she paid for the meat she'd intended to buy but left empty-handed—the boy Jeremiah on her heels, clutching their empty wicker basket. The driver plays Assyrian songs, and you also get little flags, she added, and then, all of a sudden, the driver jerks the steering wheel—she gestured sharply with her spoon before sticking it back into the pot—and lands the bus in the Khosr River. The passengers all squeal in terror, but the bus turns into a boat and sails right on. Jeremiah opened a cupboard. And shut it. He always opened his mother's cupboards, checking around, looking for something. I thought we could go, the three of us together; you could drive us down, but we'd pay for everything. It's on us. We won't tell Dad in advance, it'll be a surprise. We'll shove him into the river. You know how scared he is of water. We'll scare his phobia away once and for all. It'll be a shock for him, but he'll feel safe with us. Hilkiah, it's only water, I tell him, it's been forty-five years now. So what does he tell me?—she stirred with her spoon—I nearly drowned back then, he says. My body is still on that boat. He'll be turning sixty-three in the fall. This is our chance. Jeremiah looked at her in astonishment. Not only because of the prospect of this scary stunt with the tour bus, but chiefly because of her suggestion that all three of them travel together. He said, Mom, the Babylonians are gearing up to come here soon; who knows, by Dad's birthday they might have arrived; there will be an awful siege. She lowered the flame and said, as if to herself, The soup looks great, and opened a cupboard and took out pink mineral salt from the Himalayas. Nonsense, she said, what would the Babylonians want with this hole? You think the King of Babylon has nothing better to do than come to Jerusalem? He already has plenty of dough from the rest of the world, you think he needs our money, too? He's got enough trouble with all those barbarians hanging out up there. They aren't coming, she declared, sprinkling salt: We're going to Nineveh, I've already ordered our tickets. There will be a siege, Jeremiah repeated. And you won't be able to go anywhere. All at once he saw it again, as though in miniature: legions trudging slowly across the kitchen table, where the Formica turned into a three-dimensional map, with mountains, boundless plains, dry riverbeds, crumbs advancing like ants toward the edge of the world between boulders of coarse salt. His mother said, I don't understand you. On the marble counter, next to her, he caught sight of an old guidebook to Assyria. Well, you won't catch me moving to Babylon, his mother said brusquely, after a long pause. One exile in a lifetime is enough for me. They can do whatever they want.

His father entered the kitchen silently. Jeremiah slipped a folded newspaper on top of the guidebook. His father said: They announced it on the news. It's happening. Egypt's been smote hip and thigh on Babylonian soil. First the Assyrians, now the Chaldeans. Why say Chaldeans? If they're from Babylon, call them Babylonians. Jeremiah mumbled, They're an Aramean tribe who gained control over Babylon. They're the new Babylonians . . . They're all the same, his father said. Wave after wave. They're coming. They all want to ride out into the distance in chariots and on horses. Demolish and destroy. I'm sick and tired of all these invasions. Your great-grandfather saw Assyrian troops take these highlands by storm. They're fighting over there on the Euphrates, Egypt and Babylon; sometime or other, they'll fight here, too, face-to-face, there'll be a bloodbath in our own backyard. You tell me, eh, why should the Egyptians want to wade into the Euphrates? It's insane! In our own backyard they'll slaughter the— But Esther, his mother, suddenly burst into a song by Naomi Shemer: In our yard / In the shade of the olive tree / —she sang gleefully in a thin soprano, in order to put a stop to this gloomy lecture—Lots of guests / Regularly drop in . . . Each in his own tongue / And his own way / to say: Hel-lo. When she lifted the pot lid, steam covered her face and fogged up her glasses. Jeremiah remembered the pot he'd seen in the sky a couple of hours earlier and realized, to his amazement, that this was the very same pot, his mother's pot, except that in the sky it was as large as the moon, and then as large as the setting sun, but maybe not, maybe as small as a coffeepot, like Broch's *finjan*, but all of a sudden he couldn't recall the exact size of the pot he'd seen earlier, and understood that he needed to jot down what he'd seen or he'd forget everything. His father said, Did you bang your head? And Jeremiah said, I went through a low door.

His mother stopped singing, because she remembered she

had some complaints about the plumbing. She struck her fore-head with her spoon. The cold water, she said. I mean the hot water! That is, sometimes it's too hot, and then, at other times, the boiler's running for hours and yet the water's as cold as ice. When's the plumber coming? The bathroom sink is clogged again, too. Jeremiah's father had promised he'd get to it himself, but he was scared of tampering with pipes. For your father, she said, a few cheap pipes are more complicated than the digestive or circulatory system. He might know how to fix a heart valve, but a valve in a washing machine terrifies him. A tube in a dish-washer, a tube in a dryer? Forget it. But artery buds—now, *there* he feels comfortable. I tell him, Hilkiah, it's all the same thing! Jeremiah got the message and said, Okay, I'll take a look.

He stooped under the bathroom sink and gripped the Swed-ish wrench that had been left there since his last visit, three weeks ago. He dragged a bucket under the siphon and struggled to loosen the threads. His mother brought him an orange melon on a tray. When she had set the melon next to him on the floor, she poked it with her fingertip as if to say, There's a melon. The melon, which was overripe, ripe to burst, simply popped open at the touch of her finger. The stench from the sink grew worse with each turn of the wrench, and Jeremiah jerked his face to one side and almost puked into the green bucket. His mother paid no attention and didn't remove the fruit. Their pipes always got clogged, and they were always skimping on a plumber, since they knew their son would come and visit and take care of it for them. Come to think of it, he reflected, and was ashamed to ad-mit as much, from the minute he entered the house, that was all they were thinking about: The free plumber has arrived. When his grandfather was alive, he took care of all the household re-pairs. A metalworker, he was also an amateur plumber who knew how to detect obstructions and leaks by listening to the sounds coming from the walls. Once, when Jeremiah was a boy, they lifted him so that his ear could reach way up, and he shouted, It's a mouth, I hear an open mouth in there, and they dropped him in fright. And he also kept a mongoose as a pet, Jeremiah recalled; his grandfather trapped snakes with the help of the mongoose, until his granddaughter was born and he was forced to set the mongoose free in the hills of the land of Benjamin. But it returned with a viper between its teeth.

His mother knocked at the door. Anything new with my pipes? she asked, or so he fancied. He didn't answer, but poured a blue liquid into the drain and glanced at his watch. He looked for the burst melon and realized that he hadn't been served any melon; it must have been some sort of fleeting dream that took hold and let go in a single second. In a quarter of an hour, he'd have to run the hot tap for a good while. On the other side of the bathroom door, he could hear his father shouting to his mother: While we wait for him to get the job done in there, slice me some bread and a mango—I'm all dried up. And his mother was surprised: Again? Jeremiah wasn't sure he'd heard right. Bread with mango? Why's he eating that? Something in his father's request, something in his tone—a mixture of cheerfulness and dread—depressed him as he crouched under the sink. How will they manage in exile? After all, they're so helpless when it comes to anything practical. They don't even know how to unstick the float in their toilet tank. Don't even know how to change a lightbulb. Behold, I will give this city into the hand of the King of Babylon, and he shall take it. And Zedekiah, King of Judah, shall not escape out of the hands of the Chaldeans, but shall be delivered into the hand of the King of Babylon, and shall speak with him mouth to mouth, and his eyes shall behold his eyes. Jeremiah had no idea who Zedekiah might be, since Jehoiakim was the current King of Judah, and he reckoned that Zedekiah was the name of a future king, but he didn't know anyone called Zedekiah apart from the Zedekiah of Zedekiah Delicacies in the Mahane Yehuda Market, where he'd buy green and black olives, and where his father would taste the cheeses. His wife wouldn't allow animal products into the house, and Hilkiah was constantly tormented with his cravings for hard, salty cheeses, so he'd lay hold of what he could on the counter, and the vendors, familiar with the situation, showed him all due deference—he'd been a senior physician at Hadassah, so it was worth their while to stay on the best of terms with him. They'd offer him their wares and delight in the keen pleasure he'd evince in savoring, with his eyes closed, the kashkaval and the gouda. And Jeremiah, in a flash, beheld his father being led in fetters from the cheese counter in the Mahane Yehuda Market to endless colossal palaces with hanging gardens and inscribed towers, and a lofty blue wall topped by huge, roaring lions, and he knew it was the city of Babylon, and he saw his father kneeling, in his white cloak, spattered with the blood of his patients, at the feet of a king seated on a great white throne.

Jeremiah glanced again at his watch and turned the hot-water faucet. Adjacent to the door, on the other side, his father sat on a stool and ate a chunk of dark bread with thin slices of juicy mango. Fibers stuck between his teeth. An hour later, he'd have to floss them out. On the plate beside him on the floor rested the mango's pit, and it was plain to see that it had been thoroughly chewed. His teeth and his mouth and fingers were stained orange. Jeremiah's father felt the first signs of decay in one tooth; the sugar bore through, close to the nerve, causing him pain.

Jeremiah left the Swedish wrench in its place and plodded out of the bathroom. Though the hot water streamed into the sink, he took no notice. His father shot him a quick look, at once nonplussed and annoyed. Once Jeremiah leaves, I'll get up to turn the faucet off, he mused, but he knew he would forget to do so in the twinkling of an eye, and the water would keep running for hours, and they'd wind up with one hell of a bill. Jeremiah pointed behind him: Pour in a quarter bottle of blue liquid once a week. How about we try sulfuric acid? his father asked. Jeremiah was planning to leave and return to his apartment in Nahlaot with another stack of books. He'd been moving his belongings in stages. But, all at once, he felt exhausted. He glanced again at the mango sandwich that lay, docile and nibbled, on the tray, flung out a word to his mother in the kitchen, who was absorbed in listening to a raucous talk show on the radio, and went to his vacated room. He needed desperately to lie down.

The angel was lying on his childhood bed, his face turned toward the wall. Jeremiah sat beside him like a father watching over a sick child's sleep. The angel said, without opening his eyes, You can sit on the edge of the bed. And it began to dawn on Jeremiah that he had indeed been appointed, that the matter was serious and not just a passing daydream; that there were indeed heavenly messengers in the world doing their work and entering without knocking; that there were vast, distant forces banding together around him. Neither the pot, nor the voice, nor the melon, nor the almond branch sufficed in itself—only the angel on his bed truly hammered the point home. Jeremiah wondered whether it was an angel with a long history—for example, the angel who was present at the binding of Isaac, or the angel who fought with Jacob and refused to reveal his name. The angel was stretched out at a slight angle, on his side. There was nothing out of the ordinary about him at a glance, but Jeremiah knew at once that this wasn't just anybody. The light told him so. His room was plunged into darkness, as if to keep him from seeing anything but the angel, with only the new star outside shedding light from its habitual place. Someone holding a torch passed by the window, and for an instant Jeremiah caught sight of the angel's countenance, and it was his own childhood face, the boy's face he'd lost years ago, with bright, shoulder-length hair. He didn't quite get it—why hadn't he been terrified by the figure lying on his bed and burying its face in his pillow? To be sure, a Jeremiah deep within him was indeed filled with terror, but this voice of panic seemed very distant: Jeremiah's heart wasn't even racing, though all contemporary accounts of such visitations tended to make a big deal out of how thrilling they were. He was pretty surprised by his composure, considering all he'd seen during the course of the day; it was as though he'd been injected with some sort of anesthetic, as though he'd elected for an epidural during a long and difficult birth; even his surprise was muted. And a soft wind swept through the room. And the light in the room was like the light of the setting sun over a wheat field. The wind, too, blew as in an open field, as if the walls were nothing but clouds or even open air, presenting no obstruction to the wind rising and blowing and gliding toward you and beyond.

On the piano in the room, which had been covered for nine years now by a summer blanket, a photograph of his sister leaned on an oblique stand. She was photographed playing on this very piano, in this very room. The piano hadn't been covered back then, when she was still alive; it remained open at all times and didn't have a photograph on top but, rather, pages of sheet music and a plaster bust of Bach that Jeremiah, when he was ten, had partly painted. Later, it fell from the piano and shattered; his mother had glued the pieces back together, and it was shunted from the piano to the kitchen, where it stood to this day as a paperweight on top of the vegan recipes she diligently cut out of the newspapers. Jeremiah knew exactly what his sister had been playing when the photo was taken, because he was the one who'd photographed her. The angel said, The piano is covered. The silence that followed was so long that it seemed he must have been done speaking, but then he added, Yet you, too, know how to tickle the ivories. And there was another prolonged silence, as though time had no meaning and the conversation might continue in this manner for hours and days and years and centuries.

Beside the bed stood a small nightstand on which his father's ring binder rested. For some forty-five years—ever since the Yom Kippur War, in which he had served as a medic and nearly drowned crossing the Suez Canal when he stumbled on the roller bridge—Hilkiah would cut out a selection of newspaper articles on government corruption in Israel. He'd amassed a stack of binders. The binder on the nightstand represented only the last three months. In the margins of his clippings, Hilkiah would jot down his own comments and interpretations, cross-referencing other scraps of news, attempting to reconstruct, as he said, the whole network of corruption. Once a year, he would select the best evidence from his binders and then slip these articles into a large envelope and tuck it into a pillowcase—his Pillow of Corruption, as he liked to say—which he then slept on for the entire year. At the end of each year, he'd replace the pillow; once, Jeremiah peeked inside one of the outgoing pillowcases and saw that the scraps of paper were covered with all sorts of disgusting brown stains from his father's saliva and night sweats, which had seeped through the newsprint. His mother once burned several such pillowcases, which caused a huge to-do; she'd flung the bulky, foul-smelling pillowcase archives into the fire, a lifetime's work, and his father had shoved her in his rage, so she claimed, and the police were called in. Jeremiah only heard about it years later, from his sister, during her last days. Now Jeremiah opened the ring binder and thumbed through the pasted scraps of newsprint. Next to the binder lay a yellow glue stick, his father's plain ballpoint pen, and his large iron scissors, the seamstress scissors he'd inherited from Jeremiah's grandmother. The sound of cloth as it was diligently cut to measure came back to Jeremiah, the scissors steadily advancing, and he thought about the Chaldeans' iron chariots and how it was anybody's guess where they might have deployed their troops by now and what and whom they would slice in two when they arrived, and he imagined the battlement walls butted by battering rams and how they would also be diligently cut in two.

In the margins of the articles on corruption he read words in his father's own elegant handwriting, outraged comments like *A nice share for the finance minister!* or *The minister of defense gets two million for giving a lecture?!* or else more laconic and less explicable remarks, such as *The city is the pot and we are the meat . . .* or *Lard for lips to lick,* or *Power-newspapers-government-security,* or *Presidential malfeasance,* or *Deep-pocketed museum,* or *Safe-deposit box on fire*. And there was a photo of the opening of an exhibition in which all the guests were eating veal sweetbreads—that's what was written at the bottom of the photograph—even the curator, even the artist.

Jeremiah sat at the foot of the bed. The angel drew up his legs, to clear a bit of space for him. What's your name? the angel asked him. My name's Jeremiah, he answered. And you? The angel answered, My name is Jeremiah, too. Do you have any instructions for me? the first Jeremiah asked. The angel said, Earlier, when I was nosing around the apartment, your mother opened the icebox and all the frozen pitas she'd stored dropped like hail on the floor. Jeremiah said, I heard a voice this morning; was it you speaking? And the angel answered, But I don't have a voice. Things have been shown to me, Jeremiah said—so what now? Yes, one thing must be clear by now, the angel told him instead of answering—and he revealed his face in the dark, in the light of the new star—and that's that you don't have a chance, Babylon has already shod its horses and painted its tanks blue, and Babylon will arrive, it'll show up here, and you'll suffer, and though you don't have any choice in the matter, it can't be allowed to happen without a great lamentation; you'll be the mouth of that scream.

Now rise and go by way of the Potsherd Gate. You'll meet someone there, and he'll sell you a jug. You've got to start as soon as possible—they're galloping from one desert oasis to another, and their horses are thirsty, and they're fueling the tanks that will follow close behind the horses, to strike a second and more excruciating blow. Procure for yourself a large and colorful jug. And you will hold on to this empty jug, so that everyone can see you in the streets of the city. Carry it around for days and weeks, and never let go of its neck. Until everyone says, There's a man in Jerusalem, and his name is Jeremiah, and he walks around with a large jug in hand and won't relax his grip on the jug. This will be broadcast everywhere, it will become known, and it will astonish and exasperate. And then, when everyone knows this for a fact, you will break the jug in plain sight. And you will tell them: Thus said the Lord of Hosts, Even so will I break this people and this city, as one breaks a potter's vessel, which cannot be made whole again. That's all.

Jeremiah asked, And will this help? I'll be able to prevent the city's fall, and— But the angel interrupted and said: I don't know, but if the city falls they will remember you and the jug. They won't be able to say it was all due to chance. Jeremiah said, And what if I buy a jug and don't smash it, what if I fill it with water and say— But the angel cut in again and said: Now play me something on your sister's piano. Do you know your mother preserved your sister's dried placenta inside the piano? And it's still there. Jeremiah got up and glanced at the piano and groped for the string that switched on the lamp, but there was no lamp, and the piano turned into a large pile of dry mud, whose height matched his own. And it had a head of its own, the mud. The angel stretched out on its back and stared silently at the ceiling, and Jeremiah lingered for a moment and then fled the room through the window and re-entered his parents' home by the front door.

4

IN THE KITCHEN, his mother removed the lid from the pot and a column of steam shot up. I didn't notice you left; I had my head in the pot. The swelling has gone down a bit, she said, and he felt his head gingerly. His father, who'd been a hematologist at Hadassah, saw his wife poking at their son's head and momentarily ceased removing seeds from his pomegranate. Their daughter, Jeremiah's older sister, had been stricken with the very disease Hilkiah specialized in. When her first symptoms appeared, after a period of exhaustion and headaches, Hilkiah had started laughing, because he knew, *knew beyond a doubt*, that he was dreaming. There was no way that what he dealt with daily as a doctor would appear and infect his daughter. After all, it wasn't contagious. He thought—no, he *knew*—that she, who'd heard for years about every least detail of the disease, was amusing herself in ticking off for him the symptoms she'd heard from his own mouth during meals and while traveling or in conversation with colleagues. After all, she'd even accompanied him at times to hematology conferences. But then she'd shown him her back, and he saw the blotches and a frightened sound erupted from within him. He was no longer certain whether he was dreaming or not. He screamed in a voice that wasn't his own, but didn't wake up. And he realized that it was really happening. Even before she said a word, he knew exactly what she had, he saw death sitting inches away from her. She asked him what she'd come down with, what was wrong with her, and he realized not only that she wasn't pulling his leg, but that she *herself* hadn't made the connection between what he'd told her all those years and the disease she now had—that she hadn't yet raised the possibility in her mind that she'd become ill with what he specialized in. He explained to her a number of times, and to Jeremiah, that it's a liquid cancer, a blood cancer, of the white corpuscles. That the blood goes wild. The white corpuscles. But there's a new treatment, he'd told her immediately, back then, years ago: You infect the patient with an engineered AIDS virus. The virus can't cause AIDS, but it attacks the white blood cells going wild and butchering the blood. There's no guarantee of success. But there were children who'd been treated in a hospital in Egypt and completely recovered. When she asked what it was that she had, he told her; it took her some time to register what was going on, to register that the explanation, which bored her for the most part, and bored her brother—truth be told—had now turned into her life and body. Tomorrow we'll start with tests and treatment, her father said. And he left her after several hours, just to catch up on some sleep: he needs to sleep, twenty hours he hasn't closed his eyes. He'll sleep here, one floor up, in the doctors' on-call room, and show up the following day at dawn and open the ward and start to do whatever needs to be done, with the assistance of the medical team; he'll send for the very best. But when he came down to the ward early in the morning, after four hours of sleep, there was no one to treat, for she'd cut her veins two hours after he left her, and when the nurses discovered her she was dead; they hadn't found him at home, and down in the village his wife slept soundly and hadn't heard the phone ring, and no one knew that he was sleeping one floor up, in the on-call room. He stood before the bed and again thought, No, no, this can't be, it's without doubt a dream. And then he was obliged to wake up.

In the days that followed, he couldn't put to rest the unsettling thought that she'd killed herself not in spite of all the information he'd innocently passed on to her in dribs and drabs over the years, but precisely on account of the information he'd fed her. He knew everything there was to know about the disease; after all, he'd written a book on the subject that was about to appear in print—though this, too, he'd been saying for several years. He had intended to start with a battery of tests and treatment early in the morning, but the story had been interrupted even before it began. He didn't even have time to accustom himself to this new version—the story of a healthy girl, a gifted pianist, who turns all at once into a girl in critical condition—before he had to get used to another narrative entirely, the story of her sudden death. She was nineteen years old. The music had been cut off. That same day, he left the hospital and abandoned the ward in a state of chaos, with patients in the middle of treatment and remission; he simply never returned after the period of mourning, never got back on his feet. As soon as he was told what had happened, he was overwhelmed by a dark, deep self-disgust, though it was accompanied by laughter, too, as if all along he hadn't been able to help hearing a sort of belly laugh about their fate: A morbid joke is making the rounds, and we're the laughingstocks. A morbid joke? Esther wondered. Morbid joke, morbid joke, he repeated.

Efforts were made to speak to him, to explain that of course he wasn't to blame and so on and so forth, but he wouldn't listen. The circle was closed and couldn't be breached. He recalled how he'd instructed her about the disease, how he'd shown her enlarged pictures of diseased blood cells, how he'd explained to her about bone marrow and the awful suffering incurred when the circulatory system breaks down, and he believed—in truth, Esther thought, justifiably—that his detailed elucidations were what caused his daughter's illness and brought about her death. He had described to her what she should expect without realizing that one day it would be her own fate. Perhaps he'd intended the opposite; perhaps he'd gone into such detail precisely in order to prevent the devil, so to speak, from making her sick with this very illness, in order to find a way to cope from the very beginning with a situation that was so improbable, in which a doctor's daughter, the head of the department of hematology and a specialist in blood cancer, would fall victim to the self-same illness in which he specialized? But that's exactly what happened. Over the years, Esther began believing not only that her daughter committed suicide on account of her fear of the illness she knew all too well, but also that she became sick in the first place because of what her husband had taught her, that the words repeated over and again, and the photographs and the graphs and the accounts of patients, children and adults, that he brought home, were what caused her to fall ill, that he in a sense had infected her with all of this evidence. He washed his face and hands that same morning and descended one floor to start the process of treatment; he hadn't managed to dry his face since he couldn't find a hand towel in the staff room, and he almost used his sleeve, and then he saw the head nurse, who was completely red in the face. He'd been certain of his ability to cure his daughter, since he knew she would be receiving the very best help, knew that he himself was the best possible help. But his daughter didn't let him treat her, she hadn't given him a chance, and two hours and a quarter after he'd left her that same night and went up one floor to get some sleep, she'd taken a razor blade that she'd noticed lying on an adjoining bed and had sliced the veins on her wrists, and her sick, thin blood had gushed out, and by the time she was found she was already lost. While I was asleep, her father reflected, she'd already reached her death, and he suddenly realized that his room was exactly above her room, and her ceiling was the floor on which his bed stood.

They lied to Jeremiah, who was nearly thirteen years old, and told him his sister had died from the illness; it wasn't a complete lie, but neither was it the complete truth, and until he heard the true version by chance from someone or other, he believed his sister had succumbed to blood cancer—an illness that he, too, was thoroughly familiar with, and for the same reasons—within twenty-four hours of the moment it had been detected in her body. After he heard the truth, he quietly approached his mother, without feeling any anger, and sat next to her, and didn't say a word, and she didn't speak, either; they briefly exchanged glances, and the matter was seemingly settled. He turned thirteen. They didn't celebrate his Bar Mitzvah. They buried his sister in an empty, untended field abutting their home, which belonged to Jeremiah's uncle, his father's brother, and they didn't raise a tombstone, they only planted an olive sapling over the grave, not at its feet but directly on top of the mound of earth. And after many years, Esther understood the obvious—namely, that the roots of the olive tree would pierce through and cleave the corpse. It hadn't occurred to her while she was planting it. At the time, she thought only of the trunk and the branches and the fruit. And the memory.

Esther looked up and switched off her talk show. The sharp kitchen knife was on the table, its blade stained with the juice of another mango. She cut tiny slices for herself, close to the mango's head, but left her fruit uneaten, then handed over to Jeremiah a saucer on which she crisscrossed some larger slices with the point of the knife. He ate, making a mess like his father. He still keeps dreaming that he's drowning, she told Jeremiah under her breath. I don't know what to do. Because of his constant drowning, I, too, have started dreaming of drowning. His dreams are inundating my own dreams. He keeps a scalpel in his bedside drawer. It's worse than a loaded gun. The scalpel won't rust. He also keeps her blood samples in the fridge, she whispered. Everything's there, in a Styrofoam container, sealed with insulating tape, behind the legumes, deep on the right side. I've ordered a new fridge; I told him the fridge broke, even though it's in perfectly good order. I thought that once we got a new fridge it'd be possible to finally bury the blood. He arrived moments before the movers, removed the blood, put it in a cooler, waited for them to install the new fridge, then stuck the blood inside. He's been holding on to it for nearly ten years. Jeremiah glanced at his mother and said: I beheld the earth, Mom, and it was waste and void, and the skies, they had no light. I looked at the mountains, and they were quaking, Mom, and all the hills moved to and fro. His mother said, Exactly, *moved to and fro.* And she thought, His voice has changed. Jeremiah said: Why don't you leave the house for a bit, go into town? I noticed there's a dance performance at the Jerusalem Theatre tonight. I'll come with you, if you'd like, he wanted to add. It's been close to ten years, Mom, he said. Not seven days, or a month, or a year. His mother said, Yes, I know exactly how many, and she took a Diet Coke out of the fridge and poured herself a drink and gulped it down with revulsion. He remembered in alarm that he was supposed to go purchase a jug. It amazed him that he had nearly forgotten this only minutes after the revelation had been granted him, as if there were, in these revelations, or in the miracles that had taken place throughout the day, something at once highly charged and yet altogether feeble and worthless, so that, if you didn't want to think about them, it was a simple enough thing to turn the gaze of your memory elsewhere and it all faded away at once.

Hilkiah entered the kitchen, holding the empty plate in his hand, and took a box of dates out of the freezer. He liked them ice-cold on his teeth. The mango rind he'd thrown by mistake into the toilet, where it would float until his wife noticed and fished it out in disgust with rubber gloves. Lately, he'd been making such mistakes from time to time. His father looked over at the fridge, forgetting for a moment what it was he'd been looking for, and then remembered, yes, the dates, to rinse. And once more there rose in Jeremiah's ears the words he'd managed to forget. They came to him now as if whispered anew: Even so will I will break this people and this city, as one breaks a potter's vessel, which cannot be made whole again. The water in the bathroom sink was still running. The three of them heard it but didn't make any move to go shut it off. They hovered over the dates.

5

THE OLIVE TREES OUTSIDE seemed to be growing at full speed. All of a sudden, a branch would put out a leaf; within minutes, a fruit would ripen as a bird flew by above and was followed by more birds, who streaked through the skies like the tip of a brush dipped in black ink, inscribing something with the clouds as background, but moving too fast for us to discern the shape of the letters. Jeremiah shaded his eyes with the palm of his hand, and the birds' shadow slipped between his fingers. He couldn't remember whether the light rail stopped next to the Potsherd Gate, because he didn't remember whether there was a gate with such a name in the first place; he wasn't in the habit of visiting the Old City that often, and he worried about boarding the train for fear of encountering once more the wrath of that prophet.

Guinea pigs and other small creatures scurried between the trunks of the olive trees. Jeremiah bent forward to pet them. He discovered to his surprise some breadcrumbs in his pocket, which he fed to the sparrows bunched together on a branch. A triplet of crows flocked down, and he fished out of his shirt pocket a fistful of sunflower seeds for them too. Directing his voice to the small animals and the birds, Jeremiah said: Do not be afraid of the King of Babylon, of whom you are afraid. Be not afraid, says the Lord, for I am with you to save you and to deliver you from his hand, and I will grant you mercy, that he may have mercy on you. The crows nodded. The guinea pigs diligently licked their fur.

He turned away from the olive grove and set out for Queen Helena Street, leaving behind him a trail of crumbs. Over there, where the public-broadcasting buildings once stood, in a lane where the radio security guards used to like to kill time and the broadcasters and technicians would stroll by, nodding their heads, a little falafel stand was established after the earthquake: Queen Falafel. Whenever the blind vendor heard a new customer passing by, he'd turn to him and say, in a questioning, semi-querulous tone, even before offering him, as was his custom, a single free falafel ball: You're standing here on Helena the Queen, but you don't know the first thing about Queen Helena. And nobody knew. Nobody. And even if someone knew, the person would say, You're right, I have no idea. That was the ritual over there. Some would ask, Isn't she Miriam the Hasmonean? Others said, just for the hell of it, She was Herod's wife, no? And the vendor would serve up the sample falafel ball and nod sadly at his customer's general ignorance. Jeremiah entered and asked for a falafel. Hunger yawned within him like a small pain. He hadn't touched a thing at his mother's; his parents were in the habit of taking hours to prepare their salads, and he couldn't wait any longer. The vendor asked, And Queen Helena? And Jeremiah answered: Queen of Adiabene—that's in northern Assyria. She converted to Judaism with her son King Monobaz. Distributed figs to the poor of Jerusalem when she arrived on a pilgrimage. Her coffin— But the vendor cut him off and said: Enough, shut up, Jeremiah, have a falafel ball, it's piping hot. For a minute I didn't recognize your voice. If I wanted to hear a lecture, I'd go to the university. Boring us to death with Queen Helena—everybody here knows the story. And Jeremiah laughed, and pulled a hundred-shekel bill out of his still-moist sock. The vendor ran the bill between his thumb and fingers and said: One hundred shekels for a falafel— what have we come to? The end of days. Have a drink, too, and take another half portion. I don't have any change. Jeremiah said, Keep the change, and the vendor said, No, no way. And someone dressed in white priestly garments pushed his way through the line and said, Hurry up and give us half a portion for a hungry priest on his way to serve the Holy. And the vendor answered him, as he would always answer: We don't have half portions. With us, a portion is *two* pitas, and half a portion is one whole pita. What should I put in your half portion? And the priest said, Everything. But the vendor wanted to make things difficult. Define *everything*, he said. Heap on the cabbage, the priest said, and also— But this cabbage, the vendor said, this cabbage. Did you ever think about cabbage? Anybody ever give it some thought? How a leaf covers a leaf covers a leaf covers a leaf? One wing concealing another, and all in the shape of a ball. Did you ever wonder, as a priest, why we use the same word in Hebrew for both cherubim and cabbage? And one of the soldiers said, Cabbage? Number one reason for soldiers' farting in the barracks. The vendor said: That's real funny. What causes farting is your lousy digestive system, not the cabbage. Why don't you check out your stomach, your bowels, your spleen? I can see with my blind eyes that you have an inflammation down there, a fire. You eat dead animals, and then you blame some innocent cabbage. Stop stuffing dead animals into your intestines; eat falafel with a salad every day, believe me. Sabich without an egg. Spinach burekas. Lentil soup with lemon and cumin in winter. Beans with rice and roasted pine nuts. There's plenty to eat in the world, plenty—there's no need to keep slaughtering. I'm also talking to you, holy priest-o. You want to tell me you all still really believe God digs the smoke of grilled meat? Haven't we made just a teeny bit of progress? The priest kept silent, and the soldier picked at something spicy. And Jeremiah thought of his sister, and her intestines bloated with bad blood, and felt nauseated. Oh that my head were waters—and he bit into the pita—and my eyes a fountain of tears—he bit into the falafel balls—that I might weep day and night—he clutched the spicy falafel—for the slain of the daughter of my people.

The soldier told the blind vendor's hired hand, I'll take two orders, one with white cabbage, the other red. He stepped out of the booth cautiously, his hands loaded with cabbages. I don't get it, the vendor said, the cabbages are either green or purple, so why does everybody say *white* cabbage and *red* cabbage? You say, Lay on some white cabbage, lay on red cabbage, and I'm telling you, even with no eyes to see with, it drives me crazy. You asked for white cabbage? There's no white cabbage in the world. You asked for red cabbage? I don't have any. People ask for what doesn't exist; this is what I've learned from cabbages. His employee was all the while hacking at cabbages of both colors for the portions for the priest, who kept pointing with his finger at what and what not to fill his pitas with. The soldier asked: What's that music? I've never heard classical music in a falafel stand. The blind man said: It's coming from the rear; I worked in the record library before the earthquake. You know that the public-broadcasting radio building used to stand here before the earthquake. I was in the record library when the earthquake struck. Jeremiah already knew the rest of the story; he'd heard it told many times. Old records fell and cut the falafel man's eyes and blinded him, and the public-broadcasting people offered him the corner stand as part of his compensation. No one really believed that he'd manage to prepare falafels without being able to see, but he stuck to it; his grandfather had sold falafels in the Old City, and after the earthquake and the accident, he suddenly got it into his head that he needed to follow in his grandfather's footsteps—his grandfather who'd been expelled from the Old City during the last war—and not only in order to savor the taste of those falafel balls every day. For years, he'd tried to re-create the taste of the old man's falafel and salad and failed. He'd change the mix every couple of days, and was the first to taste and make adjustments, but would always say, Tasty, but Grandpa's it isn't.

A black cabbage dropped and rolled away, and Jeremiah bent over to pick it up. And, thanks to one of those flashes of insight in which we see the disaster that's about to befall us a split second before it actually arrives, a yelp burst out of Jeremiah a moment *before* he managed to strain his back. He froze, his hand stretched out toward the loping cabbage, which was gaining momentum down the steep lane; he was scarcely breathing, his face contorted partly in pain and partly in astonishment that he'd done it to himself once again: It's happening to you once more, you've gone and pulled a muscle in your back, and now you know all too well that you'll be out of commission for several days. Meanwhile, the cabbage kept on rolling down Helena the Queen and burst against a boulder. A jackal trotted out from between the ruins of the public-broadcasting buildings and looked at Jeremiah for a moment. He wasn't going to eat his pita, even though the blind vendor held it out to him, waiting with boundless patience for him to take it; Jeremiah said, I'm sorry, I can't eat, I've thrown my back out, I've got to lie down right away.

With stifled moans, he dragged himself into the ruined radio-broadcasting compound and slowly lay down in the shade of one of the walls. Broken records and compact discs were scattered everywhere. He tried to move his legs to the right and left, using some of the Feldenkrais exercises his mother had taught him in order to relieve the pain. Ponderous piano music could be heard from within the ruined building where the record library had been housed; then again, maybe the music came from the falafel stand. He saw crates of tomatoes and pickled cabbage and gallons of cooking oil. Lying down alleviated the pain, but Jeremiah knew that as soon as he tried to get up it would return. He again forgot all about the Potsherd Gate, forgot all about the jug. He didn't remember that he was forgetting.

From a certain distance, inside the record library, he heard someone talking, apparently into his phone. But I don't know what to do, I'm telling you, the voice said. I've been driving that scooter you sold me—yeah, you, don't play dumb with me—for how long now? And I keep hearing a sort of whistling coming from the front variator, or more like the sound of a plane taking off, so I decided today to find out what's going on, yeah? So I opened the belt cover. And I took out the front variator. I looked and looked. And I noticed the crankshaft rod that connects to the variator, yeah? At the end of the rod there are supposed to be these sorts of teeth that engage the cogwheel in the kick? So what do I see? The teeth are completely eaten away! That's something, isn't it? That ever happened to you? I'm not blaming you, why are you shouting at me right off the bat? I have no idea why and how! I'm a wreck, I'm telling you! How'd the teeth get eaten away? Then it hit me—hey, I've got a crankshaft from my late brother's scooter, which is just sitting around waiting to be taken apart! Question is, how do I change the crankshaft? How do I remove the magnet from between the coils? The voice at the other end of the line answered what he answered, and the man said: So you're saying change the crank and it'll all be okay? Remove the magnet with a gear puller? But where can I get a gear puller—what am I, a mechanic? A good gear puller costs some five or six hundred shekels, if not more! What, Boris has a gear puller? So talk to Boris. Why should I have to lose business? This envelope's special delivery, okay? Right, right, for the palace for sure, I go up and down there fifty times a day—I'll bet *that's* how the teeth wore down. So talk to Boris—what? No, where am I? I'm at the falafel place by the radio, they give me a free order every day, the suck-ups.

Jeremiah shut his eyes, and the owner of the scooter apparently started to eat, since the voice went silent. Jeremiah dozed off, and when he opened his eyes the angel was there, sitting on a stack of dusty old records, and he wore on his head a black motorcycle helmet with flame stickers. Jeremiah recognized the angel's eyes behind the slit. And he was afraid, because once again he remembered, and realized he'd been putting off the purchase of that jug at the Potsherd Gate for too long. He told the angel defensively, I was hungry, I stopped for a minute for a falafel, and then my back went out. The angel said, Don't move, stay here for a while, and he removed his helmet, and Jeremiah was so taken aback on seeing his face—for it was a completely different angel now—that he jumped, despite being flat on his back. And a stone dug into his lower back, and he gasped, unable to take a full breath. The angel said: Good, relax, it's sprained; there's pressure on the nerve. It's the domino effect. It hurts—you've got to rest. Forget the jug; there's no hurry about the jug. What you need is a hot-water bottle, not a jug to smash. You'll buy the jug, but not now. For now just lie down, there's plenty of time. Jeremiah moaned in pain. In the midst of the pain caused by his wretched back, he also realized he had no way of getting out of this place; he had foolishly wandered into the deserted ruins of the public-broadcasting buildings, and no one was going to pass by for who knew how long, and who in the falafel stand would hear him even if he hollered? It was pretty far away, and there was a constant racket over there anyhow. He tried to relax and breathe, enveloped by the nauseating smell of frying; again he moved his knees to the right and left while turning his head in the opposite direction. He'd left his shoulder bag at the falafel stand. If only he could manage to reach it and then pop a tablet of Arcoxia, which he always kept in his bag, maybe he'd manage to crawl home in a couple of hours. You yourself are now a broken jug, the new angel told him. Should the smashed jug envy the new jug? Jeremiah asked: Can you save me from this? The pain's killing me. I'd get right up and head off to buy the necessary item. The angel said, You're not listening to me, you're not listening, you're only making it more difficult for me, I'm saying the exact opposite, I'm saying jug, jug—forget about the jug, okay? Jeremiah said, But before— And the angel-helmet said, There's no before. Before—before's dead. But suddenly the angel with the helmet vanished, and the bedside angel appeared, and a 120-milligram tablet of Arcoxia was resting on Jeremiah's tongue, and he swallowed it with cold water that seemed to gush into his mouth, and the bedside angel went up to him and placed the motorcycle helmet on Jeremiah's head, and in doing so brushed his shoulder blades with two fingers. He stuck the helmet on backward, with the visor at the back of his head, and Jeremiah opened his eyes inside the helmet.

HE HOVERED AT LOW ALTITUDE over the streets of Las Vegas at night. In the limousine cruising down the main street below him, he noticed a number of senior politicians. Minister of Finance Baalzakar was there, Minister of Defense Baalgezer, temporary Deputy Prime Minister Achmelech, King Jehoiakim, and other factotums, workers, eunuchs, and concubines. He was familiar with some of them; they'd studied with him in high school and had made their way up. The car was so big he reckoned it possible that the entire royal retinue and government staff was present, and that a ministerial meeting was taking place in the limo. And it came back to him that, indeed, as much had been reported: they'd all flown together to Las Vegas in order to relieve some of the tension in managing the last small war, or the one to come, or both—but what's the world come to when an Israeli minister of finance needs permission from the attorney general just to try his hand at blackjack?! The minister was quoted as saying: I lose everything anyway, I won't pocket a dime; my Swiss bank accounts are all empty, and inevitably the casino will guzzle everything up. I'm sucked dry in the casino, he roared, and then the media arrive and suck away what's left! And everyone was reassured with a sparkling smile that they wouldn't gamble away public funds, but everyone knew that the money they brought with them in black attaché cases was earnings from lectures—which is to say, bribe money allegedly earned fair and square and in accordance with the law. They've all suddenly become senior lecturers, brilliant rhetoricians. One mute minister received two hundred thousand dollars for a lecture he delivered in sign language, except that he spoke in Egyptian sign language, and his Assyrian auditors thought he was kidding them and didn't understand a thing. One lecturer raked in millions for a forty-minute talk whose title was "My Opinions on Life." The temporary deputy prime minister stuck his head out the window and then pulled it back inside and told someone—perhaps the king himself, who was sitting in front, next to the driver—Look, there's Jeremiah the prophet, a gray crow flying over us. It chased after us all the way here. This greatly amused them all. One of the ministers dug a square chip out of his suit pocket and flicked it with his fat fingers at Jeremiah, as if he were tossing away a cigarette butt. Jeremiah swerved, but the token struck his face and hurt like a poisoned needle. Caw-caw, the deputy minister screamed, and the eunuchs laughed. The big car picked up speed, and Jeremiah flew after it until it disappeared into a huge underground parking lot belonging to one of the hotels. He could still see the face of Aaronson, the deputy minister of construction and housing, in the rear window, pressed against the glass, as though someone had shoved him there.

Jeremiah wrested out the black chip that lodged in his cheek like a razor. It was a one-dollar chip. He buried it in his pocket. Blood trickled from his cheek. There was an ice-cold water faucet in the street, but in order to get a drink you had to gamble for it. Engraved on the faucet were the verses *Oh, they thirsted for water / like gamblers in the heart of the desert*. Next to the faucet's water tank was a small slot machine. The crow alighted on the faucet, inserted the chip, and rinsed his face, leaning his wounded cheek on his shoulder. Similar slot machines were everywhere you looked: beside street benches, at the bases of streetlamps, next to garbage bins, against tree trunks. The people who passed on the street spoke only of money: Yesterday—are you listening to me?—I said, I'm going to Vegas with a penny, and I stuck my penny in a machine, it was all I had in my pocket, and I ended up losing it, ha. And his friend said: I like to put up a minimum of one grand; I don't feel comfortable playing with anything less . . . The casino respects me, gives me free drinks, flies me in, so I respect it back, right? I decided, let's start with one grand, and then I heard myself say, five thousand. There was a bank across the street; its façade shone and flickered with thousands of colorful lights. Next to it was the Luxor Hotel, with its sphinx crouching there in the dreadful heat of the Egyptian desert of Nevada. This wasn't, of course, the original Vegas, but a replica built by the Egyptians. The Eiffel Tower soared not far away, and a couple of pharaoh types ascended to the top in an elevator, to gaze down at the city in the gloom that spread beyond the last lit home into the depths of the desert and the night.

Later on, he was inside one of the casinos, shaped like an upside-down Egyptian pyramid built atop a Babylonian ziggurat. By then, night had descended. The interior of the pyramid was lit up in a pale-purple light, and all the casino employees were dressed in immaculate white clothes. Waiters passed between the tables in silence, offering beverages to the gamblers. Someone placed a glass of water on a silver tray opposite Jeremiah. His pockets were suddenly filled with hundreds of hundred-dollar chips. A man of enormous dimensions sat next to him on one of the casino's indoor ramps that broadened as it sloped up to the sides of the room, and in his hand was an ice bucket filled with bills. Jeremiah didn't look at him at first, but when he stole a glance he was astonished to see Baalzakar, the minister of finance: the minister blown up to giant size, in width and height, whereas in reality he was a gaunt apparatchik with a ledger always under his arm. He was eating a chocolate-vanilla cone with one hand and rummaging in the cash bucket with the other. Minister of Energy Egeliahu sat herself down at the other end of the table, next to Minister of Outer Space Achnoam; two young gigolos wearing sombreros sucked their toes and slowly crept up their shaved shins and their knees, while the ministers stacked red chips on the roulette table. The minister of the interior turned to Jeremiah and said, in high Akkadian: Look at those two frauds. They've been made senior ministers; all our energy and our entire space program are in their hands, but why were they appointed? After all, that one doesn't know a thing or even half a thing about energy, and as for outer space, let's not mince words, that one there thinks the sun burns on crude oil—I've heard her say as much with my own ears. At least I have a B.A. in business management, and I was raised to know the value of money. The roulette wheel spun around noisily; the minister of outer space bet on red, the minister of energy on black. The minister of outer space hit the jackpot. One of the gigolos comforted the loser by buttoning up her shirt and bearing her away to a nearby alcove with soft armchairs, located at the top of the inside of the upside-down pyramid. A whore on stilettos trotted behind them, balancing toast, Persian whiskey, and tasty morsels of meat on a gilt tray. The minister of energy stuck by the roulette table, increasingly enthusiastic as the enormous stack of chips opposite her grew taller and taller. The minister of outer space had already lost everything in the first five minutes of their evening at the casino, which had been slated to go on till late. Jeremiah saw her approaching the minister of defense's secretary, and after a few minutes with him she stuffed an envelope into her shiny purse. The minister's secretary extended to her his beguiling finger soaked in Cognac, which she licked with the tip of her tongue. Every now and then, people stopped in their tracks and salaamed a statue of Baal. A racket could be heard coming from the lobby; Jeremiah saw Deputy Director General of the Prime Minister's Office Hannibal and Minister of Defense Baalgezer standing there and counting a wad of bills with spittle-smeared fingers on their way to the cashiers. I'll fuck you in the ass on the ministry's table, I'll strip you in the Cabinet office, you piece of shit, someone shouted. The ministers smoked super-fat Assyrian cigars that black prostitutes kept, needlessly, relighting with gigantic lighters, lest—heaven forefend—they go out. Someone said that once again a war had erupted at home, on the border, and the honorable minister, his eyes riveted on his winning card, commanded in a voice of steel: Mobilize everybody—I mean everybody. Follow the usual procedures. I've said it a thousand times, don't bother me with routine stuff, for the sword will devour so-and-so, and so-and-so will be destroyed by the card. He really did have a good card. People held banknotes up to the open cigarette lighters and moaned in sham pleasure, as if having orgasms, when the bills caught fire. Smoke filled the casino. The finance minister, next to Jeremiah, also took out a cigar, and Jeremiah saw to his horror that it lit itself, without any flame. The stupefying smoke buffeted him toward the small-change slot machines, similar to the ones he'd seen in the street. King Jehoiakim's younger brother was standing there with his back to Jeremiah, hesitantly sticking coins into the machine and quickly losing all his change. There was something touching about this kid sticking in coin after coin, bending over, and peering despondently at the empty payout bin. It was clear that he'd been forbidden to engage in any serious form of gambling. Jeremiah approached him from behind, dreaming and yet seeing everything sharply, utterly real, and he leaned over and whispered into his ear, For death has climbed through our windows, it is entered into our palaces, to cut off children from the streets, and young men from the squares. But the king's chubby brother, completely absorbed in his petty gambling, didn't hear a thing, as though a transparent, sealed screen had risen between Jeremiah's mouth and the gambler's ear. One of the ministers stretched out on one of the couches, and Minister of Transportation Yichueli sat next to him, puking up something on the upholstery; a waiter, or another servant, spoke to her softly, explaining to her that she must go on having fun, that she mustn't ruin the party by throwing up, because the king was about to pass through, and he had specified that he wanted her as his first pick. The king wants you, Yichueli, the waiter said, he's hot for you, you have no choice. After the surgery you underwent, how could he not be hot for you! he added. You enlarged, and now he desires maximum size; you colored, and he likes the color! You bet he wants you. No, no, he doesn't want a whore. He told me: Yichueli is better than a whore. Yichueli was the youngest minister in the history of Judah, a minor minister, all of fifteen years old. Why say whore? someone said. On the one hand, Yichueli freely bestows her love; on the other, she isn't averse to receiving gifts. Jeremiah noticed bruises on her exposed body; clearly she'd been beaten. He wanted to shut his eyes and wake up and find himself elsewhere, but he knew he had to stay and keep looking, this was his mission, and there was no point in screaming, since no one would hear him anyway—he felt his head throbbing under the helmet—and even if someone did hear, who would pay attention to more screaming in a place like this? Jeremiah saw King Jehoiakim, a ruddy-colored mountain of a man, yawping next to the main poker table downstairs when he won a huge sum (they'd fixed the roulette wheel and the cards in such a way that he would keep on raking in the cash). And he saw Minister Baalzemer shouting at a waiter for more and more drinks, and the waiter brought him a can of beer with a tube dangling from its side, and the minister tilted his head back, and someone stuck the tube into his gaping mouth to the sound of gleeful whoops all around, and Jeremiah heard Minister Baalzemer's wife yelping as she was being strapped to some sort of apparatus—she was tricked out in leather with buckles and zippers and a leather mask over her eyes, and she'd been shot up with something and started to twitch—and the minister himself, her husband, approached with a whip in his hand, and he unzipped one of her zippers, and she squealed as he flogged her, and he, too, had a zipper, and Hannibal soon joined in, holding a lit cigar between his fingers, which he brought close to the minister's wife's body, and then, biting this cigar, he unzipped his fly and waggled a sausage out of the opening, to the apparent astonishment of all present. The music beat like a pacemaker—

tam, tam, tam, tam—shaking everyone to the core. There were also crooning waiters there, trilling in Egyptian. Jeremiah felt death was surging up from within and filling him up; he realized that the orgy, which was taking place in a private casino, had just begun, that scarcely an hour had passed, and who knew what might happen in the wee hours of the night; he didn't know whether he'd be forced to witness it all. Someone sat down next to him and opened a suitcase, which was stuffed with cash, and the faces on the bills were of well-known poets and writers, and the man—he was governor of the central bank—counted the bills with clammy fingers and slipped them into envelopes and came up and distributed these to the ministers and their spouses, and Jeremiah thought that the money was certainly being printed somewhere on the premises, which is to say that there was no limit to the amount of gambling the ministers could indulge in, and they won and they lost, and they roared or they shouted in dismay, and now and then they retreated to small upholstered bedchambers, and now and then freshly recruited prostitutes of both genders arrived in the casino, the females in sailor uniforms and the males in sombreros, and the temporary deputy prime minister suddenly broke into song, something about a sailor, and his assistant answered, He's *my* sailor!, and then the temporary deputy drew an automatic rifle and started firing into the air. And two of the female sailors went up to Jeremiah and leaned over him, smiling, and their good looks astonished and overwhelmed him, and all his defenses and his objections and his raging admonishments melted, and they asked him only one question: *You want some, too?* And his mouth longed to say that, yes, he wanted some, and he had nearly said so when one of them turned him over and massaged his sore back with her fists, and the other drew out a riding crop and lashed the air above him, and he clenched his teeth and bit his tongue, and he awoke, and got to his feet.

6

HEAR AND GIVE EAR, be not proud, for the Lord has spoken. Give glory to the Lord your God before He brings darkness and before your feet stumble on the mountains in twilight. And you hoped for light. But if you will hear not, Jeremiah muttered, my soul will weep in secret. Let us lie down in our shame and let our disgrace cover us. His back was still sore, but a sort of stupefying numbness sheathed his pain. He thought he saw a lion stepping out of a thicket next to one of the buildings. The king spoke on the radio from where he was vacationing and said, You will not see the sword, nor will you have famine, but I will give you true peace in this place. Shalom-shalom. The king spoke of his willingness to arrive at a historic compromise, but what wasn't clear was a compromise with whom exactly. Jeremiah asked the cabdriver to turn off the radio, but instead of killing the radio the guy turned the volume up, and the king repeated emphatically, Sword—and famine—won't come—to this land. And the driver said: Now there's a real stud. They say he's got thirty centimeters at least. Jeremiah imitated King Jehoiakim's voice and said, If—I go forth—into the field—then behold—the slain—with the sword—and if—I entered—into the city—and behold—them that are sick—with famine. The driver said, What's that? Jeremiah got out by the Potsherd Gate. The jug stall stood out conspicuously among dozens of vegetable and fruit stalls, and every now and then blinding flashes of light shot out from the stall and pricked his eyes.

A Phoenician merchant ship was docked in the Jerusalem port in Hinnom Valley. Galley slaves rubbed down the deck with the blood of slaves who were several rungs lower on the scale of subjugation. The port had been connected to the sea canal thanks to the brilliant engineering feat initiated by Deputy Minister of Construction and Housing Aaronson (a seventh-generation Moabite on both sides who'd converted, as was widely known, to the Jewish faith, though in fact he only really Judaized his name, on the advice of his public-relations consultants). An envelope full of cash, dispatched, allegedly by mistake—the mail is so unreliable, these days!—to the assistant to the deputy director general of the prime minister's office, Victor Hannibal, had been the push necessary to secure the required authorizations and alter all the relevant zoning laws. Sometimes certain envelopes just fall into certain mailbags, you know? Hannibal guffawed. There was this black car he'd dreamed of since childhood, and the stash in the envelope was plenty for the car and a couple of refuels, too. And even though no one stood to gain personally, and there was absolutely no bribery involved, the contractor who got the bid wound up, quite by accident, being Aaronson's brother, Kosmelech! In time, Aaronson would ask, in court: Look, just because he's my brother, does that mean he has to scrounge around looking for work? Besides, the moment my name was legally changed and I turned into a bona fide Jew, he wasn't my brother anymore anyway—certainly not when it comes to business matters. And the court accepted these claims, accepted them with open arms. The canal was inundated with seawater, and ships sailed daily from the Dead Sea to Tyre and Sidon and beyond, bearing merchandise and slaves. The lowliest slaves were obliged to draw a bit of blood from their veins and smear it on the deck, a sacrifice to the spirit of the ship. That was the custom. The Phoenicians believed that a blood sacrifice before embarking would prevent blood from being shed out at sea, and who could convince them that they were mistaken and should take responsibility for whatever disasters might befall them en route? In any case, it wasn't their blood: the slaves were Amorites and Moabites and Philistines and who knew what else. The higher-ranked slaves smeared the blood around and dressed the wounds of the venesected, and then served them tea and cake and took them to their places among the other rowers. Jeremiah recognized two renowned prophets—the sort who frequently appeared in the news—about to set sail on a southbound vessel to Egypt. What would make them head south to Pharaoh? he wondered. And then he looked north, into the heavens, but the bulging pot wasn't there: only the new star sparkling behind a cloud.

The ship anointed in blood unfurled its sails and set off due west in the broad canal. A flock of gulls flew overhead as Jeremiah walked up to the small market adjacent to the Potsherd Gate. Moabite, Edomite, Ammonite, and Midianite merchants ran the market. If business were conducted here as in any other market, a medley of arcane tongues would dazzle the ear and make it impossible to understand anything. This was why most of the merchants and customers made do with hand gestures alone—why the market, overflowing though it was with foreign tongues and voices, was for the most part silent. Conversations were out of the question. People pointed at what they wanted, the merchants stuck out their fingers to quote a price, the buyers offered their own price in turn, and they haggled until they reached—shouting inaudibly—an agreement . . . or not. And there were wizards and witches here who offered to tell Jeremiah's fortune: Come here, mister, I'll treat you with my shofar, one blast of the horn and you'll be cleansed of all your filth. Mister, don't be tempted by those charlatans—*shofar treatment*, come on! But I can offer you some absolutely scientific and verified training in the Kabbalah, which will do you a world of good. No thanks, no thanks. Young man, over here, over here, behind the curtain: tantric massage inspired by Isaac Luria, have you tried it? No? You should try it, it's much better than shofar treatment, whose effects are short-term and work only during the High Holidays. Hello, mister—what, you want shiatsu kabbalah? Pahhh, it's just a foot rub, not even a very good one. Come to us and you'll even get a rebate from National Health. We're the only ones to offer a full menu of services: Light of Life healing as an entrée, hot stones according to Hanoch ben Yered for a main course, spiritualism with Huldah the prophetess followed by tarot reading for the second course, and as for dessert—consciousness-raising in the spirit of feng shui. It's two hundred twenty shekels for forty-five minutes, cheaper than a dental hygienist; we've been written up in the weekend supplement. And there was a potter there from the Pottery Workshop who was spinning his potter's wheel, and there was an oven blazing next to him, but the clay kept crumbling and bending out of shape, and his work kept being ruined, and he told himself, Hold on just a little longer, just a little longer, wait a bit longer, and you'll have yourselves a kettle.

In the glassware stall stood a skinny young woman whom Jeremiah didn't recognize at first, on account of the change in her hairstyle—her head was shaved. Her skin had darkened considerably from the fierce sunlight, and she was talking in a fluent, lilting Moabite; meandering tattoos now covered her left arm and right leg; she was speaking quietly to someone beside her, probably the assistant who helped her produce her glass and ceramic wares. But he recognized her when he got closer. Her name was Noa, he remembered now; he had known her in high school. She had disappeared, setting out on one of those in-vogue journeys to the East—that is, to Edom and Moab. And there she went native and stayed to live with some community or other between the border and Rabat Moab, and there she worshipped, like everybody else, the goddess Anat as well as Baal

Peor. This in itself wasn't out of the ordinary; many of his pals and acquaintances hung out in Moab and took part in all sorts of strange rituals. The goddess Anat in particular was popular among young girls, because she wasn't lorded over by any male gods, and her worship fit in neatly with the spirit of the times (from a feminist point of view). But others chose different gods, Ammonite and Aramean and Egyptian and Assyrian gods; there was a sort of free market of gods and holy sites, and scores of people were always heading out to find themselves in the open expanses neighboring Judah, astounded to discover how different—and how comfortable!—the world was beyond the Jordan River. Out there, people weren't imposing so many demands on them anymore: not forcing them to study, or to read, or to fight. All they were asked to do was simply to wake up in the morning and eat some fruit and till the soil and worship some idols—as they were called back home—and maybe lend a hand with some chores, such as mending a roof or putting up a shack or preparing lunch. By then they were likely to start feeling the heat, so they'd take a nap, alone or in pairs, and they'd rise in the afternoon and drink coffee, and set off for a stroll, and smoke, and stare at the stars at nightfall—it was possible to gaze up at them for hours since the air was so clean out there, compared with back home—and they'd fall asleep with the stars in their eyes and on their lashes. After three days, a week tops, they'd completely forget the awful weight of Judah—a pressure cooker on top of a barrel of gunpowder inside a train that's gone off the rails on a dynamited bridge—and they'd calm down and start to breathe again, and learn to take everything in stride, and acclimatize; and so is it any wonder that they should sing the praises of the local gods, be they the gods of Moab or the gods of Edom, thanking them for their hospitality and protection, and for having enabled them to live—what's the word?—so *simply*, so differently from their former selves. But the majority came home after two or three years, when they realized that a ramshackle commune on the outskirts of Rabat Bnei Ammon and the worship of Moloch or Asherah wouldn't put butter on their bread or bread under their butter. They came home and removed, or at least concealed, as well as possible the tattoos that had been pricked on their bodies there, and reintegrated themselves into the local workforce, which was, after all, somewhat more developed than in most of the neighboring countries, and they studied law or business management, setting their sights on managing an office in one of the Mesopotamian cities, or in Egypt, or in the land of the Hittites, and they would dismiss their Canaanite or Moabite or Sidonite episode with some embarrassment as a youthful folly, with only the graven image of some god or goddess on their desk in one of their office towers—sometimes as a paperweight holding down money and documents, or more likely secreted in a locked drawer—to reveal and stand as a testament to those wayward years.

And so they got talking, though Jeremiah didn't introduce himself, and she didn't recognize him at first, what with his scruffy beard and the years that had piled up behind them both. He asked what the name Potsherd Gate meant, and she said, Well, it was actually called the Dung Gate when it was out behind the current gate, but the Potsherd Gate sounds nicer, and, anyway, broken pieces of earthenware were dumped there. And she picked up a shard to show him. He asked whether she had a cheap jug for him, and she gave him one, and he asked if it was imported, and she replied that she herself had made the jug. It's a clay jug, made of the scraps of other jugs; in this jug there are a whole lot of other jugs that died, and so you might say it's a kind of miracle, my putting them back together again. Noa spoke quietly, earnestly: The vision of the dry bones is a complicated affair for human beings, but for jugs it's simple; for a jug it doesn't matter if its neck once belonged to some other jug, and if its body is nothing more than the remnants of ten different shattered bodies. As long as it holds cold water without leaking, it's a whole vessel, she said. And he told her, I'm Jeremiah, you forgot me; and she stared at him, and covered his beard with one hand, and peered into his eyes, and said, It's been years.

Later, they sat beside the stall and caught up with each other, filling in the last five long years, ever since they both turned seventeen. Of course, he didn't speak to her of the events of the last two days. She, too, skipped over several episodes. She let slip several words in Moabite to her hired hand: I'll be back soon, she said, as she wrapped Jeremiah's jug in rustling brown paper. But for some reason Jeremiah asked her to keep the jug's neck exposed, so she neatly removed the wrapping paper and folded it into her embroidered shoulder bag. She looked at his locket and asked him if there was something inside, and he said, I'm carrying an almond, and she touched the locket with her finger and asked if she could see it, and he carefully unfastened the necklace and sprung the locket open and removed the almond and placed it in his open palm and then closed his fist, and she saw the photo of a girl inside the open locket, and asked wordlessly who she was, and Jeremiah answered in kind.

As they skirted the harbor and crossed the Cinematheque bridge, a school of fish darted around below, and after a few paces, short of breath, Noa said, Maybe we can sit down for a bit. All the while, Jeremiah was carrying his jug. They turned left and made their way up to the Scottish Hospice, where there were outdoor tables and shade. Clouds scudded overhead. It was possible to sit back for a while, sequestered, listening. And Noa remembered Jeremiah's sister, and asked, How many years has it been? She'd forgotten his sister's name and asked him, and Jeremiah said, Mom decided that we wouldn't mention her by name anymore. You can call her *your sister*. And Noa remembered all sorts of things, such as how Jeremiah's mother once came to school to talk to them about dancing. What is dance in the first place? Why dance, she asked; after all, one can walk and sit and lie and run, the body doesn't force anyone to make this kind of a movement. And then she did something strange, abrupt; Noa imitated the movement, facing Jeremiah. Your mother is such a good-looking woman, she said. You can see that she isn't from around here. And Jeremiah, who had no recollection of his mother's visit to their school, said: She told me that all dancers were very beautiful people when they danced. That dance made them beautiful. And at times something of that survives when the dance ends; the beauty of the dance movement lingers when they go to the grocery store an hour, a day, a month, a year later. I never saw my mother's beauty, Jeremiah said. She was simply my mother. But my sister—now, she was beautiful. I didn't inherit their good looks, he added dryly. I resemble my father; only the color of my eyes comes from her. Everything else is from him. Noa looked at him and wanted to say something, but held back. And your mother? Jeremiah wanted to ask, but didn't, because he'd now remembered her mother's misshapen hand and went pale. And Jeremiah wanted to tell her something about the Babylonians and the exile that was about to take place, about the long march, but he held back. After all, he didn't know whether she would have to go into exile or not, and most of all he wished she'd just stay with him a bit longer—no, a lot longer—and he knew perfectly well what would happen if he made even the slightest reference to destruction, exile, and prophecy.

She showed him her hand and said, Look how much dirt has collected between my nails and fingers. And he said, There are guest rooms at the hospice, and they must have bathtubs and hot water . . . It must be great to lie in a hot tub facing the harbor. She said, You've grown a beard. He said, Yes, it's been growing this last week; my electric razor broke. And she said, That's no excuse, and laughed. I can shave it off for you, she said, with fingernail scissors. Just kidding—it suits you. And what happened to your head? I bumped it, he replied. When I woke up.

She took out a cigarette and smoked silently. I've got to go back down to the stall, she said. Maybe we'll meet again? You're around? Are you still living with your parents, over there in the village? And he said, No, I rented a one-room apartment a while ago on Ha-Yarmukh Street. She didn't know where that was. And he heard himself say, Forget it, it isn't important; it's pretty far. A shadow of surprise clouded her face, and she wondered what had happened, and told him: I'm staying at my mother's apartment. You remember where that is, don't you? In the Wolfson Towers. And Jeremiah, on account of the wave of murkiness that was suddenly sweeping over him, said, I forgot everything, Noa, I've completely blotted everything out.

He accompanied her down the slope in the direction of her stall, and stopped on the bridge and apologized: I'm feeling anxious today, he said; it'd be great to see you again. He wanted to tell her that he'd loved her five years ago—it wasn't true, but the memory of the love he conjured now felt like true love. After all, looking back, he could have loved her, he certainly could have. He wanted to please her in some way, so he told her, as though mockingly, Next time, give me a snapshot of you and I'll put it in my locket. And she said, A thing or two has to happen before we get to swap locket photos, no? And he got frightened and said, Yes, yes, you're right, they'll happen, those things will happen—maybe tomorrow? Maybe we'll meet again tomorrow? And she said, Tomorrow is so far off. I'll close up the stall and we'll hang out. Okay? And though he wanted to run for it, he said, Great.

7

He waited for her, staring into space at the corner of the city wall, and then they made their way to the cable car and ascended to the Bookworm Café and Bookstore, overlooking the water and the Hinnom Valley basin. From the height of the cable car, Noa had caught sight of her stall and her Moabite assistant, who was slowly arranging the merchandise before closing the shop early. And she felt the stare of—for a second she forgot the name of her assistant—latch on to the scruff of her neck, on to her body, and a fleeting vision surged up within her, the sight of herself leaping out of the cable car and hovering in the air over the valley.

The waitress smiled at Jeremiah from behind the counter and admired his jug. She removed two tea bags from a wooden box. Jeremiah nodded. The waitress had a twin sister, and Jeremiah never knew with whom he was talking. One of them he liked, and the other not; that is to say, there was one who knew him and was likable, and there was one who didn't know him and who made a show of ignoring him, and in this way he could tell the two apart—except, of course, that he couldn't be absolutely sure that the one who ignored him was the sister who didn't know him. After all, maybe the first sister, the one who knew him, had chosen that day to ignore him? They waited for their tea, staring at the table, staring at their hands resting on the edge of the table, not talking, their thoughts turned inward. All of a sudden, he wanted to put an end to it: Who's got the energy to start dating? You're not sixteen anymore, he thought. And he caught her glancing at her watch and wondered whether he hadn't been typically overhasty in making plans with her. The jug stood on the table. Jeremiah told Noa, I can identify with this jug: one half's its father, the other its mother, but Dad and Mom are also half and half, and so on and so forth; we're all puzzles of shards from earlier jugs, and, seen from such a vantage, he said, your jug speaks the truth. And he wanted to add: I'll smash it now, and from the man will reemerge his parents, and his parents' parents, all the empty dead will return, and the man himself, the jug, will disappear. All that remains of the man's bones and innards will be spread on the rooftops as food for the fowl of the air. He completely forgot that he'd been charged to wander around with the jug for several weeks. Now he wanted to rid himself of the jug as soon as possible. He thought that, with the smashing of the jug, his own task would end as well, and he started to ask Noa, What would you say if I smashed . . . But just then a pair of thick legs pushed their way through to the back of the café-bookstore, and Jeremiah suddenly felt a powerful wallop on his shoulder and raised his head. It was a poet—the name escaped Jeremiah just now, though he knew that this guy was one of King Jehoiakim's younger and disparaged brothers. The selfsame poet had invited him, Jeremiah, about a year ago, to take part in a small literary soirée. And Jeremiah had agreed. Though there's no money in it, the poet had said—we're not paying and we're not getting paid, our wares are despised, there's no demand. Literary evenings are a huge bore, and depressing to boot; ninety percent of the poets are depressives and ten percent are manic-depressive, the poet had said a year ago, or maybe he was saying it at this very moment—it was all the same. He exchanged glances with Jeremiah and Noa, picked up the jug, and examined it with an expert eye, turning and turning it between two fingers. You made it? Noa nodded, and he said, Amazing. This is museum-caliber ceramics. And what gorgeous hands, too. He placed the jug on Noa's paper napkin, carefully. To read poetry is mania or depression, mostly depression, and there's no money in depression, none.

A well-known model entered, accompanied by her manager and by an unattractive friend of hers, who never left her side, in order to highlight her beauty. The poet stared at her, dumbfounded, because he kept a magazine photograph of her in a drawer at home, a picture of her lying on the beach in the sun in all her voluptuousness and parting her lips toward his own. At the adjoining table sat three female poets slotted for close to a year now to be named Young Female Poets of the Year. The poet shot a sidelong glance at them and said: Poets; I'm telling you, someone needs to send a black Mercedes to their homes in the middle of the night and drive them to some empty lot in the industrial zone and make them disappear. That's the Assyrian style, and it's proved itself, in Assyria they feed their poets to the lions, he said, that's the best literary criticism ever, the maw of a lion. It's far more effective than old man Broch. Broch is a wet kitten compared with critics in the Nineveh cages, and those cages are the sharpest and most piercing literary supplement around. He pulled a chair up to their table without asking permission, sat down, and looked at Noa, extending his sweaty hand, which she shook feebly as she glanced at the tattoos on his arm. The poet—whose name Jeremiah could not for the life of him remember, even though he thought that he'd seen him around lately—grabbed the menu and ran his eyes down its contents. They've got a superb eggplant-and-tahini tortilla here, he said, but, no, nothing for me, I can't allow myself more than tea; I've got to lose weight, I need to get back to the gym. Yeah, most poets are nothing more than poetasters, and then you've got the poetesses, whom I divide, the poet told Noa—all the while taking in her figure as best he could in spite of her coat—into various subcategories. For instance, you have your herbal-tea poetesses and then your chocolate soy-milk poetesses. Rarest of all are your coffee or black-tea poetesses—most, to be frank, fall into the soy-milk category. Bahhh, I could puke, he said, and, you know, the herbal-tea poetesses wear brightly colored clothes, baggy linen pants, and they sport straw hats with two-meter-wide brims, and they smear their faces with *maniacal* levels of sunscreen, and stroll around in the streets, and frequent the cafés, and order herbal tea and spill it all on their baggy pants, and then they say, Oy, I've got to go now! And anyway, the poet added, sometimes they just *don't feel so good*, and in the middle of a reading or a meeting or a salon they just get up and split, leaving you in mid-sentence. And, you know, as it happens, you were all for them, you were even considering publishing them, but, no, all of a sudden they *don't feel so good*. As he spoke, he looked at Noa, not at Jeremiah, and now and then at the window, as if addressing the artificial lake gleaming through the glass. But most of the time they sit at home on antidepressants, he said; after all, they're *smoking women*. He stole a glance at the model, who was indeed smoking and twisting her lips to guide the smoke toward the crack in a nearby window, laughing euphorically. You're familiar with the expression *smoking woman*? the poet asked. I invented it—and I also use another one, *well-built woman*, you know, black clothes, a small tattoo on her shoulder blade, more wide-brimmed hats, a hundred bracelets on her wrists, a lot of Timna copper in her ears, raven-black hair, well, and they, too, drink only chocolate soy milk, actually *hot* chocolate soy milk, you know, with just a bit of powdered chocolate and plenty of soy milk with a sticky film on top. Bahhh. I don't want to name names, he said, we all know whom we're talking about.

Jeremiah thought of asking the guy what *his* classification was, as a poet, but he knew it would only provide an opportunity for the man to go on holding forth, and consequently he didn't say a word, but only kept stealing glances every so often at

Noa, who didn't show any signs of impatience—on the contrary, it appeared that the young poet's pronouncements fascinated her, as indeed proved to be the case when she asked the poet, What about Yona Wollach? The poet slapped the table and said: Yona Wollach! Come on, really—hhhaaa—at her best she was a coffee poet, one of the rarest, but later she planted herself squarely among the soy milk. Most of them finish squarely in soy milk, he said, deep in the soy milk, and that's only when they didn't start there in the first place, from the very first moment, from their first book, from the first poem they sent to a literary supplement, faxing it in, of course, because poetesses always have a fax machine at home and they communicate with the world via the fax machine. They haven't heard about e-mail yet, and they don't like to talk on the phone. They're scared to hear a stranger's voice; hence all that's left is the fax machine; sending a letter by snail mail is out of the question; leaving the house, after all, might take a month of preparation.

Jeremiah stared at the jug on the table, and his heart started thumping as though he were about to walk onstage under glaring lights. The poet pounded the table every so often as he delivered his diatribe, and Noa steadied her jug on the napkin lest it fall. Jeremiah admitted to himself that he wanted to keep in touch with her—no, to renew their relationship—but he knew that breaking her jug would only hamper his chances, even though he had bought the jug and it was now his. He wanted to press the jug against his chest; he wanted to stand on the table and announce to everyone that there was a sort of earthbound Leviathan on the prowl, and that its mouth was open wide as it approached from the north, that it was creeping along the roadways and would soon arrive and gulp them all down, that the days of the kingdom of Jehoiakim under the protection of Egypt were about to end, that everything that was now happening was already the end, the last lines on the last page in the last chapter of the book that had been persistently written over hundreds of years. He gestured to the waitress.

Noa, who'd never met anyone like this poet, was stunned and utterly captivated; it didn't take long for Jeremiah to feel put out by his monologue, which droned on and on, like a mosquito's insistent buzz close to the ear that won't let you fall asleep. All that remains is the fax machine, the man buzzed on, an old fax machine, with that old acidic paper, yellowing within a day, crumbling like papyrus from the days of Pharaoh Amenhotep IV. They feed their poems into their machines, the voice buzzed, and send them to a literary supplement for the Passover holidays; they fax the supplement, and their poetry flickers and hums as it passes through the machine, line after line, dzem, dzem, dzem, and they ask to look at proofs, which they never receive, the poet said with a sigh; and anyway, by the time the proofs finally do arrive, they've committed themselves to a psychiatric ward, where they're served hot chocolate consisting of a cocoa substitute and water and a god-awful whitener. That's the sad story, that's the whole sad story of the new Hebrew poetry. The poet spoke in all innocence, seemingly, as though stating the obvious, talking about the weather. And he stuck his hand out of the window and said, It isn't raining.

There was a blind waitress at the café, too; they did their best to let her work, and it was a wonder, the way she carried her tray and tea without sight and never spilled a drop. The waitress served them two cups of tea and moved the jug aside, and Jeremiah shot his hand out in fright to rescue the jug, as it were. The poet said, I'll have the same please, a cup of tea like Jeremiah, and Jeremiah, in order to change the subject, without thinking twice, simply wanting to liven this pathetic poet up a bit, this man with his curly beard and his tall Assyrian pointed cap and the cuneiform tattoos that covered his nape and his arms and who knows where else they reached under his clothes, said: So you're actually a tea poet yourself, is that right? And the poet froze, glared at him in alarm mixed with contempt, and said, That's very funny, that's brilliant, Jeremiah, what you just said, but, look, I know how to insult people, too. He went silent for a second, recalling an incident from the after-school youth science club they'd both attended, he and Jeremiah, a decade ago, and how Jeremiah once swiped some blood from the laboratory and sat on the stolen test tube, and the instructor asked what's that, and Jeremiah told her that he'd pissed blood. I peed blood in my pants, the poet recalled Jeremiah claiming. Now, however, he didn't say a word of this to Jeremiah, but, rather, enjoyed the advantage that the humiliating memory gave him, and laughed at Jeremiah squatting on the bloody beaker. His laughter boomed and disturbed some of the Bookworm customers, including four other poets sitting at a corner table, engrossed in a fresh pack of cards from which they were drawing and shuffling the queens. The waitress approached with his tea and served it and said, Mattaniah, if you don't mind lowering your voice a bit—people are trying to read here. And Mattaniah (Right, that's his name!) looked around and said, as if speaking over Jeremiah's and Noa's heads, I'm done with you both; bye, now. He took his tea from the blind waitress's hand as she stepped back so he could pass by, and without as much as a nod made his way to the table of his four bosom friends, who looked up at him in slight disgust.

Jeremiah stared at him as he left. Mattaniah, yes, that was his name. His poems had been accepted for publication under every shady tree and in every cultural and literary supplement; the fact that he was the current King Jehoiakim's younger brother and the son of the former, deceased King Josiah probably didn't hurt his acceptance rate. After his father's death in Megiddo— tales were told of his heroic deeds, but Mattaniah would discover in the days to come that Pharaoh Neco, who was on his way to assist the Assyrian army in the waging of its war against the Babylonians, simply gave an order to shoot his father, Josiah, and that no battle to speak of had taken place but, rather, an incidental death sentence—he became all the more determined to build up his life from scratch, to prove to the world the worth of his poems independent of his family pedigree. After all, what sort of

pedigree are we talking about here? His father was more absent
than present in his life, and dealt in national matters, and in the
Book of the Law he'd discovered, which he couldn't stop reading
and talking about as though who-knows-what, and in the never-
ending intrigues against Egypt and Assyria. When his father
passed away, it was for Mattaniah as though a distant cousin
had died, or maybe a brother-in-law. Great is the wrath of the
Lord that is kindled against us, because our fathers did not obey
the words of this book, to do according to all that is written concerning us, his father once told him, in his old-timer's Hebrew.
Mattaniah said, But you said that today we were going to go sailing in the canal, and his father said: Mattaniah, didn't you hear
what I just said? Great is the wrath of the Lord. The canal won't
dry up; sailing isn't going to go away. But sailing did go away, and
the canal would indeed dry up in the years to come, and Josiah,
Mattaniah's father, wouldn't be around to see it. A year later, Egyptian archers pierced him through; Pharaoh himself shot the first
arrow, and to his own surprise got a bull's-eye, and they brought
the wounded king back to Jerusalem in a chariot, but by the
time he arrived all his blood had spilled onto the upholstery,
leaving his body drained, and the king said to his servants, Take
me away, for I am badly wounded. So Mattaniah was orphaned,
and grew up without a father after his father's death just as he'd
grown without a father before his death. Mattaniah once read a
new book of poems and wanted to please his father and tell him
how he'd fathomed something in one of the verses, and even
started describing to him the strange new music that the poem
had opened up to him, but his father only glanced at the book
and said, Listen, Mattaniah, this doesn't interest anybody one
bit apart from you.

AFTER THE DEATH OF JOSIAH, no one raised the possibility, even
for a second, that Mattaniah might receive the crown, it goes without saying. They'd have crowned a jenny ass before Mattaniah,

they'd have imported the King of Sidon rather than crown him, and they told him so quite bluntly. And so he retreated, rejoicing, it seemed, in his own affairs—that is, in poetry and all that revolved around it, the little magazines and the publications and the galleys and the prizes and the intrigues and the festivals—and every now and then he invented a whole new past for himself in order to cleanse himself of his kingly origins and be *a no-frills poet, a bare-bones poet*, in his own words. He colored his reddish hair and beard black and told everyone—and even wrote in the bio for his marginally renowned cycle of poems, *Nineveh Palms*—that his mother was Assyrian and that he didn't have the slightest idea who his father was. He grew Assyrian curls and a groomed shovel-beard, and he pumped iron in the gym in order to make himself match the wall reliefs in which the Assyrian kings were always depicted with bulging arms and calves.

In time, Mattaniah began to believe in his invented half-Assyrian origins, which were supposed to blot out all traces of the kingly pedigree that only wearied him and stood as an obstacle, in his eyes, to the objective recognition of his literary achievements. He wanted to be important, that's all. For what's the opposite of important? he asked. The opposite of importance is nonexistence. To exist is to be important; I want to be important, important to somebody, it doesn't matter to whom. At first, after his father's death, his younger brother, Jehoahaz, was crowned king, and his kingship was celebrated with great fanfare, it was the month of Tammuz, but after three months Jehoahaz disappeared, literally. Four skinheads arrived in a black minivan, shoved him into the back at three in the morning, and drove him down to Egypt, and since then there hasn't been a peep from him—he was simply rubbed out—and so the Egyptians crowned Elyakim, his older brother. Pharaoh changed his name to Jehoiakim in order to humiliate him, but the name was actually pretty nice, Mattaniah thought; after all, they could have given him a revolting Egyptian name such as Ahmose or Merneptah. Like everybody else in high school, Mattaniah had memorized the names of the Egyptian kings of the New Kingdom as part of the mandatory curriculum for his matriculation exams in Egyptian culture and language. The disappearance of his younger and much-loved brother, Jehoahaz, greatly distressed him, and for many months he went on hoping for and expecting Jehoahaz's return from Egypt. But, then, he also believed that at any given moment he, too, would be whisked away, and he avoided minivans as though they were monsters, forever seeing his brother Jehoahaz, head covered in a burlap sack, being forced into a black minivan, its sliding door slammed shut after him. And he decided that he had to distance himself from all this political turmoil, and from all ties to the royal family—in other words, from his own family—in order to protect his life and safeguard his soul, because to be a major poet—or even just any old poet—in the incessant bustling of the royal court was impossible.

So he gradually drifted from the court to rentals in Rehavia and Talbiyeh, and adopted a mastiff to protect him on the day they showed up to take him to Egypt. The dog calmed him down somewhat and made him feel more secure. But it also reminded him that he needed it, as a bodyguard; hence the watchdog caused him to remember that he was in danger, just as a humming electric security fence reminds the person defending himself of his prospective assailants. And Mattaniah dyed his hair and his beard, and he tattooed his arms and also his back and his chest and his legs with wise Assyrian sayings and poems written in cuneiform, and he started working out in the gym even before the tats, in order to firm up his body, make it into a solid writing tablet. After getting tattooed, he made sure to keep working out, but every now and then his spirits would break and his barely concealed apprehension of Egyptian kidnappers would return, and he was seized with horror, his heart frozen by the old thought of his younger brother being snatched away in a minivan, his head covered in a burlap sack. When overcome by his fear, he'd quit working out in the gym and building up his body for months, since he knew it would be of no use when the Egyptians showed up in the middle of the night to take him away and rub him out, and all the wise Assyrian sayings faded and his flesh sagged, until he pulled himself together and returned with renewed vigor to the barbells and the elliptical machines and the isotonic protein drink and the morning jogs, and the cuneiform on his skin—which he barely knew how to read, much as he admired its shapes—would regain its recognizable contours.

Now Mattaniah sat himself down next to his four poet friends. They all had smartphones in their hands and were taking pictures of one another, as well as of the other customers sitting in the café or browsing its bookshelves. They hardly exchanged a word, for the most part snapping their pictures in silence, and then they'd show one another the photos they'd taken, or they'd upload them to their social media accounts and silently write comments beside the snapshots and hit *like* under their own pics. Suddenly all five of them turned in Jeremiah's direction and photographed him and Noa. And Mattaniah leaned forward, spilling a handful of yellow soup nuts he'd dug out of his pocket, and took pictures of the lake and the Old City above it, and then added some filters to the shot when he posted it on Instagram in order to create a more romantic atmosphere, and then he uploaded the same picture on Facebook, and then he also e-mailed it to himself and opened his incoming message. Jeremiah caught snippets of their conversation. The five had recently founded a new literary journal and were engaged in deciding who could and could *not* participate and publish in the journal. They wielded a pen of iron and wrote down who was a yes and who a no. You want to publish Gunkel? Gunkel the graphomaniac? Over my dead body. When you get right down to it, his poems are, at best, the immature overflow spilling out of a starving yeshiva student's pen, and at worst they're megalomaniacal spasms at the level of a religious secondary-school girl. Gunkel? We've set up a literary mag for *him*? After all, he was formed out of the dirt between the fingers of Pinchas Sadeh, who, *entre nous*, was no beacon in exile, either. Perhaps, while we're at it, you'd like us to print the kitsch of, what's his name, that grade-C poet, the Cohen, and the guy stood up and recited with pathos, *A voice is heard in Ramah / Lamentation, and bitter weeping / Rachel weeping for her children / She refuses to be comforted—for her children are gone.* Gone, they're simply gone! They're gone, so I guess I'd better sit right down and dash off a limerick about it!

It took Jeremiah a fraction of a second to grasp that they were quoting his old poem, his own poem, from the book of poems he had sent to Broch. They were quoting it, or so it appeared, guilelessly, as if they didn't know that he, the poet, was sitting at a distance of several tables. And a second poet said, *Rachel weeping for her children*—forgive me, but that is without question stylistic scum, a sort of precooked cornstarch quiche warmed in a microwave until it turns all rheumy. Nothing easier to squeeze out than tears. Here's a surefire recipe: take a historical figure—Rachel, Leah, Dinah, say—and let her shed some tears in a poem, and, rest assured, your book's bound to go through three print runs. Why not *Rachel weeping for her deputies*, this poet suggested, trying his hand at improvising a witty parody. Surely she had deputies, too, no? And if she didn't, why not, is it so hard to deputize people? And a third poet raised the stakes and said: I suggest *A broomstick sweeping its underling*, and then a fourth said, Nice, but whose underling? And they shot back, Rachel's, what d'ya mean, *whose*? But she didn't have underlings, one of them insisted. And his friend asked, She can have deputies but not underlings? And they laughed and laughed, and Mattaniah, who hadn't joined in so far, took courage and said, The Lord licking her stamps. The other four stared at him and said: What? Mattaniah, what's the connection? Where did you get that one from? This isn't a post office, and anyway there were no stamps in our forebears' time. Look, one isn't obliged to write and talk at all costs . . .

Noa, who had no idea that all this banter revolved around the man sitting next to her—his poker face betraying the faintest hint of his discomfort—was browsing through the latest edition of one of the newspapers' literary supplements. There was a review of the new journal edited by the five poets over at the other table, with further details provided by Broch, a literary critic whose name she'd undoubtedly never heard before. The write-up in the supplement was the reason for their get-together, even though they hadn't dared open the journal as yet, and couldn't bring themselves to read the critique; in the meantime, they were steeling their hearts against what must surely be—so their instincts and experiences told them—a death blow. Noa drew Jeremiah's attention to the write-up, and he was surprised to see them there, a photo of the five poet-editors of the new literary journal *Muscle* (the original name that Mattaniah proposed, *No*, had been unanimously rejected by a show of hands). In the picture, their ever-present smartphones and cups of coffee and strong tea were visible, and Noa saw that the headline heaped praise on the review and mentioned the five by name.

One of the poets raised his hand, and the blind waitress sensed something in the air and came over. The poet asked for a glass of water, and the waitress, her arm stretched out in front of her, brought him a glass of water with a floating slice of lemon. The poet, short and adept at mimicking the cries of rats—his day job was actually doing this routine at birthday parties and stag nights—winked at his friends, poured the water into a vase, and after a moment again called the blind waitress and said: Waitress, what about my water? There are thirsty customers here, can't you see? And he pointed to his empty glass. The waitress, with her sightless, embarrassed eyes staring over his head, apologized and fetched him another glass, her arm again thrust forward and her fingers fumbling at the empty space ahead of her, and he silently poured this glass, too, into the vase and winked at his friends, who were on the verge of cracking up, though he was making sure to keep a straight face. Once again he called the waitress: Waitress, what happened? What about my water? And the waitress again approached the table, this time with a carafe balanced on a round tray and filled with bits of lemon and ice cubes, which melted inaudibly save to her own ears.

The rat poet called out to the blind waitress, Say, come over here a minute, I've got a question for you. She turned around and looked a little over their heads. You can't see us, he said, right? She smiled apologetically. The poet said: What's intriguing is that we can't see you, either. Can you see her? he asked, and his friends said, No, no, there's no one there. I can't see anyone, they can't see anyone. And so, the poet said, squealing for a moment like a rat, and so it seems to me there's been some mistake here; it looks to me like you, in fact, don't exist. Someone who doesn't see and can't be seen—well, she's empty, nothing, zilch. No? I must be speaking to myself right now; maybe you're only a thought in my head, in which case, you should know, my thoughts replace each other pretty fast, so soon enough you'll be replaced, too. But where's our waitress, the real waitress? one of the friends asked—this sounded like Mattaniah. And the rat poet answered: Excellent question. Our waitress is at home; there's no one here. So there's no point, then, the rat poet told the waitress, in your going home today. Imagine going home and seeing yourself—or, rather, not seeing yourself. Imagine letting yourself find out that you're blind! She'll get the shivers there at home—what a pity. But no harm done, since we've agreed you don't exist, he finished up. Best if you simply stay put here, and she there. And now bring us something sweet.

Jeremiah buried his face in his hands. He picked up and held on to the jug with his eyes closed, and then opened them wide and looked at the people sitting in the café. There was a microphone hooked to a ring on the wall near his seat, intended for literary readings; he picked it up, switched it on, and said, One-two. Ah . . . Oh that I were in the desert in a travelers' lodging place. That I might leave my people and go away from them, for they are all adulterers, a band of traitors. And they bend their tongues like bows of falsehood, Jeremiah said, and they have grown strong in the land, but not for truth, for they advance from evil to evil, and they do not know me, says the Lord, Jeremiah said. He couldn't bring himself to establish eye contact with his audience. Beware of your neighbors, he hissed, and put no trust in kith and kin, for they are all double-dealers, and every friend goes about spreading lies. They deceive their neighbor and no one speaks the truth, they have taught their tongues to speak falsehoods, they wear themselves out acting vilely. He slurped some cold tea, for his mouth had gone completely dry. You dwell in the midst of deceit, Jeremiah said, through deceit they refuse to know me, says the Lord. Therefore thus says the Lord of hosts, Behold, I will smelt them, and try them, for what else can I do with my poor people? Their tongue is a deadly arrow, it mouths lies, they speak kindly to their neighbors, but in their hearts they ready an ambush. Jeremiah mumbled this in a monotone, speaking practically to himself, his mouth not properly aligned with the mike, which every once and a while whistled shrilly. He looked around at the customers lounging in the Bookworm; some were staring back at him, but most were busy with their own affairs, reading or writing or browsing through newspapers or eating or sipping their hot drinks, as was the practice at the frequent poetry-reading evenings that took place there. Shall I not punish them for these things? says the Lord; shall not my soul be avenged on a nation such as this? Jeremiah whispered: For the mountains will I take up a weeping and a wailing and a lamentation for the pastures of the wilderness because they are laid waste so that no one passes through, and the lowing of cattle is not heard, both fowl of the air and beasts have fled and gone. And I will make Jerusalem a heap of ruins, a lair of jackals, and I will make the towns of Judah a desolation without inhabitant, Jeremiah added hoarsely, gasping for air, his throat parched. And he raised his head as though rising from the deep, and stared at the mike like someone who suddenly discovers he's holding a serpent.

Now everyone was looking at him in dumbfounded silence. The twin waitress took several steps toward him, and he realized that she meant to ask him to leave. In a far corner, the blind waitress wept while the model hugged her and tried to calm her down. Noa, at his side, covered her forehead with the palm of her hand and looked fixedly at the table, as if she wanted to be shoved in and buried between the narrow slits of her five fingers. The poets drummed on their table with their sharpened pencils or with the ruler that served them in drawing up their classification tables. A large, charred chunk of liver was frying on the grill, and smoke began to spread throughout the café and bookstore. A veteran writer—recipient of the Israel Prize, one of the fixtures at the Bookworm—got up, hesitated, like someone who knows the worth of his words, and declared: *Bullshit*. Then he hesitated once more, enveloped in thin layers of smoke and the odor of cooking oil, before saying again: *Bu-hul-shit*. His two attendants supported him on either side; he glared at Jeremiah and slowly sat down again.

Jeremiah raised the jug. He wanted to stand on the table but of course didn't. He displayed the jug before the eyes of all the seated customers the way a magician flaunts an empty top hat. And someone said, Are you an idiot or what? Titters, chortles . . . The blind waitress had returned to work in the meantime and was bringing bread and olives to one of the customers when one of the poets stretched his arm out as she passed by him and in a single motion snatched a black olive from the bowl, tossed it in the air, threw back his head, bit sharply into the olive as it dropped into his mouth, chewed out the pit, and spit it out in an arc. The pit landed on Jeremiah's table, and the other poets applauded in amazement. So Jeremiah stood on the table after all. Noa flinched and got up and moved toward the window. She could see her stall down there, closed for the day and covered in a gray tarpaulin held fast by several rocks lest the winds sweep it away.

Jeremiah was barely managing to keep his balance. He

smashed the jug on the floor. It shattered loudly. The twin waitress hastened to sweep up the pieces with a broom and dustpan. Thus says the Lord of Hosts, Jeremiah shouted, without a mike. Even so will I break this people and this city, as one breaks a potter's vessel, so that it can never be mended. And they shall bury in Tophet, until there is no room to bury. Thus will I do to this place and to its inhabitants. Even making this city like Tophet. And the houses of Jerusalem, and the houses of the kings of Judah, like the place of Toph . . . The rest of his words were swallowed up in the din of tables being dragged and customers rising and stretching and the espresso machine putting on steam like a locomotive, and Mattaniah, raising his lips from Noa's ear, told Jeremiah, Listen, that was sure one hell of a speech. It was actually pretty funny, he said with unexpected generosity, but get a grip on yourself, come join us, we'll make room for you at our table. There's no future in imitating the Bible, believe me, there's no public for that sort of thing; no one understands most of the language anymore, it's a generation of ignoramuses. I understood everything, natch, said Mattaniah, but I don't count for much. And he pretended to hear the sound of barking coming from behind and turned around to look, like someone worried about his dog . . . and the veteran writer stood up with the help of his two attendants and ever so slowly—commanding due reverence—strode calmly toward the elevator that led to the rooftop helipad above the café. He, as was his habit, *forgot to pay*, and the blind waitress fumbled after him and called out, Motta, Motta, the bill. From his place on the table, standing high up like a tightrope walker in the emptying bookstore, Jeremiah caught sight of Noa through the large window overlooking the wadi, with her Moabite embroidered shoulder bag, surrounded by the five poets. From where he stood, it appeared to him that she was engrossed in explaining something to them, as she gesticulated and swept her arms broadly, while they, in their turn, matched their own strides to hers and listened to her attentively.

8

THAT SAME NIGHT, Mattaniah went down and opened the front door of his home on Yishai Street in Abu Tor, although it was 1:00 or 2:00 a.m. and he hadn't heard any knocking. Undoubtedly, there had been some sound or other, barking or scratching at the door, he'd think several hours later, in the first flush of morning, but in all honesty he couldn't remember hearing a thing. Tukulti, his mastiff, was standing on the front step, just as he'd stood countless times in the past, whenever he returned from one of his solo strolls through the neighborhood, or from a quick exit into the courtyard to peer up and howl at the moon. Mattaniah had adopted his dog in response to an appeal by the old critic Broch, whose dog, Sargon, gave birth to a litter of six puppies—it turned out that Sargon wasn't a stud but a bitch, though, for whatever reason, the critic insisted on addressing her as male; who can know the ways of the righteous or look into the hearts of the pious? And so six young writers hastened to unburden the old critic's senior, four-legged aide-de-camp of her puppies, adopting Sargon's six offspring, and they could still be seen in town, or at book launches, trailing their dogs. Broch christened the puppies with proper Akkadian names, in order to continue the dynasty: Mattaniah received the puppy Tukulti-Ninurta, named after Tukulti-Ninurta I, King of Assyria, it goes without saying. But the name was far too long, and hence got shortened the same day to Tukulti, to the indignation of both Broch and Sargon.

This time, however, the dog wasn't meant to return. Yet here he was, hobbling into the house. He wheezed, went to his habitual corner, laid his head on the floor, and shut his eyes. Mattaniah stared at him, astonished, clasping the knob of the half-open door. That very morning, making his way to the Bookworm to meet his friends, as was his habit, he'd stopped next to the city dog pound, tied Tukulti to a nearby drinking fountain, opened the lowest spigot, the one intended for dogs, and beat a retreat without looking back. Several days earlier, a critique had been published in the book-review supplement in the popular section devoted to what were called *negative recommendations*. Broch was the endorser. The section aimed to zap out of existence works that were considered particularly harmful to the culture, and Mattaniah's last book, *Assyrian Hymns*, won the place of honor. No one was surprised. Everyone was waiting for the blow to fall: This collection of poems of ecstatic praise to Sennacherib, King of Assyria, apart from being pure trash, objectively speaking, cannot be said to have appeared at the most opportune of moments, given that the Assyrian Empire is on the verge of collapsing, and, in our learned opinion, its monumental pseudo-Assyrian style only worsens the insult to our national poetry, opined Broch in his dispassionate and measured tone. But Mattaniah had chosen Sennacherib because he was the son and heir of Sargon II, the great King of Assyria, and in doing so endeavored by implication to sing the praises of Broch's dog, and by way of metonymy to praise Broch himself, of course, and perhaps afford him a little pleasure alongside whatever other intangible dividends had been yielded by his lifetime as a critic. But Broch wasn't able to follow such twists and turns of thought, and his spirit did not rest, nor did it remain silent. Greatly inflamed, he flew into a rage and tipped the scales in Mattaniah's disfavor. If our poet was at least familiar with basic Assyrian, Broch carried on, dispensing his usual words of praise—that is to say, of scathing attack—if at least he knew the fundamentals of cuneiform and the basic declensions in Akkadian . . . But this poet, apart from his family lineage—doubtful in itself, not to say fabricated—doesn't have much to offer us wretched readers, writing on a newfangled laptop even as he pretends to be carving into ancient clay tablets. Indeed, it's like someone singing opera in a shower of sewage, the critic said, moderating his words. Though, indeed, in this case, we haven't even been lucky enough to be presented with sewage but, rather, absolute, dissolute aridity. The shower is dry, alas, but the stench won't go away, and the Assyrian hymns of our dear friend Mattaniah—a chariot of Israel, and its charioteer!—amount to nothing more than a hard stink between soft covers. Or perhaps even *soft* isn't a fitting description for this book, Broch remarked—now as though muttering to himself as his strength deserted him. After all, we don't call a looseness in the bowels *soft* but simply *wet*. That, in a nutshell, dear reader, is the fundamental contradiction at work in the oxymoronic Assyrian hymns of this poet—we forgot his name in the process of writing this review, Broch added, but it is of no import—it is a malodorous aridity that can also be described, from a different vantage, as a product of the runs, or perhaps a watery dysentery; we won't split hairs on this last point. The common ground—Broch clarified—is, of course, the stench, oh, the dreadful stench. There are telltale signs. You look at a pair of stained briefs and can't remember precisely when you had such terrible diarrhea, and out of embarrassment you fling them into the garbage or the fire, not into the laundry. Thus, into the rubbish I flung these *Hymns*, Broch wrote, but I have yet to feel any relief, and who knows whether I will ever feel relieved.

The title of the article had been "There Came No More Such Spices," a title whose full irony was revealed only upon a second reading. And Mattaniah, who read and reread the review—he might even have been able to pretend it didn't actually concern him were it not for his photograph adjoining the article, under which was the caption STINKS—rose to his feet, and without a second thought put his huge dog on his leash, drove out to the dog pound, and, lips pressed tightly together, tied the creature up and swore that he'd drive straight to the critic's home and strangle old Broch then and there: with both hands he'd clutch his crooked neck and crush it like a sheet of scratch paper. But on his way over, his brother—May His Glory Be Exalted—called, his brother whom he hadn't heard from for at least two years, and said, I read some kind of write-up on you in the paper. So Mattaniah didn't drive out, needless to say, to Broch's place; he only managed to abandon the dog, and if anyone asked what happened to Tukulti he'd say the dog got run over, and he would smear his spare leash with mud and dip it in the bloody juices of a steak purchased for the occasion—this was how he planned to corroborate the supposedly deadly accident. And he convinced himself that within minutes someone was bound to arrive and take the dog into the pound and feed him some dry food, and, hey presto: Peace unto Israel. Let the high praise of God be in their mouths and a two-edged sword in their hand, he thought, seething, to execute vengeance on the nations. He returned home and picked up the paper, hoping the review would somehow have dropped out of sight. Indeed, to his stupefaction, it was nowhere to be seen, as though it had been erased from the back page of the book-review supplement; but then he realized that he'd glanced at one of the old holiday issues he kept around, and he slowly directed his gaze to his own eyes in the current issue, eyes that gazed back at him sternly, ringed in Assyrian curls, above the stink and below the spices.

Mattaniah realized, as he tore down the multi-lane Begin Expressway, that what had been done was done and the dog wasn't coming back. He suddenly recalled with a certain affection how Tukulti used to pick up sticks in the street and bring them home, like a bird building a nest that never gets built but whose components only get endlessly masticated, and how Tukulti used to wake him up every morning by licking his ears, and how Tukulti would howl at the moon. Doubtless he'd be sold to Moabite merchants, and what they did to dogs Mattaniah didn't know, nor did he want to know; that is, he knew perfectly well, because in the vicinity of Dhiban tens of thousands of dogs were annually slaughtered for food; an entire village of workers from the Far East chase after and catch dogs every year in order to slaughter them.

Mattaniah took a wrong turn, and all of a sudden he found himself heading for Mount Scopus. The light rail sped by on schedule and almost collided with him; he slammed on his brakes and turned around and drove back, tears welling in his eyes because he was remembering the time a nightmare shook him awake on the couch and Tukulti was standing there beside him and laid his paw on his cheek, careful not to scratch; Mattaniah had fallen back asleep, and the nightmare faded away. What's got into your head, you idiot, abandoning a dog because of a review?! After all, everyone knows that a book Broch savages is without any doubt extra special, inasmuch as hatchet jobs are Broch's way of pointing out the novelty of a book, his way of signposting a literary breakthrough, while he lavishes praise on the mediocre in a sort of witty contrariness. And, in any case, why take revenge on a dog? Are you out of your mind? Mattaniah made a sharp U-turn and steered his car back to the dog pound, making plans about how he'd spoil the abandoned dog with snacks and a bowl of cottage cheese and he'd prepare all of Tukulti's favorite delicacies. But when Mattaniah returned to the water fountain—ah!—Tukulti was not there. He made his way back home and swore that as soon as he got back he'd grab the spare leash and use it to hang himself in his bedroom, but, needless to say, he neither grabbed the leash nor hanged himself. He sobbed bitterly over his rotten heart, and over the dog that had undoubtedly been snatched by now and locked in a van on its way to the slaughterhouse in Moab. And he reread the review, and suddenly he saw how accurate it was, how very precise, and in effect constructive and helpful, how Broch had written it for Mattaniah's own good, and had said these things only to spur him on, with nothing less than the highest professional integrity, mixed with humor—what, is humor only a tool to use against one's enemies? No, Mattaniah was finally catching on, and he realized that it was unquestionably true: pseudo-Assyrian poetry wasn't going to save him. He took down from his shelf the twenty complimentary copies of *Assyrian Hymns* he'd received from the publisher and burned them—or he intended to burn them, but told himself, I'll reread it tomorrow at dawn before making my final decision, and then, undoubtedly, I'll burn them all.

He fell asleep, crushed. And in his dream he saw a large crocodile creeping closer and closer, and the crocodile was the size of Jerusalem, or maybe the city had shrunk to the size of a dollhouse, and the crocodile opened its jaws, but Mattaniah awoke and the crocodile vanished. He stumbled to the door, expecting the devil to be waiting there, holding a small hatchet with which he would chop out Mattaniah's wicked heart. But only his dog was there, after some twelve hours gone. Tukulti's leash was chewed and hung on him like a tie. He padded in, skulked to his corner, and laid his head on the floor. And Mattaniah approached and stood over him and then lay down beside him on the floor, and there they both slept, Mattaniah's brawny, tattooed arm resting on the dog's back to protect him from all possible harm and from fear of the encroaching night. At the break of day, they got up, and the dog didn't show any signs of ill will; he proceeded to his bowl as he did every day, and Mattaniah measured out his helping and added more and more snacks. The dog ate, but only the exact amount he was accustomed to. Mattaniah noticed that he still hadn't removed the leash, so he removed the leash and saw that it was now considerably shorter. He tied it to the spare leash that he'd planned to dip in blood, and they stepped out in silence, and circled the neighborhood just as they'd done only yesterday. Tukulti took a long time peeing alongside the cypress, as was his custom. When they bumped into acquaintances or poets, Mattaniah lowered his head and didn't say a word, as if he had taken a vow of silence.

And they returned home, and for the first time Mattaniah called out to him to jump on his bed, and again they dozed off together, as though sleep-deprived. In his new dream, someone was about to die in some hospice or another; it was Mattaniah's mother, his Assyrian mother, as it were. And she was about to die in Nineveh, where she lived in his dream, and next to her there stood a gigantic Assyrian dog, who always sensed when someone was about to die and would comfort those about to depart. The dream escaped him when he awoke, and the dog he'd dreamed of, too. But in the dream Mattaniah had asked his mother, who'd rested her hand on the hospice dog, Where are you going? And she replied, Over there.

THE FOLLOWING DAY, Mattaniah and Tukulti once again strode down the streets of Jerusalem. He caught sight of Jeremiah from afar as the latter entered a hummus joint, slumped into a chair, and pushed aside the sports pages. Mattaniah had applied ointments to and bandaged his dog's leg, which he'd discovered had been injured. And he remembered that he had an appointment at twelve, though he couldn't recall with whom or where. Whomever he was supposed to meet, he wasn't going to make it. Their legs bore them to the light rail, and they sped to the Dung Gate station where they got out and headed for the gourmet pet store nearby.

He immediately recognized the same young woman he'd seen two days ago at the Bookworm sitting next to Jeremiah. She stood at a stall alongside a worker who was wrapping several plates as he stared at her from a short distance, his dog at his side. He tried to imagine the way her inner thighs would feel, leading up to her crotch, as well as the taste of her lips. Her hair was clipped short, and she was slender and tall, with a copper earring in one ear. He shut his eyes and imagined licking the lobe and the earring. Her ass was so narrow, he thought he'd be able to cover it with his palm and lift her one-handed. He was certain she'd spent time in Edom or Moab, so he rolled up his sleeves, reckoning that his foreign tattoos would impress her. He approached the stall and casually examined the jugs, bowls, and ceramic pots. She didn't remember him from the café, he noted instantly, and felt surprisingly relieved. He bought a bowl, handing her hard cash; she made out his tattoos, and her eyes widened. To his astonishment, she could read Akkadian. She held his hand and slipped her fingertips to the back of his arm and read and translated the words on his arm, and then she did the same for his other arm; he told her that unfortunately the rest was under his shirt. Not to mention his pants, he muttered, turning his head aside. By the following day, she'd already read him his back and his chest and his legs and his entire body, and she showed him her own scant tattoos. And when she mounted him, her eyes looked fixedly at the cuneiform on his chest rather than into his eyes. Mattaniah had a scented candle, and he lit its black, crooked wick in the little bowl he had bought from her and pulled down the blinds. The light glittered for a moment in her earring, and he saw the green fleck in the copper.

On the balcony, facing the Valley of the Cross, Tukulti stood guard. And in his latest dream, Mattaniah drove northeastward, up to Haran, and there was a large well there, in effect a water tower the height of a skyscraper, and he was told that all the Assyrian waters of the Tigris and Euphrates were stored there. And someone he couldn't identify arrived and told him, There's a spigot at the bottom, and it's okay if you drink—the water here is boundless, and after all you'll only take a sip. But he was scared to drink, thought it was forbidden.

9

ESTHER, JEREMIAH'S MOTHER, took a quick look over her shoulder like a burglar, even though no one was home except herself. She opened the kitchen cupboard and took out the old sugar jar. Inside, there was something wrapped in newspaper. She unwrapped it and again looked around, like someone cracking a safe, then removed a little woman made of clay. Though the hands were broken off, it was clear that they had once propped up her small breasts, one of whose tips was chipped, too. Her face smiled and glowed, and her curls, which were partially crumbled and damaged, reminded Esther of hairstyles from long ago. The little woman's body was a small column of sorts, and Esther set the column's base on a chair, placed a cushion next to it, lit a candle, and started talking rapidly. An old vendor from Ugarit had sold her the little woman, years ago, in the souk adjacent to the Potsherd Gate. Esther pointed: Asherah? Asherah? The wizened vendor of figurines didn't speak any Hebrew, and only nodded and said, Ath'rat Sea, Ath'rat Sea. Esther said, I'll buy it, and the old woman nimbly wrapped the little woman in newspaper, and then pointed repeatedly at Esther's crotch and at her own crotch. Esther smiled nervously and departed, her heart pounding. She hastened to buy a sugar jar in another stall, and placed the little woman wrapped in newspaper inside that. As soon as she returned home, Esther drew her out of the jar and noticed that now only one of her breasts was still intact and that both of her arms were broken. Esther didn't know where to find glue, and it seemed to her that she heard the sound of Hilkiah's footsteps on the path; in fear, she flung the crumbs of clay out the kitchen window into the yard, tucked the broken little woman back into the sugar jar, and quickly hid it behind several rows of glassware.

10

AFTER SMASHING THE JUG, Jeremiah walked across the bridge above the Cinematheque. He stopped in his tracks for a moment and looked around to where the separation wall encircled all of Greater Jerusalem, as well as the walls of the Old City, as though immersed in a protracted and serious conversation. And all he wanted was to stumble upon a hummus joint and order in quick succession two helpings of hummus topped with fava beans, to wipe his plate clean with two fat pitas, drink a bottle of cold juice, wolf down five falafel balls soaked in tahini, round it all off with a cup of black coffee, and then find himself a tree or a bench and doze off for a while in the open. He felt like a deflated balloon. The lack of response to the shattering of the jug lowered his spirits; the indifference to the shards and to his words building up to the shattering had been just about unmitigated. A hatchet job was preferable to silence, he recalled Mattaniah once telling him. You write and publish and listen, but no voice comes, no answer, and if you do hear a voice it turns out to be nothing more than an echo of your own insipid mutterings. And who said that, Jeremiah asked himself, you or him? But he couldn't remember.

He found himself on Bethlehem Road, walking south. It was past four by now, and the long day was already way too much to process. Maybe peace and quiet would finally win out; maybe he was done with all those divinely inspired visions and the attendant running off at the mouth. After all, just between us, he thought, what's any of this got to do with me? He caught sight of a dog in the distance, loping along alone, and Jeremiah could easily tell that it was one of Sargon's brown-coated offspring. His meeting with Broch yesterday came to mind, and he remembered that he had to buy a new keyboard for himself, although he had no intention of writing anything in the near future. He was glad to remember that next to the nearest hummus joint was an office-supply store, and he deliberated for a moment whether to purchase the keyboard before or after eating, but, hunger getting the better of him, he entered the joint on Bethlehem Road, at the corner of Gedaliah, and sat down, waving to the waitress, who was—as he now descried and all but burst out laughing—the twin sister of the waitress at the Bookworm. Apparently, there's no way to avoid the sisters, he thought, and was suddenly struck by her beauty, the waitress sister; her large eyes were like pools in a poem, he mused. And the hummus–fava beans arrived, and he tore his pita in a frenzy and dug in. Oh, the delight of polishing off your first helping of hummus when you're already determined to order a second.

There was another restaurant adjacent to the hummus joint, and, while Jeremiah was absorbed in cleaning his plate, his mother walked into the other place. Jeremiah didn't notice her. His mother—who did catch sight of her son, hunched over his plate of hummus—seated herself behind a column by the windowed partition separating the two restaurants. She was served, as every day at four o'clock, a cup of red-hibiscus tea and a slice of spelt cake. Immediately after the death of her daughter, Jeremiah's mother had stopped eating meat and dairy products; she wouldn't even eat harvested vegetables and fruits. To everyone's astonishment, she didn't lose but, rather, gained weight. Jeremiah and his father, too: everyone put on weight after the death of Jeremiah's sister, even though they'd all cut down on their consumption of food. Jeremiah and his father, Hilkiah, would suddenly break down, jointly or separately, and begin to wolf down cheeses, and then stop, and start again, even sneaking some fish on the sly, and his father would have these sudden cravings for different kinds of foods, such as mango, or kasha, and his mother, too—kasha, yes—and they'd eat lots of kasha, and then they'd stop with the kasha and they'd consume (both of the men, not Jeremiah's mother) goat cheese and tuna, and then they'd feel sickened by the cheeses and by the suffering of sheep and goats and fish, declaring all at once, Enough! And they'd switch to legumes and crude tahini. Once, on one of the anniversaries of his sister's death, his father returned home with a large steak in his bag, which they tore into, a steak and fries, and Jeremiah didn't sleep that night, because his stomach had not digested meat for years; at daybreak, he threw up in bed while asleep. When he woke up early, he took the filthy sheets, and, instead of dumping them into the laundry basket, went out, half asleep, and set fire to them in the open field near his parents' home. The sheets blazed there, and the smell of the charred steak and fries filled his nostrils for a second time, and he let the fire be and fled and didn't return home that entire day, but waited until late. At two in the morning, he entered without making a sound, and, crossing the corridor, he caught sight of a dark silhouette sitting in the kitchen; the silhouette was slowly eating a cake.

They'd decided back then, his parents, that they'd never bring up his sister's name again, for her name was too difficult for them to bear; and so many years passed and they'd only say to Jeremiah, Your sister, and to each other, She, or Our daughter, and after several years, when someone asked Jeremiah, Come to think of it, what was her name, his sister, he didn't immediately remember; it took some time to recall.

His mother sat in the restaurant adjoining the hummus joint

and watched her son ravenously polishing off the helping of hummus, and she sipped her tea, the lenses of her glasses steaming up. In a minute, she'd rise and knock on the window between the two restaurants, she thought, but in the meantime, she would look at him a bit longer. The recurring shock stabbed at her once more, how her child had grown up and in effect vanished—a baby, a boy, a teenager, a young man. When did it all happen? She knew it was a banal thought, but it truly astounded her: Twenty-two years, when did you slip by? At home he never ate with such an appetite, not even the hummus she'd prepare for him. She always felt that at home he ate in anger— entering the kitchen and uncovering her pots like a customs inspector looking for stolen goods, or like a kosher-food supervisor grudgingly tasting some product. As she watched him tearing a pita and cleaning his plate, for a moment she saw his sister sitting opposite him and looking at him, and wanting a taste, just a bit, at the end of a fork—but, no, his plate was empty.

In recent years, Esther had been in the habit of joining customers wherever she found a vacant seat; she'd sneak a look at their plates, and if she saw something there that hailed from the world of the animate, so to speak, she'd start up a conversation with the other diners, or start talking to herself, and quietly describe the wretched suffering of these creatures, slaughtered merely to please the palate and gratify the gullet. She'd start a conversation and say something like: Where are you from? From Sidon? I have an uncle from Sidon; he got caught in a fishing net, and he was strangled in it, and they left him there, suffocating, for ten minutes, and then they stripped him to his skeleton, and they beheaded him and removed his brain, and they ground his skin to a paste, and what remained of his flesh they crammed into a tin can. Or she'd sit next to an Egyptian tourist who'd ordered coffee with *a lot of boiling milk*, and say: I visited Egypt once. My mother was with me—I was a baby then—and they took my mother, and they forced her to leave me behind. My mother screamed and wailed, but it didn't help, because they had to have her milk. She nursed me, and they needed her milk. And the tourist asked, What, to nurse other infants? Esther replied: No, for their cappuccino. I was left behind, and someone came and struck me on the head, and they turned me into the meatballs being enjoyed by that young man sitting over there, across from us. And then she'd get up and walk over to the young man's table to continue. In this way, she'd spoil the appetite of not a few customers, and she was declared persona non grata in a number of restaurants in Jerusalem; in one place, they stuck her photo up at the entrance above the words NO ENTRY. She didn't always talk, though; sometimes she'd simply mimic the sound of the animal that was being eaten, clucking like a chicken, or lowing like a cow, or baa-baaing like a sheep. The imitations were uncannily precise. She'd pass by a table clucking, to her own delight, or she'd sit down and glare pleadingly at a boy absorbed eating ribs and snort like a slaughtered pig.

Jeremiah browsed through the sports section in the paper. The sportswriters explained the symbolic value of Assyria's crushing defeat, six to nothing, by the Babylonian team. When an empire is collapsing, your soccer team isn't all that great, either, and after the first ten minutes, Babylon's ten players began to rout the team that had been, until recently, and for hundreds of years, the terror of all the teams in the world, to the extent that it was customary to define soccer as *a ballgame that lasts ninety minutes and ends with Assyria winning*. But times had changed, and the Assyrian players, with their curly beards and their bulging muscles, suddenly appeared little more than bulky and cumbersome, and the tall, lithe Babylonians made mincemeat of them with their exacting, mathematical footwork, perhaps because they were playing, for the first time, without having to worry that a goal in the Assyrian net might sooner or later cost them their lives. Jeremiah recalled how the sportscaster Yoram Arbel had once explained, during a live broadcast: They only know how to attack, not to defend. Two or three goals in their net and they come apart, but usually nobody gets that far.

Assyria is on the attack so ferociously that, ten minutes in, they're already three or four to zero, and the game's over.

Jeremiah thumbed through the paper. He read in the real-estate section that King Jehoiakim had purchased for himself, if *purchased* is the appropriate verb in this case, the entire enormous Holyland Park building complex, to turn it into his private, royal residence, since the palace in the Old City wasn't much more, in his own words, than a nook, and certainly didn't bring any honor to the royal family or to the people that family represented. The tenants were forcibly evicted at night, with the assistance of Egyptian soldiers. They weren't happy to go, but, as it is written, Give unto the king what is the king's—and, anyway, it wasn't as though anyone was being thrown to the dogs: everyone was relocated to a tenement. In Egypt they'd throw you into the desert without water, so be grateful and say thank you. Of course, the King of Judah, Jehoiakim, was an Egyptian puppet, although he tried to conceal this fact. Even his name, Jehoiakim, was given to him—or, to be more precise, was sprung on him like a net over a butterfly—by Pharaoh Neco, who called him Jehoiakim the way a person might give his little mutt a fearsome name like Rex or Herod. Lots of people didn't bother to keep track of the kings anymore: they were appointed and then exiled from one day to another, and it wasn't always clear exactly whom they were serving. But in the case of Jehoiakim—who regularly made his way around Jerusalem accompanied by two Egyptian chariots, and dressed according to the latest Egyptian fashion, including eye makeup—there was no doubt.

Pharaoh Neco was called Neco the Cripple by some, because he was missing both his hands and his feet, like shattered statuary, thanks to the sharp sword of the King of Babylon, Nabopolassar, or, according to a less reliable source, thanks to the golden lions on King Solomon's throne, who leaped at him and tore off his hands and feet when he attempted to sit there and worship his native idols. Whether thanks to Solomon's lions or to Nabopolassar's sword, Pharaoh Neco II was borne from one place to another in the arms of a servant as large as a boulder, and when he sat on his throne he would sit on this servant's lap, and they would always wear identical clothing, and the servant would operate his monarch's hands and feet from behind. Seeing him brandishing a scepter or a sword, one could almost believe the king was in perfect health and possessed four dark-brown brawny limbs. Neco was the one who'd dismissed Jehoahaz, the talented son of Josiah, and replaced him with his brother Elyakim and, as stated, changed his name to Jehoiakim, which caused a certain amount of confusion: people spoke of Elyakim but meant Jehoiakim, though many still thought that the king was Jehoahaz, or even Josiah, although Josiah had met his death in Megiddo some time ago, thanks to the Pharaoh's arrow, whose accuracy was nothing short of miraculous, and which was fired from a hand that was not his own. It wasn't as though anyone really knew with any certainty who the king was at this particular moment. Nor did they care. Jehoiakim, Elyakim, Jehoahaz, Jehoshabaz, Jehosabitch? Do me a favor, I've had it; in a minute, you'll expect me to know who the current minister of transportation is, or the minister of the postal system. Consequently, most subjects simply said *the king*, and in doing so covered all the possibilities from now till further notice.

Jeremiah perused the report about turning the Holyland complex into the king's new palace. The city, already more than adequately embellished with hideous architecture, was being turned into a monstrosity of unsightly construction, unheard of from the Euphrates to the Nile, and delegations of architects from the entire region, Persians and Hittites and Elamites and Egyptians, would arrive every year in order to nervously applaud this extreme urban unsightliness, and to write doctoral theses and professional tomes on the subject. Of particular noteworthiness was a book by one of the most recent Assyrian kings, who was also a certified architect, Sin-sar-iskun, *Toward a Theory of Urban Unsightliness*, a book that summarized all relevant research into his subject up to the present day and concluded with practical recommendations, which included—and here the Assyrian king exchanged his theoretician's hat for that of a politician—changes to many different cities, not least Jerusalem. This city, which had been one of the most beautiful in the world, was being built up at a monstrous rate and with amazing and grotesque insensitivity. Land was being parceled out piecemeal to foreign investors, who would in turn destroy the ancient buildings that were already on their sites and build pseudo-ancient buildings in their place, in Jerusalem stone, with only one thought in mind—namely, to keep enlarging the already densely built-up area without any consideration for the view, the history, the people, the location—and all the real-estate billboards were in Egyptian, since no resident of Judah could afford to pay such high prices.

Jeremiah was engrossed in the paper, and in its depiction of how Jehoiakim's real-estate kickbacks found their way into his pocket by means of a branching network of couriers on scooters and envelopes and safes and bank accounts and tax shelters on various islands where it was doubtful anyone had ever set foot. Not that the king had ever agreed to pay his taxes; his refusal had assumed a religious character, as it is written, Should the Lord's anointed pay taxes? Jeremiah finished his salad and sipped some of his lemonade and tore out the article on the Holyland project's takeover, and he wrote in the margins of the paper a short sentence that came to mind, with the intention of developing it further later at home: Woe to him who builds his house by unrighteousness and his upper rooms by injustice, that makes his neighbor work for nothing, and gives him not his wages.

In the adjoining restaurant, two waiters grabbed the cluck-ing lady under her wings and cast her out, telling her to go to hell, but Jeremiah was absorbed in formulating his sentence and dotting in some of its vowels and didn't notice what had hap-pened. Someone sat down next to him, ordered a minced salad, and, glancing at the torn page and at the sentence written in blue ink, asked Jeremiah offhand if he'd written it, and if he had by chance written it, whether it might be referring to the King of Judah, or just to some figment of his imagination. Jeremiah replied that it wasn't any of his business, and the man said that it actually was his business, and he pulled out his policeman's identity card, took the paper with the sentence as evidence, and slipped it into a sheet protector. Within minutes, a van stopped in front of the restaurant, and Jeremiah, who didn't have time to pay for his hummus and drink, was handcuffed and led to the van and driven to the police station in the Russian Compound. A small salad came out of the kitchen, and since there was no one to claim it, the waiter sat down and ate, for the first time that day, with a torn newspaper serving as his place mat. He held Jeremiah's second pita in his hand instead of a knife. The police van's siren wailed a bit as the van pulled away, but then—once the driver realized there was no reason to use it—ceased.

11

A ND SOMEONE SAW THEM TOGETHER several days after they
met and said to her: The king's brother, no less. Ha—good
for you! And Noa, who didn't have the faintest idea about Mattaniah's family, of whom he never spoke, said: What nonsense!
He doesn't even have a brother, and certainly not a king. His
mother's Assyrian, anyway—haven't you read his poems? Do
you think the king's brother would live in a rented apartment in
Abu Tor? But she immediately called him up, and Mattaniah
admitted his royal origins with some embarrassment. Filled
with joy to realize that she really hadn't known, he sheepishly
explained his story and his tattoos. That's the end of that, he
thought to himself. After two, three days that had been pretty
terrific, he'd finally met someone who hadn't known a thing
about him, who looked at him and accepted him and his poems
for what they were, and didn't make fun of the cuneiform on his
pale skin but even got excited by it, who understood his body, his
need to build up his muscles, not as some sort of scrappy belliger-
ency, but as a form of cultural aspiration. Right away she saw
what he had wanted to say, to cry out, all those years, but couldn't

manage to express, and so wrote it out on his skin and body instead, and she understood that he didn't pump iron in order to beat anyone up but, rather, to make himself look like a picture, like a stone relief in a palace in Nineveh—in order to be, with his body itself, part of a world in which the presence of kings and gods and winged creatures is made palpable all around. We must grant ourselves at least the minimal right to be alive and active in such a world, because there's no other world worthy of human habitation, and poetry isn't possible in any other world, Mattaniah said to her and to others. Our world is a world that's on its way out, on account of the changing times, on account of the fact that history has begun to replace mythology, and on account of the soldiers and politicians who have begun to replace the People of the Name and the heroes and the giants and the sons of God. What's left now? The King of Assyria, the King of Babylon, the King of Egypt, buying and selling, giving and taking, subclauses in standard contracts; neither God nor an angel nor a prophet, only their pale replicas. Mattaniah didn't want to be a copy, and didn't want to be pale, either. And he told her: Take, for example, that Jeremiah—I noticed that you were sitting with him at the Bookworm. I've known him since we were ten. We weren't close, but he was always like that—skinny, unkempt, stooped, bursting with thoughts and talk, rat-a-tat, palaver here, palaver there, self-intoxicated, exhilarated by his own thoughts, gazing at the moon at night and listening to the bugs singing to the moonlight, that sort of thing. I mean, I'm not putting it all down, I'm just saying, take a look at yourself, man. You've got a body; show it some respect. You've got a pair of eyes; they're not only there to gaze up at the crescent moon. And you've got a phallus—a gift!—so, please, go ahead and use it properly, not just to piss out a little trickle now and then, and from a squatting position at that. If you want to live a full life, it's not enough to read books, you have to clothe yourself in them, Mattaniah told Noa, even though he imagined she'd tell him that she was through with him, because of the hush-up on his part. After all, he'd have told her soon enough about his origins, and would also have explained why it had taken him so long to say anything.

She didn't dump him, however, but came to him at once in a taxi, and sat facing him and told him that she understood perfectly, that she, too, during her time in Moab, sought out the same sort of connection, and idol worshipping had been nothing less than the desire to touch the sacred, and not only verbally. She told him, Make use of Him. When he didn't understand, she said, It's a quote. He still didn't get it, and then she explained it to him. She had a silver statue of Baal Peor in her motley shoulder bag, while in the closet where he stored his bodybuilding contraptions Mattaniah kept a pair of life-size statues of the god Ashur and his consort, Ishtar. It was possible to order surplus statues from some archive in Babylon, and this is what he did. Mattaniah told her, Ishtar is the queen of the heavens, and he left the god Ashur in the closet and took out Ishtar, and stood her up beside the bed, next to Noa's statue of Baal, which she placed on a sheet of plain brown paper. Her idol was only ten centimeters high, and his goddess was practically as tall as a human being, but this didn't bother them. They laughed and tumbled onto the bed and, under the protection of the two gods, they made love fervently. Afterward, she rolled them both cigarettes, which they lit up on the balcony, and they both petted the dog, and she told him they were a king and queen without a palace and without servants, a king and queen in strict confidence, without pomp and without honor or flattery. He went to his study, cut her a crown from ruled paper, and stapled it together, then returned to the balcony and crowned her. Tukulti whined quietly, and she called him *our prince* and placed the paper crown on the dog's head. A few days later, she moved into Mattaniah's place. Her hair, which had been shorn in Moab, began growing back, and her body, which had been awfully skinny from eating nothing but roots and beans, began to fill out a bit. In no time, it was brought to their attention that she was pregnant. Mattaniah and Tukulti would accompany her daily to her stall near the Potsherd Gate, and sometimes they would stand in the not-too-distant distance and gaze at her, in all her splendor, as she leaned over the counter and arranged cups and jugs on the bright embroidered tablecloth.

At the end of workdays, they'd come and pick her up at the gate, and the three of them would walk home, circumventing the outlying neighborhoods. They'd tarry on their way, to get some food and even to feed the strays and alley cats. And one day she stopped in her tracks in the middle of the street next to the box containing the security system for a haberdashery on Jaffa Road. With the light rail noiselessly gliding by them, she told him, I remembered a dream. And they walked on in silence, and she said: You were onstage at a literary reading. There were all sorts of journalists and photographers—you must have written something good. And you sat there onstage in your red sweater, and, strange, you were without a single tattoo, but it was you, no doubt about it. And you spoke quietly and nicely, but you suddenly got stuck—you were missing a word and you couldn't find it. And there was some sort of gadget, Noa said—pointing back to the shop's alarm box—on which it was possible to type words. And I knew the word you were looking for, she said, but I can't remember it now. So I started typing the word, and my fingers shook, and I got confused, and I typed the wrong letters, and the word wasn't broadcast, and you were still there onstage, sitting like you wanted to hide from yourself. I'm sorry, she said, glancing at him, and Mattaniah told her how, back when he was a kid, two days after he'd gotten sick and thrown up in bed—in bed, he stressed, and not in the bathroom, which would of course have been better—his mother, Hamutal, told him: You're someone else. You're not Mattaniah. And he lifted his astonished eyes and asked, What, you didn't give birth to

105

me? And she told him, in a completely matter-of-fact tone, No. The next day, he went up to her and said, Mother, listen, I really am the same boy.

ONE DAY, AS THEY REACHED BEIT HAKEREM on one of their walks, Tukulti, contrary to his usual practice, jerked his leash toward a side street, and they followed him. They were deep in conversation, and Mattaniah didn't notice that they were being led to the end of Broch's yard, which the *Muscle* poets had named the Deathyard. Tukulti planted himself opposite the gate and wailed like a baby, but Mattaniah tugged at the leash and told him: No, no, on no account are we going in here, this is the Deathyard, do you want to be swallowed up in the Deathyard? There are open sinkholes here. Let's scram. They had to drag him away. Mattaniah was certain that the critic was peering out at them through a curtain or some aperture, even though the house was as silent as a grave. Noa didn't understand what the fuss was about, so Mattaniah said: He's a literary critic, more or less senile. If he comes out, he won't let us go for an hour or more; he could stand there for six hours easy and recount the entire history of his critical oeuvre, and what success he's had in Germany, and how in France thirty translators are working on his complete works, including the reviews he wrote in the children's and youth papers when he was seven years old, and how the Swedes are bonkers over his book on Agnon, and how in Ecuador—of all places!—there's already a school of thought that's influenced by his book on Kafka, and how in the West there are already other schools influenced by the Ecuadorian school, and in Egypt and Saudi Arabia, for example, any research on Kafka is indebted to his book, that is to say Broch's book—Mattaniah had a hard time stopping—except that, in all innocence, they believe they're merely continuing the Ecuadorian project. In the heat of his peroration, Mattaniah didn't notice the door opening a crack, but Tukulti did and tensed up.

Mattaniah saw a white foot sticking out of the crack, and he told Noa, Let's get going, he's coming out; we've got to get out of here. And they fled, whooping joyfully, even as the house shoe—like the snorting snout of a mole returning to its hole—retreated and vanished into the pitch-darkness of its lair.

12

THE FIRST SLAP HURTS THE MOST, the cop told him. The first slap is like a frightening trapdoor that opens onto a new world. Jeremiah, who'd never been slapped—neither by his parents nor by anyone else, maybe only by his sister once or twice—got smacked even before the interrogation began. The slap was dealt by the duty officer in the police station, for no particular reason, with much the same attitude as someone greeting his fellow man. After the slap, which was meant to soften him up, they took down his details, and his fingerprints, and they filed the article on the king's palace with its incriminating note in the margins, while the cop who'd arrested Jeremiah completed his report in the proper form, the tip of his tongue poking out of the corner of his mouth and tickling his mustache. Jeremiah waited next to the vending machine, before which a policeman would stop every once in a while to slip in a coin and remove a can. He sat there with one hand shackled. The vending machine had a sort of handle crudely welded to its side, and he was handcuffed to the handle, which he now realized was the fixed spot where the apprehended were always made to wait, alongside the machine, and that the handle had been welded there specifically for handcuffing. His cheek stung. And the visions and voices from that same early morning came back to him, the pot and the almond tree and the angel, but it was three o'clock now, and all the revelations had vanished, or he at least didn't feel their presence anymore, as though all at once they'd abandoned him. Instead of the thrilling sensation that had overwhelmed him at the onset of that day, after the vision of the bulging pot and of the almond, and even after the smashing of the jug, he felt empty and dispirited, although as yet he didn't quite grasp the gravity of his situation. This morning God spoke to you, he'd reflect later on, and all it took was a cop's palm to blot out all the glory of His speech. He tried to awaken the presence of the voice and God, so that He might appear and save him from the vending machine, or at a minimum imbue him with inner faith and endurance and peace, but nothing came, nothing at all, and the voices and the face of the angel that several hours earlier were alive and present within him turned into a mere memory, like the memory of a dream, alien and distant. He was filled with the humiliating thought that he'd been sent on his mission only to be abandoned as little more than prey for the police, and his cheek ached from the duty officer's slap, which happened not to have been that hard but which nonetheless made it clear, to his dismay, that he'd been abandoned, at least for the moment, and even if—best-case scenario—this desertion was part of the plan, all that he had to hold on to were those same visions, and who knew whether they'd ever return, and who knew whether they weren't just a dream or a psychotic attack, on whose foundations he'd now be forced to go on living, fighting a losing battle from the start against forces that were doubtlessly far more powerful than himself, though he still had no idea exactly who and what they were. And he hoped for another sign, for nothing more than another small sign, so he would have the strength to go on. But no sign of any sort appeared.

A woman entered the police station, her head covered by a scarf on which was printed a map of the world. Jeremiah noticed that her glasses were broken and that she was barefoot and was holding an empty bottle. When she entered, she strode right up to Jeremiah and asked him, Do I file a complaint with you? And he asked, astonished, Complaint? And she explained, For rape. Jeremiah said, Oh, I'm sorry, but no. And he jangled his hand-cuff. I thought you were a plainclothes policeman, she said. Otherwise, why would you be sitting here at the entrance to the police station? He said, No, no, I've been arrested. She said, Why? And he replied, I wrote something. About the king. She said, Who's king these days, anyway? And he muttered in a low voice, The real king is Pharaoh Neco, but on paper—the king is Jehoiakim. She said, I hope they release you soon, and he said, This rape, it . . . it happened a long time ago? And she said, Yes, quite a long time ago, as far back as yesterday evening. He didn't understand why she seemed so offhanded about it—he would have expected her to be agitated, shouting—but all he said was: Why are you barefoot? It's not a good idea. Maybe you want something to drink? In the meantime, a policewoman approached her and took her to the duty officer's counter. The duty officer opened a new file and commenced to ask the complainant a couple of questions, and he asked to take her fingerprints, but she put her hands on her head and refused to continue. I'll only talk to a policewoman, she said, and only inside; you want me to tell you everything out here in the corridor, the smallest details? And the policeman said, Before you go in, you've got to give me your particulars, okay? It's routine. The complainant said, Particulars? What sort of particulars? The word r-a-p-e has all the particulars you need. Yes, the policeman said, but who, and what, and where, and how, and why, and from when to when, and how much, and wherefore, and at what angle . . . ? The complainant looked around helplessly. Jeremiah, his wrist beginning to smart from the handcuff, called out to the cop who had slapped him: Can't you see she's all by herself here? She's got no one to comfort her. Leave her alone—enough already. And the cop said, Another word from you and I'll fix your other cheek, too. The woman turned to Jeremiah and said, I cried all night, and none of my friends called. They've all turned their backs on me; they're all my enemies now, from the moment they heard about the rape. I ran, she said, turning to the vending machine that half concealed Jeremiah, I ran, but they caught up with me, they shoved me into some alley. There were two of them—not one, two. I was a good-looking woman once, and now they've stolen all my beauty, they've wrung out all my splendor and all my beauty. I want my life back, I want to go back in time. And the cop hummed a popular song that went *Come back, come back to the orchard*, but the woman didn't look at him, and continued talking to the vending machine, as it were, on which was printed a gigantic picture of a chilled-to-the-bone bottle sweating in the heat. Suddenly she screamed, Everyone had a peek down there, everyone—they saw everything—near the theater. And Jeremiah was sickened, because he remembered his sister screaming that same way, suddenly going berserk. A Xerox technician approached to reload the copier with paper, and the woman made room for him to service the machine. I've gone to the dogs, she screamed, and no one cares. I've gone to the dogs, his sister had said, and maybe the complainant, too—I've gone to the dogs. There's no pain like my pain, the complainant screamed. It's not a toothache, it's not a headache, it's not menstrual pain, it's not lower-back pain, it's not a pain in the neck, it's not a stomachache, it's not labor pains, it's not the pain of a burn, it's not the pain of a hammer hitting your head. Her voice got louder from *pain* to *pain*, and Jeremiah wished he could completely disappear behind the vending machine; indeed, he tried to squeeze between the machine and the wall, which was coated in oil paint, and rest his head there. The woman shouted at the duty officer: You slap around your prisoners; I read about you in an investigative report, how you were acquitted on reasonable doubt. Go ahead and beat me up, too—my pain couldn't get worse anyway—smack me, smack me, you big hero, smack me one, it doesn't hurt, my insides are already scorched, my bones are already scorched, my entire nervous system is scorched, so your slap won't knock me down and won't hurt me.

Banished, banished, I'm banished forever. I've turned into an eternal pariah. I saw waterfalls of blood, waterfalls in Canada of red rushing down! Policemen and detainees and lawyers stared at the complainant as she bemoaned the bitterness of her fate; they didn't say a word, just gaped at her as if they were looking at a strange flowerpot. In the end, she spun on her heel and left the police station at a run. The duty officer said: Bravo, time to break it up, *finita la commedia*. Tomorrow there'll be a repeat performance. And he knew what he was talking about, since the complainant had been dropping in for several weeks now, every day, at about seven in the evening, to deliver a more or less similar monologue before leaving the station without filing a complaint, All things considered, it breaks the routine, and the entire harangue, which she changes a bit each time, isn't ever longer than three minutes, after all, so why not. The Xerox technician opened the paper trays and loaded up five hundred fresh sheets of paper, but as he made to rise he couldn't straighten himself up: his knee had locked when he bent down.

A new cop arrived and removed the handcuffs and led Jeremiah to the interrogation room at the end of the corridor, one floor down. He sat him on a plastic chair. Opposite him was an enormous vibrating armchair that gave massages; it stood empty, waiting for the interrogator. And Jeremiah stared at it with longing. If only he could lean back there for a while and get a massage. His back had started hurting again as the pill he'd taken that morning gradually wore off, and he imagined himself reclining there, and confessing to everything, to everything they wanted to know, in exchange for the luxury of pressing his back, the painful parts, against that vibrating armchair, which would massage all over, releasing the pressure on the nerve there in his right hip. Then the interrogator entered the room quietly and dropped into the armchair with a sigh. As he raised its footrest and pressed the button that started up the massage, Jeremiah saw that it was Broch.

13

MR. BROCH! Jeremiah said in relief, and he stood up and stretched his fists out in front of him, even though they were no longer shackled, as though asking to be set free. But Broch ignored him, rose from the armchair, walked up to the soft-drink machine that stood in the corner of the interrogation room beside a snack machine, and slipped in a coin; a freezing-cold can tumbled down noisily. Jeremiah then saw Broch fishing his money back out of the coin return, and realized that the soda had been, in effect, free. Broch opened the can and threw his head back, to empty his soda in lengthy gulps. He was obviously thirsty. And Jeremiah said, If I have found favor in your eyes, would you mind giving me some water? Broch paid no attention. Jeremiah tried again: Mr. Broch, I'm Jeremiah; yesterday, at twelve o'clock sharp, I was in your home, I'm so glad you're here . . . But Broch didn't respond, just stared at Jeremiah as though he'd never laid eyes on him before and hadn't even heard what he was saying. He crushed his can with one hand, returned to the armchair, switched on the massage, and without warning flung the crushed can at Jeremiah's head. The can struck Jeremiah's forehead and fell onto the table. Shut up, I'll do the talking,

Broch said. I'm the interrogator here, and you haven't received permission to talk. For this offense alone, interrupting a senior interrogator during an official interrogation, you're liable to get up to a year and a half. In fact, let's take it as read that you've already been indicted under the interruption clause—and, by the way, I have the civil authority to judge you, and there's no contesting my verdict. You've been accused, he read from the file, of disorderly behavior on public transportation, of assaulting a minor but helpless prophet, of disturbing the peace and vandalizing personal property in a bookstore, and of inciting regicide in the national press, a grievous act of treason in itself and an offense whose sentence is death, of course. Tomorrow you'll be judged, and presumably you'll also be executed. Do you confess? If so, it'll be noted in your file. And Jeremiah said, Mr. Broch, enough with the jokes, this isn't the book-review section, I . . . He mustered up what remained of his courage and said: Look, I was given the gift of prophecy, okay? All those things I said were . . . I was told to say them.

Broch froze, his eyes still on the file, and then he raised his head. No, he said after a prolonged, stunned silence. You haven't received any sort of prophecy. No. Hold on—he narrowed his eyes—but I know you, you're Jeremiah. You published the . . . He gestured gracefully, as if brushing away a mosquito. No, that's it. That's the limit. You can fudge a police investigation, you can remain silent, you can lie—after all, I'm only here on reserve duty—but not, not in poetry! You have no right to remain silent in poetry, and no right to cheat the interrogator, and no right to disrupt an interrogation, certainly not. No right at all, and I know this perfectly well, because *I'm* the one who determines such rights when it comes to poetry and its investigation. He pulled out his phone and browsed briefly before tapping the wrong letters, which ticked him off; he tried again, and cursed the sluggish Internet, because the thick walls of the interrogation room disrupted the wireless network signal. But in the end the poem was uploaded, and Broch read several lines from Jeremiah's first and only collection: *They shall come with weeping and with supplications will I lead them / I will cause them to walk by rivers of waters / in a straight way wherein they shall not stumble / for I am become a father to Israel / and Ephraim*. And there was a dead silence. Of course, Jeremiah identified the words immediately, and Broch said: Tell me, please, I'm all ears—what's the connection between this printed graphomania and the word of God? Explain it to me. No, because, if this is prophecy, then we might as well throw Isaiah right into the trash. It's either this—or Isaiah. And I won't allow, he suddenly roared, while the armchair shook his entire body, I won't allow anyone to throw Isaiah into the trash, even though you and your friends at that literary journal, whether it's *Muscle*, or *No*, or *Leave*, or *Wow*, or any of the other literary journals you keep starting up and that last for two issues and then shut down without anyone's noticing except the founders and the editors, are always endeavoring as best you can to throw Isaiah into the garbage, and Amos, too, and Joel—those are the names of *real* prophets, in case you don't recognize them. I won't allow it, no, I won't let you. I'll stand in your way, I'll block you with my very own body. I'm an old man, it's true, but I've got strength enough left to thwart someone like you from galloping off to the garbage dump with the book of Isaiah in his hand. Indeed, your text is little more than a mishmash of clichés; to compare it to high-school verse would be to praise it to the heavens. Tears, entreaties, the straight-and-narrow path, father, firstborn, water, Ephraim. You're aware that this is all dreadful, right? Well, maybe you weren't aware when you published it, you just scribbled it down and sent it right off, but today you're aware, right? Tell me you're aware of it; I'll make a note of that in your file. Broch browsed his phone for a moment, then stopped and said: We're fortunate to be in a soundproof room; otherwise, I'd be ashamed to read this aloud. Look, look what you've written, Mr. Prophet. You're like the Medusa—all one needs to destroy you is to put a mirror in front of you, you'll crack under interrogation, your own poems will break you, I won't need to beat you up at all. Now Broch intoned, like someone reading the Torah on the Sabbath, though in a strong Iraqi accent of sorts, peppered with consonants: Who gives the sun for a light by day / and the ordinances of the moon and of the stars for a light by night / who stirs up the sea that the waves thereof roar / the Lord of hosts is his name; if these ordinances depart from before me / says the Lord / then the seed of Israel also shall cease / from being a nation before me forever . . . Maybe you can explain to me the connection between the laws of nature, of the moon and the stars, and the laws of the Torah? After all, the connection is entirely fabricated and arbitrary . . . and what's this incipit rhyme: Light / By night . . . Excuse me, but come on, when you get right down to it, your style is simply abysmal. Do you know how to read, or did you skip that stage and proceed straight to writing? Explain it to me, please, because, when it comes to literature, after all, I don't understand a thing—I flunked all my exams in literature—and of course I've never been invited to teach at Harvard; nor was I made an honorary fellow at Oxford; nor was I offered a second sabbatical year at Ann Arbor, Michigan; nor was I offered a seat as professor of Hebrew literature at the Center for Jewish Studies at the University of Nineveh. So, please, go on and fill me in, I'm all ears. And Jeremiah replied, It isn't connected to my literary work, which may well be a failure; the prophecy came much later; there's no connection. And Broch said, Right, there's no connection, none. You're a prophet like I'm Maria Theresa, Her Royal Highness the Archduchess of Austria and Queen of Bohemia and Hungary, who, anyhow, is long since dead. Nowadays, everyone caught red-handed committing a crime, not to mention every lunatic on the street, they all say, I'm a prophet! Every thief, every burglar. You know, we have a rape victim who shows up here every day lately. I interrogated her, and she, too, told me, over and again, that she's actually *prophesying* here and that we're not listening, *that she herself wasn't violated*, the rape is merely an allegory for the anticipated destruction of Jerusalem, so that if we only listened to her and read the signs carefully we'd be able to foresee the future and know what to do about it. Come on, what am I supposed to tell her? That she's right? That we'll record her allegorical complaint and publish it in the newspapers? What? Today every child that steals something tells me the Lord of Hosts sent him. So, what, I just release him, let him go on pilfering chewing gum, maybe offer him a job here with the police, or maybe also a post as a senior lecturer in the Hebrew Literature Department? After all, even though I retired a hundred years ago, I'm still hiring and firing at Mount Scopus, as you know perfectly well. You, too, tried your luck; you, too, were rejected; I personally jotted a tiny little *x* in your file, and now I know I was right—that would've been all I needed, having you start prophesying at departmental meetings on Sunday in the Institute of Jewish Studies conference room. So, yes, I can snatch you away from the police and free you, and drive you in my car straight to the dean's office and arrange to get you tenure, and tomorrow you can start teaching the major introductory course on Hebrew literature, and you can even choose your own curriculum. You'll set the canon—why not, after all? Indeed, you're a most deserving appointee, a deserving appointee. And I, too, am a deserving appointee, Broch said modestly, I'm a deserving appointee to the Hebrew Literature Department, and to the police as well. I've been volunteering for reserve duty for years; after all, I was an interrogator in the Military Criminal Investigation Division, and then an officer in the CID, and then a deputy officer at CID headquarters. You may be surprised, but I had a life prior to literary criticism, thank God, he said, mainly to himself. And Jeremiah said, Just let me go; I'm so thirsty. He was fed up with Broch's speech, fed up with the entire day; he only wanted to get away, to be released, to clear out. He hadn't asked for any of this, and he had no intention of putting up with it, either. Let's get back to the interrogation, Broch said. You should know, he said, that that's a two-way mirror over there; we can see ourselves reflected in it, but on the other side are a couple of very senior priests and prophets, and the entire proceedings here are being broadcast live to the Temple, since they expressed interest in your case today. One could even say that they've been following you, but everybody is being followed, all the time—it's okay, it's only natural. Even when you visited me, you were under surveillance. Broch stood up and leaned over and whispered in Jeremiah's ear, That vending machine is jam-packed with cameras; after all, the king himself is being monitored twenty-four/seven by Egyptian satellites, and the entire Holyland complex is swarming with thousands of Egyptian mikes. Then he snapped upright again and began pacing. So, he said, you thought you could upset commuters and smash jugs and go home as if nothing had happened. It doesn't work that way. Too bad I didn't choke you to death yesterday at my place; we'd be finished with all of this and would have saved ourselves an interrogation. So you claim you've been gifted with prophecy. Come on, then, and prophesy something for me right now, for example, Broch said, and signaled at the supposedly two-way glass. Jeremiah noticed a red bulb lighting up and realized he was now being recorded by yet another camera, perhaps of higher quality. He said, Now I've got nothing to say. Broch approached at a leisurely pace, grabbed the crushed can, aimed it at Jeremiah like someone threatening to throw a stone, and said, Wrong answer, try again. He smiled his familiar smile, fish-eyed and tight-lipped. And Jeremiah said: It doesn't work that way. It just comes to me; I can't decide when I— Broch roared: Now, or else I'll stick you in the vending machine and you'll spend the night there with the Coke cans. Jeremiah said, Go ahead and kill me, I'm not saying a word from now on, and Broch got up and shoved Jeremiah's forehead against the Formica and bore down on it with all his weight, and Jeremiah said, the words escaping his mouth with the speed of a fleeing chariot, Thus says the Lord: if you will not listen to me, to walk in my law which I have set before you, to heed the words of my servants the prophets whom I send to you urgently, though you have not heeded, then will I make this house like Shiloh and will make this city a curse to all the nations of the earth.

Broch released his grip, but Jeremiah kept his head on the table and was still. Broch said, So that's it? Jeremiah clasped his palms behind his neck and closed his eyes. He didn't see Broch shrug his shoulders at the coated pane as if to say: What can I do? That's all I got out of him. The red bulb flashed and went out.

When Jeremiah opened his eyes, Broch had left the room, and the door was propped open by a chair on which a bottle of iced tea had been placed. Jeremiah grabbed the bottle and gulped down its contents. Apparently, they'd decided to release him, he reflected mistakenly. He ascended the stairs and walked back up the corridor and swiftly strode out of the station; the duty officer, exerting himself over a Sudoku puzzle, appeared not to notice him, and someone else was now handcuffed to the upstairs vending machine. Jeremiah strode down Jaffa Road and Shlomtzion Ha-Malka Street in the direction of Customs Square, catching a glimpse of the new residential complexes in the Mamilla neighborhood, and of the mall that had been built opposite the Old City walls and which had crumbled during an earthquake, turning within minutes into islets of ruins, while the Old City and its ramparts had remained in one piece. And he strode on toward King David Street, heading for Liberty Bell Park, where he meant to take cover like a mouse from the shadow of wings.

A crescent moon dragged in its wake an enormous fleecy cloud, like a tugboat sailing into port. I looked and there was no one at all, the birds of the air had fled, Jeremiah thought. Part of the walls of Jerusalem had been destroyed to make room for a new neighborhood half within and half outside of the walls. Land was appropriated—for the public good, of course, though most assuredly for the good of its confiscators, for are they not a deserving public themselves? The earthquake had been disastrous—which is to say, a prime opportunity. Real-estate sharks silently swarmed to the derelict plots of land and promised to remove the rubble and smiled from ear to ear, and in return

they received limitless building rights—up, down, and across—
and the earth's lemon was squeezed to the last drop, and jam was
made of its peel, and they prepared beads from its seeds for the
children of their bondsmen.

The ruins of the YMCA and the King David Hotel stood on
either side like twin mounds, and Jeremiah stopped for a moment to gaze at what remained of these two buildings that he
remembered so well from his childhood. For a minute, they
seemed restored and rebuilt in his memory, the rubble like a
movie played in reverse, going from a heap to a solid edifice. And
he glanced at the YMCA, which was almost completely destroyed—
only its central tower remained standing, leaning slightly to one
side—and at the bulldozers that stood there, reluctant to begin
shoveling, since they didn't know where to dump the debris: the
city was pretty much covered with shattered Jerusalem stone,
and there was no point in starting to build before the earth
calmed back down, but they'd been saying this for two years already, ever since the quake. And then the king set out on military expeditions to the East and along the coastal belt at the
command of his lord on the Nile. There was inevitably some
tribe or other, or some pact between nations, that it was necessary to suppress and eliminate; there was always a rumor of a
particularly good crop somewhere, and the King of Judah would
sally forth to claim his share, discarding sheaves at the corner of
the fields, as ordained. And every new suppression and elimina-
tion brought on the next war, fortunately! The oppressed demanded vengeance and equipped themselves with light as well
as heavy firearms, and then some Judean soldier was killed, so,
after another plentiful yield of crops, it was time for another pu-
nitive expedition, to avenge the blood of this selfsame slaughtered soldier. And bulldozer drivers were conscripted to destroy
homes in faraway cities and to clear ramparts in order to facili-
tate a secure entryway for the army, and they abandoned their
large vehicles in Jerusalem, instead riding on the king's own
bulldozers in faraway cities, and some of them would never

return—that's how it is in war—and their bulldozers remained orphaned on construction sites for many more years, like huge yellow headstones, like their children, who wouldn't remember much about their fathers save the gigantic bulldozers in whose driver's seats they'd once been allowed to sit.

Someone wearing a kaffiyeh dragged a bum leg while pushing a large coop across the street, with chickens crammed between its bars. From his place on the low stone wall, which alone had survived the earthquake, Jeremiah heard the coop man haggle on his cell phone in elegant Hebrew about the price, one assumed, of his chickens. The chickens were packed so close together that it seemed as if they'd turned into a solid block, like an oblong chest of drawers. Their cackles sounded to Jeremiah like sobs, and he shook his head. Like a cage full of birds, so their homes are full of deceit, therefore they have become great and rich, he muttered. As soon as he stops talking on his phone, I've got to ask him about buying his chickens, Jeremiah thought; from what he managed to catch of the heated exchange, the price wouldn't be too high. He waved at the merchant, but realized that he had no idea what he was going to do with the chickens once he released them from their coop. Where would he leave them, in Independence Park? In the botanical gardens? In his parents' yard? Would his mother accept them? And what would they eat, and what would they drink in summer? It was cold, and it might snow soon. Surely, by releasing them he was sentencing them to death. And he understood something obscure that flashed through his brain for a moment and vanished. He wanted at least to say something to the chicken merchant, like: Look how you're bunching them together, they're providing you with a living and you're crushing them and making them suffer, but even this he couldn't quite force through his feeble lips. Anyhow, the merchant was engrossed in the heat of his negotiations. What sort of prophet are you, he reflected, if you can't even save one chicken? Not even one chick, not even a dog or a flea, never mind a boy or a girl. Jeremiah imagined tearing the cell phone away from the chicken merchant's hand and smashing it to pieces like the jug. Good for you, you smashed a jug. See how far it's gotten you. What now? His release from detention had been too easy. It dawned on him—and his low spirits sank even lower—that it wouldn't be so simple to escape Broch's iron claws, and that he'd been released for a reason, perhaps so they could catch him red-handed in the act of an even graver offense, and it hit him with no small measure of fear that undoubtedly he was being followed—indeed, this was pretty transparent— and he knew with certainty that the matter wasn't settled yet. He glanced back, and nobody was there, or so it seemed.

The slender Kislev moon rose above Liberty Bell Park. Realizing that the day was drawing to a close, he told himself, I've got to get home. Those early-morning hours, with their almond and the pot that had veiled the sun, seemed to Jeremiah as if they hadn't been so much another day as another year, another century. His detention, too, and the interrogation seemed distant, even though he'd been released barely half an hour ago. The hummus–fava beans weighed on his belly like a cannonball on a feather pillow.

The chicken merchant moved a short distance from his coop and continued his business transaction. Can we say two hundred ninety-five? Give me two hundred ninety and we'll call it quits. The merchant was pacing to and fro in the soft rain, and Jeremiah knew that he could, if he so desired, make a run for it, grab the coop, and dash off; the merchant limped badly and wouldn't be able to catch up. Grab the coop—later on you'll figure out where to set them free. You couldn't possibly condemn them to a worse fate. Give them, if nothing more, an hour of freedom. Listen to them crying. Behold the voice of the cry of the daughter of my people from a land far off, is not the Lord in Zion? Is not her king in Zion? One hour of freedom—when did you last have one free hour, an hour of quiet, without any obligations, freedom with no future knocking on the door and no past piling up behind you and making a terrible racket as it falls? He endeavored to visualize the neighborhood, to plan his flight, to retreat back to Agron Street, or maybe he'd keep walking south, toward Liberty Bell Park. But where would he spring the chickens after carrying them off? And he knew that he wouldn't do a thing; in admitting as much, he was spared having to make the decision, be it in front of the pet store, in front of the cages in the zoo, in front of a butcher shop, in front of a window display of fur coats. The harvest is over, the summer has drawn to an end, and we haven't been saved. When he turned five, his mother had brought him an aquarium with two goldfish as a birthday present. The following day, his father woke him up at daybreak, and they stole out of the house; in his memory, his sister was with them, too, though all of a sudden he wasn't sure if she had indeed joined them on the fish expedition. They'd driven to the botanical gardens in Givat Ram and had sneaked in through a gap in the fence and turned the fish loose. Jeremiah remembered the fish and the guard who advanced toward them waving his truncheon, and how they stood there, stock-still, mute in the chill air of a fall dawn, calmly waiting for the guard, who was Ammonite, like most of the guards in Judah, and how they let him approach at a run, how they waited for him to come to halt, and only when he drew up close did the guard notice the small boy standing next to the adult, and the empty aquarium. Jeremiah's father held the guard back, waving cash in front of him like a paper sword, with a picture of King Solomon under the *100*. The guard calmed down at once; he put the "sword" in his pocket and stood beside them, and together they waited for the sun to rise. They gave the empty aquarium to the guard as a present, and he in turn filled it with earth and ants for his son; his son nurtured generation after generation of ants inside it, for years on end, even after his father's death, even when he, too, grew old.

Behold, I will make my words in your mouth fire, and this people wood—and it shall devour them, Jeremiah remembered being told, though he couldn't remember when he had heard it.

Was it today, was it years ago, perhaps even before he was born? And he understood that he would never be able to speak softly, like his father, because someone had stuck fire in his mouth this morning; harsh and unyielding fire had burdened his tongue, had placed a glowing coal on his lips, and his mouth was the bulging pot, and he suddenly understood his vision: It was my head and my mouth and my spirit that I saw there. And his speech would have to burn, flame, ignite. It won't be nice. It won't give you any pleasure, nor will it bring you any recognition. The days of poetry are over, he admitted sadly to himself. You won't publish anymore; nothing will get printed. No, from now on, all your words will be words of fire. Blazing and burning up in a flash. Devouring both themselves and the speaker. He beheld the nation at first as firewood placed in front of a hearth, but then he pictured the nation as trees in a forest, an immense forest whose dimensions stretched from horizon to horizon, and he uttered a word, and the crowns of the trees caught fire. Okay, give me two hundred and we'll close the deal; you're killing me here, the chicken merchant screamed into his phone. Jeremiah, who suddenly found himself standing close to the man, told him, as he was turning off his phone, An appalling and horrible thing has come to pass in the land, the prophets prophesy in the service of falsehood. The merchant replied: Believe me, every word is true. You can't open a newspaper without seeing it: here an envelope full of cash, there a few building permits; here a new central bus station, there a sex bribe or a winning lottery ticket. Nobody ever offered me a sex bribe, let me tell you, the merchant said. I think it's because of my bum leg. But my middle leg isn't fucked up one bit—in the middle, I'm hung like a donkey, you know? Jeremiah peered at the chicken coop from up close, and only then did he notice how wide he'd been off the mark: there weren't any chickens in the coop, there were children in the coop, six or seven small children around three or four years old. Some of them were screaming and wailing, and the merchant told him: Look at them; they'll be fed to the flames in an hour or so, but when it comes to me getting paid—no, I have to wait till the end of the month, if not later. Net sixty EOM. But I have to pay VAT on the fifteenth of every month. And social security—maybe you can explain to me, why a ten percent surcharge—that's a tax, for all practical purposes. Ten percent, fifteen percent . . . two hundred a head, that's practically giving them away, I'm such a sucker. Even when I was a kid, I was just as pathetic, a sucker, a chicken. And Jeremiah said: What? You snatch children? He was astounded, even though he'd heard, like everyone, of such people, like body-organ harvesters and sex traffickers and dog snatchers and child slavers, but he'd never seen one with his very own eyes. You deliver children to idol worshippers? And the man said, Snatch? *Snatch?! Purchase*—I buy them from their parents, *purchase*, the parents get a few shekels and perform a good deed in the bargain, instead of just dumping these brats in the garbage. Don't you start with me like my wife—knock it off! Everyone lays into me from their moral high ground, but there's an unregulated birthrate here; millions are being born, and sometimes one comes out malformed, okay? Take a look at that one in the corner, for example. The merchant pointed. He's so sick, he'll die in a week anyway. And look at this one, yellow as a chick—what can be done with her? You want her? Take her, take her for free, bring her up yourself, Mr. Goody-Goody. D'you know what it means to raise a girl with a shmatte for a liver? D'you know how much her daily medication costs, for one day? So take her! Take her for free! And he went up to the coop and bent over and grabbed the girl, who was clearly sick with yellow fever or cirrhosis. Jeremiah said, Leave her alone, don't touch me, I mean her—and rage welled up within him, and helplessness. And the seller said: Don't worry, you couldn't have taken her anyway, she's already sold. That's how I make a living. I buy them from the parents and sell them to the Ammonite workers here in their tenement project. There's a nice demand from the Tyre and Sidon sailors, too; in such matters they're of one mind—the Phoenicians and

Ammonites—I don't know who taught whom the ritual, and it doesn't interest me. They believe in this, not that I understand it, but it's their religion from time immemorial, so—what?— I should tell them what is and isn't right? Based on what? We don't have our own difficult customs? So, granted, they put boys and girls into Moloch's fire; they let the flames caress them until a faint odor ascends to heaven, as they say . . . I was once here, in Sultan's Pool, when they performed the ceremony, and I admit, it's not a pleasant smell, but who am I to decide what's right, who am I to decree what's good or bad based on what's pleasant or unpleasant to me? So my nose should be the standard? Besides, I mean, the kids don't exactly smell like roses *now*, he said, and wrinkled his nose at them and kicked the coop in an effort to silence their screams. When the kids are Moloched, the wor-shippers beat on drums so as not to hear all the hollering. All those drum circles aren't there to soothe the mind, as they say— oh no, they're a diversion. I bring them the children, they wash them, they treat them nicely, they give them hot goat milk and tetanus shots and antibiotics, and then they're fed to the flames. I bring my guy a kid, and he sells him to their high-ranking clerks. See, if a high-ranking clerk has a substitute child, then the clerk doesn't have to put his own kid into the fire, you get it? I'm talk-ing about gold merchants, diamond dealers with mines in Sheba; you can't expect someone like that to feed his own daughter to the flames! His daughter has to go and study business adminis-tration at Harvard, and while she's out there she'll get breast implants, before returning to manage the family business. So, naturally, her father procures a child from me, a child who'd have been dumped in any case, and that way everybody's happy. But when you come right down to it, they're not actually burned alive. It isn't true, what's written in the papers; I've seen it with my own eyes. They only *pass through* the fire—it's like a shower, it's like a warm douche. And you should know that if a child *survives* the fire they turn him into a prince. Did you know that? He becomes a demigod for them. The Ammonites are a real pious nation, not like us, a bunch of hucksters. But, then again, if the child doesn't come out of the fire in good shape, well, forget it.

I can see that you're touchy. I was like that once, too. Why blame them? After all it's not like we don't feed our own people into our own fires, in our way, yeah? What about Menashe, our king's great-grandfather? I mean, he went into the fire, no? He sure as hell did—big-time, like on a conveyor belt he went right in, my grandpa told me stories . . . And I heard on the radio that King Mesha of Moab passed the son of the King of Edom through fire, but I call that just being neighborly, yeah? As we say here, better a close neighbor than a distant brother. There's no denying, it's one powerful spectacle. They've got an altar that's out of this world, coated entirely in copper, with the bull and horns, everything burning hot. They run the child through from one end to the other; if the child comes out alive—I swear, sometimes the child comes out fine, if they run him through at the speed of light, but, well, if they wait an three extra seconds, in order to say the blessing, then that's that. I've got kids of my own, don't think I'm callous, but if I had to pass my own kids through fire, and I could pay chicken feed to buy your daughter instead, I don't think I'd count my pennies. Would you? But, what, you got any kids? Be reasonable for a minute. You wouldn't save a healthy child, with a future ahead of him? You could say these kids here in the coop are already dead, for all practical purposes. I'm giving them a chance to turn into demigods. What's a bit of Tophet fire? Tophet, that's the word—they call it Tophet. The tent they put up there in Sultan's Pool isn't a circus tent, okay? Anyway, what's Moloch compared with years of hunger in some hole in the Katamonim or in Gilo? What? Toiling in the Timna mines is any better, or clearing stones in Ezion-Geber? Timna isn't a Tophet itself? Were you ever there? I worked there for three years, from the age of ten; I'm copper-toxic from head to toe; every so often, late at night, I radiate heat. Mining copper with the temperature up to 122 degrees, drinking filthy warm water from a rusty canteen doesn't count in your eyes as Tophet? And it's all within the law! A booming business! I plaster the coop with feathers for people like you, to let them think I'm selling turkeys here. I've already had run-ins with inspectors and the police. I don't want any trouble, I pay my business tax a year ahead of time, he said, and then added: I used to play professional soccer; that's how I got my bum leg. I used to be right fullback, but I once kicked a victory goal. He pulled out an old clipping, kept between plastic covers for safekeeping, and gave it to Jeremiah to read. The article was indeed all about this miracle, how the right fullback scored a goal from the outfield, and in the photograph someone was bearing him up on his shoulders. The fullback told Jeremiah, That was the King of the Goals that season—the King of the Goals himself lifted me on his shoulders. Jeremiah told him, And they shall bury in Tophet, for want of room to bury, and the houses of Jerusalem and the houses of the kings of Judah shall be as the place of Tophet. And the merchant said: You're one hundred percent right, but keep this in mind, just between us, there's a big market in children, not only among the Ammonites—oh no, let's just say that nothing human is alien to our king, okay? I've noticed they've fenced in Sultan's Pool, they've put up some sort of tent, sure, like a circus tent, and I saw limos going in, and, believe me, it wasn't an Ammonite license on the Mercedes, it wasn't a Canaanite number, it was a Jewish number, glatt kosher, yellow plates. A black Mercedes drove into the tent; I delivered the merchandise and then tried to take a peek inside. There's a bookstore not far off; it's closed at night unless there's a book launch, so I climbed onto its roof and saw the smoke coming out of the tent top. They flew in all the apparatus, as well as an Ammonite priest in his fancy getup, by helicopter from Rabat Bnei Ammon, and the priest taught them the ritual ceremony point by point. You wouldn't believe what's going on in this city in that big top. They also use the tent for . . . And he fell silent, noticing a city inspector approaching on an electric-powered scooter from the other end of the street. I saw them leaving, he said hastily to Jeremiah. They were wearing what looked like hoods in bright colors. I saw the plume of smoke. I also smelled the smell, the merchant said as he got ready to clear out, harnessed to his coop like a horse, his limp suddenly and miraculously cured.

14

MATTANIAH RIPPED OPEN A PACKAGE of soup nuts with his teeth and poured the yellow heap into his large hand. Eating junk food was for him a matter of principle. Until the age of eight, he grew up on delicacies prepared in his father the king's residence—that is to say, until the day he watched a foreign TV channel and was informed that his father the king had been killed in the Battle of Armageddon against the Egyptians. He'd already learned how to read, and still recalled the headline in the paper: And the king said to his servants, take me away, for I am badly wounded. He understood that his father was ill; he thought he'd caught a cold. And when he was told that his father had fallen in a critical battle against Pharaoh, Mattaniah imagined his father swooping down on the pyramids and thrusting his sword between the Sphinx's eyes. He didn't understand the words *Take me away*; he didn't understand where they took his father. He didn't really know him, he reflected, but was only familiar with the stories about him: the discovery of the Book of the Law, the smashing of the pagan altars, the roasting of the altars' high priests upon those same altars. As a child, he didn't think any of this was especially significant; it even made him laugh. In particular, there was talk of demolishing the Tophet in Gai Ben Hinnom, before they'd channeled in seawater and flooded the entire valley, which then turned into a harbor, and before they'd revived the Tophet in an adjoining valley, not as an improvised primitive bronze altar, but as a mega-altar, covered in galvanized stainless steel.

But now, as Mattaniah crossed over Gai Ben Hinnom, which had been converted into a lake, and as he passed by the large circuslike tent that had been pitched in Sultan's Pool for the last couple of years, he realized that his father's efforts and all his altar smashing were in vain, for the Tophet was restored post-haste and even improved after his father's heroic death, and all the appeals to the Supreme Court and public demonstrations didn't help a bit. They said that the matter was outside of the court's jurisdiction; an expert in international law claimed that the area was in effect extraterritorial Ammonite territory within Jerusalem, and that local law couldn't be applied within its perimeter, whereas, on the other hand, in order to maintain a balance between Ammonite religious freedom and the fundamental principles of Hebrew law, and weighing in private property rights as well—to be sure, everything was backed up by contracts and affidavits—it just wasn't possible to issue a restraining order against the big top. (Truth be told, envelopes changed hands, fat and prudently sealed, sent along to the prosecutor and a high-ranking judge—not that it reached him directly, not at all, but by means of a limited-liability company that his adopted daughter founded to handle the matter; she was, in fact, legally adopted in order to set up the LLC, and soon thereafter the judge's ruling was subtly tweaked, and everything was nicely sewn up: Nope, nothing to be done. Sorry, there are extenuating circumstances, see?)

His father died twelve years ago; Mattaniah had now lived far longer without a father than he'd lived by his side, though, to be honest, he didn't see him all that often during those first eight years, either, and even when he did see him it was for the most part from afar. That was how he'd always remember his father, Josiah, from a great distance, not emotionally speaking but in point of fact: on a high throne or on a dais, almost featureless.

Take me away. Your father was anointed king when he was eight years old, Mattaniah was told when he turned eight; prepare yourself for the possibility that this will happen to you, too. He clearly remembered the months between his father's death and the crowning of his younger brother, Jehoahaz, months during which he imagined that he, Mattaniah, would be the one to rule. And the term *child king* resonated in his head, perhaps because his mother had told him, Yes, you'll be the child king; you'll hold a scepter as tall as you are, and a crown will be placed on your little head, and it'll slip over your neck and shoulders like a spring-loaded trap on a rat, ha-ha, and I'll draw a partition and hide behind it and talk, and you'll sit out front and repeat your mother's words. But his brother Jehoahaz was crowned instead, and Mattaniah recalled the excitement during the coronation, as well as the affront and then the dread when, only three months later—the festivities alone lasted close to two months—his brother, who'd become king, disappeared, and all they told him, told Mattaniah, was that his brother had been *taken to Egypt.* He never saw him again, and no letter ever arrived. During the following years, he'd imagine himself boarding a bus to Egypt and looking for his brother in Pharaoh's palaces, and then in the local jailhouses. He thought of Joseph in the pit and of Joseph in Potiphar's home, but Mattaniah knew that he'd never go, he'd never search, never meet, and never Joseph . . . His brother Elyakim was crowned in place of Jehoahaz, who'd disappeared in Egypt—though, to be perfectly honest, Jehoahaz was simply shot down in the outskirts of Ashkelon—and Elyakim's name was changed to Jehoiakim by Pharaoh, and on no account was it permitted for anyone to call him by his old name. He'd ruled for five years already, which, compared with Jehoahaz's three months, felt like an eternity. Indeed, it seemed as if the kingdom would last forever and that, at long last, there might be some peace under Pharaoh's aegis. Elyakim, which is to say Jehoiakim, quickly took over the multi-tower high-rise building project on Jerusalem's southwestern hills, above the soccer stadium, and shut himself up on one of the top floors, with bodyguards on every floor below and sentinels in the surrounding watchtowers, too, so that it was practically impossible to reach him. He shut down the elevators in all the buildings and lived on the twentieth or thirtieth floor—needless to say, no one knew which one for certain, and he would also change floors from time to time, for security reasons—and in order to pay him a visit it was necessary to use the stairs. Only one elevator was in use, exclusively for the king and his Egyptians, the ones who gave him his orders, and on every even-numbered floor it was obligatory to pass a security check, with X-ray machines, dogs, body frisking, preliminary inquiries, fingerprinting, retinal scans, document verification, personal questionnaires, and who knows what else. It didn't matter if you were an ambassador from a foreign country or the minister of defense or the king's younger brother. After Mattaniah attempted to visit his brother the king to ask for his support in setting up a new literary journal and was forced to endure the humiliating ordeal—he was fed up by the time he reached the fourth floor and beat a retreat—he gave up on ever trying to visit his brother, just as his brother had lost any interest in keeping tabs on Mattaniah.

And so, when he was seventeen years old, Mattaniah decided to seek out—this is how he put it to himself—his own path, and to forget his royal origins once and for all, or so he said, and leave behind his brother and his childhood memories, cleansing himself as much as possible of the blood of kings which pumped through his veins, so to speak. He began to fabricate, at first to himself and in due course to his new acquaintances as well, a new life story, including semi-Assyrian origins, with a mother exiled from Assyria to Israel as part of the two-way forced deportations that were at the time customarily agreed upon to the supposed satisfaction of all the nations in the region.

And he tattooed his body in some hole-in-the-wall in the Armenian quarter in the Old City with black, archaic, florid Assyrian cuneiform that he didn't really understand, and whose design the tattoo artist had downloaded from the Internet. And he grew his beard and hair accordingly, and studied beginners' Akkadian in an Assyrian dialect, and in his room he hung an enormous square poster of the King of Assyria, whom Mattaniah made sure to call by his proper Assyrian name, Tukulti-apil-Eshara, which means *My trust in the son of Assur*, and not by the Hebrew corruption, Tiglath-Pileser. He worked to build up both mane and body until they resembled those of the figure in his imagination: letting his beard and hair grow long, tinting their reddishness black to match the color of his tattoos; lifting barbells and pulling spring chest-expanders and slurping down protein shakes and energy drinks. Within twelve months, his muscles had bulged and solidified, and he had come to resemble the Assyrian in his poster far more than the boy he'd been several years earlier. He mail-ordered a wristwatch like the one Tiglath wore, and a matching hat. When people saw his profile, they couldn't help remarking that he'd become the spitting image of the poster in his room.

Except that, against all odds, Assyria's standing in the region kept deteriorating, pretty much in inverse proportion to the development of Mattaniah's muscles. One day, a match was struck, so it seemed, in some remote corner of the empire, and Assyria started tottering like a house of cards (made of iron). Envoys and refugees bruited rumors of the empire's imminent fall, though it took several years to grasp properly and take to heart the fact that Assyria was gasping its last breaths. It was as strange as a dream, like waking in the morning and seeing that the sun had gone out, or that it had turned into a triangle. Mattaniah would still walk around Jerusalem dressed up Assyrian-style even when Assyria no longer existed, when Babylon and Egypt were already fighting over the carcass of an empire everyone had believed would last forever.

And Mattaniah continued, after several meetings with a psychologist, along his journey of self-renewal, of which his Assyrian getup was only the external expression. He began to devote himself to writing and reading, and he began eating, after years of nothing but palace cuisine, a wide variety of déclassé foods, including lots of junky snacks. Above all, he had a constant craving for yellow soup nuts, a packet of which he always kept in his pocket and every once in a while would open and pour into his cupped palm and shove into his mouth and swallow. He didn't object to saddle-shaped Pringles, either, and candy-coated peanuts were a staple, and the thought of Apropo Corn Snacks made his mouth water, and he'd eat strawberry cobbler on a regular basis, not to mention family-size packages of peanut-butter-flavored Bamba puffs, their scent promising precisely what their taste delivered.

Encouraged by his psychologist, he adopted Broch's pup, and started to publish pseudo-Assyrian poems under pseudonyms and then under his own name, and he insisted on eating falafel and shawarma and grilled meat—always out. Eat out, the psychologist told him, you've already eaten *in* plenty. You ate at home enough—you were weaned on plenty of cream from the palace's udders—the time has come to eat street food, the time has come to eat standing up, the time has come to eat cheaply. Junk-food time is here. He'd start, for example, with a cheese bureka in the morning—over at Musa, by City Hall—with some grape juice, which of course didn't contain even one molecule from the fruit of the vine; at noon, hummus–fava beans or musabaha or hummus with meat, most often at Hummus Abbas, at the pedestrian mall; at four o'clock, after exercising, he'd slurp up a super-large glass of fruit juice through a straw, date-banana-melon with mint, which he'd drink with abandon, especially in summer; in the evening, another bureka—if in the morning his bureka had been cheese, he'd finish the day with spinach, and, conversely, if in the morning he'd had a yen for spinach, he'd settle in the evening for cheese—though sometimes he felt like having a falafel or an eggplant sabich instead, or just any old combination of sushi, and between meals he'd gorge himself on a tube of Pringles or Bamba or Apropo or Time Out white chocolate—chocolate that was, so he was informed, completely chocolate-free—or a tortilla or a Cadbury Flake Bar, or maybe American peanuts or four-fingered Kif Kef bars or, again, Apropo, or Till Midnight cookies—half biscuit and half supposedly high-quality chocolate.

His food expenses were huge, and were, naturally, paid from public funds that reached his bank account indirectly—he didn't know how, nor did he ask why—but this didn't bother him in the least, which was understandable, considering that he saw his wild street-food habit and his ravenous consumption of snacks as signs of the overall strengthening of his distinct personality and his growing independence. He was no longer at the mercy of his mother or the palace chefs with their healthy, nutritious, and delicious meals! Each time he wiped clean a plate of hummus, its spiciness biting into his tongue, he knew that he was distancing himself from his earlier life and becoming more and more his true self, and he knew, too, that it was only from within his true self that the poet would emerge, not just any poet but a poet in the great Assyrian tradition. A few years hence, he mused, he would board the express train to Assyria and settle there and start a family there and work the land in the shadow of the northern mountains and utterly forget his origins and his cushy, upholstered past. He'd be able at last to eat balanced, nutritious, healthy, tasty, simple food over there—venison you kill and devour like a lion or leopard. With this thought, he used his teeth to rip open a new family-size packet of soup nuts.

When, one time, Mattaniah managed to reach his brother the king on the phone and asked him, How goes it, Elyakim?, his brother would have strangled him over the line if he could have: There is no such name, he said, that name is forbidden, that name is bad. From now on only Jehoiakim is allowed. Jehoiakim—

that's the name Father gave me, repeat after me. Mattaniah was astonished. Father? But Father's dead. And his older brother said, Pharaoh is now my father, and yours, too; he's everyone's father. And Mattaniah realized the line was tapped, and that his brother, in his high tower overlooking the soccer stadium, was caged in Pharaoh's hand, like a frightened, shuddering bird. Mattaniah wanted to please him and call him by his new name, this name that Pharaoh Neco had imposed on him like another mandatory tribute, but he couldn't get himself to force it out, and only said, See you, bro, and hung up.

He sat at the southwest corner of the Old City walls, between the Zion and Jaffa Gates, between two arrow slits, and looked down at the circus tent, which, at this time of day, was practically shut down. At night, though, things over there started hopping. And he took out a notepad and started to draft a poem. He would call his next book, or so he told himself, *Like a Bird in a Cage*. This made him think of his dog, waiting for him at home, maybe hungry, and he quickly scrambled down the walls and hailed a taxi to Abu Tor. His dog licked his face and ears in greeting, as though what had happened yesterday hadn't happened, as though he hadn't been abandoned. The treacherous deal treacherously, the treacherous deal very treacherously: Mattaniah called to mind Isaiah's obscure poem, which he had learned in school. Isaiah was everyone's downfall during matriculation exams. You go try to understand Hebrew a hundred years or more after it was written—*archaic* isn't even the word. And Mattaniah, well, suddenly something snapped inside him at the sight of his all-merciful dog. It seemed as if the creature bore him no resentment whatsoever for having been disgracefully abandoned, wasn't even asking Mattaniah to make amends, and terrible tears welled up in Mattaniah's eyes, and he opened a can of tuna and emptied its contents for Tukulti and sprinkled a fistful of the soup nuts left in his pocket on top of the fish, like a shower of gold, and hugged his dog. Tukulti put his paw on Mattaniah's tattooed arm and ignored the food—they both preferred to wait for Noa to come home so that they could all eat together—and if there had been a witness to this scene, it would have appeared to him or her that the dog was actually trying to read the Akkadian on Mattaniah's thick, bright limb, or was in the process of copying it down with his claws.

15

THE CHILD MERCHANT SLIPPED AWAY like a lizard behind the small heap of rubble that had once been the flour mill, and Jeremiah, who'd bolted after him, determined to do something—but what exactly?—lost track of him pretty much immediately, and stopped to catch his breath at the corner of Keren Ha-Yesod and King David. It was close to ten o'clock at night, he was sweaty and exhausted and hungry, and on the spur of the moment he decided—a decision that brought him instant relief—to catch the light rail for his parents' home in Anatot and sleep there that night. He didn't remember that there was a station at Liberty Bell Park, but a passing train stopped directly in front of him, and the big Liberty Bell replica rang in perfect coordination. As he strode forward, the doors appeared to slide open to the rhythm of his breathing, and before he knew it he was inside. He made his way through the car, which at this late hour was predictably empty. He seemed, in fact, to be the only passenger in the car, at least at first, but when he turned his head he noted one more person at the far end, sitting with his back turned away from Jeremiah, facing opposite the direction of travel. Jeremiah looked for a seat as far as possible from the passenger, worried all of a sudden that this guy might be another one of those light-rail prophets, and dealing with another light-rail prophet—or *any* prophet, for that matter—was about the least appealing prospect in the world right now. Jeremiah sat down. The light-rail air conditioner, which always blew too cold and too strong, began to freeze his head, and a voice resounded from the rear of the car: Sir, you haven't validated your ticket; riding with an unvalidated ticket is like riding without paying. And Jeremiah said, Shit, a night inspector! It started to rain, the drops striking hard against the polished windows. Jeremiah raised his head, and it was only his father there in the car, standing and laughing in delight and waving a multi-use electronic fare card, which he swiped in for his son.

He sat down next to Jeremiah in the cold, and they traveled in silence, thigh brushing against thigh. Jeremiah remembered the expression *fruit of his loins* and shuddered. His father stared straight ahead for a long time. Few passengers ever boarded at such an hour, and fewer still wanted to travel to Anatot or the other stops in northeastern Jerusalem at night. His father pulled out his large-screen smartphone, which also served him as a mobile library now that he'd had his hundreds of books converted and scanned and then nearly vacated his home of all printed matter, and took never-ending pleasure in the thought that everything was on his mobile phone, backed up in the Cloud, so lightweight, so mobile. He was delighted by the notion that his books had become bodiless, that they'd turned into an invisible essence, intangible but nonetheless present, that a Jew could carry his entire library with him wherever he might be going. He would read the thickest possible tomes on his phone, relishing the thought of holding unwieldy encyclopedias, shelves, entire libraries in the palm of his hand. And Jeremiah was under the impression that his father wanted again to show him an interesting passage from this or that volume, but in fact there was an article on the screen from *Ha'aretz*'s main page in which all the events of the day were recorded in a few lines—of course, without mention of God's instructions or Jeremiah's visions or the angel, but his speech in the bookstore was mentioned, as was the broken jug, and his interrogation, and how he had been released only to be placed under house arrest. And his father said, So you're coming to stay with us for your house arrest? I'm glad. And Jeremiah, who didn't know that he'd been placed under house arrest, repeated after his father, *House arrest*, and fell silent. There was something else in the news that Jeremiah didn't know: that he was to be put on trial, and that his trial was scheduled for tomorrow morning. Broch hadn't said a word about house arrest or about any trial, let alone set a date for it, but the court reporter knew all, apparently. Jeremiah looked at his father as though for advice. He drummed his fingertips on his knees, as was his wont, playing nonexistent music on his knees' keyboard, and his father watched and said, out of the blue, She told me: Dad, hold me up and I'll sit in front of the piano one more time and play that difficult twenty-minute stretch of the *Hammerklavier*. And I held her up, but she didn't have the strength by then to lift her hands, she just dropped them on the keys; she couldn't play the piano any more than a pillow could. And I took the pillow back to bed, and the next day I took her to the hospital. By then, she wasn't making any sense. She asked that I bring the piano along, that I hire movers—after all, I'm a senior physician, and if only I made the effort they might allow the piano into her room, or at least an electronic keyboard, and what's all my seniority worth if I can't even get her a piano? But I didn't seriously consider carrying out her wish, and I didn't move the piano into her room, even though I guess that's the sort of thing you might expect from me. Okay, enough said, enough, it's not her we're concerned with at the moment. She's dead, and none of the angels who occupied our dreams when you were in your mother's womb visited us when your sister took ill, or after her death. Nothing. They didn't come to comfort us—it was as though she didn't exist for them. If only one of them had shown up, a morsel of a dream, half a tiding, three words, a quarter of an explanation. But nothing. Jeremiah, who'd never heard his parents talking about being visited by angels when his mother was pregnant, didn't respond, and only said, Did you pray for them, did you ask? And his father looked at him and said, No, but neither did we pray or ask for those dreams of your mother's of an infant prophet when she was pregnant. When they care, they know how to make an appearance without any invitations. Oh yes. In droves.

And silence. At the Yekutiel Adam stop, some twenty villagers boarded. At the next stop, Pisgat Ze'ev Center, the line split, right to Anatot and straight to Sayeret Duchifat and Heil Ha'avir, which was the last stop. Jeremiah and his father knew most of the villagers and nodded their heads as one, in greeting. The flute teacher was there; and the junior-league soccer coach; and the olive-oil merchant; and a prostitute; and the millionaire tutor who gave private lessons in math; and the translator from Akkadian and Persian and Moabite and Elamite and more, who translated the languages of the East one into another and one from another, and published all over the place, and even mixed her languages up, until you couldn't be sure whether some Persian poet wasn't actually an Ammonite, or whether this great Sidonite playwright wasn't after all the national Elamite playwright—she herself was starting to confuse them. My polyglotism is a bitter curse, she said. I never intended to become a translator; my profession was forced on me by circumstance, just because I happen to be familiar with all the languages of the area. Personally, I dreamed of being a bookbinder, but there's always a demand for translation in this region swarming with nations. Jeremiah looked at the people that he knew, village neighbors and friends of his parents, who for the most part were older than he by twenty years or more. And he said in a gentle, even friendly tone, as his gaze took in his old-time neighbors: A conspiracy is found among the people of Judah, and among the inhabitants of Jerusalem. They have turned back to the iniquities of their forefathers; the house of Israel and the house of

Judah have broken my covenant that I made with their fathers. Therefore thus says the Lord, For sure, I am going to bring upon them disaster from which they cannot escape.

The passengers stared at Jeremiah in embarrassment, not least his father, who buried his head, so to speak, in the book he was reading on his phone, paying scant attention to what was going on. Okay, enough of all that, go to sleep, dumb kid, the math tutor told him with a mixture of compassion and disdain. Jeremiah's parents had dished out thousands of shekels to this man, since the boy couldn't for the life of him understand the language of numbers and sums. What is *three*—three—what does it actually mean? And the teacher had replied, What do you mean, *What is three*? Three apples . . . And he raised three fingers, but Jeremiah said: But what is three without the thing, not three fingers and not three coins but three, what is three plus three, three *what* plus three *what*—I don't get it. And what is a negative number, how does a negative apple look, or three negative fingers? And what does the square root of an apple look like, and what does the root of a negative apple look like? And, come to think of it, what is x? We always talk about x, but each time the answer is different—how can that be? I don't get it. And the teacher grabbed an apple and brought it up close to Jeremiah's face, like a loan shark waving his brass knuckles in the face of some deadbeat. Jeremiah got a 100 on his matriculation exam, and the teacher, who met him by chance several days later, said, Three you didn't understand, but you don't ask questions about one hundred, eh? And the prostitute said to the translator, Well, since his sister . . . But she didn't finish her thought. She remembered seeing the sister walking with a piano score in a downpour once, a downpour like the one outside right now, and her pages were completely wet, and the whore, who'd found shelter under some roof, called out to her to join her there, where it was dry, but Jeremiah's sister continued marching proudly in the rain, holding her score out as though it were thirsty, as though she were taking a stroll with a flowerpot, letting it slake its thirst in the blessing of the heavens. Next stop: Pisgat Ze'ev Center. Change to: Anatot, final stop. The automated sign announced this in several languages, and the translator smiled to herself like a cat warming itself in front of a heater in winter. My dear friend, Jeremiah's father suddenly said to the math tutor, whom he'd feared all these years, even though, when they were students together, they'd shared the same bench and desk: after all . . . But Jeremiah cut in and said to his tutor, What right has my beloved in my house, when she has hatched vile deeds? Suddenly he saw his math tutor's soul as if via X-ray, and it was like a pit of filth, filled with lust for his confused pupils, who were unable under any circumstances to solve an equation by substitution. As he stared at the forehead of the polyglot, he saw through the fraud. This famous translator wasn't familiar with even one language, apart from Hebrew and a smidgen of Aramaic; and the whore had once kicked a cat and killed it, just like that, because it was keeping her awake, but since she refused to entertain sweaty clients she'd consequently acquired a name as a high-class operator; and the oil merchant would tell people he was selling them pure olive oil, but always made sure to blend in a third, sometimes two-thirds safflower oil, and his oils won prizes in contests, and with each win he increased the quantity of safflower . . . etc., etc. All the small lies of the inhabitants of his village were revealed at once to Jeremiah, as if the surveillance dossiers on each of his neighbors had been revealed to him all in one instant: idol worship was as common in his neighborhood as watching TV. In fact, everyone watched the idol-worship game shows on the Idol Worship Channel, and this was the real work of idol worship, not the anointing of some hilltop statues with oil— that belonged to the past, to the era of ancient Israel. Now, for the most part, it took place on the screen. No, there were no murderers or child merchants there—simply normal people with the same run-of-the-mill human contaminations that everyone is familiar with and which everyone calls their *complex personality.*

And then a Bible teacher approached Jeremiah. He'd taken cover all that time behind taller neighbors at the rear of the car, since he'd had no desire to be seen, to reveal what lurked behind his smug face, but now he said: No. No. You shall not prophesy in the name of the Lord, or you will die by our hand. The fact that you keep saying *Thus says the Lord* doesn't make your act any more convincing. I saw in the paper as well—*Thus says the Lord* this and *Thus says the Lord* that. Right, the math tutor added, I can say it, too, Thus says the Lord: twenty-five squared is six hundred, not six hundred twenty-five, because six hundred is a number that I find more pleasing, I like big round numbers. It doesn't work that way. And Jeremiah said, Oh, Reb Birnbaum, I'm awestricken; how can I say another word? And the teacher said: Enough, shut up; aren't there bigger crooks in Judah for you to pick on than the inhabitants of this quiet village? People who taught you, and brought you up, and fed you in their kitchens . . . You won't remember, he said, but the gym teacher here once saved your life. You were in your stroller, and the stroller started rolling downhill, and he broke into a sprint and caught the handle, while your father—who's reading with such supreme concentration—stood there talking to someone about something of great import. Back then, too, he was engrossed in some idea. Today the gym teacher is a mountain of a man. All gym teachers end up overweight men in track suits— that's what they call the mockery of fate, but you know that our gym teacher once held the Jerusalem record for the hundred-meter downhill sprint. Jeremiah said, And the whore? And the teacher said: Enough. You're committing an awful injustice. She isn't a whore—not every woman who lives alone is a whore, not every woman who decides not to get married is a whore—you can't go on making such accusations, you're no longer a boy of six. Pull yourself together: grow up. And, needless to say, Jeremiah, you should be the last person to rage against whores— people who live in glass houses and all that. Jeremiah blushed; the teacher was alluding to the ridiculous rumor about his family being related to Rahab the famous whore. His father had responded to that sort of talk with a snort of contempt, but Jeremiah's sister had stubbornly insisted that it was true, and there was a touch of pride in her voice when she said as much. You better watch out, I'm a spectacled cobra, the Bible teacher said, and I have a poison tooth—I was born with it—and in any case it won't be on account of your ridiculous accusations that I'll bite you, but because you're trampling all over the Bible. Shame, trampling on the Bible! someone screamed, and Jeremiah recognized Sophia the Bulgarian dental hygienist. How assiduously she'd polish his teeth, digging through mounds of tartar with her steel pick as she leaned against him, scrubbing away layer upon accumulated layer with her electric brush. The things you're saying today are nicely formulated and well polished, said the Bible teacher, and in today's world, where everything goes, and there are no literary standards to speak of, some inexperienced editor is bound to come along and publish your *prophecies*. He'll copy them down from the papers and list you alongside the true prophets, like Isaiah and Samuel. Sure, such things have already happened. After all, they'll set the seal on the Bible one of these days, lock the doors, and every scribbler wants to get in while there's still time! This I won't allow to happen. Jeremiah stared at his forehead but didn't detect any blemish; perhaps he was a hidden tzaddik, a saint. And this saintly person told him: Sit down next to your father. If it weren't for him, and the medical aid he provided to a number of neighbors all these years, and to my wife, too, we'd have thrown you off the train a long time ago.

A motorcyclist in a helmet revved alongside the light-rail car, swooped up close to the window without slowing down, and shouted out to Jeremiah, Thus says the Lord concerning the people of Anatot that seek your life, saying: Behold, I will punish them, the young men shall die by the sword, their sons and their daughters shall die by famine. And not even a vestige shall be left of them. For I will bring disaster upon the people of Anatot. Jeremiah wanted to implore: No, no, it isn't necessary to bring famine and the sword to every math tutor and dental hygienist. Enough is enough—it's only a squabble between neighbors. I can manage them fine without any disasters, without any crushing penalties. But the motorcyclist cut away and vanished, and the light rail stopped at the Pisgat Ze'ev Center stop, and Jeremiah and his father pushed forward to be the first to leave the car and wait on the platform for the connection to Anatot. Jeremiah glanced up toward Mount Scopus, which stood above them to the southwest, and on whose slopes he'd climbed as a child, during his vacations, when his father would take him along to the hospital. He neither remembered nor knew about the incident of the stroller rolling down the street, and his father, as if reading his thoughts, said aloud, Yes. And a chill wind blew, and the night creatures sawed and chirped away in the patches of grass between the tracks and on the leaves of the few trees casting down shadows like parched refugees in the moonlight. And cats fixed their large eyes on the waning, late-Kislev moon. Their neighbors passed by them on their way to the platform to change trains and return home, and the math tutor stopped for a moment and said, I'm sorry, Jeremiah, I got carried away. Who knows, maybe there's a bit of holiness in you after all. Everyone's entitled to prophesy a little—who am I to decide? All I know is how to solve binomials and integral equations, and I've got to tell you, the tutor said, that I don't understand everything, either; I know how to rattle off solutions like a parrot, and I know how to teach my pupils, he confessed, but I've never grasped what it all really means, what it stands for in reality, and even what that word really means—*binomial*. So forgive me. And you, too, forgive me, Hilkiah. You saved Orna from certain death, even though we were getting divorced. Why'd she have to go off with that Sidonian? What sort of place is Sidon, anyway? What's she doing there, what?

The sound of a millstone and the light of a flickering candle rose from one of the homes, and Hilkiah took out a cigarette and offered it to his son, as he was accustomed to do at moments of crystalline nighttime purity. Though Hilkiah objected to smoking and generally refused to smoke, there were moments in which smoking turned into something otherworldly for him—not the beastly wheezing of nicotine addicts walking the streets and dragging on their cigarettes, oblivious to their own habit, as he liked to say. In the last five years, he must have offered a smoke to Jeremiah—who also hated smoking—three or four times at the most, always in moments of well-being and quiet. Hilkiah had a toothache, and he tried to divert the smoke to the tooth, curious whether the nicotine in the smoke would kill the germs. In recent years, the materials needed to fill cavities had gotten so expensive that only the well-heeled could afford the procedure. In fact, getting ill had almost become fashionable among the poor, though a poor sick person made no social sense at all. Being both poor *and* sick is a tiring affectation, explained Minister of Finance Baalzakar, railing against protesters: You stuffed your mouths with sweets, and now you want me to fill your cavities for you? Sorry, I don't have any money to spend on your rotting teeth—in the future, be sure to floss.

Jeremiah's parents lived in the last house in Anatot, which was farthest from the university and faced northeast, overlooking the hills and summits. At times, it seemed, thanks to a strange optical illusion—a fata morgana of sorts—that the Dead Sea extended right up to their doorstep. And the memory of hiking, one winter, from their home to the northern end of the Dead Sea came to mind, how they trekked, he and his sister and father, for some six hours, how light burst out from the clouds, coming and going, streaking the hills with blotches of shadow; they walked in the shadowy blotches, protected for the most part from the sun; by early afternoon, they beheld the sea, and it wasn't an illusion, but the actual salty waters.

Hilkiah inhaled his smoke and told Jeremiah, I saw from the train window today the son of King Josiah, who was with you in your youth science club. And Jeremiah asked, baffled, What? And Hilkiah said, You know, what's his name, Mattan, Mattaniah, Josiah's son. Jehoiakim's brother. And Jeremiah said: Ah yes, Mattaniah. I saw him today, too. But what's that you said? He was with me in the youth science club? And his father said: Yeah, for sure, but he signed up with a made-up name to keep other children from teasing him. He was called something else in the club, something like Zahi, Zadok . . . no, Zedekiah. And the name Zedekiah sounded familiar to Jeremiah, and troubled him, and he said: Sure, the boy Zedekiah I remember . . . but what are you saying? Zedekiah from summer camp is Mattaniah?! Wow. I'm in shock. I didn't make the connection; he was, like, a chubby, quiet kid . . . He had reddish hair—what happened to his hair? And how'd he get so burly, with all those muscles and tattoos . . . ? And his father said: Maybe he's been hitting the gym all these years to buffer that quiet little boy with a lot of macho racket. Anyway, tomorrow's your trial. Don't worry, I've already spoken to a lawyer; he'll meet you in the morning at the entrance to the courthouse. He's a patient of mine. If your life is going to depend on a lawyer, it's always best to hire a lawyer who owes you his life . . . Otherwise things are liable to turn sour. Jeremiah said, What did we study there, at the youth science club? And Hilkiah said, Astronomy, geology . . . And Jeremiah raised his head for a moment, as though he could see the same stars he'd seen then, lying on his back in a field with the rest of the children.

He didn't really succeed in calling up Mattaniah's face as a child, so he imagined him as he appeared today—broad-framed, whether brawny or flabby was open to question; tattooed in cuneiform; sporting an Assyrian beard and an Assyrian hat; his large brown dog beside him—sitting there in the classroom at the youth science club, under the retractable ceiling, under the stars, which drifted in as at a planetarium. All of a sudden, he remembered how they'd walked together after one of the group activities and stopped at the entrance of an apartment building. They'd gone up to the intercom panel, and Mattaniah had pressed all the buttons, and the neighbors started blathering through the intercom speaker: Hello, hello, who's that? Pincasi, what do you want? First things first: Did you pay your building maintenance fees? So why are you buzzing me on the intercom? I buzzed? You buzzed! What? Your garbage is still sitting there dripping on the first floor. Hold on, who's that? What? Shulman? Shulman's dead! Who said Shulman, I said Fichman—you deaf or what? Fichman? Didn't he move to Sidon with the—? What? Who? Why are you buzzing me between two and four, asshole? I've told you a thousand times, I need to sleep. I buzzed? *You* buzzed! You piece of shit, I'm coming over in a minute with a cleaver to cut up you and your retarded daughters! Seven daughters you bore, and they're all retarded and hideous, with horse teeth and the brains of a horse to match—how proud you must be! You're going to cut *me* up? What daughters are you talking about? I'm a single widower—let me sleep! Let me sleep! A hundred and thirty shekels, don't you go playing dumb! I'll cut you up, imbecile, go back to your Ammonite slut and don't come back. Building maintenance fees are more important than federal taxes, so when are you going to pay, when? That's right, the fees have gone up, up, and up, don't you go playing dumb; he always asks if the fee has gone up—enough already! Let me sleep, I need to sleep when I can, I'm a pilot, there'll be a midair collision tomorrow because of you. Tomorrow? Tomorrow? Again, *tomorrow*? What about your boy and his ball, that doesn't count? Might as well be bouncing right on my head! My daughter's a lawyer, a real barracuda; she'll gobble you up without salt—you just wait—and I'll bet you don't want anyone talking about that hose you've got running right into your kitchen, do you? Slut, slut, you called me a slut? Me? What about your wife, ho-ho-ho, does she really have to moan right into our ears every night? All the rent I pay just to listen to a porn soundtrack, and you have the nerve to ask me what the problem is? It stinks, that's the problem, it stinks. You think you could get away with not paying your taxes for as long as you've been ignoring your maintenance fee? Your daughter doesn't scare me; I'll send over my Moabite handyman and, believe me, he'll calm her right down, okay? I'm saying that it isn't—

Jeremiah and Mattaniah stood there, Jeremiah recalled, and laughed wildly in front of the neighbors' unending symposium, speaking to one another without knowing exactly to whom they were speaking, and then they left, the two boys, while behind them the conversation continued, shouts and insults and bitter curses. Even when they boarded the bus to the center of town and parted there with their schoolbags, the conversation was probably dragging on, and who knows, Jeremiah reflected, looking at his father for a second, maybe it's still going on to this day. Jeremiah almost laughed, and quietly entered the house with his father. The door was unlocked. Behind them, it resumed raining. His mother was watching the news on TV with the sound muted, and Jeremiah and his father stood there, dumbfounded at the sight on the screen of the city of Ashkelon in flames.

16

MATTANIAH BEN JOSIAH leaned over Tukulti-Ninurta, his large brown dog—who lay on his back with his paws bent and his eyes narrowed to slits—and slowly, gently scratched his belly. The mastiff gave himself up to this scratching and stroking, but Mattaniah's hand was tormented by guilt and regret; and there were moments in which Mattaniah wanted to bite it, his own hand, since his dog clearly wouldn't. You don't deserve to be the vessel for such kindness. Everything you do is soaked in lies, every stroke. But the dog, it seemed to him, had shrugged off the past, had forgiven him for everything. Mattaniah glanced at the TV out of the corner of his eye. The camera zoomed up onto a helicopter, and it was obvious from its bold blue color that it was not an Egyptian but a Babylonian chopper. The chopper was blue, but Mattaniah thought that it was most probably some kind of mistake, for why should the Babylonians sack Ashkelon? It all had the tinge of a misremembered dream: wrong from the bottom up. Like a blue crow alighting on the full moon. Babylon? Babylon?! But the camera panned farther up, and more choppers were there, coming into sight, blue choppers bearing the emblem of a roaring lion, and soldiers in pointed helmets that Mattaniah recognized immediately as Assyrian, and after a moment he understood that they were nevertheless Babylonian helmets—these helmets were the spoils of war. They were wearing the headgear of their former enemies.

His manual of ancient Assyrian was on the low stool beside them, and Mattaniah patted his dog with one hand, feeling Tukulti's ribs through the dog's thin skin, while the other hand opened the book to the table of basic logograms, which he then went over out loud. Sun. God. Mountain. Man. Bull. He thumbed through the pages for a while, enunciating with some effort, *Madatushu amhur*. And translated, His tribute I received. And continued, *Itishun amdahitz*, I fought him. He repeated these phrases, endeavoring to improve his accent: *Itishun amdahitz, madatushu amhur*, I fought him and received his tribute. He stroked behind the dog's ear and told him, kiddingly, Tukulti, *Itishun amdahitz, madatushu amhur*. And he added, *Sha la iknushu ana niryah*, Who does not surrender to my yoke . . . And the dog also glanced at the book and, as though reading from its pages, replied, *Atama rabbi*, and even translated, Only you are the big. And added, standing on all fours, *Muhalik za'iri*, Destroyer of enemies. Mattaniah froze, and then got up and fled in quick, short strides to the kitchen.

Henceforth, they'd sit together and speak Assyrian and Hebrew. For it turned out that the dog knew how to talk, and his Assyrian was better than Mattaniah's. Yes, he'd known how to talk even before he was abandoned. Yes, many dogs know how to talk, he said, but they would never admit to it, since it was clear what would happen if they did: they'd be taken to a lab and would spend the rest of their lives under observation—that is, being tortured. We know all about you human beings by now, he said. A dog that knows how to talk knows how to think as well, and has enough brains to realize that a human being is about as likely to let go of a talking dog as a dog is likely to let go of his favorite leather sandal. Doggy not drop sandal! the dog said—that's a well-known old Assyrian saw. He taught Mattaniah how to pronounce High Assyrian properly, as well as the Babylonian dialect. And Mattaniah asked his dog: If that's the case, why are you talking to me? When I treated you so poorly, after all the good you've done me? And the dog said: Poorly? I can't say anything especially terrible comes to mind. You were always good to me.

Noa came home, so they shut up. She showed Mattaniah a new jug she'd made that very day, a jug as black as night. Tukulti didn't say a thing. Mattaniah noticed that it had been six hours since they'd last gone for a walk, so he strapped on the dog's collar and clipped on his leash and gave Noa a long and fervent kiss, and she rummaged in her pocket till she got out a package of snacks for the dog that she'd bought for him in the market at the Potsherd Gate. Then she went to take a shower, and man and dog glanced at each other and went out for a stroll around the lower slopes, behind the darkened streets between the far end of Abu Tor and the beginning of Wadi Kidron. And they shared the tasty doggy snacks between them, and raised their eyes to the sickle moon and to the new star as they both stood a moment to relieve themselves on either side of a cypress.

PART TWO

JEHOIACHIN

17

SEVEN YEARS AGO, he recalled, under this or that headline, there were these outsize photographs of Babylonian soldiers beholding the sea for the very first time, standing there facing the waves on the shoreline of the great Philistine city of Ashkelon, or swimming in those salty waves that so filled them with surprise. Their iron helmets were arranged in rows on the beach. Back at home, so far away, water was sweetness itself. Here they filled their mouths with seawater and spat it back out, laughing in disgust.

Jeremiah folded the sea that was in the paper that was in his memory, and the roaring of the surf ceased. He raised his eyes to the palace. New floors and buildings had been added in recent years, and additional canals branched out from its base, Venice-style, as it were, and at night, it was said, gondoliers had once plied about and sung to amuse the king and his retinue. In recent years, Jeremiah had made it his custom to show up at the palace every couple of days, like a postman, and shout into an intercom, each time to a different intercom at the door of a different building within the palace perimeter. This time, he went up to the tallest building in the compound, even though he didn't know whether the king lived there, and pressed all the buttons, and again uttered the words he'd written down seven years ago in the margins of a newspaper, for which crime he'd been arrested and sentenced: Woe to him who builds his house by unrighteousness and his upper rooms by injustice, that makes his neighbor work for nothing, and gives him not his wages. You're still alive, Jeremiah told himself; in other words, they let you go—after all, you were prepared to die back then, which let you put your mind at ease, thinking death would relieve you of your burden, just like Jonah thought he'd be free inside his big fish. You don't need to prophesy in the belly of a whale, after all, or curse anybody, or preach. Inside a whale, it's utterly quiet, among all those doomed sardines and who knows what other sorts of fish that were sucked inside to their death. Who says I will build myself a wide house and spacious chambers, Jeremiah went on into the intercom, and who cuts out windows for it and panels it with cedar and paints it with vermillion? Will you reign because you strive to excel in cedar? Did not your father eat and drink and do justice and righteousness? Then it was well with him. He judged the cause of the poor and needy—then it was well. Is not this to know me? says the Lord. But your eyes and your heart—Jeremiah's lips almost grazed the plastic mesh— are only on dishonest gain and on shedding innocent blood and oppression and violence, to act swiftly. Therefore, thus says the Lord concerning Jehoiakim the son of Josiah, King of Judah, they shall not lament for him, *Ah my brother!* or *Ah my sister!* They shall not lament for him, *Ah lord!* or *Ah his glory!* He shall be buried with the burial of an ass, dragged off and cast forth beyond the gates of Jerusalem.

Jeremiah struck the mesh with the heel of his hand and gave up. Pathetic, he thought. Ah my brother . . . Ah my sister . . . The words bounced back like an echo. Ah sister. Seven years, seven years spewing out words in vain. Each day and its prophecy, each day and its dreams. A gardener, a man from Cush, watered the flowers below in the compound, along the length of the

Venetian canals that were now empty, and Jeremiah saw him bending over and attentively sprinkling drops of water on the palace's vibrant violet petals. And once again a fire began to burn in him, and he took out one of his scribbled-down prophecies, and he opened his mouth and turned to the blue and red potted flowers next to the intercom, and he told the flowers, Stand at the crossroads, and ask for the old paths: Where is the good way? And walk in it, and find rest for your souls. Rest—for your souls, he told them in all seriousness, and he wondered whether what he was preaching to the king's flowers wasn't in fact meant for himself, only himself, whether he wasn't the one seeking some form of solace for his soul. Only him, nobody else, all this prophesying nothing more than an interior monologue. Even if he shouted, he wasn't ever going to be heard, because his words all sounded so different outside his own skull. The flowers nodded their heads in the breeze. Beetles crept in and out of the corollas.

From where he was standing on the hilltop, Jeremiah could see below, in the soccer stadium, troops of workers preparing the largest bowl of hummus in the world, for the upcoming Middle East–wide hummus competition; the newspapers had been reporting on their progress for the past month, and cement mixers were pounding and mashing and pouring enormous quantities of chickpea paste into a bowl that had once been the dome of an observatory, which the king himself had ordered dismantled. Why on earth gaze at the stars? Night after night, it's just the same old thing up there—and the moon, look, spare us, waxing or waning, enough, we get the idea. The financing of all this astronomy and astrology and who knows what sort of idolatry wasn't going to come from the king's treasury . . . The Lord's anointed suddenly turned all sanctimonious. I want this dome, and that's all there is to it. Tomorrow.

The cement mixers backed up a long incline to a ramp that had been placed around the bowl, and steadily poured in thousands of liters of freshly ground hummus, while a representative from *The Guinness Book of Records*, who'd arrived especially from

Hattusa, filled out his report, and every once in a while leaned over the bowl with a spoon whose handle was as long as two broomsticks in order to sample the dip, deep in concentration.

The intercom was sparkling clean. Blank paper slips appeared in the slots reserved for the names of the nonexistent residents, and the board was still entirely covered with a thin sheet of plastic, which Jeremiah had a hard time removing. Behold, I will make my words in your mouth fire, and this nation wood—and it shall devour them. When he first heard those words, he'd thought of a dragon. Now he thought: What fire, what woods, what dragon in your head? A man stands in front of an unconnected intercom and presses this button, that button, and talks to a wall day after day, week after week. Prepares his speech at home and edits and corrects and rehearses and then shows up at the palace to shout into an intercom that isn't working. Consider your situation. He stepped back several paces and sat on a rock. A beetle landed on his head, but he took no notice. He understood that the king had such extensive vertical security that there was no need for sentinels on the ground, much as a falcon has no need for guards when it raises its nest to the skies. Above him rose huge towers connected by an impressive network of bridges and vertical and horizontal elevators and cable cars, in order to minimize the needs of its residents, members of the royal family and their servants and slaves.

And he remembered Mattaniah, who grew up in the palace, which hadn't yet relocated to the Holyland but was still back in the Old City, and how once, when they were children, Jeremiah had been invited to visit—that is, visit the palace—but Jeremiah was frightened, he simply got scared, and although they'd arranged to meet, he forgot, as it were, and didn't show up. They met at the youth science summer day camp in Givat Ram; Mattaniah would arrive every morning, escorted by two Egyptian bodyguards, and one guard would hang around the entire time and watch over the boy and his conduct from a distance. One time, after some kid roughed Mattaniah up—as will happen with boys, nothing too serious—the offending child was caught in a stranglehold within seconds by the Egyptian guard, and no one ever bothered Mattaniah again. Using the smattering of Egyptian that the guards and governesses and cooks had taught him, little Mattaniah had shouted at the guard to relax his grip, since the man had almost choked the attacking boy to death, not to mention the astronomy teacher who'd rushed to the scene holding an inflatable moon. Jeremiah didn't know what to make of the term *puppet king*, which his sister had used then, nor did he know that Jehoiakim, who was soon crowned and promoted in the papers as a new David or a new Solomon, was in effect Pharaoh in disguise, a sort of hand puppet behind which wiggled the Pharaoh's own fingers, which only said what Pharaoh told it to say, and only moved its fingers and its head when Pharaoh moved his own. Now Jeremiah thought how strange it was that Mattaniah had indeed loved hand puppets and assorted marionettes, and how, at the youth science club, he'd sometimes sneaked out to go next door and take part in the youth puppet theater instead— accompanied, needless to say, by that Egyptian man-mountain tattooed in hieroglyphics, his permanent shadow.

But your eyes and your heart are only on dishonest gain and on shedding innocent blood and oppression and violence, to act swiftly. And I, Jeremiah reflected, am I not to act swiftly? Everyone's in a rush to do something. What better metaphor for the entire human race than a marathon? All and sundry running in their own lanes, the fast and the slow, parallel to each other, but there are so many lanes, and one can't always see the competition. And then he saw an enormous Olympic stadium of sorts, and its racetracks, and on them he saw kings, kings running around and around: the King of Babylon, Nabu-Kudurri-Usur, whose name was corrupted by the Jews to Nebuchadrezzar or Nebuchadnezzar, and whose appearance Jeremiah knew only from the newspapers; and Pharaoh Neco, who, if the rumor was true, was armless and legless, and consequently had to run along borne on the back of his servant like a royal schoolbag on the back of a child; and Jehoiakim, King of Judah, and his brother the missing Jehoahaz, and also Josiah the dead king, too, dragged along in a coffin, blood sloshing over his chariot. And that wasn't all—it seemed that more and more kings were running in Jeremiah's vision: Assyrian kings in an unending column, nearly filling their entire lane; and the kings of Elam and Media, too, in the farther and wider orbits; and Menashe, Mattaniah's great-grandfather; and Ammon, Mattaniah's grandfather; and Ahaz and Hezekiah and Ahab and Adonijah and others still, and Jehoiachin, too—Jehoiakim's eighteen-year-old son, who'd been living for a decade now in Vienna—even he was running there. As Jeremiah watched him running, he suddenly knew, knew for sure, that he'd be seeing him in the flesh soon enough. And he himself, Jeremiah, was there on the track now, too, walking at a rapid pace, not really running, for the poets, young Mattaniah among them, were also in the race, running as one body and at more or less the same speed, one behind another, all sharing the same track, and Broch was jogging alongside them, keeping time. And there were more and more lanes there, for his parents, and his grandfather the priest, who loved to speak over and over again about Evyatar the High Priest, who was perhaps the first in their family line, and about David. And farther back were the tribal heads and the patriarchs and Adam and Eve, who were now there, too, running with a limp after they'd been expelled from Eden, on the farthest-flung lanes of the stadium—like comets circling some solar system—with the serpent hot on their heels.

Woe to him who builds his house by unrighteousness and his upper rooms by injustice, Jeremiah repeated, unable to keep his mouth shut. Seven years ago, he had been tried on account of these words, but the building that was built by unrighteousness continued to be built both up and across, skyward and sideways, and the king up on who knew which floor marveled at his sliding window, which opened at the touch of his fingertip onto a grand view of the Holy Temple. He could slide open the window and see whatever was going on out there, not to mention the flat screens in his chambers on which he could observe the people worshipping up close. He even had cameras installed in the Holy of Holies for his private use, although he was far from interested in religious matters, a complete bore. As for animal sacrifice, he couldn't bear the sight or sound or smell of it, though the stench and the screams reached him even here, thanks to his screens. He preferred his meat grilled and silent, thank you, without blessings and Levite hymns, and without any ritual sprinkling of the animal's blood. When Jeremiah was tried for what he'd written in the newspaper—that is to say, what he'd scribbled in the margins of one particular article—the king was watching the trial on one of his flat screens, even though he wasn't particularly interested. Such things happened every week—trials of prophets and traitorous army officers and spies—and who could keep track of them all?

But now Jehoiakim was standing and listening quizzically to his intercom receiver and the words of prophecy that were erupting from it, which rather resembled the prophecies delivered by one of the people whose trials he hadn't paid much attention to, several years back—and maybe they were being spoken by that very same prophet. The prophet who had stood trial, all the while repeating his tired and irrelevant mantras, such as: Amend your ways and your doings and hearken to the voice of the Lord your God, blah-blah-blah, and how it was a good thing God had changed His mind about the calamity that He'd said He would bring upon you, blah-blah-blah. And as for me, Jehoiakim remembered, the prophet had said, Behold, I am in your hands, do with me as seems good and right in your eyes. And Jehoiakim had shouted, seven years ago, at the plasma screen: Hey, great, so let's hang him and that's that, you said so yourself, smart-ass. And Jeremiah, as if in reply to the king's bellowing, which of course no one could hear in the courtroom, had said quietly, Only know for certain that if you put me to death, you will bring innocent blood upon yourselves, and upon this city, and its inhabitants. And the courtroom had fallen silent, and Jeremiah had said—his voice suddenly as innocent and thin as the voice of a child, one of the judges thought, a man by the name of Ahikam—For *in truth* the Lord has sent me to you to speak all these words in your ears. *In truth*, the king thought. Enough already, really. Come on! Swat the fly, he's annoying the horse.

The king replaced the intercom receiver on its cradle as delicately as he could, lest he be caught eavesdropping thanks to the click. It was interesting stuff, actually, pretty words if nothing else, and he jotted some of it down on a scrap of paper, which he stuck into his pocket. Still, what bullshit, he said. If I had to listen to every prophet and quasi-prophet out there, I wouldn't be king but a talk-show host. I could sit in the palace and broadcast all day every day, he said to one of his eunuchs, who'd just come in—unless he was there all along, watching the king listening to the intercom. And let's suppose, the king said, just let's suppose that I *wanted* to listen to them. Do you know how many prophets hang around Jerusalem? Hang around this apartment complex alone, which people keep calling a *palace*? There isn't a day, not a day that they don't come around and prophesy to and about me. On the radio, in the papers, and now this one even managed to get access to my intercom. What's going on? Isn't there any security here? Anyone can come and press all the buttons and drive not only the neighbors but the king himself crazy? Look, there's an old prophet here who turns up every Sabbath and asks to come up, and I actually let him in and offer him a cup of tea, the king said. I respect everyone; my door is always open. I've proclaimed as much, even though scarcely a soul ever tries to take me up on it. Why doesn't anyone ever come? Why don't more people frequent the king's open house? So, anyway, this old prophet arrives every Sabbath and utters four words: Palace of the Lord, Palace of the Lord, Palace of the Lord. And then he leaves. What am I supposed to do with that? What am I to make of it? I suppose he means that the palace was, is, and will be? Like in the days of Isaiah? Isaiah, now there was an honest-to-goodness prophet; you could rely on him. He saved my forefathers from Assyria, after all. But, okay, common sense would say—Jehoiakim told a second eunuch, who had replaced the first, who'd slipped away unnoticed—that the House of God can't be destroyed or harmed. No, please, correct me if I'm wrong, Eunuchvitch, but if God dwells in X's house, can X's house be destroyed? That's ridiculous. It's like someone saying, Look, if you ever stop eating poppy-seed cake—and I'm crazy for poppy-seed cake!—the skies will fall.

He raised his head and looked at the sky outside the sliding window. And the eunuch looked at the day's agenda and said, Your Highness, this morning the king has a dental hygienist's appointment, five months overdue. And the king was afraid and said, No, no, push it back a month; the pain was excruciating; why did you schedule that murderess for first thing in the morning? Let's get out the scale. The royal scale was brought, and the king stepped on, and was again dismayed to see that he weighed only 196 pounds, whereas he knew that his weight should be at least 286. You didn't fiddle with the scale, did you? he asked his scale attendant suspiciously. Heaven forefend, my lord king, that I should ever do such a thing—though the attendant had, it goes without saying, fiddled. It was a digital scale, and he'd programmed it to show only two-thirds of the actual weight registered, so that the King of Judah always weighed in at a reasonable and healthy level. I eat and eat and don't gain weight, he rejoiced. But if we're already talking about weight and teeth, it's not a big jump to the subject of breakfast—as in, where's mine? What, the king doesn't get a bite to eat in the morning? Do I have to order myself a pizza? And the eunuch chuckled and asked, Wouldn't my noble king prefer to hold off just a bit and eat from the giant hummus bowl? My I remind His August Majesty that the ceremony is scheduled to begin a mere two hours from now, right after your canceled appointment with the dental hygienist? Perhaps we should start getting dressed, so that Your Highness will have sufficient time? The king stood up. He was dressed in short floral-patterned shorts, and his feet were like twin loaves of white bread, the eunuch reflected. The king said, But the king wants a drink first. And the eunuch said, Oy, my lord is thirsty. Apple-carrot as usual, great king? Large or medium? I'm off to squeeze the juice. And His Royal Highness King Jehoiakim pondered at length, and then decreed majestically, his voice resounding loudly: I'll take a large.

18

Noa and mattaniah's wedding was as modest as it gets. That's how they planned it, anyway: a wedding followed by a small vegetarian reception in the courtyard of the old Bezalel building, on Shmuel Ha-Nagid Street, without music and without dancing, and with guests invited strictly on the basis of the bride and groom's wanting them there, not according to official family ties. One of their poet friends was supposed to take photographs, and they also intended to read some poems, so that in the end the entire event would be conducted more like a modest book launch than some ostentatious nuptials. After eating slices of quiche and a green salad, the bride and groom would sit in a circle with twenty or thirty close friends and family, and they'd talk about this thing called marriage, and they'd read passages on marriage from the Midrash, and they'd recount how they met, and what they saw in each other, and in this way set out together on their new path surrounded by the love of friends and relatives.

But the wedding was brought to the attention of the king, and, burning with fury, he was ready to blow it all to pieces. Over my dead body, he declared. All of a sudden, Jehoiakim was reminded that he had a little brother, after having barely exchanged a word with him for years. And he told his majordomo eunuch: It's not going to happen; I won't let him tarnish our reputation. It's no skin off my back if he wants to hang out and write poetry—no one reads the stuff anyway—but photographers are bound to show up at his wedding, and TV people, too, and there's no way I'm going to be seen sitting there surrounded by poets munching on green leaves. You can be sure he's chosen this sort of ceremony just to humiliate us, Jehoiakim told his majordomo eunuch, and I won't be party to any of it. Consequently this selfsame eunuch appeared in Mattaniah's home a month before the wedding and explained to the bridegroom, after blessings and niceties, genuflections and bootlicking, that the organization of the wedding was now out of the couple's hands, that from now on Mattaniah needn't worry about a thing, or pay for a thing, that the court would be taking care of the wedding, and that they would even bring their own paramedic along. Mattaniah asked, Paramedic? And the eunuch replied, Yes, people inevitably suffer attacks and strokes of one sort or another at weddings, from all the food and dancing. And Mattaniah said, Attacks and strokes? And the eunuch replied, Yes, heart and brain.

And Mattaniah was delighted with this arrangement, because he assumed, perhaps naturally, that he'd be the one to make all the decisions while his brother had only to foot the bill. And he and Noa were assured that everything would be fine: After all, it's *your* wedding, of course, and your preferences have been jotted down point by point. All you need to do is show up and get married, they were told; we'll worry about all the rest. And they set out for a monthlong, all-expenses-paid sailing trip down the Nile, to the cataracts in the land of Cush.

THE FIRST THING THAT GUESTS SAW when they arrived at the wedding was the cow. And the paramedic sitting quite bored by the entrance eating a pita. Noa and Mattaniah didn't see either, however, since they'd been sequestered immediately in the private chambers to which they'd been herded through the building's back door. The cow stood in an oblong, fenced-off area, and above her head was a sign that read: I'm your cow. Congratulations!!! In another hour I won't be here anymore! Ha-ha-ha! The three mischievous exclamation points were colored blood-red, and whoever got the hint—well—got it. The animal's various cuts of meat were drawn on her body in different colors. A butcher was standing beside her and explaining to the guests the virtues of each cut, and every guest chose according to his or her own taste, and their orders were written down. Almost every hind part has a matching fore part, the butcher explained to Noa's parents and sister. The hind part of the animal works harder than the fore part, which causes the hind parts to be more fibrous and less fatty, and consequently they need to cook for a longer time. There's a connection between the tenderness of the meat, its texture, and the part of the body from which it's taken— that's the main thing to understand. And Noa's father said, I want sirloin, I love sirloin. And the butcher said, An excellent choice, sir—the cow lowed—sirloin is terrific for roast beef. Apart from that, sirloin is suitable for steaks, or stuffed schnitzel—if, of course, one uses a thicker cut. But we won't be smoking it today—no, no, smoking is hazardous to your health, ha-ha. Besides, if we all smoke up before the wedding, we'll probably doze off before it's over, am I right? At this, Noa's mother cracked up and wiped away a tear. Oish, it's my only daughter getting married, she told the butcher, even though Noa's sister was standing right next to her, chewing gum: No smoking or stroking your meat during her wedding, please. And the butcher asked, What'll it be, Shoshanna? Noa's mother pointed at the cow with her cigarette holder, and the butcher said, Why am I not surprised by madame's choice? Filet mignon—or, as we call the cut in our profession, filet medallions. Classic. It ought to be clear to madame, then, that it isn't recommended to cook filet more than medium-rare. If a little blood isn't visible, it's a sign that we've made a mistake; roasting too long will result in a tough and stringy piece of meat, and hours of picking at your teeth with the ole toothpick. And *that*—the cow lowed again—we want to avoid at all costs. It's most advisable to use a cut of veal, of course, but I'm sorry to say we don't have a veal calf available at the moment; still, even with regular calves and older cows like this one, it's always possible to get a decent filet mignon. It's just that veal meat is more delicate in texture and therefore in taste. But we don't have a veal calf—a calf could hardly feed this crowd—it was simply a matter of insufficient size, and we have so many guests, thank God! And Noa's mother, Shoshanna, said snidely, Well, they only invited fifty or sixty people. The butcher stared at her, baffled, and said, What? not seeing the joke. And then he continued: Filet of a mature cow will give you a stringier but nonetheless juicy steak, with a stronger taste of meat. You'll lick your fingers, Mom, the butcher promised. And Shoshanna said, But only on one hand. And the butcher didn't get it, and Shoshanna said, As far as licking, and raised her right hand, which was gnawed away up to the wrist bone. Her husband, Jacob, explained to the butcher, She used to work in a fish-canning factory, and one day she dropped her purse into the machine, and so she stuck her hand in. I mean she shut off the machine first, natch, and only then stuck her hand in—she isn't as stupid as she looks—but the blades were still turning even after the current was off, from the inertia. One silly slipup, and—oop!—off went all fives of her fingers, and someone got some extra-nutritious fish spread. And Shoshanna corrected him: *Five*. All five.

The wedding area was organized by the majordomo eunuch so that the guests—their numbers had swelled from exactly fifty-two to, grosso modo, four thousand—strolled down a path that led to the reception hall, where they were offered an assortment of tidbits. There were the customary lamb kebabs, and sushi platters, and half portions of falafel, and little sweets, and cheese platters, and fried fish, and burekas with all kinds of fillings, including, of course, a vegetarian option—namely, mock liver, which was mainly stir-fried mushrooms. It was all meant to look moderate, discreet, so as not to provide any sort of target for the media who'd been invited to report on the event. Once the last of the guests had entered, they led the cow away and took her back to her shed, since all the cuts of meat had actually been prepared in advance, and the entire business of selecting one's preferred cut had been intended purely to whet the guests' appetites—even though this cow, too, was slaughtered, it goes without saying, several weeks later. When one woman saw the cow being led away by a rope, she asked her husband, Say, d'you think they'll be serving parsiman? And he said, What, Parmesan? And she said: How stupid can you get? I said *parsiman*. And he said, What the hell is parsiman, you moron? And she said, What the hell do you mean by *What the hell is parsiman*? You acting stupid or what? You know, that sweet stuff, made of sugar and ground almonds? He stared at her for a long time, and at that very moment knew that he'd leave her. But they stayed married for another thirty-six years.

Mattaniah's mother, Hamutal, arrived at the wedding accompanied by thirty girlfriends who weren't on the guest list; this led to a polite disagreement with the majordomo eunuch, which ended with the thirty girlfriends' being loaded onto a truck and sent back to the center of town, although they were told that they were being driven to the bridal canopy platform. There they waited, in the locked truck, for three hours, until the end of all the celebrations and dancing. Hamutal searched in vain for her son and the bride, to bless them and bestow on her son her late husband Josiah's ring, a ring that had been handed down from generation to generation, beginning with Solomon, and within which, so it was said, Asmodeus, king of the demons, was still confined.

But Mattaniah wasn't among the guests; he was still in their private chambers. Tukulti was there, too; he understood perfectly what was going on outside; he didn't need to see it with his own eyes, and didn't say a word, either. He and Mattaniah had agreed that they wouldn't talk to each other in the presence of anyone else, apart from Noa. The majordomo eunuch told Mattaniah, I'm giving you an hour, you've got to impregnate her now. And Mattaniah said, She's already . . . And the eunuch looked at Noa again and saw that she was pregnant, which he hadn't noticed under her broad wedding dress, and he yelled: What, already in the family way? In that case, you've got to plow her again—that's the custom—don't spoil everything. I'm going outside now to proclaim it, so don't go and make me a liar. And Mattaniah said, Okay, I'll see what I can do, and Noa, stunned, said: *Plow? Plow?* What sort of vulgar idiot is this? And the eunuch said, But it's a vulgar sort of thing, isn't it? Maybe it's all hidden under silk and crinoline and muslin right now, but, as far as I know, once you start poking into a tube of paint with your paintbrush, once you start picking at your nose with your pinkie, once you get in there . . . He demonstrated on his own nose what he meant. And Noa said, A tube of paint? And Mattaniah said, Okay, okay, can we be left alone now? The eunuch licked his pinkie clean and said, I see that the groom's already hot—what month is the bride? Noa replied, Beginning of the ninth, and Mattaniah estimated, She's giving birth in another month. And the eunuch said: Just try to make some noise— I want the moans to be heard outside—and do me a favor, come at the same time today, just for me. Everyone's milling around and waiting for it. Then, later, only when you hear the song, enter. But, please, please, I'm begging you, make sure there aren't any stains on your clothes, okay? I've been at weddings where the groom and bride make their grand entrance and she's been sprayed all over. There's a change of clothes and some towels here in the chest. The king has already arrived, and there's a diplomatic emissary from Babylon here, too, so do your part, okay? After all, it's *your* wedding. And Mattaniah asked, When are the butterflies going to be released? And the eunuch said, When you hear the butterfly song. Male singer. When you hear the words *I want to paint the world with a paintbrush / in the colors of sweet honey*, the eunuch sang, you stand by the door, and then there are a few seconds of music without words, he reminded them, and then comes the refrain, *White butterflies*, et cetera, et cetera. The eunuch wiped away a tear: Such a perfect song, such beautifully epistemological metaphors. Anyway, that's when you come out, and that's also when the butterfly hatches will be opened. It was Noa's idea, and Mattaniah had agreed enthusiastically: they'd invited an entomologist, who brought with him in perforated boxes several thousand cabbage white butterflies. As soon as the bride and groom stepped out of the private chamber, they knew that, all at once, to the guests' utter surprise, the cabbage whites were to be released to the sound of "White Butterflies." They, Mattaniah and Noa, were dressed in white, and the message was clear and impressive—white on white, there was no mistaking it. The eunuch left, and Mattaniah sat in a corner and read from Rilke's letters; he intended to read a passage out loud during the ceremony. Noa sank onto a pile of cushions, exhausted and stressed out, and in spite of her being in her ninth month of pregnancy, she smoked half a cigarette—she couldn't help herself—and the fetus inside her coughed and cringed. And they waited tensely, without exchanging a word, until the first notes of the song were played; then they quickly got up, and together reached for the doorknob, and her hand touched his, and he drew back his hand timidly. Outside, the guests were eating hors d'oeuvres, ready to burst even before the main course, and the butterfly man, who was standing directly on the other side of the door, raised the lid of one of his boxes for one last look-see, and his face turned as pale as his butterflies' wings, for they were all—how to put this—corpses now, simply dead, lying in heaps. There had been some sort of mistake; maybe they got too hot. He examined box after box, and the situation was the same—all his cabbage whites were stone dead. The song began—strings, drums, a guitar riff—and the butterfly man realized what he had to do, as the bride and groom stepped out at precisely the right moment, to hoots of delight from the crowd.

Far more than four thousand people were present; half the city was there to have a look, and the celebrants were spilling out from the courtyard into the surrounding streets. Noa and Mattaniah registered the sheer number of people present only after standing awhile, trapped under the bridal canopy. The butterfly man and his assistant began to release the cabbage whites, flinging them in the air haphazardly over the bride and groom as they accompanied them up the aisle on their festive walk to the bridal canopy. Noa's mother said, Amazing, ingenious, butterfly confetti—it's such a beautiful idea. And Jacob, her husband, said, At our wedding we had chicken leg quarters and white rice; why be fussy, Shosh? And she said, At our wedding we also had your parents there, but they're not around anymore, are they? He'd have smashed her face with his elbow if they weren't in public, and, in the midst of the high decibels of the sweet butterfly song, he told her, What a pity it wasn't your head, rather than your hand, that got left in the fish machine. And she, who hadn't heard a word, said, That's so right, exactly what I thought, too; we've been blessed, Yankele, we've been blessed to marry a daughter into the royal family. The butterfly man returned to his boxes and began to clean up, covered in sweat, shaking. He was dumping his remaining butterflies into the trash when he noticed, in one of the final boxes, live butterflies— the butterflies in this box had somehow survived. And he was about to release them then and there, but one of the majordomo eunuch's assistants caught on, and said, Hey there, what do you think you're doing, Butterflyvitch? And the butterfly man said, I'm setting them free. Forget it, said the assistant. You want them to go flying into people's food? First course is quartered brain over cabbage—are you crazy? And the butterfly man said, I'm setting them free; they've got to be released; if they stay cooped up, they'll die, too. And the assistant said, You know what, hold on a minute, I've got an idea. He went to the storeroom and brought back some bug spray and sprayed it generously through the air holes in the butterfly boxes, and then he split and returned the spray to where he'd found it, even though the can was nearly empty.

The ceremony under the bridal canopy was lovely. Tukulti held one of the canopy poles, and consequently the whole business slanted backward. The chief rabbi looked at the dog and bristled—Oy, where's your yarmulke? Show some respect here. But there wasn't any time to deal with it. The voice of joy and the voice of gladness, the voice of the bridegroom and the voice of the bride, the chief rabbi trilled. We are gathered here today to rejoice in the joy of the virgin Noa, daughter of Shoshanna and Jacob, with the choice of her heart, Mattaniah son of Hamutal and Josiah, may the memory of the righteous and holy be a blessing. I am my beloved's and my beloved is mine. All of Israel is responsible one for another, not including a third-party guarantee for a mortgage, hey? No one laughed at the joke, and that was a pity, since the silence only encouraged the rabbi to try out another: So why is the glass broken under the canopy? Someone said, In memory of the destruction, but the rabbi said: No, what destruction? We should ruin a wedding because of the destruction of the ten tribes, may the Holy One, blessed is He, revenge their blood? You think *they'd* ruin a wedding because of *us*? Still no one laughed, and the rabbi said, One breaks the glass on the principle of *You break it, you buy it*! He turned to Mattaniah, choking with laughter. And I'll end with another joke, the rabbi said, turning to Noa: Why is a woman's period called a period? Someone shouted, Knock it off, hurry up and get them married so we can go eat, and the rabbi said, Because *mad-cow disease* was already taken! And he couldn't hold back—ha-ha, he gagged with laughter yet again at his own joke. But this time King Jehoiakim, too, laughed raucously: He's great, that rabbi, he mixes spiritual authority with a sense of humor, he said to his attendants, who nodded. And the rabbi, convulsing with laughter under the canopy, had to excuse himself for a minute, and ran off to the adjoining room to rinse his face before returning and conducting the rest of the service without a hitch, even though every now and then he was seized by stubborn little bursts of laughter, when he couldn't help remembering how funny he'd been. Then, seconds before the breaking of the glass, he tried his luck one more time—he really felt that he was in excellent form today—and, playing what he thought would be his trump card, asked the bride's father: Sir, Pop, maybe you know the number one cause of divorce? Think hard, it's an important question, under the circumstances. A young couple is standing here and waiting. And Jacob, Noa's father, turned crimson, and was unable to speak a word. His wife told the rabbi, Let him be, he's *decreepit*, he doesn't know anything. And the rabbi said, I'll tell you, the number one cause of divorce is marriage.

A speechless silence fell on the crowd, like a hand grenade into a sniper's nest, and then someone guffawed, and everybody glared at her. No one seemed to know who she was; it wasn't clear who could have invited her. Maybe she was a friend of Mattaniah's—that was probably the most likely answer—one of his erstwhile young female poet cronies. She squeezed her way through the crowd and stepped up to the dais and took the shrill mike from the rabbi and told the crowd—who were shrugging off a few last titters—Good evening to all the guests and to the young couple. The speakers screeched for a moment, as if a dagger had been plunged into the sound system. I would like, with your permission, to file a complaint, I want to complain. And the rabbi, who felt like thwacking her in the face, restrained himself and asked beguilingly, About what would madame like to complain? And she told the crowd, I want to report a rape. And the crowd shouted, Get her out of here, she goes around everywhere in the city with this same story, she doesn't belong here, this is a wedding. But Mattaniah said: Leave her alone. Please, go ahead, but make it short, and then we'll eat and celebrate, and you'll have a good time, too. And the complainant said: I'm a woman who's been beaten by the lash of misery. I've been driven, I've been led into the dark, there was no light there. He turned his hand against me, and then he ruined my blood and my flesh, and he crushed my bones. He shut me in the dark like I was dead; he fenced me off and shackled me. I screamed and pleaded, but he shut out my prayer. He shut out my prayer, he shut out my prayer, she said. He built me a brick wall; he screwed up my way. He left me wasted. He strung a bow in front of me and set me as a target for his arrow, he annihilated me with all the arrows of his quiver; everyone laughed at me, composed poems about me. He gave me to drink and . . . But the honorable rabbi said: Okay, that's enough, we get the message. Will somebody remove this nice auntie from the stage, and let's have a round of applause for Auntie, please. Someone did escort her down, to general applause, and Mattaniah, who wasn't sure whether he and Noa were indeed married yet, asked the rabbi, Your Honor, when are we getting married? And the rabbi replied: We're already in overtime. You were married even before the nutty woman got onstage to make a fuss. I know her; she also shows up sometimes in my office at the rabbinate. It's a nightmare; it isn't funny anymore. There are people who should be locked up for their own good. And the eunuch signaled, and the orchestra began playing Sephardic music, and the rabbi, who had to get to another wedding, began to make I'm-about-to-leave gestures so he would receive his envelope. But there was some sort of misunderstanding regarding who was responsible for the rabbi's envelope: Mattaniah was under the impression that his brother had taken charge of everything, whereas Jehoiakim—with all due respect—didn't think that he, of all people, ought to be the one to pay off the honorable rabbi. Consequently, the rabbi lost out on both fronts, and it transpired that the wedding ceremony, in retrospect, and against his will, had been conducted as *a good deed for its own sake*, to his great regret.

Afterward, those who were equal to the task pounced on the food as if they'd just been released from a forced-labor camp, piling their plates upward and sideways. A woman screeched, You moron, leave some room, wait for the brain. And her husband replied, What, there's brain? And the wife said: Yeah, quartered brain in marinated cabbage—didn't you look at the menu? Why don't you do a little reading for once? And the husband repeated, in exactly the same tone of voice, What, there's brain?

And Noa, who'd gone off to one side during the complainant's speech, shouted, Mom, I think my water just broke, but no one heard her. She was the bride, but no one was paying any attention to her. She screamed, and her mother came up to her and said, Nonsense, that's not possible, it's too early. And Noa leaned on someone from the catering service, and there was a doctor there, and he crawled under her crinoline and stuck his head out and said: She's giving birth. Make some room, and get rid of this tent of hers—I'm choking. The guests and Mattaniah, who was making the rounds, shaking hands, didn't take any notice—everybody was famished, and the food was flowing freely. A kitchen knife was brought over, and the doctor covered Noa with a huge sheet.

And thus Mattaniah and Noa's child was born in the midst of their wedding festivities. The doctor delivered their son, and Jeremiah's father, who saw it beamed live on TV, drew closer to the screen to get a better look, because the doctor who delivered the baby had studied with him, at the same medical school. Most of the guests continued to make their way to the buffet so as not to spoil their appetite with the bloody spectacle, or perhaps out of modesty, and King Jehoiakim, who saw the birth from a good ways away—his table laden with both sweet and savory—told Mattaniah, who was sitting there sipping beer from a giant goblet, all dressed in white, with long sleeves to hide his embarrassing tattoos, that there was no point in waiting eight days for the circumcision, having to bring all these guests back from all over the world: The rabbi's already here; for the same price we'll get both a wedding and a bris. Mattaniah had no idea what his brother was talking about, so the king told him: Your wife just gave birth. Finish your drink—no need to get excited. She'll be giving birth plenty more times, your boy isn't going anywhere, but your beer will definitely get warm. Still, Mattaniah got up and ran toward the bawling, and the king tottered along after him. Later, Mattaniah told his brother: Are you crazy, a bris now? It's dangerous as hell. And his brother the king said, As though on the eighth day it won't be dangerous.

So they circumcised the boy two and a half hours after he was born, and they really did save a *lot* of money, as well as sparing the guests a lot of bother. After all, they'd shut down the entire city for the wedding, and if they'd been forced to close off the streets for the second time in a month, there probably would have been a revolution. After the fact, an official statement about the birth was dispatched to the papers, and people spoke in praise of King Jehoiakim and of his great piety and honesty, and reporters sought out Mattaniah to ask him what he was going to name the little newly circumcised boy. And Mattaniah stared in fright and didn't know what to answer. He was sweating so profusely that his clothes stuck to his skin and his black tattoos showed through his clothes, leaving him streaked like a white leopard. And King Jehoiakim, from his place behind a heap of meat, decided without further ado, The kid's name is Eliazar.

19

JEHOIAKIM URGED THE COUPLE to come and live with little Eliazar in one of the dozens of empty apartments in the palace compound, but Mattaniah enjoyed his apartment's proximity to the desert and to the city and cheap restaurants, and for Noa it was near her stall.

Eight days after the wedding, Mattaniah went out with Tukulti for a hummus in town. From their corner in the hummus joint, they noticed Jeremiah entering and making his way between the close-set chairs to eat. During the last couple of years, they'd barely seen him. And they weren't the only ones. After the trial, even though he'd been acquitted, albeit tenuously, people chose to keep their distance. The acquittal was baffling, since the conviction appeared certain, and Jeremiah's lawyer stood there in the courtroom and didn't say a word—that was his tactic. Perhaps, if he didn't build a defense of any sort, he thought, the court would show mercy, and who knows, perhaps he was right all along. He did, nonetheless, charge a fee for his silence.

Needless to say, the verdict was by no means a tacit validation of the prophecies and warnings the defendant had spread. The court made its case on the grounds of freedom of speech, basing its decision on the famous Supreme Court ruling concerning the controversial newspaper *Kol Ha'Am*. The judge cited this legal precedent extensively—a case that had been cited so many times over the years that it was now worn as thin as a wooden doorknob or the heel of a thousand-year-old sandal—reading from his decision as follows: The test of reasonable doubt, to which we subscribe, does not require that the minister of the interior be convinced, in any case, that the public good is certain to be endangered by the publication of the aforementioned material . . . The determination of *certainty* in the sense of *probability* is not even to be necessarily interpreted as the determination of possible danger from the vantage point of time, that is to say in the sense of *proximity*. Even though taking into account that, as a result of its proclamation, a danger to the public good has been brought about, which is imminent—the judge read this, realizing that he didn't understand a word of what he was saying, but pressing on nevertheless—strengthens the estimation that the said danger is indeed undoubtedly proximate, even as taking into account that the proclamation is liable to effect the public good only after considerable time lessens the possibility that such a thing would even occur. And yet, if the minister of the interior will be convinced, under the circumstances, that the proclamation will cause with near certainty serious damage to the public good, assuredly he will have no other recourse but to exercise the authority in his power according to clause 2(19)(a), even if he estimates that this is not a matter of causing said damage immediately, the judge concluded his explication.

No one, it goes without saying, understood the circumlocutions of his argument, including the high priests and the prophets and the ministers of Judah who were present, and Jeremiah, too, stared blankly at the judge and tried to understand from his tone of voice whether he was to be killed that same day or set free. But the court decided in favor of the freedom of speech, since in any case the public was hardly likely to pay much attention to the words of yet another new prophet, or—truth be told—to any other prophet, either. Consequently, there was no lawful reason—or, alternatively, there was no real use—for putting this loser to death over a few words scribbled in the margins of a newspaper. Jeremiah saw Broch sitting in the courtroom taking notes. To his surprise, Broch didn't stand as a witness for the prosecution. The judge peered at Jeremiah for a second and asked, with obliging impatience, Why have you prophesied in the name of the Lord, saying, This house shall be like Shiloh, and this city shall be desolate, without inhabitants? And Jeremiah replied, Because that's what was told to me, and it's exactly what will happen if a meaningful change doesn't occur immediately. And the prosecutor reared up, as the saying goes, on his hind legs, and shouted, There you have it, even in the courtroom, Your Honor; I'm shocked! And the judge stared at a fixed point in the air above the prosecutor's head and told that point: I suggest the counselor calm down. Whether the counselor is shocked or not doesn't make an iota of difference from a legal point of view.

Mattaniah read all of this in the paper. How did the children we once were grow up into such creatures? he now muttered to Tukulti, who sat at the foot of his table at the hummus joint and every once in a while ate a chunk of fresh, hot pita dipped in hummus that Mattaniah made sure to cool off by blowing on it. Mattaniah stroked the dog with his heel after removing his sandal, and peered at tiny Eliazar, asleep, all bundled up, in the stroller beside him, partially blocking the way. Jeremiah sat down next to the toilets, and Mattaniah noticed how the atmosphere in the restaurant had become a bit chilly. People continued to eat, but to all appearances without appetite; the waiters, who'd generally shout out orders to the kitchen, turned taciturn and nervous. The diners, one and all, stole glances at this prophet, whose trial had made him far too well known. Once, he'd stopped at the Bookworm on his way to the Cinematheque and was told, in so many words, that they would prefer it if he'd purchase his books from them by phone from now on, since they had some sensitive clients who objected to his presence. Well, what do you expect? No one wants to be told over their morning coffee that their children are about to be torn to pieces and that our bookshelves are to burn. So he stopped dropping in at the Bookworm, and he also stopped attending films at the Cinematheque from that day on, after someone in the audience said volubly—at the screening of a lengthy, melancholic Hungarian film in black and white—Not only is this movie depressing, but that guy sitting in the aisle seat there, you can be sure any moment now he's going to give us a real mouthful, too!

And so, little by little, Jeremiah retired into himself, and he asked to have the phone in his rented apartment disconnected. One day, he removed all his books from the apartment and handed them out in the streets of Nahlaot: Just take them. He kept only one book for himself, which he always carried with him in his shoulder bag. This was *Leisure*, by the poet known as Zelda. He couldn't give it away. And he read the poems again and again, until the book fell apart, until the signatures separated and the poems got shuffled out of order. He'd walk around half the day with a passage from the book memorized, such as: Sail a craft / across the sea of fire. And he'd lean over to stare at a rose and realize how simple the poem was. Sail a craft. Craft a poem. And then: A chrysanthemum white as death / and quivering like longing— / you sing me plenty, Jeremiah said to the only groundsel on Zephaniah Street. He sat next to the flower and took out the pages and read to himself from *Leisure*. And when the wind nearly snatched the pages away, he entered a tailor's shop and asked for needle and thread.

Then he went to grab a bite to eat, and sat down furious, and was served fava hummus and a small salad and some lemonade, all without ordering, and two pitas were also set in front of him, in a wicker basket. He picked up a fork and paused, sensing that someone was staring at him, and he glanced to the side and his eyes met Mattaniah's, and also took in the brand-new stroller.

He waved meekly with his fork and, without making any sound, mouthed, Congratulations. And Mattaniah shrugged his shoulders as if to say, Hey, it happens. At a nearby table, backgammon players were playing for money, shooting their dice against the corners of the board.

Ever since his brother Jehoiakim the king paid obeisance to Babylon, several days after the destruction of Ashkelon, in Kislev seven years ago, and began paying a tax to Nebuchadnezzar— even though the King of Egypt hadn't released him from his previous commitments—a number of small changes had taken place in the life of the nation. Among other things, Akkadian, which had always been an elective in school, became compulsory, and high-school students were the first to suffer under its burden. Teachers enticed them by claiming the language was similar to Hebrew and a lot easier than Egyptian, which really was a nightmare. They themselves, Jeremiah and Mattaniah, like thousands of their generation, had been obliged to learn hieroglyphics in school: These aren't mere doodles, the teacher had insisted, these are Egyptian hieroglyphics! Tell me, children, the teacher had said, what is the difference between *scribe* and *inscribe*, between *scribes* and *inscribes*? Explain the sentence *The scribe inscribes the inscription in the scriptorium*, she demanded. Students failed Egyptian in droves. Even though they were able, with some difficulty, to identify the basic glyphs, such as hawk, leg, and hand, they were considered perfect morons when it came to the language of the southern empire. But several months after Jehoiakim's subjection to Babylon seven years ago, schools set out to teach Akkadian-Babylonian alongside Egyptian, and it slowly and steadily ate away at the students' brains, since they did indeed understand Akkadian better than Egyptian, if only because a number of Akkadian roots were similar to the Hebrew roots— but, then again, to say that our students succeeded in acquiring any degree of fluency or stylistic proficiency in that ancient Semitic language would be as far from the truth as the Nile is from the Euphrates. They could remember a few roots, sure, that was simple enough; but the declensions were a bit more complicated, not to speak of the wretched cases. Jeremiah, who was one of the few who chose to study Babylonian in junior high, recalled perfectly how in seventh and eighth grade he'd labored to decline the verb *to ride* the same as in Hebrew, and he muttered, over his plate of hummus, riding, as it were, over the wooden chair as he was about to eat, *Rakabaku, rakabata, rakabati, rakib, rakabat, rakabanu, rakabatunu* . . . The resemblance to Hebrew made the language a bit easier, but also complicated matters, since, beyond a certain point, the similarity merely led you astray. Failing his exams in Akkadian cuneiform cast a long shadow over its brother failure, his lack of success in Egyptian hieroglyphics. Mattaniah, however, who'd failed roundly in Egyptian, discovered that he had a special gift for Akkadian, and even represented the school in a national competition in the conjugation of Akkadian verbs, though he didn't win first place. But you don't study Akkadian, his brother the king reassured him, in order to come first in an idiotic competition like this one or any other.

Later, Jeremiah and Mattaniah walked in silence, side by side, down the tiny streets of the neighborhood of Baka, Jeremiah pushing the infant's stroller in front of him while Mattaniah held Tukulti's leash. Jeremiah had left the hummus joint first, Mattaniah shortly after him; Jeremiah understood that Mattaniah preferred that they not be seen leaving the joint together. But he was already accustomed to such conduct, and in the isolation that was growing deeper inside him every day, even an attenuated sort of contact was more than satisfying. Mattaniah went over what Jeremiah already knew from the newspapers, that only last week he'd married the woman from the jug stall whom Jeremiah had introduced to him, so to speak, several years ago, and that they had an infant boy whom he'd named Eliazar. Jeremiah had read about the wedding in the papers, like everyone else. Jeremiah inquired about Mattaniah's dog's health and told him that he thought he'd seen him once, years ago, loping along unattended in the streets. Mattaniah said, That's impossible—there must have been someone trailing not far behind. And Mattaniah told Jeremiah that his wife, Noa, was about to leave her pottery stall near the Potsherd Gate and open a large factory—not far from Anatot—for artisanal jugs, which she planned to export. And Jeremiah said, They're crowding the desert with factories and roads; it's awful. And Mattaniah replied: Urban development is unavoidable. We can't just keep to the same tiny City of David from six hundred years ago; times have changed. Besides, the desert is a desert—it's empty. And Jeremiah said: The desert isn't death, it only looks like death from a distance. The desert is swarming with life, with sounds, and all year round, not only in the fall and winter. I saw the shadow of an eagle on the boulders and crags, he said—or, rather, he wanted to say. My wife, Mattaniah said, when I first met her, was producing five to ten jugs a day. You smashed one of them back then, I remember. Today she gives a sample to her production manager and they put it into production and they then turn out thousands of duplicates a day. And Jeremiah said: Do you remember our astronomy teacher? How he was always watching for shooting stars? And Mattaniah said, I remember that as a child I didn't understand what that meant—shooting stars—how could a star shoot? And Jeremiah said, He always walked around with a Band-Aid on his finger, that's what I remember about him.

Above them, in broad daylight on Reuven Street, rose the nocturnal dome, filled with the stars they'd seen at night in Givat Ram, back in the youth science club, with the teacher who was maybe twenty years old but seemed like an old man to them. And Mattaniah, in the growing dark, asked: Are you still doing your . . . prophesying? Or are you over it? Jeremiah was silent. The new star was above them, and Mattaniah said, He's probably staring at that thing from dawn to dusk. Jeremiah asked, Who?, and Mattaniah said, Our old teacher. Though I heard he'd been injured. And that his injury was somehow connected to the sun, if you follow me. And Jeremiah said, as though answering a different question: You know what my father told me?

He was a doctor at Hadassah on Mount Scopus, I'm sure you remember. He was born into the priestly caste—which means I was, too, I guess—but decided not to work in the Temple. He wanted to study medicine and become a physician. And I asked him how come he gave up the priesthood, which is, after all, a way to be closer to God. He told me: I didn't give it up; medicine is as close to God as anyone can get. Doctors are priests of the Almighty, and nurses, too, and veterinarians. That's why we wear white. There's only one commandment in this religion of mine, and that's to prevent suffering, to save lives. The alleviation of pain is a prayer; every suture is a form of redemption, not only for the patient and not only for the physician. The world is flesh, and every wound is also a wound in the flesh of the world. Satan dwells in that very body, not only in the flesh of an individual man or animal. From our home in Anatot, my father would walk every day to the hospital, scrambling up Mount Scopus on foot. That's a good bit of walking, a good bit of strenuous climbing. That was his sport, he told me, climbing was for him also like prayer. In order to take one stride up this hill, he said, you need the entire globe under you, you press the soles of your feet on top of the entirety of the globe, and the globe itself presses on every inch of empty space around it, and in this way you ascend, in this way you slowly advance. Each step forward is a rung, my father said. And I never understood. Everything is a prayer, Jeremiah said, and now it wasn't clear anymore whether he was quoting Hilkiah, his father, or speaking for himself. I don't have to slaughter sheep in the Temple and chant songs of praise there. To ascend the hill, to sit in front of a patient, that's enough for me. The hospital is the true Temple; that's the only place where you'll find prayer filling every moment. The prayers of the sick and the prayers of the doctors and the prayers of the women giving birth and of the newborns themselves. My father taught me a prayer, Jeremiah said: Heal me, O Lord, and I shall be healed, save me and I shall be saved, for you are my praise. For I will restore health unto you and I will heal you of your wounds. He'd say it before every operation and to every patient, countless times a day. Not until years later did I realize that he was asking to be able to heal himself and not the sick—he was asking to be healed in order to be able to heal them in turn. And Mattaniah said, That's odd. I know it in the plural: Heal us, save us. And he gazed down at his sleeping infant and repeated the prayer tenderly and said: He was circumcised right after his birth. I was sure he'd die from it, but I couldn't stop the mohel.

They rested for a moment in the shade of a fig tree, and Jeremiah picked some figs, rubbed them against his shirt, and offered a soft, ripe fig to Mattaniah. They savored the taste, and ants converged on the stems they flung to the ground. Mattaniah said, At least admit that you were wrong then: The Babylonians didn't reach us. Ashkelon isn't Jerusalem. Jerusalem is something else altogether, you've got to admit that. Not some Philistine city on the coast. I've never been to Ashkelon, did you know that? And I've never seen the sea. I've also never been to Babylon. When I was a child, I dreamed of going to Assyria. Now people say that Assyria's in ruins, that Nineveh is a no-man's-land, that owls hoot there amid the rubble, and the trees—that the trees there weep, that the stones weep, too. I know, I don't believe it, either. I don't believe it. Assyria isn't going to disappear overnight. A new king will rise, and they'll sort things out. And Jeremiah said, I suddenly remembered, when we were children in the club and we slept in Givat Ram the night we went stargazing, you told me there was an owl on a tree and it wanted to swoop down and gobble you up. Mattaniah blushed and said: Back then I had all sorts of fears; it isn't impossible, although I don't remember that. They'd send me everywhere with those Egyptian bodyguards. They couldn't protect me from the owl. I think maybe I made it up, because I didn't want to feel so overprotected. And Jeremiah recalled that he'd told Mattaniah, Yes, you're right, it's in the tree, and it'll fly down and peck open your head. But he held his tongue and didn't say a thing now, wondering if Mattaniah remembered.

The fig tree provided shade, and the fruit was ripe to eat. Mattaniah bit into his fig and said, Figs are a miracle, how the earth produces sugar, a sort of honey from rock. You know, there are seven hundred and fifty different kinds of fig, and each kind of fig has a specific kind of wasp that pollinates it, Mattaniah said, so it's the wasp that produces the honey we just ate, the wasp is its foster parent, and the rock is its foster parent, the rock into which the fig tree sends down its roots, and even the bird nested in its branches. Jeremiah, who held his fig between his index finger and thumb, said: But who tells the wasp to come and pollinate the fig? And who tells the roots to grope after the water that's hidden below? And Mattaniah said: The fig speaks to itself. After all, your fingernails grow without anyone's asking them to do so. It just happens by itself, and this *by itself*, that's the real God. And Jeremiah said, Maybe you're right, who knows, even though he knew for a certainty that this was quite wrong— but no one takes care not to harm the fig tree, or anything else, because of this *by itself.* If the tree is by itself, then everything is by itself—the wasps' nest, too, and the people who eventually up- root the tree. I saw demonstrators standing around a tree once, Mattaniah said. They told the tree, You are our father. The city wanted to cut it down in order to put up a new traffic light. I re- member the hillside palace, Jeremiah said. Once there were foxes and porcupines up there. Now they've uprooted everything, everything; they've built there on top of everything. They're up- rooting every tree in Jerusalem, drying up every flowering garden, and paving it over to be a parking lot or road. And Jer- emiah felt that thing, the whispering ember, flare up within him and form a mouthful of words. Does it seem appropriate to you for the king to take over an entire neighborhood? It's like *Metropolis*, but this isn't fantasy, this isn't a movie, this is reality—they'll destroy all of Jerusalem this way, building over it. And Mattaniah said: Look, prehistoric cave-dwellers thought that straw huts were destroying the scenery, okay? After all, the king didn't build Holyland, he only occupied something that was already there and made some minor additions and repairs and added some nice scenic canals. In fact, no one wanted to live there; people were scared it would collapse after the earthquake. But it didn't collapse, so he occupied buildings that were already almost completely abandoned, and renewed the whole area. I read the accusations against him. It's easy to criticize, but even a king needs to live somewhere, too, right? And he can't live in a three-room apartment without an elevator in Kiryat Yovel. Jeremiah asked, When you're king, will you live there, too? And Mattaniah said: You know perfectly well that I'll *never* be king. He'll pass on the crown to his son, my nephew, Jehoiachin, and Jehoiachin will pass it to *his* son, who hasn't been born yet, and that will be the axis. I'll end up like my older brother Yochanan, herding sheep in Australia. History is full of brothers of kings who ended up herding sheep. A king's brother isn't half a king, you know. It's like the lottery—almost doesn't count. I once guessed five numbers out of six, Mattaniah said, but so many other players also guessed as many correctly that the prize was maybe one hundred shekels; I didn't even bother going down to the kiosk to redeem my ticket. And what's strange is that the lottery people insisted—they sent me all these notices, they kept pestering me to go over and collect my cash prize. But I stuck to my guns and ignored them.

20

THE KING WAS ABOUT TO LEAVE for the Largest Bowl of Hummus Competition ceremony when Minister of Defense Baalgezer entered, accompanied by his flock of armed adjutants. The royal glass of juice on the table was nearly empty, and the straw sticking out of it listed over, as if waiting for a mouth to come put a slurping end to the last drops. The king hoped it was something truly urgent: Because, as you'll see on my schedule here, Baalgezer, I've got to head out and unveil our historic bowl of hummus. I'm sure I don't have to explain to you the implications, tourism-wise, of winning this competition. Would you like some orange-carrot juice, Baalgezer? You yourself are a kind of juice, he told the minister of defense, who was the terror of the kingdom and its neighbors: A blend made up of two different juices, in fact. On the one hand, defense juice, and on the other, envelopes-stuffed-with-cash juice. Like this healthy concoction here. Here—finish my juice for me, go ahead and slurp it up in good cheer, the king said. And the minister of defense said, Thank you, but I'm not thirsty. He isn't thirsty, Jehoiakim roared, but he's plenty thirsty for cash, always. No, Baalgezer, you'll drink the king's juice whether you're thirsty or not. You'll drink, moreover, with the king's own straw, mouth to mouse. Otherwise, your head and your neck will part ways by daybreak, I swear on my life, the king said, and with lightning speed drew a switchblade. Call on your Lord Baal from the guillotine; we'll see if he can save you, if he'll deliver you.

And there was a eunuch present, a bit of a pedant, and he dared step forward and said, My king, if I have found favor in Your Majesty's eyes, as I pray I have, may I be allowed to point out that Your Royal Highness has committed a minor error? Silence. And then the king approached the eunuch and said, Error? And the eunuch said: A minor mistake. Half a mistake—no, an eighth. And the king asked, astonished, What sort of mistake, for instance? And the eunuch said, Merely a matter of phonology. Nothing hysterical. Nothing hysterical? the king asked. Sure, nothing hysterical, replied the eunuch. The king said: And so what's the error? We're all in suspense here. And the eunuch said, My lord said, with regard to the minister of defense, that he should drink the juice from the king's own straw, *mouth to mouse*. So? asked the king, barely able to restrain himself. The eunuch said, You turned the latter, dative *mouth* into a *mouse*, a common slip, substituting a sibilant *s* for the more difficult-to-pronounce palatal *th*, which requires a lingual retroflex. The king held his peace. The eunuch hastened to clarify: It's not a serious error, but when it comes from the king's own mouse—that is, mouth—it grates upon the ear. Thus I felt it incumbent upon myself to offer my most deferential correction, in order to avoid a situation in which we might find the general populace patterning its mode of speech after the king's, and so spreading the error despite themselves. King Jehoiakim grabbed the eunuch by the neck and said, From mouth to mouse, was it? And the eunuch chuckled and said, No, again you're making the same error, it's from mouth to— But he didn't manage to complete the necessary correction, for the king plunged his switchblade deep into the eunuch's arm. And he told Baalgezer, Now break a chair over his head. No, not this chair.

The minister of defense did as he was told, and then he picked up the royal juice glass and in one sip on the straw siphoned up the remaining juice, and even went so far as to slurp any remains from the sides of the glass, delighting the King of Judah and his servants. And the king said, How pleasant to see a person who knows his place; how pleasant to see such a resolute head bow and kiss the king's feet. And the minister of defense said, True, and, still holding the king's black straw, added, By the way, before my lord leaves for the stadium, he may want to know the reason I've come. The king said, Hurry up, spit it out, son of Zeruiah, and the minister of defense reported that some nonentity—oh, nobody too important, some Babylonian factotum, to be more precise, some low-ranking, subordinate factotum, a sort of deputy's undersecretary, a nobody named Nebuchadnezzar or Nebuchadrezzar—is on his way, is on his way, tut-tut, on his way, and not on his way to just anywhere, mind you, but, rather—to be even more precise!— he's heading *your* way, my lord. Yes, he's already rolling down the autostrada, slowly, slowly, very slowly—which is to say *quickly*, I mean quite quickly. You can see his black Mercedes advancing; we've picked up a signal from it, thanks to our excellent spies, and he's making excellent time. We calculate he'll be here within the next couple of days. Hence, if I have found favor in your eyes, it might be best that you keep your royal switchblade open and at the ready. And one of the minister's adjutants pressed a button, and the highway in question appeared on one of the king's large flat-screens, down which a small green point could be seen moving slowly toward the city from the northeast. But why let it get to you? the minister of defense said. My lord is undoubtedly in a hurry to get to the soccer stadium and taste some of his hummus, am I right? No, no, there is absolutely no cause for alarm, Your Highness. I'd say that it's more than possible that the sizable army this wholly unimportant fellow is bringing with him is entirely unarmed—for all we know, it's just Babylon's Olympic team, am I right? And the minister of defense set the royal juice glass down on a copy of the book of Deuteronomy that was lying there on top of a napkin. Jehoiakim, in order to shut him up, threw a hardback at the minister's head. It was a bulky Akkadian dictionary.

Having bought himself a moment of silence, the king collapsed on one of his beanbags. What did you say? He's making his way here? How do you know *here*? Maybe he's going somewhere else? There's no lack of kingdoms around. What does he want from me? *Whaaat?* Maybe it isn't me he's after. And, like a runaway train, the king's brain pounded on at breakneck speed: It's happening, it's finally happening. For years he'd prepared himself for this. And there was also a sense of relief, to be honest, as he felt the prolonged uncertainty of the past seven years coming to an end, though it was relief mixed with a dreadful fear surging within him, like sewage pouring through—like pipes filled with—like a sink blocked by—well, like a cistern collapsing on itself.

SEVEN YEARS EARLIER, several days after the destruction of Ashkelon, Jehoiakim had surrendered to Nebuchadnezzar by proxy. Babylonian accountants made all the necessary arrangements within a matter of minutes, and money began to be transferred via secure electronic transfer to Nebuchadnezzar's coffers on a monthly basis, starting on the fifteenth of the month of Tevet of that year. (Ashkelon was destroyed in the month of Kislev, so that people should *see and beware*, and in the following month, Tevet, the first payments were sent over just as the first rains fell.) It's far easier, for us as well as for you, the Babylonian accountants told their fellow accountants in Jerusalem, to rely on bank transfers for everything. There was no limit to the generosity of these Chaldean accountants, they were real gentlemen, their local counterparts thought—wolfing down shawarma and hummus at lunch, and more than once managing to dip their ties in tahini or olive oil, to their lasting disgrace. It will also be convenient for us, as well as for you, if we link the sum you owe to what we call a currency basket, so that fluctuations in the market don't cause us any confusion at a later date. On account of these taxes levied by Babylon, Jehoiakim was obliged to take out a gray-market loan with some disreputable financiers in Sidon. And what assets exactly did he offer as collateral to the Sidonians? Best if you don't know. Within five years, Jehoiakim knew, the time would come to pay back the secondary debt to the Sidonians, who were always— they, too—friendly and generous, at least until installments started coming in late. At which point they would hire mercenaries from Assyria and proceed to take what was theirs.

Anyway, Jehoiakim started paying taxes to Babylon after the destruction of Ashkelon, which was seven years ago now; and the Babylonians, for their part, maintained a barely felt diplomatic presence in Judah, and shut their eyes to the unfortunate fact that Jehoiakim was also paying taxes to the Egyptians. His was a deep enough purse so he could be taxed doubly, and so what if Jehoiakim passed on the fruits of the labors of his subjects to two instead of one of the kingdoms? What, should the Egyptians suffer because Babylon is greedy for more? shouted Minister of Finance Baalzakar. He knew perfectly well, and said as much in his speeches, that whoever pays taxes should be thankful for the privilege, since in the realpolitik of the region only the dead were exempt from taxation, and thus he who pays taxes—well, there's no better proof that he's still alive and kicking.

So, for three years, Jehoiakim had paid both Babylon and Egypt, but after those three years were up, he decided to cancel the automatic monthly transfer to Babylon. One telephone call to his personal banker and the matter was settled. The immediate cause of this interesting strategy was the reliable report the king had received of Babylon's defeat in its ongoing efforts to conquer Egypt. The Babylonians wished to drink from the waters of the Nile, as had Assyria in its day, but apparently they didn't properly estimate the difficulty of crossing North Sinai—oh, so much sand, there was no end to it—and then there was a sneak attack upon their west flank. Jehoiakim took a gander at the political map of the region and reasoned that, after such a defeat, the King of Babylon wouldn't have the patience to attend to one negligible red line in his ledger regarding a kingdom of relatively minimal significance, and so he stopped the payments and used the money to pay off the interest on his loan from the Sidonians, to lower those murderous installments before they came due, and above all in order not to have to cede any Judean property.

And there was at the time a Jew who came to him with a scroll covered in dire warnings, who tried to persuade the king not to take such an audacious step, which would surely be interpreted, said this same Jew—maybe he was a prophet: go figure—as a patent sign of sedition against the King of Babylon, with far-reaching implications. Better that the Sidonians should claim title to Judean assets if the alternative was burning the assets to the ground, the prophet claimed, but Jehoiakim simply grabbed the prophet's scroll and flung it into the blazing fire in his winter quarters, which were located in the palace compound, and the scroll went up—unsurprisingly—in flames. It was the ninth month, which is to say Kislev, and it was cold in Jerusalem, as was usual for that time of year. No miracle occurred—the scroll could not be recovered from the flames—which only proved, or so the king told the bearded prophet, that the contents of said scroll were not worth their ink and paper. I'm the king, I burn ten scrolls like yours before breakfast, Jehoiakim told the prophet, whose name he forgot as soon as the man had been presented to him: Barely a day goes by without my being sent a new prophecy, siding with me or against me, siding with the gentiles or against them, and let's not even talk about the doomsday prophecies and the prophecies of consolation. I'm the king; as far as I'm concerned, it all goes right into the fire. I don't play favorites.

Jehoiakim believed with all his heart, as did many others, that the day was not far distant when a new king, a descendant of the kings of Assyria, would once again take hold of both reins, the Tigris and the Euphrates, and the old order would be reestablished, and it would be made clear at last whom the kingdom had to contend with, which is to say: Assyria would reign over the entire world, its boot pressed firmly on the necks of all nations. Difficult, oppressive, costly, sure; but permanent, clear, and predictable. Not like now. Anything was preferable, frankly, to the current bewildering, explosive situation. Babylonians? Who'd ever heard of them until yesterday? Pipe down, Jehoiakim wanted to shout at them, pipe down and let us live. Assyria was the only real empire, he mused. The rest—counterfeits.

Four more years went by. The tension in the days following the cancelation of the monthly transfer was unbearable; the king had no choice but to take half a sleeping pill each night. He was certain that an hour after the next payment was due the phone would ring, the Babylonian number showing up on the king's caller ID buzzing like the lights in a cell on death row. The next day, he left the palace and looked up at the sky to see whether a blue assault chopper was already making its approach. Every glass of water was as suspect to the king as a goblet full of green poison, and in each and every meatball he imagined he could smell a pellet of cyanide. His only consolation came when he checked his bank account and discovered there the sum that he'd saved, accumulating month by month, thanks to the cancelation of his scheduled transfers to the Bank of Babylonia. And, really, what sort of contribution had the Babylonians ever made to Judah? They didn't pave a single sidewalk, they didn't asphalt a single road, construct a single reservoir—nothing, zilch. It was a protection racket, nothing more. We're talking gangsters here. I couldn't go on with it anymore—it wasn't fair, it was simply outrageous. Burning cities down in order to get us scared, then showing up to issue threats—his voice rose to a screech. Robbing me, picking my pockets! he said over a crackling phone line to his son, the musical prodigy who'd left town at the age of eight to study music at the Mozarteum in Salzburg and later settled permanently in Vienna.

And from his apartment in Vienna, this son, Jehoiachin, kept track, of course, of the goings-on back in the kingdom where—he had to admit—he'd been born, although his childhood felt so distant now that that old kingdom seemed to him like little more than a complex if intriguing drawing on display in a museum thousands

197

of kilometers away, whose details even the most powerful telescope would still leave vague. All the nations of the region—Babylonians, Egyptians, Jews, Hittites, Elamites, etc., etc.—seemed to him about as close or relevant to Europe as Martians, and the troubles his father recounted to him, like the destruction of a certain city called Ashtelon or Ashgelon or Ashperon, were about as real to him as the destruction of the capital city of one of Saturn's cold moons— something he'd read about in one of the books of science fiction he'd so loved as a child. And he turned his head away from his piano and score, and saw the new star shining in the skies of Vienna, and he got up and walked over to the blinds and lowered them. Since he was eight years old, he'd only get to see his father when His Majesty flew in once a year, generally close to the beginning of the month of Nissan, since that was when the Babylonian festival of Akitu took place, a holiday whose observance involved the high priest's slapping the King of Babylon hard on his cheek in order to demonstrate the throne's submission to the god Marduk, humiliating the monarch before all of his ministers, and he, that is to say Jehoiakim, was certain, and rightly so, that, with Akitu approaching, chances tended to be low that Nebuchadnezzar would have time to invade Jerusalem. Hence, every spring he'd celebrate the spring festival with his son, making an effort—at times successfully!—to enjoy the private recital that his son would give in his modest twelve-room apartment on Maria-Theresien-Platz, overlooking the Kunsthistorisches Museum of Vienna, the city in which Jehoiachin had chosen to live, far from the clamor of the barren hills between the rivers of Mesopotamia and the Nile, of which he'd read from time to time in newspapers and books.

Jehoiachin was eighteen years old and had changed his name to Joachim to please his admirers in Austria and Germany. In the upcoming season, he was scheduled to give concerts in Tokyo, Moscow, Shushan, Hattusa, London, and Mari. The concert in Ashkelon had been canceled, as might have been expected, after the local cultural institute went up in flames and collapsed onto its own pianos. He opened his itinerary and his tour repertoire, and the pages under his fingertips felt like a soft and reassuring carpet. But his plans were about to change. Also his repertoire.

That same morning, Joachim played the *Goldberg Variations* in the concert hall at the Vienna Music Academy. After the applause, he played Philip Glass's Étude No. 5 as his encore—a work that, in spite of its apparent simplicity, always cast its spell over him and left him amazed. While playing this melancholic piece, he noticed two gentlemen standing in the wings, waiting for him to finish. Something in their comportment and looks suggested that they came from his birthplace in the East. He slowed the tempo just a bit so as to prolong by a few seconds the interval before he would have to meet with them. He was certain that a disaster had taken place and that they were here to tell him as much, though he couldn't quite guess the nature of the catastrophe as yet. Perhaps Father has died, he thought, or perhaps one of the uncles, and they've come to tell me that I have to go home and sit shiva. And he was greatly distraught at the thought of it; for years he'd been preoccupied by the thought, the threat of having to hang out with his family for an entire week, to say Kaddish in Aramaic, to sleep in a strange house and wear a yarmulke, and not to shave or bathe—if there was one thing he despised, it was poor grooming, beard stubble or long nails—and, anyway, he couldn't fall asleep in a house full of strangers, he couldn't even take a shit in a house where another person was present, though in recent years such a situation had never arisen. He finished the étude and immediately started playing it again. Because of the music's circular and repetitive nature, he knew it was unlikely that the audience could anticipate when he was supposed to finish. But the two in the wings, they apparently caught on at once that they were being duped; after waiting for a few seconds, they strode onstage and stood beside the piano, like two tardy and heavily armed page turners. Joachim stopped playing, rose, and bowed. Silence from the audience. The two gentlemen led the pianist to his dressing room. Just before they reached the door, and without any apology for interrupting his encore, they told Joachim that he was needed in Jerusa-lem. Has someone died? he asked (this entire conversation taking place in German), and they said: God forbid. On the contrary, there's going to be a big celebration. The king your father wants you to come and play on the occasion of his sixtieth birthday, in the concert hall of the International Convention Center in Jerusalem, of course; surely he'd scheduled the event with you some time ago, they said courteously. It's only a matter of two, three days away from home, they told him, and then, it goes without saying, you'll return to Vienna. You won't even have to cancel your next concert, they said.

And Joachim laughed. No way was he about to set out for Judah, and he didn't remember making any sort of arrangement with his father. He would certainly have remembered such a thing. What's more, he hadn't heard from the king in at least half a year—undoubtedly, a mistake had been made. They couldn't convince him there weren't plenty of pianists already in Judah. Plenty . . . even some who weren't that bad, perhaps? . . . The gen-tlemen made no reply. Then: This isn't easy for us, the second gentleman said. You played the most difficult of all the *Goldberg Variations*, the fifteenth, so nicely . . . And Joachim said, Won-derful of you to notice . . . Heartbreak sweeps over the intervals and silences . . . And the man went on to reassure him: The handcuffs won't hurt at all, sir; I made sure to pad the steel with velvet. And Jehoiachin asked, on the verge of screaming: Hand-cuffs? What the hell are you . . . ? But he didn't finish his sen-tence, and in no time he found himself whisked into a car and driven to the airport and seated in a private jet, and in no time they were racing east, exceeding the speed limit in spite of all the traffic signs and speed traps in the sky, and in no time they were landing at Atarot Airport. After some light refreshments, he was driven to the palace in a car identical to the one they'd used in Vienna, still wearing the tuxedo he'd worn at his recital.

And when he entered the royal household, his father didn't spread his arms wide as he walked toward him, nor did he grin broadly at the prodigal son: he didn't even greet him, save for a curt nod. He and his retinue left the apartment immediately, and Jehoiachin was dragged behind them. You're not dressed properly, his father declared. Jehoiachin, take off your tux already; tuxedos and hummus don't go together. Jehoiachin had no idea what hummus he was talking about—wasn't there something about a birthday celebration?—and anyway he despised that local dish. Hummus stood in his eyes for everything that was wrong with the Middle East: *It has no taste*, he used to tell his parents over and over when he was a child. They eat a tasteless paste and it's their greatest pleasure—it's pathetic. Look, said the king, it's not that I'm not really glad to see you, but let's leave all the catching up for later; we're already very late. You're coming with me to the Largest Bowl of Hummus from the Euphrates to the Nile Competition, Jehoiakim said. Have you found something to wear? Very well, he said, but get rid of that smelly tuxedo of yours, he hollered, and promptly leaned down beside his son and cut off his jacket's tails with the royal switchblade. We can talk later, as long as we don't miss the ceremonial hummus tasting. We'll be the first to dip in; our pitas are already being warmed, and they're huge, his father said anxiously, holding up the shreds of black cloth—as big as tables!

21

EASTERLY WINDS WHISTLE in the cracks of the desiccated shower stalls in a distant military base on the border between Babylon and Elam. There are three battlement walls, in concentric circles, and a ziggurat that once rose arrogantly until it was knocked over by the Assyrians some forty years ago is still there, waiting for better days. On the lower floors, however, there are sufficient rooms with ceilings that were spared, and so the place was transformed from the temple it once was—no one remembers anymore whether to a Babylonian or an Elamite God—into a Babylonian military base, which in turn was made over into a royal archive. It is so dreadfully far to the east, so dreadfully far from anything, that one measly old guard is all that's needed to safeguard the site. He and his dog have been living there for twenty years now. Evenings, they sit on the battlement walls to breathe in the air after spending long hours below in the archive, and they play chess, or, rather, a *kind* of chess, a different version of the game, as is customarily played in such far-flung outposts. There's no king and queen on the board but, rather, a guard and a dog—always a guard and a dog—they're the center of the world, and they must be protected, and he who strikes at the guard or at the dog wins the game. The chessboard is older than they are. When they arrived and were appointed to guard the site, the chessboard was already there, waiting: it had been waiting since the days of Uru, which is to say Ur, which is to say City—the city whose name was *City*. The rules of the games were written on the sunbaked board, but since they were written in ancient Sumerian, the guard and his dog could only stare at the signs that they were unable to read, and in the end make up the rules for themselves.

This is where they keep the documents and other plunder the soldiers of the Babylonian king bring back from their campaigns of rape and pillage at the far ends of their expanding kingdom, from the neighboring nations, which are slowly but surely being condemned to servitude. The stuff accumulates here as in the basement of a museum. Soldiers take their booty and transport it to Babylon in order to catalogue and secure it—which is to say, in order to save it from destruction in the now subjugated lands. If it were possible, they'd ship every one of the Egyptian pyramids to Babylon. Here you'll find an entire wing dedicated to fallen idols and various temple utensils. There are statutes of the Moabite Chemosh, of Anat from Tyre and Sidon, and now of the Assyrian god Ashur, too—thousands of figurines of Ashur, newly deposited in the archives: small ones as well as some pretty gigantic ones, all bearing his terrifying beard, wings, and hooves, hooves that have been trampling over nations and peoples for generations; but in the light of the Assyrians' crushing defeat, this king of kings has become little more than . . . an objet d'art. There are altars to Moloch here, too, uprooted from their places in Ammon and carefully transported, intact, eastward, fashioned of burnished brass, as well as thousands of private statuettes catalogued as *unidentified gods* and wrapped and stored in itemized cartons. Some are large and upright and intact and on full display; others, including the smaller, broken ones, lie all heaped together inside their cartons. Many of the female deities are clasping their breasts and spreading their wings: O mighty fertility, the consolations of which have, sadly, been eradicated. And then sometimes gods that set out for the archive in one piece and in good health wind up being crushed or shattered during the long journey to their new home, and upon reaching the Babylonian archives are no more than pulverized dust—and, indeed, are preserved as dust until the holy day on which they will, some say, rise again from the dust and return to life . . . Amen. They're all tightly swaddled in padding and bubble wrap, though even so some will get damaged along the way. Some are as tall as buildings, still wearing their plastic robes, fettered by brown masking tape. The smaller ones, some as small as ancient coins, piled up in their cartons, are labeled not only according to their provenance but also according to their reputed powers. This god walks upon the stars. That god makes purple flowers bloom in winter. This goddess provides for the poor and unloved of a remote village in Ararat. Here's the god of travel. The god of self-actualization. The god of all donkeys in distress. The god of sick children requiring amusement. The god of poetic inspiration. The very angry goddess of a large Egyptian beetle long since extinct. The god of pyramids. The god of the praying mantis. The god of camels. The goddess of lost youth, the goddess of blessed pencils, the dog god and his friend the monkey god. The goddess of the shortsighted, the goddess of libraries and archives, the god of the carpenters of Assyria, the goddess of the stone quarries from which the statues of the gods must slowly emerge.

The cartons are arranged impeccably. The gods are many, but the years are long, dozens of years, and there's nothing else to do but categorize them, apart from chess and stargazing. It was as if the missing top of the ruined ziggurat had absented itself specifically to make room for the spectacular night sky. Not a single bulb was lit within a radius of more than one hundred kilometers of the archives, so there was no light pollution to obscure the nightly bonfire. The new star beamed down, casting short shadows in the stillness of the archives. The gods, too, gaze at the stars at night, biding their time until they can return home. They will remain hostages until the king, in his mercy, decides to go a little easier on the conquered nations from which they've been plundered.

The man in charge of the archives is unsealing some new cartons this morning, accompanied by his dog. The archivist is always given lots of warning before a new shipment arrives. The procedure is for the military always to alert the archivist to make ready to receive new artifacts from wherever it is they've set off to on a new campaign. And so the man and his dog proceed to the library and read up about the gods of the nation that the King of Babylon is about to engage in battle, in order to learn a little something about their new guests. The King of Babylon is always the victor, of late. According to the royal fortune-teller, if he found a fish with a missing left fin, his enemies would be swiftly defeated. And, indeed, such a fish was then hauled up in a net. That was the sign.

Not that anyone is even certain who the king is, nowadays; the old man thinks probably Nabopolassar is still the one exiting and returning through the gates of Ishtar. It's not important. He receives a memo faxed by the adjutant in charge, who gives them an evaluation, based on intelligence reports, of whom and what to expect, how many and when. Today the fax noted several gods from the city of Tyre and a number of temple utensils from the city of Judah, also known as Jerusalem. The archivist estimates that he probably won't need more than six large cartons to store them—six for Tyre, six for Jerusalem—though at the last minute he orders not a dozen but fourteen cartons, adding one carton for each city, just to be on the safe side. But then he only assigns eight: four and four. Spare cartons he can always fold and return to the office-supply warehouse. It has happened before that he ordered cartons for spoils that wound up being negligible, and consequently, having already labeled all the cartons, he was obliged to throw away a brand-new one—such a pity. Tyre and Jerusalem. He looks at the map. The King of Babylon must be heading south to wage war in the Land of Hatti. The old man has by now become highly proficient at his job and can estimate how many meters of bubble wrap and masking tape he needs to have ready. He prepares two shelves, and the dog helps him and writes place-names in his own unique calligraphic paw—the penmanship of someone for whom writing is hardly second nature, who indeed learned to write with some difficulty—on new white labels. The dog likes to stick the labels on the aluminum shelves. The old man spells out for him the name of this or that place, and the dog repeats the name after him, bow-wow, and writes in the appropriate cuneiform, while at the same time sticking his tail straight up and sticking his tongue partway out of his mouth.

They'll have approximately half a year until the gods and the temple utensils arrive, but they like to be prepared ahead of time. Order and preparation are the bread and butter of the new empire. It's as vital for the king and for the captain of the guard and for each and every eunuch and for each and every talking dog. When the trucks arrive in the middle of some night after a week on the road, there will already be room for whatever they contain. There will already be an empty carton waiting. For half a year, the man and his dog will be keeping the carton clean and dusting the shelf and dreaming of the spoils. There is no greater excitement in their lives—understandably so!—than the moment the trucks unload their merchandise and all their dreams at once take form and no less quickly are stored away in cartons: gold and wood, copper and flint, ironwork and textiles, embroideries and silverwork, calyx and petals, a statue, a mask.

And sometimes, at night, the guard and his dog stroll side by side past the shelves in the enormous hangar and gaze at them all. Hundreds of high-powered gods, amassed, exalted, pillars of strength, and the guard whispers to them softly, even prays to them. Yes, to all of them. For he knows perfectly well that his warehouse is the largest temple on the face of the earth, containing an unparalleled concentration of gods from across the entire world. He doesn't know who among them might still wield his or her full divine power and who has become irrelevant; consequently, he assumes that they are all thriving and robust. He doesn't ask any of them, Are *you* the one true god? He accepts the burden of worshipping every one of them, and he sings to every one—actually, the dog is the one who does the singing—songs of praise. And he consults with them about his health and his good dog's health, and about the souls of his parents who descended into the World of No Return a long time ago, below the sweet waters of the abyss surrounded by the seven ramparts, and about his son and his daughter, whom he hasn't seen ever since he was assigned to this wretched position by order of Nabopolassar, so many years ago now it's no longer possible to number them. I want to see my children, they're undoubtedly old by now, he tells the exiled gods swaddled in masking tape and bubble wrap. I want to see them and then return and fulfill my duty until the day I die, without complaint. I take careful care of you. I wash you like babies. Every morning, I push aside what remains of the roof and allow you to breathe in the sunlight, even though I wasn't instructed to do so, even though it might even be forbidden. Won't you help me just a bit? Maybe *you* can, eh? Or maybe you, Your Ladyship?

I bought presents for my boy and girl, he said. They're still wrapped and still sitting in the plastic bag from the toy store in Lagash, the city the old man was born in, where he bought them twenty years before—in fact, on the very day he was assigned to this post. The king sent a car to collect him, and he told the driver, Wait a minute, I want to give my children their presents. And the driver said: Oh no, there's no time. Bring them later, when you're on leave. But he never got any leave, and even if he had, the time it would have taken to reach Lagash and to return would have been longer than the vacation itself. So he's kept the plastic bag containing the toys—not on the shelves alongside the gods and sacred utensils, to be sure, but in his bedchamber. Two small boxes in gift wrap whose colors have long faded. After a few years, he couldn't remember what he'd bought them. But he'd never tear open the gift wrap to peek, needless to say.

His private pantheon hasn't answered him as yet. And even if they did try to respond, the languages they represent are so numerous, how could they ever conduct a conversation? So the old man just goes on devoting himself diligently to their well-being. Even the little gods pulverized to dust in their cartons receive a monthly airing. He opens the lids, each in its turn, to let in some sun and air. And there are even gods here who are shaped like dogs, so the old man shows them to the dog who assists him, and the dog, as you might expect, kneels and howls.

22

MATTANIAH AND TUKULTI pushed their way through the multitude thronging the gates of Teddy Stadium. As they stood in line, the odor of hummus—tons of the stuff—was borne through the air like the lush scent following the first rains of the season, but not very much like it: in fact, it couldn't have been more different. It's like standing by an active volcano, someone blurted out. The ceremony was supposed to start at twelve, but in light of the ongoing holdup—which wasn't explained to the crowd, but which would soon enough be understood as having been the result of flying in the forlorn crown prince from Vienna—the grand opening was delayed by close to five hours. Many wanted to turn back, but the area had been sealed off on orders of the king. That would have been all he needed, empty bleachers at such a major event; it would have made him a media laughingstock the whole world over. Mattaniah was put in mind of how he'd stepped onstage once at a poetry reading and found there wasn't anyone in the audience, not a single soul; the few who'd attended had taken advantage of the interval after the poet who'd read before him and quietly slipped out with her in search of the nearest beer garden. So the hummus crowd was gently herded in, and loudspeakers blared orders to stay put for a couple of minutes while water and small portions of pita with hummus, leftovers from the decanting of the hummus, were distributed to the multitude who'd been corralled into the dense shadows cast by the bleachers. Mattaniah tried to feed Tukulti half a pita with hummus, but Tukulti growled and turned his muzzle away in disgust. Mattaniah ate the dog's portion and then his own.

What chutzpah! Listen, they promised us an enormous plate of hummus. I thought they were going to fill up the entire *stadium* with hummus—isn't that what they said? C'mon, *the entire stadium*? What's got into you? It couldn't be the entire stadium. It's a huge bowl *inside* the stadium; does it look to you like anyone could fill the entire stadium? For *this* you dragged me here? Look, I've got big bowls at home, too, okay? *Big?* Not as big as this one—don't be a blowhard. A blowhard? Me? No, no, you're not a blowhard, you're just plain conceited; for all I care you can get up and leave, Mr. Balloon—I married a helium balloon, cut you open and that's all I'd find. Find? Find? What are you going to find, what are you talking about? Helium, helium! Cut it out, why don't you shut up, how long have we been waiting? Let's go home—whose idiotic idea was it anyway to come and see a plate of hummus? You're such a drag. Well, I never, you're such a baby! What's there to see, yeah. You run everything down, nothing excites you; it isn't the hummus, it's the size of the thing, the spectacle, knowing there's something bigger than us in this life, making room in our hearts for a grand and bountiful purpose, a great human enterprise; it isn't eating just for the sake of staying alive, it's food at its most grandiose; I mean, it's an embodiment of the divine! You must be joking, *the divine* in hummus tahini? Hummus that slaves lugged here on their backs in sacks and poured into cement mixers—that's what you call a great human enterprise, that's what you call divine. So you're saying the pyramids and the ziggurats have no value? After all, they, too, were built with slaves and cement mixers—I guess none of that is of any significance to you? It isn't without significance, but, yeah, they stand on blood and bones. I'm not going to stand there like you did on that tour on our honeymoon, applauding the royal tombs in Ur where slaves were locked up and forced to drink poison so they could accompany the nobility to the next world. No way, I'm not about to take a vacation and gawk at the pyramids and ziggurats, thanks very much; I'm not buying any tickets; I can die a hopeless death here, too, and free of charge, okay? And while I'm at it— Say, you two, can you shut your traps? For an hour now you've been drilling a hole into my head, like it isn't enough that my head's already stuffed will all this foul-smelling ground chickpea and ground cumin, I've also got to listen to you two grinding away at each other? An hour already, and you haven't shut your mouths—an hour! Why'd you get married if you can't even agree about something stupid like a plate of hummus? An hour jabbering. I checked my watch—you started an hour ago. An hour? An *hour*? So I talk in a whisper for something like thirty seconds and already you're the conversation police? Fascist! We're talking, a husband and wife are talking; so a husband and wife aren't allowed to talk anymore? But my ear's right next to your mouths; I'm stuck here, waiting, with the two of you, and I'm not married to either of you, thanks be to Baal, or Asherah, or to you—so what did I do to deserve you both as punishment? Hey, buddy, what do you want from them, let them talk; I've been listening to them and actually find it pretty interesting; it's a sensible argument; my wife and I never argue, but neither do we agree on anything, I mean we just don't talk, we're silent as Pharaoh's tombs for ten years now. And I visited those tombs on a package tour, by the way; the hotel was amazing; we really got royal treatment, there was always a bonbon waiting on the pillow— Oh, can you give me the name of the hotel with the bonbons? My daughter's going to Egypt and she's looking for a nice place . . . Oh no, that's all I need, Jews camping out in my secret hotel; when I find a nice, classy hotel I keep it to myself; I don't need your daughter, forgive me for saying so, in the room next to mine, partying all night with champagne and Persian coke and keeping me awake! Believe me, you're right—I know his daughter, and when she parties, she parties; I mean, *parties*? She *goes wild*, is more like it, I lived next door for ten years, and every Friday afternoon she'd bring someone over to have a good time, like clockwork; I wouldn't hear the male, but her, ho-ho, what a concert; she'd always say, Yeah, baby; yeah, baby; yeah, baby; yeah, baby. The babies kept changing, but her dialogue stayed the same: Yeah, baby; yeah, baby . . . One more word and I'll throttle you; I knew you looked familiar; you still owe me that building maintenance money, you pervert, eavesdropping on neighbors . . . *I'm* a pervert? And what's your daughter? Do you want me to tell all these people the sorts of things I've heard her say? Every week a different guy, I swear to you, no repeat customers! It wasn't a different guy every week, you louse, it was her boyfriend all the time, the same steady boyfriend for ten years, a modest yeshiva student; sometimes he'd cut his hair and grow a beard, and then he looked like someone else. That's a good one, a beard! Let me tell you, he also grew twenty centimeters week to week, and got an amazing tan, and then turned totally pasty-faced—I saw everything. When are you going to Egypt? *I'm* not going, though I'd like to go. So why are you squeezing hotel info out of me for a trip that's not going to happen? I told you, my daughter is going! They swallowed poison and lay on their sides and waited, and then the tomb was sealed. Maybe the hummus they're handing out is poison and we're going to drop dead and they'll shut us up in Teddy Stadium? Hey, it's a bit late to think of that, you've already eaten three pita halves. Oy vey! Don't worry, I'll say Kaddish over your grave, and one day they'll come here and dig you up, archaeologists from the future, and they'll let you into a museum for nothing, you'll live in the museum; I'll come visit you on free days . . . Hey, enough, be quiet. Enough, what *enough*? What *enough*? Let me talk; I haven't said anything yet. Enough is enough, will you shut up? I'm begging you. Sir, take care with that dog of yours; did you see the size of that dog, like a donkey? Dogs aren't allowed in the stadium in the first place. And you, you're *begging* now? I only wanted to say . . .

And when it looked as if the day was about to turn and the event would be canceled, the soft voice of the herald was heard. Eyes were borne up toward the helicopter, and it seemed as if a hand was waving at them, and there were some who even swore they identified Jehoiachin, the king's son, who hadn't been seen in the city for the last decade—all that remained was his portrait as a one-year-old infant impressed on one-shekel stamps. And there were those who said, Certainly, Jehoiachin, and how he resembles King David, and he's such a brilliant musician, just like David was. And the hummus contest was all but forgotten, as the mounting stench from the tons of paste wafted over them and turned sour in the stadium from inside the inverted observatory dome. And the herald announced that, to compensate for the delay, the Prince of Judah would play for his people on the piano. And, indeed, a second helicopter appeared, bearing a grand piano fastened to cables. It started drizzling, but there was nowhere to go, and the slanting stands provided some protection, and many simply dozed off in the meantime; hearing the king's son playing was after all a once-in-a-lifetime opportunity, though, to tell the truth, they were far more interested in *seeing* him and ascertaining whether he actually did resemble King David, whom no one alive had ever set eyes on, of course, though pictures of how people imagined him to have looked were spread all over the kingdom, in schools and at military camps and in the palace itself and on stamps and on money, too.

King Jehoiakim glanced over anxiously. He was riding in the first helicopter, and his son was in the second, to which the piano was fastened. He clasped his beloved switchblade in his pocket. The blade wouldn't open. The grand piano dangled lightly in the air below the second chopper, the one bearing Jehoiachin, who was agitated and perspiring freely. He had no desire to appear before the assembled crowd, nor did he want to play for them, nor, for that matter, did he even want to be in Judah. Jerusalem from high up appeared rather unsightly to him. He looked in vain for the river coursing through the city; he was certain there had to be a river. It was only a few minutes' flight from the Holy-land helipad to the stadium in Malha, but that was more than enough to make the prince feel like throwing up. They've brought me here like stage décor for their big hummus-bowl cer-emony. This is no sixtieth-birthday party—what a liar, what a crook. He brought me over to provide musical accompaniment for his dopey ceremony, for a gigantic bowl of hummus; he dragged me here for an idiotic dog-and-pony show, just unbe-lievable. This putrid kingdom, this failing subprovince, this land of tin ears. He wants to show his virtuoso son off to the masses, that's all, Jehoiachin thought. He was always telling me, Go on, play us a little something, something short!

Thirty thousand spectators were gathered in and around the stadium, and Jehoiachin stared at them from the circling chop-per as it got ready to land. The piano was slowly being lowered, and was almost touching the grass when, at the very last minute, someone miscalculated and the piano dropped, free-falling the last two centimeters. Jehoiachin thought he heard, across the din of the rotary blades, the piano scream. He hid his face in the palms of his hands. The thousands of spectators outside the sta-dium had no idea what was going on inside. And no one could understand the connection between a piano and hummus. We didn't come to a concert, they said. No, definitely *not*.

The second helicopter landed, and Jehoiachin stepped out. The roar of the rotary blades was deafening. Jehoiachin's ears, which for years hadn't heard anything louder than the fortis-simo of a symphony orchestra, were numb with shock. I'm sure to go deaf here, it crossed his mind—I'll lose my hearing entirely. The helicopter slowly rose and pulled away. He ran to the piano.

And the piano was somehow patched together—its legs were reconnected with steel brackets and screws—and with lightning speed it was roughly tuned. Jehoiachin glanced at his father, who was surrounded by his attendants, whom for the most part the prince hardly knew, and all at once his rage subsided, and he even felt a certain pride that his father had insisted on bringing him to perform at a ceremony of such great import, and he told himself that he'd play, and even play well, and give his father some satisfaction—birthday or no birthday—his father, who all these years had provided for his education and kept him away from the cauldron, whose bubbles were the Judean hills. Not that any music was appropriate here, save perhaps for the *War* Symphony, the *Revenge* Sonata, the *Murder* String Quartet, the opera *Nebuchadnezzar in Egypt*, and the cantata *The Destruction of Assyria*. And he looked at his father, who suddenly wasn't *the king*, and not even *his father*, but, rather, a not-all-that-healthy-looking sixty-year-old man, preoccupied, overweight, stressed out. Above them all loomed the cursed, largest-ever bowl of hummus. Jehoiachin realized that it was the reversed dome of an observatory and started to laugh. The crack in the dome intended for the telescope hadn't been sealed properly, and Jehoiachin stared at the bits of paste that were dribbling down and streaking the lawn. His father was talking with one of his ministers and kept pointing north, and it seemed to Jehoiachin that his father's face was soaked in tears. And he felt like rushing up to his father to ask him what was going on—if only he could break through the ring of bodyguards and ministers and advisers—and hug him and find out what had gone wrong, but he remained transfixed in place beside the crippled piano. Jehoiachin lifted the lid and sat down to try it out. The sound, to his utter amazement, was clear and sonorous, and he played a number of phrases with his left hand—the PA system hadn't yet been activated—and he raised his head for a moment and saw his father, flushed, looking in his direction through the ring of guards and advisers, and his father's eyes said, Yes, just go on, go on playing, and Jehoiachin remembered the encore he'd played at the end of the concert in Vienna, Philip Glass's Étude No. 5; suddenly he thought of the work as the wailing of someone who no longer has the strength to cry, and the fingers of his left hand began playing, and someone activated the sound system, and all at once the huge soccer stadium was filled with notes—just as night turns to day when floodlights are switched on, instantaneously—and the crowd softly filed in, the multitude haltingly passing by the grandstands and listening as if in a dream, and among them were Mattaniah and Tukulti, who glanced sideways from a great distance at their forgotten Austrian nephew. And Mattaniah sat down, and three or four rows away he noticed Jeremiah's father and mother, whom he hadn't seen in years, ever since the days of the youth science club, when he'd been a guest for the night in Anatot and had set off with Jeremiah and his father, whose name he now couldn't remember, to hike in the hills and gaze at the moon and the fireflies who took cover in its light (to use Jeremiah's father's words). After several minutes, Jeremiah had gotten tired and returned home alone to sleep, but Mattaniah and Hilkiah had lingered for a long while, just the two of them, in the white light.

The lanky woman whom Mattaniah remembered perfectly from his wedding was pushed toward the bleachers and plopped herself down not too far from Mattaniah and Tukulti, and in a thin, shrill voice told Jeremiah's parents—Mattaniah only managed to catch her words in snatches—I know you, I know your son. I saw him a hundred years ago in a police station. He was under arrest; they let him go, but he'll be caught and arrested again and again, and he's right, without warning the robber will come upon us. I was a senior pollster in the Central Bureau of Statistics, she said, but the principal statistician raped me, I was a senior pollster in the Central Bureau of Statistics, and one day they held a concert for the bureau employees, and I walked out of the Jerusalem Theatre, and that's where he assaulted me, the principal statistician. Disaster overtakes disaster, the woman said, everyone calls me *the complainant*; maybe you've heard about me—there was a profile written up about me in the paper, but that's not my real name. And she pulled a faded newspaper clipping out of her purse and gave it to Jeremiah's mother, who glanced at it and passed it on in embarrassment to Jeremiah's father; he cast an eye over the article, and for a moment he thought of asking her for the clipping to add to his own files. And Jeremiah's mother, Esther, told the complaining woman, Come, madame, sit here. And the woman said, No, there's no room. And Esther told her, We'll make room.

And a crown was set on King Jehoiakim's head, and a royal cloak was hurriedly draped over his shoulders, and the chief eunuch breathed onto and misted over and polished the royal scepter before placing it in the king's outstretched hand, and Jehoiakim ascended the steps that had been raised next to the bowl claiming for itself the title of Largest Bowl of Hummus from the Euphrates to the Nile, an attraction that would bring thousands of hummus tourists to the city from the entire region, even luring in devotees of the Dip from beyond the sea, allowing Jerusalem to be declared the Capital of Hummus. And Jehoiakim stood there, his entire body shaking, above the enormous bowl, whose diameter was at least ten meters, with a huge pool of olive oil converging at its center, and large sacks of cumin and sweet paprika being poured in from shore to shore, and Mattaniah recalled all of a sudden that his brother's real name was Elyakim, and he wanted to call out to him, *Elyakim*, for no apparent reason, just to call him by his name, but he remained silent.

The hummus had partly solidified during the long period of waiting for the prince, and a haze rose from the paste as from an old, thick bog. The stench was unbearable. And then the king, from the height of the bowl's rim, thought he saw Nebuchadnezzar's black Mercedes approaching. Jehoiakim realized that he'd betrayed the King of Babylon, had grievously broken a personal pledge, for which crime there could be no pardon and no mercy, for what would happen if all the local kingdoms could cancel their standing orders in a moment of wild caprice? After all, we in Babylon need to live, too, do we not? The chicks are screaming in the Babylonian nest, and I'm counting on you to provide me with worms, Nebuchadnezzar's translator had told Jehoiakim affably over the phone. An obligation must be fulfilled, you promised me *personally* a substantial offering, and it's already been four years since I first saw the missing line in my bank statement, the translator told Jehoiakim in fluent Hebrew, and I waited a month and I waited a year, and another year and another; maybe the King of Judah will turn from his evil ways and live? I loved the King of Judah as a brother, and the King of Judah sank his teeth into my offering and swallowed it. I thought there must have been some sort of computer glitch, but I was naïve, the translator's voice continued through the black earpiece. I know everybody makes fun of my naïveté, Nebuchadnezzar said in the car to his son-in-law Nergal-Sharezer, who sat up front, next to the driver, and was working on an Aramaic crossword puzzle, and who would himself, in the years to come, be King of Babylon. And Jehoiakim imagined stuttering in Akkadian and begging for mercy, and how he'd be punished and gruesomely tortured. He couldn't stop thinking of a pair of pliers crushing his thumb. He could actually feel the iron.

The years that had passed since his rebellion against the King of Babylon had been more than enough time for his imagination to work up detailed scenes of Babylon's horrific retribution—alongside the undeniable pleasure of his bimonthly savings—and he knew for certain that he couldn't endure it, that there was no way he could endure being tortured. He was even terrified of having a tooth pulled, or just getting a filling, even eye drops made him cringe—the moment before the drop falls into your eye, forced open by a eunuch's fingers. And as the days flew by, he sank further and further into these grim fantasies, and suffered at night from nightmares, and he understood, too, that he wasn't to suffer alone, but that the entire city and all of Judah would be hit just as hard. He beheld it all in his mind, and even wrote in his notebooks and on random scraps of paper how the city would fall, how it would go up in flames; he wrote of the terrifying massacre by the Chaldeans and their allies of all the members of his family as well as his friends. There were legions of Aramean mercenaries whose cruelty surpassed even the Babylonians', and the rules of war and the Geneva Conventions were no concern of theirs. He knew that they would arrive, that they would rape and pillage and dash children to the stones and hack people to pieces with bucksaws, and yet all that wasn't the problem—he knew he could somehow live with all that, albeit with a kind of dolorous grief—but the thought that he'd be stripped stark naked and lashed to a breaking wheel, or maybe on the *king's grill*, or that they'd cut off his thumbs and tear out his hair, this was unbearable, even if only as noxious food for thought. Jehoiakim knew perfectly well that there was one way out, and only one way, and the way out was to die as quickly as possible, for if the obligation that had been broken was personal and the obligator was no longer around to be there to be rebuked, maybe Nebuchadnezzar wouldn't destroy the city. And he couldn't punish me, either—I wouldn't be there to receive his blows. It will cool him off, his rage is personal, Jehoiakim thought: I must cool off his Babylonian rage, because I won't be able to save myself no matter what.

And he knew perfectly well that there was only one course of action, one and only one. That way, he could also avoid the pain and . . . and . . . He didn't manage to finish the sentence, for he realized in terror that even if he died painlessly they would mutilate his body, that if he fell on his sword or shot himself in the head in his palace they'd display his naked body or his head on the walls of the city, and if they chose his head they'd exhibit it on a pike with his purple tongue lolling out. This terrified him no less than the possibility of their tormenting his live, sensate body. I must disappear, not only die—I need to disappear and save my body from these hellish torments and from any further humiliations, he thought. He stood, shaking, at the brim of the bowl, holding the banister with one hand, his other hand clasping the locked switchblade in his pocket.

The crowd overran the grandstands and waited, and the king

had no idea how much time had passed, but all of a sudden his son was there beside him; he hadn't removed his mutilated tuxedo, but his father didn't care anymore. And Jehoiakim whispered, though everyone heard him through the PA system, and every word he said echoed back to him like a shot: Don't worry, don't worry, it won't happen that fast, it won't happen so fast. I am leaving you today, my people, I'm leaving you today my people. I know that you think only good of me. And he glanced to the south as if expecting to see the cavalry on the way, and for a second he did indeed fancy he saw Pharaoh's chariots there, kicking up a cloud of dust, coming to his aid, coming to watch over him heroically, to embrace him and protect him from the dreadful king of the north, but it was just dust, dust without chariots and without Egypt. In fact, what he saw there was a herd of donkeys who'd escaped their pen and run wild, and he stared at the sight of them, for it reminded him of something, something he couldn't quite put his finger on, something he wouldn't have time to remember. And he took out his speech and cleared his voice and read into the microphones, Stand at the crossroads, stand at the crossroads, and ask for the old paths, and ask for the old paths, where the good way lies, where the good way lies, and walk in it, and walk in it, and find rest for your souls. The technicians finally fixed the echo, so his last words sounded naked and solitary, and he choked them back and looked fixedly at the scrap of paper that was supposed to contain his speech, because this was not the note he had intended to read from, and he had no idea now how this note had ended up in his pocket, but it was already too late to do anything about it; besides, the note was, without a doubt, written in his own handwriting. And the king cast one last glance over all the Jews in the stadium, and he took the hand of the rep of *The Guinness Book of Records* and shook it warmly, and then he raised his head and saw the new star burning up in the skies, beyond the dark clouds. And in the galleries the complainant said, *It's happening*, but Jeremiah's parents paid no attention, and all at once a scream was heard, and as though this was a prearranged signal, Jehoiakim immediately turned toward his son and thrust the royal scepter into his dissenting, clenched fist, and draped the robe over his shoulders. And the king climbed over the banister, then turned toward his son, his back to the bowl, and said only this, *Never mind*, before pitching backward into the bowl, headfirst, his feet and the soles of his black leather boots appearing for a second, heels up in the muck, before he sank farther and immediately drowned in the pool of hummus as surely as in cement. And Jehoiachin was left there, wide-eyed, standing next to a number of officials, the crown slightly askew on his head, and the scepter held aslant, and the robe hanging over only one of his shoulders, and he fixed his gaze on the piano below on the lawn and then raised his eyes toward the people in the topmost seats overhead. He thrust his hands into his pockets and felt a pain in his right pocket, and blood dribbled over his fist. It suddenly occurred to him that he still hadn't seen his mother. He didn't dare to look at his hand, to pull it out. And he realized, to his horror, that he'd been crowned king.

23

JEREMIAH FELL ASLEEP in the light-rail station. In his dream, the familiar voice told him to wake up and go buy a linen belt, and to make sure not to wet it with water. The instructions didn't make any sense—made even less sense than the smashing of the jug. When he got up, he quickly wrote down what he'd been commanded to do. And he stood for a long time in front of a mirror and stared at himself as he grimaced and gnashed his teeth. He then went to buy the belt in the market where he'd bought that jug, and discovered, to his surprise, that Noa, the girl who'd sold jugs in the pottery stall, was also the vendor at the belt stall. She dashed from one stall to the other, back and forth, and he was happy to see her; maybe now he'd be able to talk to her a bit, but she tells him: Jeremiah, no. You won't find a wife for yourself. Nor will you have sons and daughters in this place. There's a silver crown on her head and he understands. And he hears the voice telling him, Now set out for the Euphrates and hide the belt in the cleft of a rock. And he wants to propose she accompany him but remains silent. Someone else has already entered the stall; for a moment, he thinks the buyer is his father, but he knows, in the dream, that this is impossible.

He stares out the window at the desert scenery rushing by. He's alone in the train, and the linen belt is strapped around his waist. And he arrives in Uruk without knowing why or wherefore. No one sees him doing it—it hardly seems worth all the effort. And all at once he realizes that he's doing it for himself. A moment later, he turns around and there's a range of mountains close to the station, and he beholds the broad river and the corpses of Egyptian soldiers rotting there in the sun, and eagles casting their shadows over the bodies' empty eye sockets. He wants to dip into the Euphrates and gulp down lots of water. He's never bathed in the sea, or in such a wide river, only in the Dead Sea, not even in the Jordan. But instead he heads toward the mountain range, trudges wearily up, and hides the belt; within moments, the belt left there in the rock is ruined, it is totally worthless, all that remains are a few strands scored with cuts and gashes . . . And the voice tells him: Just so I will ruin the pride of Judah, and the great pride of Jerusalem. They stuck fast to me like a belt, but the belt has fled from my waist, the belt desired another waist, the voice said. And Jeremiah woke up, and the dream weighed on him like a smothering blanket, and he tried to pray, quoting from memory a few verses that he recalled from the Torah portion on Abraham and Sodom—Maybe there are ten just men, and that sort of thing—but the voice said: Shh, don't pray for them, enough, end of story. Listen, please . . . Jeremiah tried. I'm not listening to you, came the retort. And now arise and go to the Western Wall.

Jeremiah got up, choking back his rage, strode off to his apartment, rinsed his face in cold water, and grabbed a can of red paint and a Swedish wrench; with that, he left his apartment, which was still half empty, half of his belongings still being back at his parents' place, leaving his new place looking like a flophouse. He meant to pack up and clear out in a hurry. He dragged himself to the light-rail stop at Mahane Yehuda, got on board, and sat down. Here he dozed off again and woke up again, and for the first time he felt pretty much fed up. If no one paid him any mind, why speak up at all? The light rail traveling east was empty, but the cars traveling west were packed, because everyone was in an awful hurry to get to the gigantic-hummus-bowl competition at Teddy Stadium. Jeremiah watched the crowded cars traveling west, and for a minute he thought he saw his mother pressed against a window. He got out at the Western Wall stop; the city seemed to have emptied, like on the morning of the Day of Atonement. And he strode boldly toward the plaza. Jeremiah shot a quick glance at the Temple, which rose above him with all its chambers and turrets and its low inner wall. He'd run through his plan many times over in the last couple of weeks. He knew there was a fire extinguisher in the plaza, and he meant to arrive there with his gallon of red paint and to unscrew the extinguisher's top and pour the paint into the cylinder. Then he'd write four short sentences in huge letters across the Wall: Such as are for death to death—and such as are for the sword to the sword—and such as are for the famine to the famine—and such as are for captivity to captivity. That's all. He'd written down many such short passages on scraps of paper that he carried around with him everywhere—short passages like those he dreamed, or heard, or thought he'd heard; he couldn't tell the difference anymore. He didn't know if something he wrote for himself, thinking it was a poem, was his own or had been passed on to him as a prophecy. His pockets were crammed with jottings that he planned to copy or to shout out or graffiti or get printed in the newspapers in the classifieds and then Xerox and staple onto university bulletin boards and distribute in the synagogues in their Sabbath newsletters, such as *Give glory to the Lord your God before it grows dark,* or *But if you will hear not—my soul shall weep in secret.*

He approached the plaza and strode up to the extinguisher, and there was no need to figure out how to get inside it, since it looked as if someone had already decided to smash it open. He looked at the Wall as if it were a blank page and calculated how best to divide the page and distribute the letters, and how much space he could afford between the lines. When he had removed the extinguisher from its dock and uncoiled its hose, someone called out to him through a loudspeaker, Whoa there, buddy, nothing's burning yet, so why bother spritzing? And Jeremiah was scared and glanced around, but he didn't notice anyone until the plaza guard in his sentry box on top of the Wall, seeing that he hadn't been seen, flashed his spotlight at Jeremiah. Jeremiah waved back in embarrassment and replaced the extinguisher in rage. He walked over to the Wall, fished a note out of his pocket, read it, and stuck it in the cracks between the stones, as was customary; he then drew out another note and another, and wedged them in. The cracks were crammed with notes, and once a week the same sentry would come with long-nosed pliers and remove the notes in order to make room. Jeremiah knew this, and so he knew that his own notes were fated to be removed as well, but even so he kept on drawing notes out of his pockets and sticking them into the cracks, some of them merely fragments of poems from his failed collection: *And death shall be chosen rather than life by the remnant that remains of this evil family,* stuck in. *See, I am letting loose snakes among you, adders that cannot be charmed and they shall bite you,* stuck in. *The harvest is past the summer is ended and we are not saved,* stuck in. *Their tongue is a sharpened arrow it speaks deceit,* stuck in. And Jeremiah glanced at the last note that he'd pulled out, which was written in enormous crooked letters; though he remembered that he'd jotted it down in his sleep, it felt as though someone else must have written this poem, and Jeremiah shuddered as though he were not its author: *For death has come up into our windows, it has entered into our palaces, to cut off the children from the streets, and the young men from the squares.*

The Wall, the guard, the extinguisher, the spotlight, the notes, his emptying pockets—suddenly everything seemed like a story someone else had written. He felt that something had given way inside himself, some simple hold on reality, some fundamental understanding of the solid as opposed to the ethereal, of the palpable as opposed to the phantasmal, of the foothold as opposed to the chasm. And he realized then that he was longing, truly and completely, for the coming of the Babylonians, as for the coming of the Messiah, if only to put an end to this hassle once and for all. He wasn't even sure it would be so terrible if he himself were among those who would fall in battle, since he knew all too well that, after what he'd been doing and saying these last few years, he would never again find a place among the people of Judah and Jerusalem, that he'd be despised everywhere, that no woman would ever marry or befriend him, because how could it be possible to have a relationship with a belligerent and querulous fellow whose pockets were crammed with nonsensical notes? And suddenly he also longed to be deported to Babylon. There were rumors that the Philistines from Ashkelon who'd been deported seven years ago had built a new city in Babylon, on the ruins of a city the Assyrians had destroyed years earlier, and they called the city Ashkelon City, and the Babylonians were allowing all the exiled kingdoms to do the same. Every kingdom was allotted a ruined quarter or a city in Babylon that had been razed to the ground, and they permitted the exiled to restore what had been destroyed. In this way, all the exiled petty kingdoms in the region were being re-established in the land of Babylon as miniaturized, renewed, duplicate kingdoms that were reaching, each in its own way, a magnificent zenith of degeneration. And there were those who said the Babylonians were certainly a painful blow, but painful not in the sense of an attack so much as an unpleasant but necessary medical intervention, like a dentist pulling a rotten tooth before your whole jaw putrefies. And tales began to circulate of a restored, utopian Ashkelon rising again on the outskirts of the city of Babylon, along the banks of the river, where they picked almonds, preserving the good ones and leaving the bad ones to rot and stink, on their way north, and how they built their new city there on the good river with the aid of a ruler and a pair of compasses, and conducted themselves according to the prophets of justice of all the world's nations and cultures, and lived according to their lights.

The guard called from his perch, If you've finished with your notes, please clear the plaza. And Jeremiah stepped back and saw throngs of people approaching the plaza from the west—the celebration in the stadium had apparently ended—and he stood there with his back to the Wall and watched them stream in. The heart is devious above all else, and exceedingly weak, Jeremiah thought. What can I do? On the other hand, he thought, on the other hand, I've got to turn my life inside out.

People were walking silently, in pairs or alone, and Jeremiah realized that something had happened. He looked the people over, so as to understand, as they headed straight for the Wall and now and then raised their heads toward the Temple. And Jeremiah threaded his way through the crowd in the opposite direction and hearkened to what they were saying and thinking. He immediately heard that the King of Judah had died, just as Jeremiah had prophesied into the Holyland intercom that morning, and this unnerved him and weighed upon him, for he felt once again that wheels had been set in motion, that something was under way that till now had been only jottings. He stopped in his tracks and saw the sentry, who'd descended from his sentry box with his long-nosed pliers, speaking to someone in hushed tones; it was a priest named Pashhur, whom Jeremiah had once seen being interviewed on the five o'clock news, his graceful but scarred face filling the TV screen. The guard pointed at Jeremiah with the hand holding his pliers, and Pashhur looked at Jeremiah and started to walk toward him; Jeremiah pretended not to notice and continued on his way at a halting pace, while listening in on what people were saying around him. But Pashhur managed to open a path through the crowd and caught up with Jeremiah and knocked him over with a smack while running; then the priest blew into a pennywhistle, and three more priests or cops pounced on Jeremiah, dragged him off, shoved him into a van, slipped a burlap sack over his head, emptied his pockets, and drove off in silence. And Jeremiah, sitting stricken, could barely breathe, and imagined to himself that they were finally going to do away with him—now that Jehoiakim was dead, a state of emergency had been declared, and all the dams had burst. He mumbled prayers under his breath: Heal me and I shall be healed, for you are my praise. Arise, O Lord, save me my God, for you strike all my enemies on the cheek, you break the teeth of the wicked. The policemen and the priest appeared to hear his prayers, though he was trying to keep them as inaudible as possible, and someone slapped Jeremiah through the sack, cutting him below the cheekbone. And they spoke about his forthcoming death completely without guile, as it were. One cop said, We'll go by the book, one bullet in the head. A second cop said: Why waste a bullet? Better to shove him off a cliff. After all, accidents do happen. If you walk along the edge of a chasm, you fall—it happens, right? And someone else said, Let's light up his beard, and Pashhur said, Hunger is free, let's just throw him into a pit and finito, and a third cop said, Let me choke him with those notes he was sticking into the Wall; we'll cram what came out of his mouth back into his mouth. He rustled what must have been Jeremiah's notes close to Jeremiah's covered ear, and then he blew into a paper bag and burst the bag inches away from the sack.

It was a short drive; when they ascended a hill, Jeremiah realized they were taking him to the Temple, or at least somewhere in its vicinity. The van stopped, and he saw, in spite of the sack over his head, that they were at the upper Benjamin Gate, located at the northern end of the Temple compound, and he nearly stumbled over a manhole cover or something of the sort; he fancied for a split second that he could see his parents' house far to the north, and the soft midwinter light slanting through thin clouds over villages and towns, some empty, others populated, over Anatot and Ramallah and Neve Yaakov and over Issawiya, and over the airport. Somewhere out there, in the distance, the light rail was speeding cheerfully along, gleaming under the new star, whose light, so it seemed, was glowing just a bit more intensely.

And Jeremiah opened his eyes in the sack, and he was overcome by the frightful realization that they'd been waiting for him there at the Wall all along, that someone had smashed open the fire extinguisher precisely to wheedle him into action, that someone had told them of his plans. And they arrived, and there was a room there next to the gate, and the priest opened it with a set of large iron keys, and they stepped into the dark. It wasn't even necessary to push Jeremiah—he entered like a man returning to his home at dusk—and they switched on a strong light, and he saw, through the sack that still covered his head, the machine.

24

THEY WALKED OUT OF THE STADIUM, which all at once had turned into the king's grave. And suddenly they realized they were holding hands, after years during which they hadn't. And they decided to return home by foot, as in those faraway days when they'd intended to walk across Holland, and even set out from The Hague, but stopped in Amsterdam to see Rembrandt's *The Night Watch*, and Esther told him, What chaos, and Hilkiah answered, Like life. Later, in the hotel, without exchanging a word, they showered together in silence. And one of the two wept under the warm torrent of water. Even so, they figured that the distance from Teddy Stadium to Anatot was too far to walk; undoubtedly, at some point they would have to hop onto the light rail. But even to plan this long walk across the city at a diagonal was in itself a sort of declaration, that, yes, it was still possible, the past could come around again. And light suddenly burst through the winter clouds, and one of them said: Even though the king is dead, we're still out for a stroll. Isn't it amazing? The world goes right on existing. And they were reminded of how, in Scheveningen, they'd stood facing the waves, rock-shattering waves, and Esther had placed an empty glass at the end of the wharf, and Hilkiah had poured out a little water from a bottle, and for a long while they'd sat there facing the North Sea and drinking in the light.

They said they'd pass by the market and bring home some vegetables and prepare something to eat, and they'd call Jeremiah up and invite him over. And just as they were saying this, Esther saw a sweet potato lying on the sidewalk. And it was as a sign and portent, Esther said: We'll make orange-lentil soup. And she bent over the root like someone saving a snail in the rain. And Hilkiah said, This we won't put in our soup; we'll take it and plant it in a pot. Years ago, he'd planted an avocado pit, but nothing came of it—it didn't sprout. He hadn't understood what went wrong; he'd intended to live off its fruit, to spread it on bread with olive oil and chopped onion, but the savor of this future spread never came to fruition in his mouth. And he took from her the orange lump with its pointed ends.

HE LOST HER AT THE PAT INTERSECTION, in the crush returning from the hummus competition. One moment she was there next to him; the next moment someone else was beside him, with a small dog on a leash. The crowd was grimly silent, perhaps on account of the awful death of the king, perhaps out of dread of what was to come. Prophets didn't lose any time in clarifying and commenting on all that had occurred, and in forecasting the future; they spoke of the coming of the Messiah, son of David— this was, for the moment, the ruling conception. And someone nearby told a group of people who'd gathered around him: Jehoiachin, Jehoiachin—surely that's the name of the new king. If so, let's do the numbers, let's see what the gematria says. And someone computed rapidly, and the number 111 came up. Everyone applauded: This number is doubtless a nice number, but is its niceness a good niceness or a bad and bitter niceness? And someone else quickly calculated that the words *very wise* also added up to 111, and then another gematria smart-aleck shot back, But *they won't rest* also makes 111, so maybe we'll find out that Jehoiachin's great wisdom will only bring us trouble and unrest. And someone else calculated: 111 also gives us the name of the sage Baba Sali. That says it all! If so, we're saved and delivered, the Baba has returned in the semblance of our king, the time of the Messiah has come, beyond any doubt! And someone else said: Indeed, he was crowned in a sports stadium, and 111 in gematria also gets us the name of the soccer player Eli Ohana, that's got to mean something . . . but what? Does it mean the king will score many goals? That's marvelous! And someone else said: But what if he breaches the gates to our city? That is to say, what if he's destined to lead us to utter destruction? And another prophet said: That music you heard on that broken piano, that music that just keeps repeating itself, over and over, over and over? From now on, it'll be this city's sound track. And they asked him, Then what's the meaning of that melody? And he said, Oho, don't worry, you'll have plenty of opportunities to hear all its meanings, believe me—you'll pick up every last one of its meanings sooner or later.

Hilkiah looked up for a moment at the new star that shone above them, as it did every other day, and told it, Enough already, turn off. And he raised his hand between his eyes and the star in order to hide it from sight. He was carried along eastward by the throng. He didn't see his wife. But she'll show up, he thought. Esther will show up soon. And the words *Esther will show up* brought back a medley of bygone moments, memories of her performing assorted dance movements onstage. Once, he saw her borne up in the arms of a muscular black dancer and was filled with envy, for he knew he'd never bear her up like that, would never be able to lift her up that way. And someone remarked, practically in his ear, Life's a sweet potato, eh? And he slipped the potato into his jacket pocket, embarrassed. He told himself that it needed planting, badly—otherwise, it would rot there in his pocket. He had to find some black earth. Yes, black earth, only black earth. And as soon as possible. Find a pot and fill it up and water it. Give it a home, like a fish in an aquarium. You can't carry a fish too far without sticking it in an aquarium. And a sort of picture appeared in his mind in which he saw six-year-old Jeremiah's hand holding a transparent plastic bag filled with water inside of which a white fish swam, a fish they named Avitar the High Priest. The light—he chiefly remembered the sunlight refracted through the bag.

But he couldn't find a flowerpot, or a nursery. At the head of Gaza Street, close to the prime minister's home, which was surrounded by a deep moat—where crocodiles from the Egyptian Nile could be seen swimming in circles—the ground was moist from the moat waters and the recent rains, and he crouched down for a moment and filled his pocket with several fistfuls of soil, enough to cover the sweet potato.

FROM A SHORT DISTANCE AWAY, Esther caught sight of Hilkiah crouching down and filling his pocket. She could have approached, pushing her way through the packed crowd at the head of Gaza Street, but something held her back. I'll keep him in sight, she thought, I'll go over to him in a few more minutes. His actions seemed odd to her, filling his pocket with earth. You turn your back on someone you've lived with for twenty years for just a few minutes, and already he appears in a different light, digging and filling his pocket with dirt. She wanted to see what else he would do, if anything, and whether he'd look upset and seek her out with his eyes. There was a cash machine there, and she leaned against it as she observed how Hilkiah stood up and tamped down the earth in his pocket and spoke to the sweet potato. Someone behind her said, Signora, I need to get some cash quickly. He had to flee, he said, and return home to Tarshish. She didn't understand what was so urgent. He said, Don't you listen to the news? And when she turned back around, once again Hilkiah was nowhere in sight.

The crowd thinned out a bit at the bottom of Agron Street.

Some people were heading for the center of town, and others were dribbling into Independence Park and resting in the gardens of the Museum of Tolerance, which was built over the remnants of an ancient cemetery that no one—apart from the dead and some jackals—ever visited. Out of the corner of her eye, Esther caught sight of a boy and his large dog, both of them throwing up, seemingly in sync, into an open drain.

IN THE MEANTIME, Hilkiah took out his phone, used primarily for reading his books, and was about to call Esther, but then had second thoughts and stuck the phone back into his pocket—the same pocket containing the sweet potato and wet earth. Come on, he told himself, nothing bad will happen if we walk apart for a little while. She isn't a little girl who needs to be kept in sight at all times, and this street is no desert. His feet bore him from Agron Street to King David Street. He saw the tower of the ruined YMCA looming before him, and told himself, I'll go rest among the ruins. But before he had a chance to sit down, he felt something moving in his pocket. And when he peeked into his pocket, he saw that the sweet potato covered in mud had sprouted a tiny stalk with two or three minuscule folded leaves at the end, curling inward toward the stem. He carefully placed his hand on the outside of his pocket. The earth was warm; he could feel its exhalation through the fabric.

AT THE BOTTOM OF KING GEORGE STREET, workers dangled down the side of the Bell Tower on ropes, losing no time in switching the huge portrait of the late king, Jehoiakim, for one of their new monarch. There was no decent current portrait available of the new king, however—for obvious reasons, nobody wanted to use any of the numerous publicity photos of him as a concert pianist. That's all we need, a photo of him striking the keys with his eyes shut—who'd follow someone like that into battle? So they dug up a childhood photograph of him, which they enlarged: a picture of the boy standing with a book in his hands, and two birds hovering in the light just behind him. But they got rid of the birds with Photoshop, and though they left the book, which was a book of musical scores, they changed the writing on the cover. And Esther saw how the workmen slipped hooks through the giant perforations in the poster and slowly unrolled the new portrait, top to bottom. She was riveted by what she was seeing, amazed, though, after all, it was only the supplanting of an old ruler by a new one, and nothing is more common than that, here in Judah as well as everywhere else. The boy with the book was unrolled as though he were being brought into the world, a sort of outsize birth, painless, motherless, gradually finding a place in the heart of the city.

Passersby returning from the stadium stopped in their tracks to see what she was looking at, and they, too, gazed in silence at this second public appearance of their new sovereign. In a couple more years, they said, he'll get fat and old and he'll look like his father, and we won't notice the difference at all. We'll be the only ones to change for the worse; the kingdom will stay exactly the same forever. And someone said, This isn't the Hapsburg dynasty. And another said: A pianist king—what next? He'll play the Rondo alla Turca right on our heads; he'll press the keys, and the hammers in his piano will hammer-hammer down on us, and the notes of that despicable march will ring right out of our foreheads. Everyone gazed at the portrait of the child king holding a book. Every now and then, a gust of wind passed between the giant poster and the wall of the tower, and the king shuddered and swelled. And Esther cried out, Long live the king! No one joined in.

HILKIAH SUDDENLY BROKE INTO A RUN, and then he stopped, short of breath, and resumed running, cutting to the right, in the direction of the Old City. Making his way down the lanes, and following the road signs for tourists, he reached the Western Wall and turned right, toward the entrance leading up to the Temple. Policemen sluggishly signaled to him that there was no entry, but he flashed his old priestly card and they let him pass. His cavity ached badly, and he stuck two fingers in his mouth in an effort to press down on the decayed tooth. Here, above, in the Temple courtyard, the atmosphere was completely different from that in the lower town, not because it was excessively holy, but because vague reports on the real political situation in Judah had begun to stream in, unlike in the new city. Numerous priests had decided not to take any risks, and were hastily bundling up their belongings—scrolls rolled up inside jugs, and hats, and a few holy vessels, and some cash and Visa Gold Cards—before removing their priestly robes, clothing themselves in mufti, and vacating the Temple until such time as the situation became clearer. No one had seen the high priest since the early-morning hours, and everyone was too scared to enter into the Holy of Holies, not least because they feared discovering that the high priest had absconded with the Ark. Hilkiah, who hadn't visited the Temple since childhood, found himself standing in one of the chambers; there were coal pans hanging from the wall, and a small altar at the center of the room, on which embers were burning low, and incense was borne up like a thin line from the end of a paintbrush at the center of the room. He thought that it was undoubtedly here that the priests wrung the necks of their pigeons and turtledoves—he had a vague memory that there was indeed a sacrifice of this nature on the books. And he went up to a coal pan and took some coal and placed it on the small altar, from which a foul odor erupted, bringing to mind blood and screaming. And Hilkiah removed from his pocket the sweet potato soiled with crumbled bits of black earth, his entire body heaving as he pried it out of his pocket, almost throwing his back out in the process. He held the tuber with both hands, making sure it was still covered in earth, and in the hollow formed in the bed of coals he placed this root, from which poked a real stalk, violet-green, with its leaves unfurling, small and large. He saw scores of ants swarming, drawn to the sugar in the tuberous root, and he hunched down and kissed the stem and leaves. He chanced upon some water nearby and cautiously watered the sweet potato, and the ants waited on the stalk and leaves until the end of the deluge. The water exposed part of the tuber, and Hilkiah, using his fingers, covered it back up with earth, as though he were drawing a blanket over it.

He walked out in the direction of the nearby rail stop. His phone had no reception for some reason, and after accosting some passersby, he understood that this was the case for everyone. He boarded the train. The passengers were all in a state. They said that things were happening quickly now, that Babylonian forces were massing on the outskirts of the city, that they'd cut off phone and Internet service into Jerusalem. Nonsense, someone shouted, not every browser glitch is a Babylonian assault. Cut it out with your Jewish paranoia, he screamed, cut it out with your hysterical alarm at the smallest delay! And Hilkiah recalled something his son had once muttered on the subject, and thought about calling up Jeremiah, if only it were possible, but there was no phone service, the whole system was down, every form of telecommunication was on the blink. He told a stranger, a biker who stood there in the railcar with his black helmet still on his head: Never mind—in the end, we'll all get home. As long as the train is moving, there's hope. And he remembered how the whole family had once been riding the light rail when a ticket inspector had come up to them, and Hilkiah assumed Esther had taken care of their tickets while she'd thought he'd been the one: What do we have here? An entire family taking a free ride. And he fined them all plenty, each and every one of them, and no amount of pleading helped. When the inspector left, all four of them started laughing, and all four saved the red penalty citation as a sort of memento of the moment in which it became clear, beyond doubt, that they were indeed a family.

ESTHER, TOO, HAD DECIDED TO GET ON A TRAIN, and she found herself at a stop that she hadn't known existed, where a blind man was standing all alone. He grabbed her arm, and she offered to help him board the train when it arrived, and he told her, This here is a stop for the blind, then added: I, having a handicapped pass, am exempted from paying. And now you, as an escort for the blind, also needn't pay. He said this as a way of trying to connect with her, as though explaining to her with a knowing wink that it was possible to dupe the system. Tell them you're my escort, he said, and we'll travel free of charge. He had a distinct Dutch accent, and Esther could barely keep herself from asking him where he was from. I'm not even blind, he told her frankly. I once was, but an angel healed me. I wear my glasses and keep my stick and my card, however, so I can ride for free on public transportation. I save thousands of shekels a year. I write poetry—I'm one of the better-known poets, and I can only write on the light rail. All the traveling to and fro dictates my poems' meter. Sometimes I also meet women this way, and they travel with me. Esther looked at him: he was a handsome young man. And she slowly reached out for his dark glasses; he didn't react, and she brought her hand closer and closer and thought, He can't see, and she gingerly took hold of and removed the glasses by their temples. The blind man's eyes were shut tight, like those of a frightened child in bed when the shadow of a monster approaches from the closet and is about to reach the pillow.

A faint commotion was heard near the train stop. When they jerked their heads around, they saw the first blue tank rolling prudently, leisurely, down Jaffa Road from the west. The incoming westbound light rail stopped and almost immediately headed back the way it had come, and Esther jumped aboard, just barely making it, leaving the blind man behind turning and turning like a spinning top, confused and shouting, but with no one to show him the way. Esther watched him for another moment and to her horror realized she was still holding his dark glasses; she didn't know what to do with them. To chuck them out the window would be senseless and wrong, but she didn't want to put them on, either, so she stuck them in her hair, pushed up at an angle on her forehead. The train car, crammed with terrified passengers, picked up speed and hurtled eastward on Jaffa Road, without slowing down at any of its stops. Many people attempted to jump on, but there weren't any handholds.

That first tank lifted its turret unhurriedly at their receding backs, and then fired one shell high up into the air, above their heads, like a ship whistling to announce its entry into port, welcoming the city and the encroaching night.

25

But how did he fall? Why wasn't he fastened to a rope or something? How could you let a king fall like that? Why didn't you hold on to him? King Jehoiachin screamed. Why didn't you hold his hand? What sort of place is this? You practically kidnap me, drag me all the way back to this awful place, and then what, you don't lift a finger, you don't keep watch, you don't supervise anything, you don't strap your king in . . . No one answered. They all stared at one another. And then someone told him, Sir, your father didn't fall, I think that he . . . that he simply *jumped*. But why should he do such a thing? Jehoiachin screamed. And someone with a scar on his face dared tell him that there were things more frightening than falling into a giant vat of hummus. Fear was relative, explained a certain Pashhur, dispassionately. Like everything, he added. The sun, for example, he expounded, is fairly close, relative to a distant star. What's more frightening than falling and dying? Jehoiachin screamed, and his voice was thin and worn. What the hell are you talking about?

He entered his new apartment. Only this morning, he had been a resident of Vienna, a pianist whose curly-haired portrait appeared on the covers of albums the world over. His wild reddish hair was his commercial trademark, in fact; women would come to hear his music and admire his hair, unruly and burning like a shampooed torch in the concert halls of Europe. And now he realized that all this was finished. You're stuck in Jerusalem like a bird in a cage; you're a prisoner even if you're not in handcuffs and under guard. You'll never be able to go home. And he was horrified by the thought that he'd left a cat in his apartment. I've got to go back, he said, I left my cat over there. And they all looked at him as though he were a madman.

An old piano stood against the wall in the apartment, and he recognized, with longing, his childhood piano. He sat down on the stool, on which he hadn't seated himself since he was eight years old. He asked all those present to leave, and when no one moved from his place he roared, Out, out, out of my sight already! They left, but they stood just outside the door, while he stared at the keys that he hadn't seen for ten years, keys on which he'd learned his first notes and very first melodies. He desperately wanted to play something—in an effort to calm down, and, who knows, perhaps also for his father's departed soul. But suddenly he saw that two armed gorillas had silently slipped into the room from a side entrance, and he got up without touching the keys.

The accident, the fall, was covered extensively on TV. *The king stumbled*—this was the phrase the public-relations spokesperson released to the media. THE KING STUMBLED would be tomorrow's headline in all the big-circulation newspapers. As for the TV news, they lightly edited the video in order to elide the moment when the king went over the railing. Jehoiachin watched the newscasts and listened to the full report of the king's tragic stumble, and all the commentators spoke of the son's grief as he sat at the piano and played for the nation while his father the king *stumbled and fell*, although even this wasn't exactly true, and he was quoted as saying, as it were, If only I'd been there at the top of the steps I'd have held on to him and prevented him from stumbling. The security guards stood there like statues. And he recalled what that scar-faced priest had said—that there are certain things more frightening than drowning in a vat of hummus—and wondered whether the priest had something specific in mind. Just then, the same priest knocked at the door and said, without any preliminaries, and as though answering his question, Come, come and see for yourself. And Jehoiachin said, I've already seen everything, and the priest told him, No, I don't mean the hummus bowl. There's more news.

And they drew up close to the flat-screen in the adjoining room and, with the rest of the royal advisers, watched the skies filling up with helicopters like a swarm of blue wasps, while blue tanks treaded up onto flattops along a long road on the outskirts of some city. Jehoiachin asked: What's that, what's going on? Is this live or archival footage? Who's that over there? What do they want, anyway? And someone in the room—it was the minister of finance, or of defense, or maybe both of them—burst into hysterical laughter. The king didn't understand, and said: Yeah? What? So where is this? And someone replied, My lord, against my will, I will answer your questions. His Highness asked who: it's the Babylonian army. His Highness asked where: just outside Jerusalem. His Highness asked what they want: well, I think they want, how should I put it . . . they want to destroy us. And Jehoiachin said: Okay, and we can fight them off, we can oppose them, of course. I'll give an order to . . . But whether he was making an assertion or posing a question remained unclear. From the silence that fell in the room he understood the answer. Someone said: Only the Egyptians can save us now. I propose we dispatch envoys to Pharaoh. Pharaoh has never let us down.

And Jehoiachin rose and with a loping stride disappeared into the adjoining room. His bodyguards were taken by surprise and didn't have time to bolt after him. He locked himself in the room he'd occupied earlier. They pounded at the door, yelling, Open up! But he didn't. And he also hastened to roll the piano, on its rubber casters, over to the secret passageway, and block its entrance.

They didn't want to break down the door; he was the king, after all.

Jehoiachin lay down on the floor on the wall-to-wall carpet and stared at the light-blue ceiling. And he tried to breathe. He realized with a start that this was his childhood bedroom. The piano stood there as it had a decade ago, and above it the ceiling was painted like the sky; his father had painted it with his very own hands at Jehoiachin's request after the boy had asked, at the age of seven, Why do the heavens end when we enter the house, why do walls and ceilings shut out the skies and clouds? His father, the king himself, and not a menial worker, climbed a ladder and stood on the ladder like an acrobat on stilts, and dipped a huge brush into a can of paint, and turned the bedroom ceiling into the heavens, so that from a certain angle, when lying on his bed—which was no longer present—the ceiling seemed to the boy to merge into the heavens outside his window, particularly in the morning, particularly in the autumn. But the color had faded, and the bed had been removed, and the space was now furnished as a conference room; only the piano remained, up against the wall, and the ceiling, which no one had paid any attention to, so consequently it was never repainted white. And Jehoiachin remembered something, and stood up—ignoring the shouts of the ministers and officials and bodyguards coming from the other room, ignoring the slip of paper that was shoved under the door—and went up to the piano. He saw that, just as he remembered, there were a few drops of bright blue on the black lid, exactly where, when he was seven, he'd ripped the plastic paint tarp his father had thrown over it. He shut his eyes and ran his manicured nails over the stains.

He sat at the piano and stared at the blurry image of his face reflected in its dark lacquer. Now he looked very old, now a mere kid. And he asked his reflected self: Yes? And what now? He spoke in a whisper. It's like we're doggy-paddling in the shadow of a cresting wave, and we can either turn our backs or face up to it. Wake up, he told the piano. The wave's already here. You've been brought to the wave. You can jump, you can wave your arms. You can swim into it or try to ride it out. But we don't actually know how to swim. I don't know how to swim, he said, and tears welled up in his eyes as he remembered the few swimming lessons he'd taken and how he'd been unable to make sense of the movements or even to float, and how his father had watched as he went under and had to be rescued again and again by the swimming instructress, until King Jehoiakim himself jumped into the water in a rage and grabbed him and raised him up level with the surface of the water and then threw him back in, repeating this procedure again and again, screaming, C'mon, figure it out already, get a grip on yourself, water is just water! You wanna die, or what?

And Jehoiachin stared at his reflection in the piano's painted wood and again asked, What now? And whatever he said, his face in the piano said, too. He said, Call the Egyptians for help? And the piano said, Call the Egyptians for help. He said, Flee to Moab? And the piano said, Flee to Moab. And he said, Escape to the sea and charter a ship and disappear? And the piano said, Escape . . . to the sea . . . and charter . . . a ship . . . and disappear, pausing between words, like someone just learning to speak. Jehoiachin said, Now you say it, and the piano said, Now . . . you . . . say it. And Jehoiachin said, Great, you're learning, and the piano said, Great . . . you're . . . learning. And Jehoiachin said, You're—speaking—Hebrew, and the piano said: I'm—speaking—Hebrew. I'm speaking Hebrew. And Jehoiachin said, I taught you, and the piano replied, No, no, *I* taught me, and then it understood its error and corrected itself and said, *You* taught me. And Jehoiachin noticed that when he stood in front of the piano his face freeze-framed, and only the person in the piano moved his lips and eyes. And he knelt on the carpet and leaned his elbows on the stool as his childhood piano told him: Neither the army, nor Pharaoh, nor Moab, nor your fortifications will help. After all, they have helicopters; they'll swoop down on the city like wasps come to lay their eggs. There's only one way out, it said, and that's me.

And Jehoiachin rushed out of the closed room and turned to the ministers and said: Hear me now, generals of Judah, and hearken, O officers of Jerusalem, there's only one thing I know how to do. I've discovered a way out. I must make him hear me, and my playing will be our voice. I'll make a supplication, Jehoiachin said, with music, and the music will make the necessary obeisance, the music will drop to its knees before the King of Babylon's feet, and his eyes will look into its eyes, and, who knows, maybe Babylon will have mercy. And two ministers from the military, one named Yeosh and another who had no name, started pacing nervously in the room, and tried to explain the magnitude of their king's folly to His Highness: Do you really believe that that mass murderer will listen, that he'll retreat because of a piano? Maybe we should send a company of flutists or the band of mandolin players from the vocational training school, too. Maybe then he'll hand over his own country into the bargain. You've got to understand that things don't work that way. Today we buried your father; we're not going to bury another king so soon. And Jehoiachin listened and said: Thanks for the encouragement, Yeosh. May you be blessed by the Lord, that you have shown this kindness to your former master, to my father, Jehoiakim, and have taken the time to bury him. Now may the Lord show kindness and truth to you, and I, too, will reward you because you have done this thing. Therefore, let your hands be strong, and be valiant, for Jehoiakim, your master, is dead, and the house of Judah has anointed me king over them. Now I'm going to wash up. And he went to the bathroom and stuck his feet into his father's clogs. Call up the movers, he commanded self-confidently. When I come out clean, I expect the piano to have been loaded onto a truck.

Afterward, the king traveled in an armed convoy to the International Convention Center hall, and the piano stood next to him in a chariot, padded with countless cushions and swaddled like a newborn leaving a maternity ward on the bitterly cold day during which he had the misfortune to be born, and the crown was on the piano's head. They bore Jehoiachin's childhood piano to the center of the stage and set it down on the wooden platform, and the blind tuner groped his way toward the piano and rested his brow on its black brow just as Jacob rested on Esau's brow after all those years in which they'd been apart. And he pressed his finger down on the middle C, and the note resounded in the hall like the echo of a bell at the heart of a silent temple. Everybody out, said the tuner, and he was left alone with the piano while Jehoiachin sat in the wings and thumbed through some sheet music. After a while, he walked onstage, to the muffled sound of tuning, and he bowed low, even though no one had applauded, for the rows were empty in the enormous hall, save for a handful of seats on which court attendants were parked, as well as two security guards.

Jehoiachin sat facing the keys, white breakers crowned with black foam. And he was filled with fear, even though he knew well enough that with the first touch of his fingers the fear would pass. The fear always passed—the first note always completely enveloped him. And he was already feeling the calming effect of the music he was about to play, even though he didn't know what it would be. Only when he extended his right hand did it come to him, and he was filled with a sense of peace and stillness and immediately started to play. And it seemed to him that the first notes sounded even before he touched the keys.

That entire night, Jehoiachin played through all of Beethoven's piano sonatas on a piano on which rested a crown—yes, all thirty-two. Now and then, he'd stop between the pieces to have a drink or wipe off the perspiration that streamed in runnels over his eyes and down his cheeks and neck. After the first three sonatas, he already reckoned his execution was at hand, but he regained his composure and told himself—and listened to the piano also saying—that here, here, for the first and maybe the last time, he could actually make a difference with his playing, that he could be of some honest-to-goodness use, playing not only to gratify the rich, playing not only for classical-music critics employed by bourgeois newspapers, but really *working* with music, as one might work with a hoe, turning music into something that could defy ruination and even save lives. I've never saved a life, he thought, while playing in a pained state of reverie, as though disembodied, the slow movement in the seventh sonata. This was just the beginning of the road, to be sure—the late, difficult sonatas were still ahead of him—but he would hack his way into that mountain one inch at a time, even if his childhood piano were to become his grave—for all he cared, his hands could freeze in a spasm as he and his piano were lowered into the pit and the score was flung after him.

The fixed cameras in the International Convention Center broadcast the performance on all possible channels. Judean technicians even succeeded in reviving a poky battery-operated emergency network. The music was aired, but to whom exactly? Was it like those broadcasts aimed at outer space? Jehoiachin mused, as he plunged into the waves of Beethoven's music. And he no longer knew which sonata he was playing, and whether he was playing the individual pieces and the movements in the correct order; he knew that he was making numerous errors, skipping and repeating himself, shortening, distorting, and in other places stretching the compositions out unnecessarily. And sometimes it seemed to him his fingers weren't playing and his hands were hanging slack, wasted, void of feeling, while at other times they floated unmoving above the keys as the piano played entire passages on its own until his fingers regained their vigor and he again harnessed himself to the music and made some progress and finally paused. And he imagined the King of Babylon, whose face he knew only from newscasts, and his attendants, too, engrossed in what they were seeing on the screens, or maybe slipping earphones on and becoming immersed in the music, their hearts shuddering, their eyes opening wide, their swords stilled, and their helicopter pilots seated in their choppers, staring at the sea Jehoiachin was creating and deepening and widening and inundating, a sea that was not to be crossed.

AT DAYBREAK, the king lifted his hands, which had lost all feeling, from the keys. Jehoiachin made to rise from his stool. And it dawned upon him that this was, beyond any doubt, his last recital. He could barely stand up to face the audience that wasn't there—everyone had left a long time ago—and he made his bow and then collapsed onstage, and the piano collapsed as well. Doctors were summoned and brought the king back to life, and the piano's corpse they covered with a sheet, and they slipped the crown into the king's bag. Two hours later, the king struggled to his feet. He needed support, and he was also given an injection before he stepped out of the International Convention Center into the glaring sunlight. And there, under the cable-stayed Chords Bridge, at the entrance into the city, a pair of Mercedes were waiting, their engines idling and their air-conditioning turned up and blowing frigid air even though it was bitterly cold outside; their windows were tinted and bulletproof, and their headlights were high-beamed and washed and polished and shining from the dew in the emerging light at the onset of the month of Adar.

26

AT THE FAR END OF WEST JERUSALEM, the new king played all night, while in the east, Jeremiah was strapped to a machine known as *the rotator*. He'd heard of the rotator from reports that had made it into the local newspapers from the Committee Against Torture, and Rabbis for Human Rights, but now here it was, in person, and in such close proximity to the Temple, too, right at the Benjamin Gate. His hands and feet were strapped to a sort of vertical cot, or simply a board, and his forehead was also strapped down. A tube had been carefully inserted into an artery in his arm. He had no idea what was dripping in there.

And the priest said, I've got some questions for you, and Jeremiah didn't answer, and the priest asked, Okay, who sent you? And Jeremiah said, I don't know, And the priest roared, Who, who? And again Jeremiah replied, I really don't know. And the priest asked, Who's funding you? And Jeremiah said, I have no funds. And the priest said, So who are you, in fact, Jeremiah? And Jeremiah only stared back and was unable to speak a word. The priest jotted down some notes to himself, and then he got up and pressed a red button and said, You'll have plenty of time to think about soiling the cracks of the Wall with venomous notes and scaring the king over an intercom. King Jehoiakim has been murdered, the priest said—that's what you wanted, eh? Way to go! If you get out of here alive, which is unlikely, we'll try you for inciting regicide—and let me make it clear to you that there won't be anybody to get you out of it, like at your other trial. And the priest switched off the light, pressed a green button set into the wall, and left. Jeremiah heard the three locks being bolted one after another, and the priest talking with someone, maybe the warden, and he heard the sound of the priest's receding footsteps. Pashhur wore wooden-soled priestly clogs, and their hammer strokes resounded from afar.

The board onto which Jeremiah was strapped began to jiggle, and then to rotate steadily on its own axis, and Jeremiah felt himself slowly revolving, counterclockwise, his head like an hour hand, from twelve o'clock to eleven and on to nine, where the apparatus stopped for a second before continuing to six, at which point his head was pointing straight down. The machine stopped. And Jeremiah felt his blood trickling down into his head. Several minutes later, the machine started moving again, and his head moved up toward four o'clock and on and on until it returned to where it had begun. This occurred several times, and Jeremiah thought to himself that he could easily endure such torment, at least for an hour or two. But then, as if responding to his thoughts, the machine gradually started going crazy, as it were, except that this madness wasn't wild but wholly intentional—it was the machine's raison d'être, it was precisely programmed, it was an algorithm of madness. After a number of rotations, the machine accelerated, all at once whirling full-circle, or for half a circle, and then braking to a stop before starting to move along other axes altogether, so that the board to which Jeremiah was strapped turned over till his nose was now facing the floor, tilting slantwise at various odd angles while varying its speed and executing sudden, terrifying, jolting stops. The machine had originally been part of the mechanism of a ride in an Assyrian amusement park; it had been upgraded and turned into a torture device. A guard sitting on the other side of the locked door didn't hear Jeremiah's screams, didn't see his face twisted in nausea, didn't see his quivering jaw. He had a small battery-operated radio, and he listened that night—not counting the hours when he slept—to music. He who'd never heard such music before listened, for the first time in his life, to the king's piano. It didn't really do anything for him, but he didn't switch it off, either.

Jeremiah longed to faint, but he understood that whatever had been inserted into his arm would prevent him from fainting or falling asleep, and as soon as he'd come to the conclusion that this was it, he was going to die, the machine stopped to give him a break—again as if it had read his thoughts, it responded at once and reverted to a slow, regular, indolent turning, like the hands of a clock. Jeremiah muttered, Cursed be the day on which I was born, cursed be the day on which I was born, cursed be the day on which I was born, cursed be the day on which I was born, cursed be the day on which I was born, cursed be the day on which I was born, cursed be the day on which I was born, cursed be the day on which I was born. He tried moving his arms and legs to rip off the straps, and he tried wriggling and jerking his body to stop the machine, all to no avail. Cursed be the day on which I was born. He realized that a good part of torture was not knowing how long you'd be left there. He shouted at the guard, but the guard didn't hear, and even if he had heard he was forbidden to open the door. Cursed be the man who brought the news to my father, saying: A child is born to you, a son. And Jeremiah told himself that one of the angels was bound to come now and save him—it *simply wasn't possible* that he'd be abandoned now, at this awful moment—and he opened his eyes and said boldly, Now, now, come now, and the almond branch and the bulging pot and all the voices that had told him what to say and had filled him with words came to mind. But no angel appeared, nor did an angel knock at the door, nor did one fly in through the wall to pull the machine's plug out from its socket, or to give Jeremiah water, and not a single word was heard in the room apart from his cursing himself and his parents and his life. And let the man be as the cities that the Lord overthrew, he said, referring to his parents. And to himself. And then a miracle did occur: he fainted. In fact, it was no miracle: the stuff that dripped into his blood had simply emptied out.

His mother rose from within the gloom into which he'd sunk. She told him, Sit down for a bit, Jeremiah. She was looking at the stars, her own particular stars, but they were speeding away through the skies in all directions. She told him the Andromeda galaxy had collided with the Milky Way; they said it would not occur until billions of years from now, but in the end it took only a few weeks. The stars from both galaxies mixed like dust from two adjoining rooms separated by a broken window. She sat in the still courtyard of their home in Anatot and gazed at the dancing stars. She had decided in her heart, so she told him, to devote at least one moment every evening to such luminous beauty. You'd think there was nothing easier, nothing simpler, she told him. And yet I didn't stand by my pledge. Why? Jeremiah asked her. Her answer faded in the murky darkness. He felt the machine's rotation still, but as though in the background, like the humming of an air conditioner while you're dreaming. And he, too, gazed at the skies and saw that the stars were moving very slowly, but all at once they accelerated, turning right and left, and the moon swirled dizzily, as well as the clusters of stars he'd known from the astronomy club; only the new star stood in place and didn't budge at all. And his mother's voice was heard, and the skies were obstructed and obscured, and she said, Even so, I believed that if I looked up, this way, night after night, the stars would turn into my neighbors in their own good time. Into my kin. Into my children. If so, why didn't I keep my pledge? Jeremiah said, Mom, they've placed me on the rotator, and tonight I will die with my feet above me, or maybe on some kind of diagonal. His mother said, I see you walking tomorrow in the light.

Jeremiah said: I don't know why I'm doing this. The price is too high, and, besides, there's no chance—why go on? And his mother stared at the stars and said: The standard for deeds is the standard of the sea and its majesty, and not of the human street, and not of the human byway. The key is not to cling to the byway, she told him. Try to remember this. You know, I, too, she told him, I, too, sobbed because I was confined between the walls of a house, between the walls of a street, between the walls of a city, between the walls of the mountains. Jeremiah said, And it's impossible to get out? You can't come and get me out of here? A moment ago, while I was still sitting with you in the quiet courtyard, she went on, I suddenly discovered that, although my home is built on the shore, I live on the shoreline of the moon and the constellations and the shoreline of the sunrises and sunsets. Jeremiah told her: I smashed a jug, but now I'm the jug. A jug without a cork, he heard himself say, but this was a voice from a long time ago, from so long ago—a jug without a cork, a jug without a cork, a jug without a cork, a jug without a cork. And his mother raised her hand, and all at once the hundreds of thousands of stars vanished from the heavens, and she vanished with them.

Jeremiah opened his eyes. The machine stood idle. And he had his face pointing the right way, and his entire body shaking uncontrollably. He didn't know how much time had elapsed. Soon the sound of a key rattling in the three locks was heard, and the priest Pashhur, reeking of aftershave and toothpaste, bent over Jeremiah's face and grumbled to the doctor who accompanied him, Shit, he's alive.

Outside, it was still dark; it was four in the morning. The guard and doctors removed the straps and laid Jeremiah on the floor. After the night's gyrations, the floor seemed to him like a tempestuous sea, and he clutched at it with his hands and his feet, and his body twitched, and a yawning nausea opened within him. The guards stood by and laughed. Like a fish in water, one of them said, and the second corrected him, *Out* of the water. As they watched him convulsing at their feet, the priest said: I think a bullet in the head right now is all that he's asking for. Isn't that what you want, you pitiful prophet? Maybe an injection? You want a shot that'll fix you up? So, here, come and sign this. I'll help you hold it in your weak hand. In your wretched hand. In your wicked hand. And you'll sign this agreement stating that you won't say another word. Nor will you, nor will you, nor will you stick notes, neither in the Wall nor in your mother's ass—or anywhere else, for that matter. Are you signing? Sign here or I drag you back to the machine. You'd like a couple more hours in my amusement park?

And Jeremiah turned his head to puke but heaved up nothing. He tried in vain to stand up, and he turned around again and signaled to the priest all blurred out of focus in front of him to bend over, and the priest stooped over beside him with the form, and Jeremiah signaled to him to come closer. I can't stand up, he groaned, you've got to come a bit closer, and the priest brought his head up close—A bit more, a bit more—and the priest held the agreement in his hand, the same form that he'd already had numerous prophets sign. Pashhur said, Here, sign here next to the *X*; I've already filled in your details, I only need your signature, only a teeny signature with my pen. And Jeremiah told him, You're not close enough, just a bit more. And the priest bent his ear until Jeremiah could see the tiny hairs inside it and the wax that had accumulated there, and Jeremiah whispered into this ear, Pashhur . . . Pashhur . . . And Pashhur said, Yes, yes, Pashhur is my name, and he looked with satisfaction at his colleagues. And Jeremiah whispered in his ear, Pashhur . . . Pashhur . . . And the priest said, Yes, yes. And Jeremiah said: Pashhur, from now on no longer Pashhur, the Lord has named you Terror-All-Around. For thus says the Lord: I am making you a terror to yourself and to all your friends, Jeremiah whispered, and wept. And they shall fall by the sword of their enemies— while you look on. And I will give all Judah into the hand of the King of Babylon, he shall carry them captive to Babylon, and shall kill them with the sword. I will give all the wealth of this city, all its gains, all its prized belongings, Jeremiah wept, and all the treasures of the kings of Judah into the hand of their enemies, who shall plunder them, and seize them, and carry them to Babylon, Jeremiah said into the cavernous ear. And you, Pashhur, he whispered, and all who live in your house, shall go into captivity, and to Babylon you shall go, there you shall die. And there you shall be buried. You and all your friends, to whom you have prophesied falsely. I'm sorry, he added. I'm sorry.

And he got up onto his feet, leaned against the wall, and bent over to vomit; for a split second, he was reminded how, once, after his sister's death, he decided to go to the freezer and drink her cancerous blood and die. He actually had it all planned, and he got up at night and stole into the kitchen to open the freezer in which his father kept her blood. But his mother was there, facing the stove and staring at the wall in front of her. And he said, from where he was leaning on the wall—and it wasn't clear whether he was speaking to himself or to those present, who were looking at him with a mixture of bafflement and hostility—Ahhh, I . . . have been a laughingstock all day long . . . And again he collapsed. And the doctor said, embarrassed, Wait a minute, we'll call you a taxi, so that . . . And Jeremiah took one long look up at the doctor from the floor and said, Thank you, doctor, but I think it'll be difficult for a taxi to get across town and make the ascent up to the Temple. His fingers jerked in spasms. The doctor was filled with the urge to step on Jeremiah's fingers in order to make them stop, and he said: Nonsense, it's five in the morning. The roads are empty—why should it be difficult? Why? And Jeremiah answered, Because of the tanks.

27

SEVERAL HOURS before the grand hummus ceremony, Mattaniah and Tukulti stretched out on mattresses under the sky, on the rooftop of the large house on Yishai Street, as was their custom. Because it was cold, they'd lit a small fire on the roof, to keep warm and grill venison that Tukulti had caught on the slopes of Abu Tor. Mattaniah lay alongside Tukulti and rested his arm on the dog's compact body. Tukulti wondered, What's it like over there, in Egypt? And Mattaniah recounted how he'd once flown to Egypt as a child. His father, Josiah, would fly over there on weekly visits: to file his report, Mattaniah said. And once or twice, he brought along his wife and sons. The plane flew low over the pyramids, which were painted green and yellow, and Mattaniah told his brother Jehoahaz that the pyramids' volume—that is, the volume of each and every pyramid—was the area of the base multiplied by its height divided by three. Jehoahaz stared out the window of the plane and said: That's maybe true for certain pyramids, but surely it isn't true for *all* pyramids. Some are wide, others narrow, some are low—what you're saying simply doesn't make any sense, Mattaniah. Later,

Mattaniah went up to his father at the head of the plane and whispered, Dad, Jehoahaz is retarded.

Tukulti laughed and told Mattaniah that his ancestors came from Old Babylon, the real Babylon, not the one inhabited by the newfangled Babylonians of our own era. You can see my kind in the ancient wall paintings, large and strong, speaking to the kings, fighting by their sides, and advising them on all matters. The angels that keep reappearing in Genesis and other books are always depicted and drawn as winged human beings, but reality was a lot simpler: they were always dogs. Three dogs announced the birth of Isaac, a dog leaped at Abraham's hand clasping the slaughtering knife, a dog struggled with Jacob and bit his ankle. Mattaniah asked, And you're an angel, too? Tukulti was silent, and then replied: Me? I'm just a talking dog.

The morning of the hummus competition, they both went to have their hair cut. Mattaniah said, First we'll go to the dog groomer, but the dog groomer told Mattaniah: I can also cut your hair; it isn't all that different. I'll even give you a discount— I'll give you a two-for-one discount, in fact. And the barber noticed, under the black dye, the yellow-reddish roots of Mattaniah's hair, but he didn't say a word. At the age of twenty-six, at the dog groomer's, Mattaniah suddenly saw in the mirror that he was beginning to go bald, and in response to his query the barber said, Of course. The process would take a year or two, and then Mattaniah would finally be exempt from all hair-cutting. And that was when Mattaniah started to lie to people who asked and told them he was only twenty-one, as if to put off the draining of his youth down the sewer, but of course that only aggravated the situation and made his balding more obvious. Soon someone told him: You must be kidding—already egg-headed at such an early age? I reckoned you must be thirty-something. Tukulti, who saw Mattaniah anxiously checking his hairline in front of the mirror, told him, Take my pelt and make of it a hairpiece. And so they sat for an hour or two in the shade of the tamarisks, and Mattaniah said, Because you haven't withheld your pelt from me, whatever is mine I will give to you, and where you go I will go, Tukulti, and half the kingdom will be given to you. Tukulti mused a bit and then said, I have only one request from my master. Mattaniah nodded, and the dog went on: I still have an aged mother, and she's penned up in Broch's home. Let us go down to Beit Hakerem and visit her there, and I shall behold her before she passes away. And Mattaniah, who knew perfectly well that it was impossible simply to stop by and knock on Broch's door and enter, said, Sure, I'll make an appointment for the summer. No, Tukulti said, for we will now rise and make our way there. And Mattaniah said: He won't let us in, man. He doesn't open the door like that for no reason. Tukulti said, God will open it for our sake.

So they caught the light rail at the Ramat Rachel stop and rode up to Kikar Denya, and Mattaniah punched his ticket twice in the ticket machine. The train was packed with large dogs that day, some leashed, others loose, and Tukulti passed beside each one of them and sniffed his or her ears and rear; it seemed as if he was telling them all something. And when they were standing in front of Broch's home, Mattaniah said, Wait a minute, at least let me give him a call and let him know we're coming by. He dreaded receiving another drubbing at the critic's hand, of being trashed again, remembering how Broch had once burned his notebook before his eyes in a Nescafé can. But while Mattaniah was still trying to find his phone number, Tukulti went up to the door and barked once, twice; the handle squeaked and Broch's door opened, but it wasn't Broch who appeared then and there, wearing his nightmare-inducing house slippers, but the dog Broch called Sargon, who wasn't a male dog at all but a bitch, and Tukulti yelped, and the bitch, just about dumb and blind and deaf now, her mouth drooling and with an ugly sore on her foot, lowered her head and took a flying leap, her paws churning air. Mattaniah rushed over in embarrassment and, standing in the doorway, bent over to pet the aged dog. All of a sudden, she barked hoarsely, and the master himself dashed out of the house, holding a whip in one hand and a book in the other, hollering: Get in here immediately, Sargon! Who's that who dared set foot in my home? Who's that who opened my door? And he raised the whip, and Mattaniah told his dog, Let's get out of here, but Tukulti stood fast between the bitch and the critic and, without warning, leaped and knocked Broch and the whip flat onto the thick carpet, and shoved his forepaws and his black claws into the old man's face. Broch screamed, Sargon! Get back into your kennel immediately! But Tukulti closed in and ran his claws over Broch's lips, etching three thin lines of blood there, and spoke into his face: Nay, Broch, her name isn't Sargon. Nay, from now on her true name will be reinstated, and it's Innana, and that's what you'll call her, too. And Broch told Mattaniah— whose name he couldn't remember, though he knew more or less who he was—Hey, young poet, get your talking donkey off me immediately, before I fuck you up for good and sell that stinking bitch to the glue factory.

Mattaniah stooped over the critic, and all at once his fears left him, and he felt all grown up, and he brought his face up close to Broch's face and whispered in his ear: No longer will you change the names of dogs and people. No longer will you throttle writers and poets. *Your fire's burned out, dragon.* And he entered into the house and penetrated into the inner sanctum, the study that no human foot had breached for decades apart from Broch's own, and began pulling out and flinging books from the shelves, at first two or three at a time, then entire rows. He raked them out and flung them—tens, hundreds, thousands of books—and he ripped at and tore their pages to shreds, and took down from the walls all the photos of Broch with the writers and poets he'd crowned and then inevitably humiliated, with the chairs of departments of Hebrew literature he'd appointed and then demoted. On one of the lower shelves, Mattaniah saw his own book, his book of Assyrian hymns, with his servile inscription, and he yanked the book from its place and opened it, and the pages were all, to the very last page, blotted out with a thick black felt-tipped pen, line after line, and then additionally effaced with large Xs. His inscription, too, was blotted out in rage. And in one of the rooms he saw a small heap of broken and crooked computer keyboards, and he kicked and scattered the heap, and in the bathroom Broch's urine sat yellow in the toilet bowl, because he'd left it there when he hurried out to see who'd entered his home, and Mattaniah pissed on the critic's own piss and then flushed away both their yellows. And there was a book there in the bathroom, on a shelf, and it was a copy of Zelda's *Leisure,* and he thumbed through its pages, and there, too, the poems were completely crossed out. The Bible was in there as well, and it, too, was erased and corrected and revised. Mattaniah was overcome with joy at the sight of *Leisure,* and he returned to the study and told his dog, Kill him, Tukulti, bite him in the aorta, eat his gullet. But Tukulti raised his astounded eyes and ignored the command. And they made to leave, the two dogs and Mattaniah in their wake, but before leaving, the aged mother dog stopped and pawed, one last time, and licked the critic's wounded lips.

28

THE CHOPPERS DIDN'T LAND IN JUDAH but flew in the direction of the Arabian Desert for a different mission. They weren't really necessary: a hundred tanks, and foot soldiers and mounted troops in iron chariots, were sufficient to conquer not one Judah but ten. From the window of his armored car, the King of Babylon and his attendants watched the King of Judah fall to his knees. To the best of his memory, the King of Judah was old and potbellied, but Nebuchadnezzar couldn't possibly keep track of all the kings who paid tribute to him, surely not the marginal king of such a negligible kingdom. Nebuchadnezzar signaled to Neriglissar, who was none other than Nergal-Sharezer, to go out to the surrendering king. From his place next to the driver, Nebuchadnezzar kept an eye on what was going on.

Neriglissar didn't want to deal with this, certainly not first thing in the morning. No, all he wanted to do was sleep. Nonetheless, he went out and approached the King of Judah and, without any ceremonial preliminaries, kicked him gently in the chest. He had to make a great effort to do any shouting first thing in the morning—he hadn't really tuned up his voice yet—but he knew that his king was watching, and that all of this was being broadcast on a host of channels, so he had no choice. It was necessary to re-establish the balance of power, and to demonstrate Judah's unequivocal capitulation, so anything less than kicking and shouting would be interpreted as softheartedness. Jehoiachin fell back and shielded his face with his hands. Neriglissar returned to the car, fetched a club from the trunk, and struck—though not too harshly—the ribs of the presumed canceler of the automated payments. He really just wanted to wrap it up and get on with things. He, too, was certain that the local king, Jehoiakim, was supposed to be at least fifty, but he wasn't going to get stuck on details. He really wanted to get it over with already. The king was always sending him out as muscle, but he hadn't been trained or brought up for this sort of thing; he was an astrologer by vocation, and in the heavens were the limit of his aspirations, not in landing blows on the King of Judah. He wasn't a particularly strong person and didn't look forward to it and didn't get any pleasure from it, certainly not at five in the morning. But one time Nebuchadnezzar had made him watch two Aramean prophets get grilled over a fire. The king's intention was more to educate Neriglissar the astrologer than to punish the Aramean prophets. Neriglissar had told his king that he'd rather not beat up the prophets, and so Nebuchadnezzar said curtly, Well, if that's the case, I'll take care of them myself. He used a kind of large copper deep-fryer that the Ammonite barbarians used to fry their infants; a blazing fire was lit underneath it, and the prophets—who, needless to say, were false prophets (they'd been mistaken in their forecast concerning Pharaoh Neco's troops and the crossing of the Sinai Peninsula)—were thrown in shackled and naked.

So Nergal-Sharezer shouted, more for the cameras than for the defeated king, Jehoiakim son of Josiah, come and declare publicly that you broke your covenant and oath. And Jehoiachin shouted back—and his words were immediately translated for the folks at home—Yes, yes, I admit to everything. So why did you cancel those payments? Nergal-Sharezer screamed. What, are you nuts? Did you think we wouldn't mind, did you think we'd just let you go wild, Jehoiakim? And Jehoiachin said, even though he had no idea what this Babylonian was talking about: Yes, of course, the esteemed gentleman is quite right. I don't know what possessed me, I canceled the payments, I guess. I couldn't manage the taxes; the taxes were more than I was earning; I was choking on them. And Nergal-Sharezer said, turning to the cameras: Now, Jehoiakim, you'll see that you made a mistake. Now you'll see the surcharge we customarily impose on any business cancelation, a surcharge and a fine and also cumulative interest, but the interest we'll demand in blood, and the surcharge in heads, and the fine in vessels from your Temple, and the stamp on your bill will be inked with blood from your own head, O Jehoiakim. And he drew a gun and aimed it at this dust rag, this kid, an eighteen-year-old at most, who would now die and be blotted out when it wasn't even five-thirty in the morning yet. But he noticed then that the king's hand shielding his head was bandaged, and, oddly enough, something within Nergal-Sharezer stirred a bit, as though trying to awaken; however, he nevertheless flipped off the safety and put it up to the Judean king's head. And a voice in the assembled cried out, in Aramaic: Hold it, hold it, drop your gun, sir. That's not the king, that's his son, *it's only his son*. Can't you see? That isn't Jehoiakim; Jehoiakim's already dead. Can't you see that he's only a boy, and wounded? And he only arrived in Judah yesterday; he didn't cancel anything, he didn't do you any harm. He's only a pianist—take a look at his fingers.

This voice was enough to halt the execution, and everything came to a stop. Nebuchadnezzar, King of Akkadia and Babylon, got out of his car. Nergal-Sharezer dropped his gun and watched as his king approached. From a carriage parked nearby came Jehoiachin's mom, Nehushta, the queen mother, accompanied by her ladies-in-waiting. Since he arrived yesterday, she hadn't seen her son close up, but she'd stood all night, eyes glued to the screen, watching him play. Nebuchadnezzar told Nergal-Sharezer: Leave him alone, it really isn't Jehoiakim. I can see it now. So who are you? he asked in front of the crowd, and the words in Akkadian were understood but seemed odd, for in the ears of the locals it sounded as if the king had asked, What are you?, and someone in the crowd cried out in broken Akkadian, *Saklo, muskeno, muskeno*—a fool and a beggar—though to the crowd's ears the words sounded quite different, thanks to an unfortunate resemblance to the Hebrew words for *execution by stoning* and *misery.* And Nebuchadnezzar looked at Jehoiachin and asked in basic Aramaic, *Sultana?* Eh? But the prince didn't understand, and the king glanced backward, and instantly his aged translator, whose hands had been cut off, popped up by his master's side. Nebuchadnezzar turned to the amputee and asked him to ask Jehoiachin, You're the son, yes? The youth nodded. And Nebuchadnezzar asked, So where's your father? And Jehoiachin said, He died yesterday; he fell. And the amputee asked, You're the one who played all night? And Jehoiachin said, That's me. And added, improvising, I'll reactivate the payments, I'll add on to them, too—even though he didn't have the faintest idea how much was in the royal coffers or how much they would need to pay.

Nebuchadnezzar's ministers stepped out of the cars to watch this unexpected spectacle: Nebusarsechim, who would be soon appointed chief eunuch, and Nebushazban, and Nebuzaradan, and the remaining ministers of the King of Babylon, though Jehoiachin didn't know them by name. They were all clad in black suits and sported long beards, save for Nebuchadnezzar himself, who was shaved and bald, a small man who looked more like a clerk, wearing wire-rimmed spectacles and with a head like a thin-shelled egg. He had a slight limp as he paced around. He seemed to be deliberating over Jehoiachin's proposal, but then he glanced at his watch, and Nebushazban finished talking on his phone, nodding to his king, and Nebuchadnezzar said, No, it's too late. Jehoiachin didn't understand why it was too late; after all, nothing had happened yet, and financial matters could always be settled amicably. He'd take out a loan or mortgage some property, or he'd give a concert and use his earnings to repay the debt, he thought. Everything can still be fixed, he told the amputee, who told Nebuchadnezzar, Give us a second chance. But then the sound of an approaching train was heard, the light rail coming back from the Temple, and when it stopped it disgorged not the usual Jerusalemites but two hundred Babylonian soldiers, with the Temple vessels in their possession—all the riches from the House of God and all the riches from the king's palace. And the King of Babylon told the amputee to tell the King of Judah: I'm sorry to have to tell you this, but while we were having our nice little chat here—and a genuine note of grief could be heard in his voice—we already carried off all the gold vessels we could find, and have confiscated the rest of your accoutrements, so we've just about finished collecting our lost revenues. I say *almost* because we're still left with the exile clause that your dear father agreed to. It's a fundamental point of the contract he signed, and I have the right to impose sanctions without having to demonstrate any proof of damage. Hence, within three months, ten thousand Jews will gather here, all your ministers and all your mightiest warriors and every artisan and metalworker, and you, too—he turned to Jehoiachin—will join them. No, no you won't die. You're a good pianist; I heard you in my car on the way over. You'll come and play for me in Babylon. Play? *Melulu*? To play? You get it? You and your mother and all your eunuchs and all the local elite. You see, your music has lightened your punishment. I won't do to you what I did to Ashkelon—the city won't be put to the torch—but I'll take all your rich people, and your professors, and your artists, and your intellectuals, and your musicians, and you'll personally prepare the list of exiles for me. That's it, that's the lightened sentence, that's my verdict, and if you go up to the palace and the Temple you'll see that all is in order, that not even a vase has been broken, the amputated translator bellowed—he had conveyed the entire translation in bellows, because that's how he believed it was proper to convey the king's words—nothing is missing apart from what we took as a symbolic fine that won't even cover our fuel expenses coming over here, sixteen hundred kilometers of travel. The music, he added upon reflection, was a nice move. I'll listen to it at leisure when I get back.

So it's agreed: you've got three months to get organized, and you'll rule for three months here, and then you'll come to my place and you'll reign from afar. I could demand that it all happen within twenty-four hours, but the King of Babylon's heart is merciful, and justice still reigns in Babylon, praise be to Marduk. Now I will depart from here, and you'll quietly get organized and travel northwest at the beginning of summer, and we'll settle the ten thousand exiles in a new Judah. By then, everything will be ready for you. We'll give you a ruined city to restore, and there you'll sit, and all your chronicles will be written down in a book. Prepare yourself; you'll get the hang of exile. You'll build yourselves homes; I'll order a grand piano for you, and you'll sit and play real nice. Ten thousand good exiles, choose for me the best figs in the basket, and the bad and rotten ones we'll leave behind. I'm sure you understand that what I'm describing as a sentence is nothing more than a rehab-and-recovery program. When all is said and done, rot has spread deep among you here. Remember: three months from today, you're out of here. Everything will be done quietly, calmly, the translator bellowed, ten thousand of the choicest figs will go into exile, and the rest of you will stay put.

Now I need to ask you, and this embarrasses me, whether you might have some relative or family member—a son, brother, cousin, niece, someone? I want to crown someone else, quickly, and I want to be certain this time that I won't have to make the same journey again and repeat what I've just said from the beginning. Believe me, Jehoiakim—Nebuchadnezzar had already forgotten the name of the king's son and so addressed him by his father's name—I've got plenty of other matters on my mind apart from this little tax rebellion.

And Jehoiachin said, No one, no one. The Babylonian whispered, and the translator bellowed, No one? No one? *There's always somebody.* And Jehoiachin remembered and replied, Ah yes, you're right, there should be someone else. And Nebuchadnezzar, whose voice softened till he sounded almost delighted, said, Good, let that one step forward, if you please. He raised his head and peered around, as if he sensed that the person in question was there in close proximity. And he beheld the tens of thousands who had risen from their beds and gathered around, standing in silence, and inundating the open space between the International Convention Center and the Central Bus Station. He didn't see Jeremiah, who had been standing there all the while, leaning against a TV van in order not to fall over on account of the dizziness, which still hadn't let up, nor did Nebuchadnezzar see Jeremiah's mother, who stood at a distance of some dozen meters from her son but hadn't noticed him among the crowd, nor did Nebuchadnezzar see Noa's mother, who was hanging around in a dressing gown. For the most part, the crowd hadn't seen or heard a thing, only rumors about what had been seen and said. Within minutes, there were already plenty of false and empty rumors clouding the true ones: The king is being beaten to death in there! They're lashing him with a whip! They're wrestling, and the King of Judah is gaining the upper hand! They're— And Mattaniah pushed his way through the assembly, flanked by a large dog on a leash, and to Jeremiah it appeared as if the dog was pulling Mattaniah forward. Nebuchadnezzar looked at the dog and said, Marvelous, a big Babylonian dog. He kneeled and scratched Tukulti behind his ears and spoke to him kindly in his native tongue, while the King of Babylon's astonished eyes struggled to decipher the passages in Akkadian on the young Judean man's forearms. The King of Babylon gently grasped the tattooee's wrist, like a nurse checking the pulse of an old man, then turned over the arm in order to continue reading. And suddenly Nebuchadnezzar had the urge to dig his teeth into the flesh of this white, inscribed forearm. And the King of Babylon stood up and ambled over to his car, and he opened the trunk and returned with a bottle of extra-virgin olive oil that was saved for such occasions, and he approached Mattaniah, who looked vacantly at the bottle, and without a moment's delay the King of Babylon shot back his arm and shattered the bottle of oil on Mattaniah's head.

29

Noa, LEFT BEHIND, watched Mattaniah and Tukulti hurry in the direction of the western entrance to the city, where the King of Babylon stood waiting for the new King Jehoiachin. Eliazar was slung close to her body, less than two months old. The night of the king's piano recital, they'd slept soundly and hadn't heard a thing, but something woke them up early in the morning; they heard neighbors leaving their homes in a rush. Noa told him: Don't worry, Eliazar. You won't be king. *You* were born at your mother's wedding; a sinful stain will always mark you. No prophet will anoint you as king with such a stain on you. It's impossible to become King of Israel with such sinful origins. She looked at little Eliazar, asleep against her, and said: No, never a king, never a prince. Neither a prophet nor a minister of war, neither the captain of the guard nor the minister of agriculture—not a magician or master sorcerer or eunuch or chief eunuch or satrap, either.

A three-minute stroll from their apartment stood a Babylonian tank that had strayed from its path and was stranded in a park. Horses that had been unharnessed from their iron chariots nibbled at the flowers in the rose garden and lapped the waters from the artificial pond as though it were a trough. But Noa didn't know any of this, not yet. These were the last minutes of quiet. She sat with Eliazar in the depths of the park, early in the morning, and sang him a song that no one else heard—certainly not the Babylonians, some of whom stood at the city gates while the vast majority were just then finishing up looting the Temple with a quiet, thoroughgoing efficiency, after first locking up the priests who hadn't managed to flee, as well as whoever else was there hiding in the broom closet so that no one would hurt or bother them. Only Eliazar heard the song, and this while asleep. What was it she sang to him? Would it be remembered in the moments to come? In even a few seconds? Suddenly her heart divined what Mattaniah refused at all costs to grasp, that they would kill Jehoiachin—who it was rumored had flown in yesterday—and that she would be, in no time at all, even today, the queen, and that this baby would be the Prince of Judah and Jerusalem. And she realized that Jehoiakim had summoned the pianist because he didn't want Mattaniah, under any circumstances, to rule in his place.

He won't rule, nor will I. Not she, and not the boy. And she told him: *Neither I nor you. Neither I nor you. Neither I nor you.* Mattaniah may take part in this screwy story, with his own free will or by force, but as for us—no way. Mattaniah can build a new palace for himself, can deploy an army of servants and slaves, can wage war against the people of the region, and sanctify the name of God or, on the contrary, do evil in the eyes of the Lord—he can do whatever he wants. But she won't budge from the house in Abu Tor, and she'll raise Eliazar on her own, and teach him only Hebrew, not all the tongues that Mattaniah promised her he'd teach him—not Assyrian and not Babylonian and not Egyptian. He doesn't need any other language than Hebrew in order to speak to her. When a boy grows up alone with his mother, he has no need for any language other than his mother tongue. She noticed some bread gone stale that someone had left for the birds in the park, and said, The bread's dry, the

270

broken bread. And she said: You're such an idiot. You knew all along that this day would come, and Mattaniah would be sucked into this boiling broth. He denied his destiny because he, too, knew in his innermost heart that this day would come. There aren't that many candidates, and given the brutality of our era they're growing fewer by the day. Suddenly she understood why Mattaniah had been in such a rush: he'd sped over there in order to reap his reward. They were going to murder his nephew, and he wanted to be there when it happened; God forbid they should crown someone else. And she imagined herself for a moment stretched out on the bed in the palace, her feet bathed and massaged in oil, but then she banished the sight from her eyes as if she were shooing away a mosquito bloated with blood shrilling in her ear. And she remembered the makeshift shacks in Moab, near Dhiban and Aroer; she'd lived there several years earlier, and then in the smaller community near Al-Karak. She told little Eliazar: We'll hop on a bus today and flee. We'll cross the Dead Sea in a rowboat, and tomorrow we'll watch the sun setting from the eastern side of the river; by tomorrow, things will be real quiet. The people of Moab hadn't ever been sent into exile—they had no tradition of exile there—so a kind of serenity fell on any traveler who had covered a distance of merely two or three hours. She felt the tang and smell of bygone days, of a thousand years ago, wash over her. You'd arrive on the far side of the Dead Sea, and the first thing, which almost begged to be done, would be to shave your hair. All the women there shaved their hair, and adopted simple linen clothes; the silence of Moab begged for a change of attire. From the other side of the Dead Sea, Jerusalem was barely visible, lost and absorbed among the hills in the colorful, blinding light, at times violet and purple— even as you, too, Noa reflected, are slowly absorbed, leaving the big cities and dwelling among the rocks like a dove. It was always possible to stumble over some flint utensils that the local inhabitants had left behind thousands of years ago—blades and awls and graters—and one could collect a handful of sharp blades, and pick vegetables and fruits in the orchards, or trade for them in the small itinerant bazaars, and slice some pears and desert apples. And within a day or two, a sort of waking slumber would descend on you, the dream of a simple and forgotten way of life in an unending summer, far from the thundering tracks of imperial horses, far from the coastal plain and the fortified cities toward which those horses were always galloping, far from all the tumult and the shouting of the Jews dwelling in that place, constantly hoping for Egypt's ascendency or the fall of Assyria. Years of tense anticipation and anxiety had turned them hard, suspicious, and bitter, suspicious toward everything that wasn't familiar. Even a woman's cropped hair was horrifying for them; even a small tattoo on the nape of your neck provoked their ire. In their friendly manner, as it were, they objected to anything deviant. Even her refusal to watch television with her parents every evening was from their point of view a sign of contempt, the first signs of madness and sociopathy. They liked these sorts of phrases: *There's a way to do things*, or *No, that's not the way.* They told her that Moab was a kind of parched desert, a cultural wasteland, filled with beggars and disease: There's no orchestra there, they told her, that says everything about the place. She decided to go anyway, and she immediately understood how they'd misled her, and how the land was not lacking in water and green, springs and torrent-beds, and cold and warm pools, as though all the water in the region led there, and she heard the water in the silence, and beheld the green, which wasn't abundant but was a very bright green, and someone gave her a slice of melon left in the cold, streaming water, and she absorbed its coolness. All this was some ten years ago, and she would go back there tomorrow, tomorrow. After all, Moab is so close, she told herself resolutely. She'd return to those days of her youth, when she was in her twenties. She'd cross that little strip of water with Eliazar, and they'd sit together in a hammock and eat cantaloupe and watermelon; she'd feed him the tasty, cold Moabite fruit; she'd find for herself a stone blade thousands of years old and slice thin slices for him. And, barefoot, she would walk in the cold water, she thought, and she would shade both their faces under a wide-brimmed hat. Tomorrow, she told Eliazar. Tomorrow we leave and cross over. But several minutes later, a black jeep arrived and some eunuchs honked at her to come over. They didn't know exactly whom they were bringing; they thought she was just some concubine. And she didn't get up, took no notice. So they honked a second time, persistently. And in due course they took her and Eliazar and brought them to the palace.

30

ALL THE ASSEMBLED JUDEANS watched Mattaniah remove his shirt in embarrassed alarm, and he was left with only his pants on, as oil mixed with blood dripped over his cropped hair and over his face. Nebuchadnezzar and his ministers crowded around him and tried hard to read the inscriptions in cuneiform on his body. He stood there with his pants bunched up at his ankles, as though he'd come for a dermatology checkup, his shirt clutched in his hand, sucking in his belly a bit. His skin was bright and speckled everywhere in whitish patches, as is common for redheads.

Assyrian and Babylonian are cognates of the Akkadian tongue, and he who knows one of the languages can make do in the other. This is a king to my liking, Nebuchadnezzar told Nebushazban, who also drew up close to read. The king didn't succeed in reading most of the inscriptions—they were in High Assyrian, ornate, ancient—but learned Nebushazban clapped his hands excitedly and shouted, Indeed, on his shoulder is the inscription from Shalmaneser III's black obelisk: Ashur, the exalted Lord / King of all the mighty gods . . . , he began reading, and then as quickly fell silent, nervously realizing that in reading aloud he was displaying a deplorable arrogance toward his king. Nebuchadnezzar inspected Mattaniah's muscles and his hat and said slowly in Akkadian, as though speaking to a monkey, Am I to understand that you're one of us? Even though Mattaniah more or less understood the question, he couldn't answer with any fluency, so he told the translator—the fib was by now routine—I'm of Assyrian descent on my mother's side, Your Highness. In order to prove the point, he switched with some difficulty to his broken Assyrian, and the king replied in Babylonian, and in this way they somehow spoke, to the king's delight.

And Nebuchadnezzar glanced at his watch and said: What I've heard and seen is more than enough. You will reign from the day your nephew comes to play for me, but you can start learning the ropes immediately. *Shalashat arhu*, three moons. You'll now make a pledge to me personally; you'll say it in Akkadian and in Hebrew, here in front of all the Jews and Babylonians, a serious vow. You'll be my vassal, but not like the vassals of Shalmaneser III—not like him whose words are inscribed on your body, who'd pulverize his many kingdoms to dust with his huge stone pestle just to brew himself some hot herbal tea with their remains—but like your nice dog here is your bond slave. Ah, finally there's someone to talk to, and he slapped Mattaniah on his tattoos. Again, to his embarrassment—though he kept it all to himself—he felt a strong urge to dig his nails into the future King of Judah, into this flesh, to scratch deep. Oh, you're cold, the king cried out—get dressed, please. Why doesn't someone bandage the future King of Judah's head? he suddenly screamed, and remove the wretched oil from his hair, and the blood. Mattaniah recognized the word *igulu*, which means *good oil*, but a picture of a frozen igloo came to mind instead, and he was there, stretched out in the igloo, naked and shivering. I'll give you whatever you need, Nebuchadnezzar said, and you'll restore the Temple and fill it up with new vessels. Whatever we've already packed away in crates—it's lost to you now; we're not about to unpack it all. If you'd only arrived a few hours earlier, maybe I'd have stopped despoiling the gold vessels and riches from the House of your God. But everything is already packed in our cartons, and the forms have been filled out, and everything is already on the way to our archivist. If we unpack the crates now—and it appeared as if Nebuchadnezzar was only waiting for Mattaniah, the future king, to ask this boon, and he'd have it done as Mattaniah wished, but Mattaniah didn't utter a word—there'll be a huge commotion here, the masses will turn to looting. Best for us to stick to our plans and not open any cartons that have been sealed. You'll be my vassal, he said, and that isn't anything to be ashamed of, but an honor. Everyone has a bond slave; and I am also a slave, of Marduk, and he, too, has lords who are greater than him, who appointed him to rule before the beginning of time.

And now, Nebuchadnezzar told Mattaniah, now begins the second and most popular act in the little play we've put on before the people. And Nebuchadnezzar raised his eyes and there were masses of people wherever he looked; most of the inhabitants of the city had come out and packed the streets as though for a state funeral. And Nebuchadnezzar said: Now I will change your name, just like Pharaoh Neco renamed your older brother. I know, I know, your father and mother gave you a very nice name, and this stranger comes along and changes it, but from now on I'll be your father and mother. And you'll love me as you love them—and maybe even a bit more. And your new name will remind you whom to love. But, as another exceptional example of goodwill and of mercy I will let *you* chose a new name for yourself. I've never done that before, Nebuchadnezzar said, but, then again, I've never seen a king so neatly decorated in cuneiform inscriptions before, either. And Mattaniah said: I, uh, would rather stay with the name Mattaniah. Because, you know, I've gotten used to . . . And he giggled as they dressed his head and tightened the bandage. Nebuchadnezzar stared at him for a moment, fish-eyed, and then snorted, and his ministers burst into laughter, and this wave of laughter swept through the crowd, as when the fans of a soccer team rise to their feet and wave their arms and fall back into their seats, and it sped down the length of Jaffa Road, which was jammed with people, and crashed into the Western Wall, and there shattered. And when the laughter subsided, the King of Babylon asked again whether the future King of Judah had come to a decision, and Mattaniah, who hadn't interpreted the laughter correctly—that is, he thought they were laughing *with* him—opened his mouth again to say *Mattaniah*. But something in the Babylonian king's eyes made him realize that one more wrong word out of his mouth and they'd shoot him then and there, so he said, When I was a child I had a made-up name, and Nebuchadnezzar said, That's great, what was it? And Mattaniah said, I called myself . . . I was called Zed . . . Zedekiah. So the other children wouldn't know who I really was.

And so his name was changed to Zedekiah. He was twenty-six years old when he was crowned king, but he lied and said that he was twenty-one, and thus was it registered. And he was given the standard vassal-kingdom forms to fill out. They placed before him the royal desk, and he entered his father's name, Josiah, and his mother's name, Hamutal, daughter of Jeremiah. Fleetingly, he remembered his grandfather, whose name was the same as that of Jeremiah the prophet, whom he hadn't seen since that chance encounter in the restaurant. And Mattaniah recalled that it was him, yes, Jeremiah, who'd given him his name in the youth club—at Mattaniah's own behest. Then, too, he hadn't been able to come up with a name for himself. The memory surged up of the full moon they'd seen then, swaddled as though in a pink fabric; it seemed like such a long time ago. Mattaniah placed his hand on Tukulti's back—his dog, who'd been there all along and had listened to the ceremony with his muzzle lowered, and when they'd smashed the bottle on his master's head he'd remained silent and hadn't budged from his place. The dog recognized

Broch in the crowd, staring at him in loathing, with flesh-toned Band-Aids plastered on his upper and lower lips, like a terrifying clown.

Jehoiachin, the newly dismissed king, who was standing nearby and taking all of this in, lowered his gaze and slowly turned around and walked away. No one, so it seemed, paid any attention to him; only Mattaniah looked after him for a moment. He didn't even have time to say goodbye to his nephew, whom he'd last seen when one of them was a child and the other a teenager. And Jehoiachin boarded the light rail at the Central Bus Station. On the one hand, he was delighted that the whole royal shebang had been forestalled before it even began, but the speed with which it was forgotten and the ease with which he was let go, on the other hand, offended him to the very depth of his soul. No one remembered, it seemed to him, his playing—all of it had already been forgotten.

He boarded the light rail, confused and drained, and it set out once again on its eastward journey, in its voyage that has no end, to and fro, like a pendulum swinging across the city, in light and darkness, for only on the holy Sabbath does it rest—or, rather, that is, it *might* rest, depending on the king, whether he doeth evil in the eyes of the Holy One or not. The multitude swarming down Jaffa Road parted to let the light rail through, like a zipper opening, and then closed ranks in its wake. And from the eastern part of the city, the blue tanks crept up Agron Street. They held their fire, as they'd been instructed to their great chagrin, shelling neither the ramparts nor the private residences. The tanks were ramped up onto flattop trucks and then disappeared at the head of the road leading westward, and the Babylonian king and his ministers were swallowed up in their cars and disappeared. Only Nebuzaradan and Nebushazban, who'd been assigned to stay behind and assist in organizing the deportation of the ten thousand—a partial and merciful exile—remained, but now, deprived of all the guards and their companions, they appeared almost like boys, dwarfed by their strange, overly festive getups. And as at a party where you don't know a soul apart from a single person, and you force yourself on him the entire evening, they both cast questioning looks at Zedekiah, and he said, in pidgin Akkadian, which would improve in the years to come: Okay, so I'll take you over to the palace in the Holyland complex, to my nephew; surely he's waiting for you there. Anyway, he, Jehoiachin, is still king for the next three months, and who knows, maybe his reign will be extended. Zedekiah didn't register that the palace was already his, that he was now obliged to live there, and that the present king would reign only officially, on paper, in the shadow of his dead father, the drowned, the great.

And Zedekiah stood there, the Chords Bridge behind him, and peered at the legions of the nation, of whom he saw only a small fraction, and he realized that, although he was terrified, there was also something warm making a place for itself between his stomach and his heart, like someone might feel after not failing, as expected, a difficult exam. People looked at him, most of them for the first time, and suddenly someone shouted, Long live the new king, long live our father, Zedekiah, King of Judah, long live! And the multitude roared in answer.

31

JEREMIAH WANDERED THE STREETS OF THE CITY like a spinning top in an earthquake. His balance would return momentarily; then the dizziness would start again, and he'd throw out his arms to hold on to trees. The city was like an enormous swing under his feet, and sometimes it seemed to him that he was walking in the sky—until, worn out and shaking, he flagged down a cab and asked to be driven to the palace. The prophecy for Jehoiachin was already set in his mind. And he knew that he had to reach the palace and choose for himself an intercom and say into it: As I live, says the Lord, even if King Coniah son of Jehoiakim of Judah were the signet ring on my right hand, even from there I would tear you off and give you into the hands of those who seek your life, into the hands of those of whom you are afraid, even into the hands of King Nebuchadrezzar of Babylon and into the hands of the Chaldeans. I will hurl you and the mother who bore you into another country, where you were not born, and there you shall die. But they shall not return to the land to which they long to return.

That was it. But the prophecy was all twisted in his head when he muttered it to himself, peppered with mistakes. He wanted to say *cut you off*, and what came out was *tear you off*; he wanted to say *to another country*, and what came out was *into another country*. And he realized that they'd scrambled his brain, that they'd swirled him around in the machine not to break his body but to scramble and craze his words and speech.

But it was impossible to reach the palace, for the multitude was blocking all the roads in the city. When he got out of the cab, it dawned on him that he didn't have any money to cover his fare. He told this to the driver, and the driver looked at him and said: I know you, you're Jeremiah. Forget it, don't pay. I heard you once speaking at the Bookworm. And Jeremiah thanked him and barely made his way to the nearest light-rail stop. He got on and sat there, his head leaning against the window, not even knowing in what direction the train was traveling. And he realized that they'd taken his shoulder bag with Zelda's book in it when they'd led him to the rotator. The amputated beggar cries, he told the window. His weeping covers the sun's eye, screens the flowers from view.

HIS FINGERS AT REST ON HIS KNEES, Jehoiachin sat, the new-old king, riding the light rail. And the few passengers in the car drew away from him. His ribs were broken—maybe two, three ribs—and he felt a stabbing pain each time he drew breath. He'd never broken anything in his body: always coddled, spared any pain. Now even breathing hurt, and he'd injured his precious hand, and the other one also ached, and he was wheezing and coughing. His fingers were intact, but for the first time in years, dirt had collected under his nails. He felt the dust in his hair. Ten thousand exiles. And he knew perfectly well that the legions of the soon-to-be exiled were weighing down his shoulders, that he was fettered to them by tens of thousands of chains, and, more, that if the ten thousand ever reached Babylon in another three months and he wasn't there to play for the king, bitter would be their fate. He coughed, and his ribs, like spikes in his chest, tormented him. He thought of Mattaniah, whom he hadn't recognized at all, even after he'd realized that this was his uncle. He didn't remember him like that.

Someone entered at the far end of the car and immediately dropped to his knees, retched, and threw up. And Jehoiachin tried to avoid looking at the man, but then he got up and limped up over to him and jerked him up by the armpits. At this, his ribs shrieked as though they were being harrowed, and he screamed and ceased at once. He fished out of his pocket a moist towelette from some remote restaurant. And the retcher stretched his hand out and wiped his mouth and neck.

Later, they walked side by side from the Anatot stop to the house at the end of the village. There they found Hilkiah, sitting all alone next to the radio, whose batteries had died during the night; Esther had gone along with the rest of the populace to witness the arrival of the Babylonian king and the crowning of the new King of Judah. And Hilkiah dragged into Jeremiah's old room a mattress that hadn't been slept on for many years, and the pair of maimed men lay down there.

First he examined the guest, whom he immediately recognized as the king who'd been crowned yesterday and who'd played and been dethroned in the morning. Broken ribs, a concussion, and a swollen eye. He brought some ice and disinfectant and sutured the king's eyebrow. As for the ribs, he said, there's nothing anyone can do, only rest and patience. The pain will pass within a month or two, and try not to catch a cold, because the sneezing will hurt—and don't laugh, either, if you can help it. At this point, Jehoiachin began to sob, crying for the first time in years except for any crying he might have done while listening to music; music made him cry a lot. And Hilkiah told him softly: Come, now, it isn't that bad. You were king for a couple of hours . . . Isn't that enough? . . . I haven't ever worn a crown in my life. And he gazed for a moment at the photograph of his daughter—or, rather, at its absence, since only now did he notice that it was no longer on the wall, that it was missing, but he gazed anyway at the photo that wasn't there. Jehoiachin sat up, raised his arm, and with some effort thrust his hand into his bag, where his crown lay, and he told Hilkiah, Here, take it, please, as a gift. And Hilkiah, before returning the crown to its owner, set it on his pate for a moment and felt the weight of gold on his bald head.

Jeremiah lay there, too, and beheld, from the torment of his wheeling soul, his father crowned for a moment. All of his inner organs, and his brain in particular, felt as though they were seeping together in his body: his heart sliding down, his liver pushed up to his throat, his lungs shoved under his colon. And to his father he said, I've been placed on the rotator, Dad. And his father was sorely afraid, but he kept quiet, and then said, Wait a minute. In a panic, he went into his daughter's room, in which they hadn't moved a thing for more than a decade; a small painting of a tree fronting the sea still hung on the wall, and her empty desk still stood, with unsharpened pencils and an eraser on which was etched a map of the Old City. And he opened a drawer and found her medications, including her anti-nausea pills; she'd suffered from nausea even before her cancer. All of her medications were still there, like the rest of her stuff. Hilkiah returned to the room with his new patients, ripped open the aluminum seal with his fingernail, cradled his son's head, had him sip some water and swallow a pill, and placed a second pill on his tongue. And he said, confidently, even though he didn't know— he didn't know a thing—that the medication would take effect in half an hour, and the pains would pass, and the dizziness would go away: It'll soon pass, son, maybe even a little sooner than soon.

After a few minutes, Jeremiah felt that the effects of the rotator really were easing off, and his balance gradually came back to him. He got up carefully and, looking at the king's head drowsing beside his crown, tiptoed to the living room and stepped out to the balcony. The moon was shining in the daylight—not so strange a sight—and on the round balcony table his father had set a glass of herbal tea. And Jeremiah told him, It passed. And his father said, Look, the moon is eclipsing the new star; they say that this won't happen again for another five thousand years.

They sat at the round wooden table that Hilkiah's grandfather had sawed freehand, and Jeremiah recounted to his father what had happened until now and what was about to happen, told him about the exile that was being coordinated over the coming months, and the despoiling of the holy vessels in the king's palace—even though they'd actually looted the old palace, which in effect was a museum for the House of David, and not the Holyland complex. He raised his eyes and told him: Dad, surely they'll take you to Babylon; they'll take most of the doctors and the educated, those are the king's orders. Maybe a few family practitioners will remain to take care of the poor country folk, but every specialist will be sent into exile. Hilkiah, without appearing to get upset, said, I've always wanted to see Babylon and the towns along the banks of the big rivers. He kept looking at the door of Jeremiah's sister's room, which he had left open, and at the medicine drawer that was still open, and at the blank space where his sister's name wasn't written on the yellowing box on the wooden table, which bore a label that merely read: NAME OF PATIENT _____.

Jeremiah drank the refreshing tea. His father gave him the package of pills but told him: You probably won't even need these; you're already recovering from it. Trust me, I understand these things. All that was necessary was to tend to the nerve centers shaken up in your concussed brain. And Jeremiah filled another glass and carefully got up, still a bit dizzy, to set the glass beside the king, asleep in the adjoining room. The king, who was exhausted from lack of sleep and from playing his piano and from the blows he'd received, had dozed off. When Jeremiah returned to the balcony, the door to his sister's room was shut, and his father said: And so we'll set out for Babylon. We'll pack tonight. We won't let them send us into exile; we'll uproot ourselves voluntarily; we'll buy train tickets to Babylon. And

Jeremiah looked at him, unable to grasp whether this was stoical serenity or utter idiocy. For a moment, he thought that exile, which would certainly be hard—a long journey, ending in one's absorption into a neighborhood or city that would need to be more or less built up from its foundations, not to mention learning a new language, a new alphabet, and all that—maybe it would distract them, at least, from his sister's closed and anguish-filled room, and the unending hope for the miracle of resurrection. Babylon might be, in effect—who knew?—their real revival in old age, or so he tried to convince himself. The change wouldn't be easy, but at some time or another, there would be a new door and a new apartment, and they'd sit on new chairs and acclimatize. Whatever the case, there was no choice. And he said, against his will: Go on, leave. I'll come later; I'll join you when I can, when matters are wound up here. And Hilkiah asked: What, it didn't end today? I thought that—

Jeremiah got up and returned inside, and he sat down on the bed to instruct Jehoiachin in the prophecy that had been laid down for him. But, though he opened his mouth to speak forcefully, he didn't utter a word; he squelched the prophecy, and only asked the sleeping King Jehoiachin's suspirations, in a voice that could barely be heard: Is this man Coniah a despised broken pot, a vessel no one wants? Why are he and his offspring hurled out and cast away in a land that they do not know? And he grieved there, in the gloom of the room, grieving not for the city, not for Judah, but for this youth, the son of the king, narrow-hipped and slender-fingered, asleep there on a worn mattress on the floor. Record this man as childless, a man who shall not succeed in his days; for none of his offspring shall succeed in sitting on the throne of David, and ruling again in Judah. And Jeremiah stood up. The dizziness had almost completely vanished, and this bothered him, for he feared that, just as it vanished, so it would return to assault him. He sat beside Jehoiachin, on whom he'd bestowed absentmindedly the pet name Coniah. Jeremiah kept looking at him until Esther returned home and entered the room. The king's son still hadn't woken. In her hand was a small bag of sorts, filled with provisions for the trip to Babylon: almonds and dates, two avocado sandwiches, and a thinly sliced radish, for she mistakenly assumed they were setting out in exile that very day, and who knew whether food would be served on the long journey. And Jeremiah saw that this was his sister's lunch satchel from nursery school, which his mother had kept with all her other belongings. When he saw her name embroidered on the satchel, he remembered that it was his father who'd sewn her name back then; he recognized his handwriting in the seven letters that the purple thread whispered: Shlomit.

PART THREE

ZEDEKIAH

32

NEBUZARADAN AND NEBUSHAZBAN entered the wine shop on Metudela Street accompanied by Zedekiah, the new king. In effect Zedekiah had already begun his reign the day after his appointment near the Chords Bridge. And Jehoiachin his nephew was given the somewhat dubious title King of Judah in Babylon, even before he was exiled there. One may as well ignore the interim period, Nebushazban told Zedekiah, and in any case, you need someone to look after you. We'll teach you all you need to know, so why not get cracking? For what, after all, does a king need to understand? Nebuzaradan began. Women and wine to understand. His Hebrew was a bit odd, Nebuzaradan's, captain of the guard. Food, however, he spoke fluently, and he loved to drink wine, loved to savor the taste; in each new province of the empire, the first thing he'd do was check out the wines and vineyards and crush a rinsed grape between his large teeth. The first word he taught Zedekiah to pronounce in Akkadian-Babylonian was *karanu*, wine. *Karanu danu*, strong wine. *Beit karani*, wine house. *Rab karani*, chief wine bearer. Zedekiah wasn't familiar with these words from any ancient Assyrian writings, so he diligently repeated them to himself. Nebuzaradan was also fond of olive oil (*shaman sirdi*), fond of dipping fresh challah into a saucer of extra-virgin oil—for him, this was an unparalleled treat. Nebushazban, by contrast, made sure not to drink while on duty, and oil nauseated him. He was more interested in the local architecture and in the primitive art of the indigenes. Since Jehoiachin had pretty much disappeared after his dethroning ceremony—and it would be a lie to say that anyone really bothered to look for him—they took Zedekiah under their wings. They, too, like Nebuchadnezzar their master, were impressed by the cuneiform tattooed on the limbs and back of the designated local king, and, not having any other acquaintance in the conquered country, they stuck to him like a pair of tourists to their guide in some dangerous, barbaric land. They appointed a local clerk to organize the list of those who were to go into exile with the King of Judah in Babylon, Jehoiachin, and bureaus of exile were opened, and the Jews whose names had been announced arrived and stood in line in order to receive their travel certificates. (And some whose names *hadn't* been announced came, too.)

During the first weeks of his rule, when he accompanied them on their tour of the city, Mattaniah, which is to say Zedekiah, was compelled to leave Tukulti behind in their new home in the Holyland complex, along with Tukulti's aged mother, the refugee from the house of Broch. Zedekiah wondered whether Tukulti also spoke to her in the language of men when they were alone. Noa, two days after his coronation, said that she had to return to the old house in Abu Tor to gather some of her belongings, a thing or two that she'd forgotten—and she took Eliazar, and a day went by, and two days went by, and she still hadn't returned. She said that there was a lot to pack and arrange there, that it wasn't right to move an infant to a new home, and to a top floor at that; she claimed she had a fear of heights. Zedekiah, who was preoccupied with his new responsibilities, let her be for the time being, thought he'd let her get accustomed to the idea. She stared at the nameplate on their old door, NOA AND MATTANIAH, and wondered whether she should change the plate, update her husband's name. Instead, she got out a screw-driver and simply removed the plate, and left it in the kitchen, beside the jars of chickpeas and lentils. And she opened a can of beans with crushed tomatoes and ate it cold.

A week later, once he realized that she'd relocated to their apartment and wasn't going to return on her own volition, Zedekiah sent for Noa. When she had ridden up the Holyland elevator with Eliazar in his sling, he greeted her warmly and told her about the view. One could see everything from way up there, through Jehoiakim's old sliding window, from the Temple right up to the Babylonian camp in Ramat Rachel, pitched on the remains of an early Assyrian encampment, and farther out, toward the city center, the old Bezalel building, where their wedding had taken place and their son had been born, and even over to the Old City. Zedekiah approached the toddler and extended his finger for him to grasp. And later Zedekiah would himself take the time to spread and tuck in the sheets on their queen-size bed on the thirty-first floor in one of the building's towers, open on all sides and protected by armored glass. And he told her: Noa, they changed my name and moved me to a new apartment, but these are trivial things. You don't have to take it so hard—you'll be able to continue your life just like you wanted, only with fewer frustrations, so why make things difficult? Sit, sit . . . There are greater forces than us at work here . . . And they went to sleep under the glass dome, and the heavens opened over her, and Zedekiah, who still remembered from his days in the youth science club several interesting facts about the nocturnal skies, told Noa: The night connects us to the infinite, because the dark that descends on us is the darkness that goes on and on right up to the edge of the universe. During the day, it's possible to believe that we aren't part of the infinite, that we're in a bubble of light, but night reminds us of the truth. And no one wants to remember it, so they hurry to shut their eyes and sleep, or to switch on a light. And Noa said, I get it, it's scary. I want to shut my eyes. I want to fall asleep. And Zedekiah looked at her and said: The problem is that the darkness that's behind our closed eyelids is a part of the big darkness, too. That's why it doesn't help. There's no getting around it, no. And she said, Are you happy to be king? And he replied, I wasn't interested, but if that's where life has led me . . . can't you see also the positive side? And he fell asleep and didn't hear the answer.

After some time, she was woken by a loud noise and didn't understand what it was, and then she understood: Oh, he snores now. In the old house in Abu Tor, he had never snored. And the following night, it happened again. She'd shove him a bit, or hiss *shhh* at him, or even squeeze his nostrils shut with two fingers. He'd stop for a moment, and then start up again. And after a several sleepless nights, she told him that his snoring was wearing her out. Nonsense, he said, I don't snore. If anything, you're the one who snores—I heard you once. You also mumble in your sleep and grind your teeth. So she waited another night and recorded him, and he blushed when he heard himself snoring and said: I should be hanged! How horrible. I'll go sleep in another room—I'm such a nuisance. And he went to the adjoining room, which was a sort of walk-in closet, since he didn't want it to be known that the King of Judah was sleeping apart from his queen, but it didn't help: the wall wasn't thick enough, and the noise went right through. Even when he moved down a floor and slept there, she heard him, and then he flew into a rage: What do you want from me, anyway? You want me to give up sleeping at night entirely? And she said, Just move down another floor or two.

Zedekiah summoned Baalgezer, the minister of defense, to seek his advice, and the fellow said: We'll take advantage of the situation to get in a little publicity coup. You'll sleep on the ground floor, and we'll make it public; we'll say that the king has decided to move closer to his people and not to lock himself at the top of his ivory tower. That the king is a night watchman to his people! And so it was, and it was made public, and Zedekiah started to sleep on the ground floor, without the stars and without the dome of darkness. They arranged a windowless basement for him and placed a bed and lamp there, and people would come and stand around the building at a safe distance. To catch sight of the king asleep wasn't possible, of course—if there had ever been windows down there, they were now sealed up—but at least they could hear him snoring. You could stand and listen, every night, to the loud snores coming from the ground floor. And people crowded around and muttered prayers and entreaties to the king's snores. And Noa would lie on the top floor, with her eyes open, under the heavens that stretched above her like a bowl, and the silence there was almost painful.

Zedekiah asked that his staff purchase a heavyweight motorcycle for him. Sometimes he was startled awake by his own snores, and was unable to fall back asleep, and he'd escape quietly and motor up and down Begin Expressway just for the hell of it, and cause an enormous racket in the city before sunrise. And he also realized an old dream: they brought him a female singer to give him voice lessons. It turned out that he was a bass-baritone, and in the morning it was possible to hear him singing outside the palace.

For the most part, he slept pretty well, with no one pushing his knees or pinching his nose or startling him with *shhh* or smacking his elbows: deeply, healthily, nine hours a night. In the morning, the two Babylonian ministers would pick him up in a Mercedes, and every couple of days they'd set out on a wine-tasting tour. They'd start, as was their habit, at the rabbinate, where the rabbinate's head vintner diluted his terror by pouring a third of a glass, and Nebuzaradan, the captain of the guard, placed the base of the glass on the bar counter and jiggled the wine in the glass, twice, thrice. Then he stooped over and, as though preparing to dive into the glass orifice, shoved in his enormous nose and inhaled without tasting. Zedekiah and Nebushazban looked at him, kind of astonished, while the vintner attended to his every movement and word. Nebuzaradan flourished a white napkin, and the vintner spread it in front of the wineglass so that the Babylonian might examine the color of the wine against a white background. He then peered, with one eye shut tight, at the drops that trickled down the side of the glass, and again inhaled, and then, with both eyes shut, sipped. A tense, brittle silence spread amid the bottles. He didn't swallow, and gazed at the ceiling, lost in thought. He turned completely red, Zedekiah noted, remembering that his father was also like that, immediately turning red even if imbibing just a sip for the Kiddush. The vintner looked at the king as if asking for help, but Zedekiah returned a blank stare. And then the captain of the guard turned toward the window and all at once spat the wine out. No . . . Nebuzaradan said, no . . . no . . . And the vintner, who'd brought out his best wine, was shaken up and asked: No? No? Nebuzaradan deliberately ignored him and said, No, I'm astounded, it's beyond all expectations, this godforsaken hole, but, hey, don't be stingy, this is great wine. Great wine. Worth you should taste, Nebushazban, he said. Such great wine has not come to our mouths since same wine in Nineveh our mouths we opened to sip. I'm almost drunk, he laughed, from one spitted sip. Not wine but winey presence. Be precise—not wine but whine-ish essence in itself. This wine deep like Babylon wells, and balanced, too, he muttered in a mixture of Akkadian and bits of Hebrew he'd picked up in the last weeks, I appreciate vines are fifty years, please correct if we're not mistake. We have body full in the mouth, tannins soft and caressing. And lo, sugar, too, came out strong! he shouted abruptly.

He moved on to the second glass. Good color, like the King of Akkadia and Babylon Nebuchadnezzar's car after a night of dew, he determined, dark-toned, almost obscure, but there's an open moist crack and sweet to the tongue and mostly for the tip of the tongue to chafe, concentrated and full-bodied, and odd, toothed tannins that sting in their calm like genitalia hairs that have just started sprouting. This wine he swallowed to the dregs—he couldn't help himself. Muscular wine like our honorable king here, Zedekiah, but, like the king, it's also round and generous, and he gives me finish especially fast. Sometimes a person just wants to finish strong, to give everything inside, without all the preliminary games, without all the pleasures of the palate . . . This is a handy and delightful wine now, he told the head vintner of the rabbinate, to drink it, to drink today, with the meat. Mattaniah sat nearby and looked at him, from time to time fishing out a peanut-flavored Bamba from its packet and placing it on his tongue.

The Babylonian passed from one glass of wine to another—he was unquenchable. Each and every wine was for him another open field of secrets and visions that waited to be translated into a treatise: here was one that was full-bodied and aromatic like strong, genial goat milk straight from the udder, and it was rich and velvety, crammed full of the savors and fragrances of Nabataean avocado and lemon, all backed by a light tannin, like a puppy's milk teeth, revealing suppressed intimations of city brushfires; there was one in which he detected a conspicuous though not bothersome woody influence, nicely blended with a sharp but enticing presence of saddle leather. At the first assault, Nebuzaradan said, the tastes of almost sharp plums and black forest-berries clearly emerge; in their wake, red berries appear, dark chocolate—eighty percent—made with Brazilian cocoa, and hinting at sweet and bleeding chewing tobacco. No, no, not sweet, he corrected himself after another moment of reflection, alive-salty. This is Assyrian wine, right? he asked the vintner, and even though it wasn't Assyrian but from Hebron, the vintner said, Fantastic, precisely, the vineyards of Ashurbanipal. Great wine, the minister ruled, and the vintner nodded: Great wine.

He turned to Zedekiah and poured him a glass. Zedekiah refused. His mouth tasted of his snack; besides, he disliked wine. But Nebuzaradan insisted, resolutely, his apparent drunkenness falling away: That wasn't a suggestion, King. If you want to rule here, you'll learn to drink, and to talk knowledgably about wine. Don't be like all the other pushovers who rule over petty kingdoms and drink beer and seventy percent rubbing alcohol and don't know how to say a thing about their drink apart from *It tastes good* or *It doesn't taste good*. Now, drink up, or else I'll break another bottle over your head! Nebuzaradan pounded the table with his fist. And Zedekiah, afraid, drained the glass of Assyrian wine, which tasted just disgusting, like a gulp of liquor mixed with sweet raspberry juice for children, and Nebuzaradan said, Well, whaddaya say? And Zedekiah, who didn't have the faintest idea, seized on some of what he'd just heard and added some rubbish of his own—after all, he'd been a poet a hundred years ago—and said, In the amazing prolonged finish emerges an alluring smidgen-hint of licorice with a trace of Hittite *lokum*, and in the margins I sensed grass that has only ever imbibed the water dripping from an air conditioner that then suddenly dried up and died under someone's cleated leather boot. And Nebuzaradan patted him on his broad shoulders.

In his corner, Nebushazban folded the financial page of the newspaper impatiently and stuck it into the book he was reading for the third time, *Toward a Theory of Urban Unsightliness*, a book that was responsible, in many ways, for his general outlook on things. What bullshit, he felt like shouting at his companions, but instead he restrained himself, and was all deference, as was his way. They got up to leave, but before doing so, Nebuzaradan told the vintner: Thank you, you've subdued the captain of the guard. This was a one-of-a-kind experience. You are my oasis here—I'll be back. Please, start packing your bottles. In three months, you're coming with us to Babylon with all your wine, every last bottle. Don't leave a drop behind you, chief of my vineyard, I want you close to me . . . Just don't forget to bring a corkscrew.

33

ONCE THE LISTS WERE PREPARED, the deportees were put on the light rail in an orderly fashion. Everyone figured that the light rail would take them to the airport in Atarot, but they soon found out that the railroad from the north—that is, from Babylon—had been connected to the Pisgat Ze'ev stop. Thousands of Ammonite and Moabite workers had toiled day and night so as not to lose a moment. Jerusalem, Rabat Bnei Ammon, Ashteroth Karnaim, Damascus, Rivla, Tadmor, Mari, and then northeast along the Euphrates on the old Imperial Assyrian railroad. When they passed by the Sea of Galilee, from the east, everyone looked out at it for the last time—though for many of the deportees this was also the first time that they'd ever seen the sea that was part of the northern kingdom of Israel. They'd seen it only in pictures till now, and because of some sort of optical illusion, the Sea of Galilee appeared to them as completely black. It was something to do with the angle of the light, they assumed.

The journey took seven days, more or less, since they stopped at every station, sometimes for a few minutes and sometimes for several days, and without being notified beforehand. It was permitted to disembark, so many deportees got out and never returned; they abandoned the exodus and settled in towns along the railroad tracks, selling the jewelry they'd brought with them, or else they rented a house and some land and a donkey or goat and planted vegetables and took a few books out of their suitcases and set up a makeshift synagogue in a deserted shoe store. And maybe someone had brought a portable Book of the Law, or else a tablet onto which the Torah had been copied by a scribe, which just needed to be plugged in for a bit so the Torah could reach full power, and there was a rabbi present who ruled that this could serve as a kosher Torah in the hour of their need, and they read from the Torah, and someone started teaching the few children with them to read and write.

The Babylonians received the list of poets to be deported from the Jerusalem Writers' Association. First they rounded up all the prizewinners; they stood beside their beds, watching them muttering in their sleep or simply breathing in and out like any run-of-the-mill guy, and then they cleared their throats and woke the poets up, shaking them by the shoulders. In a single night, they seized all of the poets of Judah, first the famous ones, and the serial winners of prizes and grants, and the habitual invitees at festivals abroad, and then the minor ones, the sort who wandered about town carrying with him the shreds of a newspaper on which was printed the only poem he'd ever published, and even then using a pseudonym, and regretting just a bit that he hadn't used his real name. But for the Babylonians this didn't change a thing. They saw through all the pen names—that is, they'd seized the vice president of the Writers' Association, and he'd furnished everyone's true name with the utmost pleasure. The handful of poets who weren't home the night of the purge were saved from exile for the time being, like deep-sea divers exploring the ocean floor while way up above them a nuclear war was raging, divers who slowly swam up from the depths of the seas to discover that their world had been nullified. After several days, one could have said that all the literature of Judah had been erased.

Jeremiah, who was registered in the offices of the association as living in Anatot, was staying in his rented apartment the night of the purge, and consequently was saved. One of the soldiers who'd entered his parents' house stared for a moment at the sunglasses sitting on their kitchen table and asked, Can I have those? Esther didn't understand the language, and he took her silence for a yes. It was night, and yet the soldier left wearing the sunglasses; he felt more comfortable this way, knocking at doors and waking people up. Several hours later, soldiers arrived from another unit, which was looking not for poets but for doctors. And he sat there, Hilkiah, waiting for them; he sat there in the living room in his white cloak. And Esther wore a doctor's cloak, too, his, because they were worried the soldiers might take him without her.

In the news, they reported on the rounding up of the poets and writers and the fellows of the Democracy Institute and the Psychoanalytic Society and the Spinoza Institute and Confucius Institute and Gilgamesh Institute and the Van Leer Jerusalem Institute—the city had a wide array of research-endowed institutes, which greatly facilitated the rounding up of the intelligentsia—and of the medical specialists, and the senior lawyers, and the tenured professors at the university, and so on and so forth, all according to the orderly spreadsheets assembled and distributed by the Babylonian computer tasked with organizing the exile. It took three hours for all the lists to be printed out, and Jehoiachin scanned the names, which didn't mean anything to him, and nodded.

Jeremiah quietly entered his parents' home through the window at three in the morning. They sat there, the two of them, in armchairs in the living room, both in white cloaks, talking softly, and he, who didn't want to scare them, hung back in the doorway and looked at them glowing there, two halves of a full moon. Yes, it's dreadful to go into exile, Esther said, but to stay here without any friends and acquaintances is no good, either. Do you remember the days after we buried her? You remember saying that you felt like running away, getting as far away as possible? You said, She sent me into exile, she banished me from life. No? You don't remember? That's what you told me. And what did you tell me when I said all that? Jeremiah's father asked, almost in a whisper. I told you we had another child, that we were like a conquered nation who'd had half of its territory devastated, and that, though it was possible to abandon the half that was left, it was also possible to stay and somehow live on it and hold on to it. Do you think we've held on to him long enough? You think he understands what it all meant for us? And Hilkiah said: Sometimes when he spoke I'd see her face in his face, and I'd hear her voice; there were sentences of his that were exactly her sentences, her intonation, the music of her speech. And once I almost told him this, but at the last minute I held back. Maybe I should have said it. I didn't want to frighten him. Esther said: Everything that happened during the pregnancy, my dreams about the dedication, now it's actually happening. It's pretty sad, this prophecy business, it's like catching a virus. Especially when it doesn't really work. He barely drags himself along. I saw him once prophesying near the Smadar Cinema, Hilkiah said. Two beggars stood in front of him, and he tried. He really tried. I couldn't bring myself to watch. I left, I slipped into the movie house in the middle of the feature; I watched the film, something about mountain climbing.

The silence grew between them, and Jeremiah, who'd been leaning his shoulder and brow against the doorjamb with his eyes shut, deliberated as to whether he should clear his throat and enter or just stay put, maybe stay put there forever. And Esther suddenly said, in the dark, I once saw some lost ducks in a cloud—they lost each other in heavy fog. Tell them that you're a nurse, Hilkiah said suddenly. That you're my nurse. That we work together.

Jeremiah quietly turned around and left his parents' home without bidding them goodbye. Esther stared after him. He realized, as he left, that those cloaks were the white flags of their surrender. Clothes of surrender, surrendering attire, he muttered. They're wrapped in their white flags. But it won't help.

The next day, Jeremiah sat on the white Chords Bridge in black clothes that he'd taken from his sister's closet, his head resting on a cable, and gazed at the thousands of deportees standing in long lines in the early days of summer. Train after train left the central station, except that this time, in contrast to the light rail's customary circular route, the cars didn't return. Jeremiah saw his parents standing in one of the lines. Each deportee was scrutinized in a quiet, businesslike manner, and his baggage was inspected, and his identity card was examined. They were then all courteously ushered into a car and led to an assigned seat; each passenger was given a cooler for the journey, a kind of serving tray, like those used on airplanes, and also a basic Hebrew-Babylonian conversation manual. Jehoiachin and his mother boarded a car just like everybody else.

A special car was reserved for prophets. Concerning the prophets, says the Lord—Jeremiah heard the bridge speak to him in the humming of its strings, like a harp in a storm— concerning the prophets, see, I am against those who prophesy lying dreams, says the Lord, and who tell them, and who lead my people astray by their lies and their recklessness, when I did not send them or appoint them, so they do not profit this people at all; who prophesy lies in my name, saying, I have dreamed, I have dreamed. The cables quivered, and Jeremiah's body quivered with them. I have dreamed, I have dreamed, Jeremiah repeated, like an echo.

HE SAW EZEKIEL STANDING IN LINE, a young prophet whom he'd only heard on the radio once or twice, and whom he'd seen years ago at the Bookworm, sitting there stooped over and writing feverishly. He looked an awful lot like Brenner, the writer. Ezekiel entered one of the cars, and, a moment before being swallowed up with the rest of the deportees, spun around as though looking for someone. Jeremiah thought about what a train full of prophets would be like—the early prophets, such as Samuel and Huldah and Natan, and the prophets that barely anyone remembers, like Gad the Visionary or Hanani the Seer, and Elijah and Elisha, and Amos and Jonah, Isaiah and Hosea and Micah and Zephaniah and Nahum and others he himself had forgotten, and then the prophets of the future, like this same Ezekiel. He imagined them seated with their backs facing the train's destination, each car provided with its own prophet, one prophet to a car, all staring, frozen, each one of them with the same word in his or her mouth, the identical word that had to be spoken as they waited for the engineer to come and start the train. And in the train on the parallel track Jeremiah envisioned the kings, from Saul right up to Mattaniah, they, too, sitting in their cars, wearing identical crowns on their heads, as though the crowns were really a single crown under which, every now and then, a new head popped up. Meanwhile, the trains slid inaudibly away.

AFTER THE LAST TRAIN LEFT for the north, and a silence fell over the station and city as on the eve of the Day of Atonement, he returned to his parents' home and went from room to room and shut off the lights they'd left on. They'd left all the lights on, he noted in astonishment, including the small night-light that his sister had called Firefly. He switched off everything. And he stood for a long moment, leaning against his parents' bedroom doorjamb, and suddenly felt like lying on their bed, felt like simply lying on his back a bit in the dark and looking up at the ceiling with his eyes shut. But he didn't step into the room, and he didn't lie down. He strode up to the fuse box closet and switched off the current for the whole house. His back still hurt a lot, but it had stopped preoccupying him a long time ago.

All at once, thousands of homes in Jerusalem had been vacated, and yet Jeremiah, sitting in his parents' empty and darkened home that same evening, saw a light go on in one of the neighboring houses in Anatot. As he peered in the dark through the shutters in his sister's room, he saw that the home of the math teacher, who'd been deported, was being silently looted. The teacher had a rare collection of shells, and someone knew about it and wanted the collection for himself. Jeremiah watched how the thief left the place with an enormous fossilized ammonite shell—two meters in diameter—on his back, as though he were a mover lugging a refrigerator. The deportees from Judah, who tended to be affluent, educated professionals, were also for the most part the owners of handsome, spacious homes, and as if by some law of nature, even as they were on their way to Babylon, the plundering and looting began. A cat sniffs out a deserted house in no time, Jeremiah thought. In another hour, no one will remember the cat that ran off. And though no one knew precisely what started it, at the same time as Judah lost its exiles, people began moving out of Edom—entire families, homeless refugees whose cities Nabataean tribes from the desert had raided. The people of Edom fled their homes by the skin of their teeth, seeing their houses confiscated by the Nabataeans, bearing effigies of their god Qos on camels. They crossed the Jordan close to the southern end of the Dead Sea, and then went westward, as a result of their fear of the invading tribes. When they heard of the deportation of the Jews, they hastened to fill the vacuum yawning in the South Hebron Hills, and some of them made their way up to the empty properties in Jerusalem. Though these properties remained fastened shut with locks and nailed shut with planks of wood, the planks that were meant to protect the houses and their windows served only to mark the homes as vacant, and it was as if the wood were bellowing to the new arrivals: Come and break in, O man of Edom, smallest of the nations! They seized upon this abandoned property with heavy hearts, and they broke the locks in shame. They were also academics and doctors and lawyers, and they told their new neighbors: It's only until the persecution passes. After all, we have no intention of settling here permanently—we'll return to our native Edom in a week or two, a month max. So their neighbors left them alone—not that there was much they could do during those days of general tumult and exile—and the Babylonians allowed it all to happen, or simply weren't paying all that much attention. But none of the squatters would ever return to Edom, neither they nor their children, and they sired sons and daughters and they planted vineyards and they opened a small school and a center for Edomite culture, which grew steadily. And a month passed, and two months, and a year, and the deportees didn't return, and the Edomites tilled the abandoned fields, and they made their pretty ceramic utensils and their copper vessels and their decorated jugs, and they sold them in due course, first as itinerant peddlers and then in a small outdoor market, and in the end they completely took over the pottery business. Now and then there was a case of intermarriage, and the younger generations of both nations began, as is the way of the world, to merge, and there was always someone who wanted to remind everyone: We're all brothers, no? Esau will not always despise Jacob. And they spoke, too, of the massacre that Joab son of Zeruiah committed, and how he'd eliminated all the males in Edom: Let them settle here in compensation. And people whose names were Qosgever and Qosmelech and Shuvnaqos and Qosbanah and Qosnadav and Qosaneh-lee occupied the region south of Jerusalem and, afterward, even neighborhoods in the center of town; within a year, the first nursery school was opened in which the only language spoken was Edomite.

A flock of sparrows would alight every morning on a tree in the neighbors' yard; before her exile, Esther regularly fed them bread, but the day after the deportation they ceased coming. Although most of the residents of Jerusalem were allowed to remain, nearly all of the artists, professionals, professors, writers, poets, artists, prophets, musicians, directors of cultural institutions, delicatessen and wine-store owners, owners of movie theaters as well as their projectionists, and pretty much everyone with an advanced degree were gone. It was clear that there was no point in keeping the university open, so they shut down both campuses in the absence of any senior lecturers. And the Smadar Cinema and the Cinematheque were both shut down, as were the music centers in Mishkenot Sha'ananim and in Ein Kerem, and the writers' cafés and the Artists House were shut down, and the Israel Museum and the Museum of Biblical Archeology and the Science Museum were all shut down; only the Museum of Contemporary Amelek Art remained open, following orders from on high. Almost nobody thought much about it, since business and agriculture went on as usual. And when Adrabah—the last bookstore in Jerusalem—closed, it was clear that that was that . . . even though they'd really reached *that was that* long before.

Along the light-rail tracks that had been laid down from Babylon to Jerusalem, a steady trickle began—one drop at a time, like a neglected kitchen faucet—of voluntary deportees to Babylon, and on the route that the deportee trains had made during the first year of Zedekiah's reign hundreds of new travelers were added during the years that followed; they embarked in order to join voluntarily the exiles who'd been forced to leave. The few remaining musicians went first, since they knew they'd be just as easily understood in that distant place as here, and it had been a long time now since they had been able to make a living in Judah from their music (aside from playing at weddings). After them went the *aspiring* artists, who saw the exile as an opportunity—the ones who hadn't published anything or had a one-man show yet, and consequently didn't appear on any lists. Shortly after the deportation, they couldn't help noticing that there was no one left who would be interested in listening to them or looking at their paintings or reading their poems. So all the artistic dregs of Judah settled in Babylon, along the riverbanks, and played and sang, and poems of weeping and lamentation were printed in the papers, but the songs and melodies they sang and played were of all kinds, and even the dirges were played with a sense of of hope. Some settled in tents close to the site of the new city of Judah in Babylon, whose foundations they started to dig, and they learned Akkadian and Aramaic, and founded clubs for the study of ancient and new sacred books, and also a printing house and a publishing firm, and they married Jewish and Babylonian women. Some emigrated farther, to Persia and Media, the lands of the sons of Japheth, and they scattered farther and farther, not because of swords or tanks but because of the locked gates of the university, and the closed bookstores and the welded-shut doors to the theaters, and the classical-music radio station whose power was shut off in the middle of a concerto.

Those who remained in Judah didn't care much: All the better, let them go, let them emigrate; our king's Zedekiah and our city's Jerusalem. But in Babylon, when the exiled Jews said *the king*, they meant Jehoiachin, the young king imprisoned there, who would come out to his exiled people from his place of confinement once a year and bless them in broken Hebrew.

34

JEREMIAH'S PARENTS DISEMBARKED at the last stop.

All the other passengers had alighted at stations along the Euphrates. To Hilkiah and Esther's surprise, beyond Damascus security measures on the train were nonexistent, and it turned out that the Babylonians didn't care at all whether their Jewish deportees settled in South Babylon, at its center, or in the north. Only the roads leading back to Judah were well guarded, and the return train was canceled until further notice. They traveled northeast. The journey took many days, during which they slept by day and kept their eyes open at night. There were almost no lights along the way, and no signs to speak of. At first light, they'd hang a sheet on the train car's window and fall asleep. There were fewer and fewer passengers; the passengers disembarked the moment they realized that there was no one to tell them where they should get out, seizing on encouraging signs, such as a palm tree or a clothing store: Surely if there's a clothing store it's possible to make a living here, if not from the peddling of sewing machines, then from tailoring; if not from tailoring, then from selling buttons; if not from selling buttons, then from selling thread. But Esther and Hilkiah went on. And when they arrived at the river, after many days, the last passengers in their car abandoned the train. The water persuaded them, like a great rhetorician, to step outside. So they alighted and drank and walked up to the water and shouted in Hebrew at the Euphrates. The water received the foreign words with sympathy. Esther and Hilkiah saw all of this from the window of the train, which they were about to cover with their sheet. They were sitting side by side and holding hands—all four hands were clasped. And, without speaking a word, they decided not to get up, and they didn't even bother to check whether there were any passengers left in the other cars. They simply sat and continued on their way. They didn't know where the train was taking them. Maybe they thought that, at the end of the line, the last car would become the first, and the train would begin its return journey, as on the Jerusalem light rail. They didn't know how many days they'd been traveling. Several—that much was certain, judging from the length of Hilkiah's beard. And then the train gave a sudden lurch, apparently switching to a different track, and the desert scenery that had lately accompanied them was replaced by water. The tracks ran assiduously along the west bank of the Euphrates. They didn't look out the left-hand window; they covered it with flattened-out boxes. This way they also blocked out the new star, which didn't give anyone a moment's rest. Here, too, it doesn't budge, Esther said of it. Maybe there's a place somewhere where it can't be seen, Hilkiah answered. Everything depends on the latitude, he told her. Maybe it can't be seen at the North Pole. But he didn't know for certain. In any case, they looked only to the right, at the river. The water, which was moving in the opposite direction to their train, served as a sort of reference point, like a banister on a darkened staircase you ascend in a dream. And they knew that this river wouldn't go on forever. Maybe there are other trains, she said. Maybe we can cut across and reach the north. What was there, north of Babylon? This they didn't know. And Hilkiah said abruptly, for no particular reason, Ararat. Esther looked and didn't see any mountain.

The light rail raced on. Now and then it stopped at various stations, and people bearing baskets boarded, and Jeremiah's parents bought food and tea from them. The tea darkened with each day of their journey north, and the languages that they heard became more and more alien. It wasn't Babylonian, or Assyrian; they couldn't identify it; they hadn't been wherever people spoke such a language, and never imagined they would be.

Hilkiah's tooth hurt, and he'd run out of painkillers. He pressed two fingers against his jaw. And she watched and asked, It still hurts? And he said, Nails. She waited for him to fall asleep, then opened his mouth and, with two fingertips, seized hold of the tooth and pulled it out, effortlessly. He didn't pay any attention, just kept sleeping. She flung the tooth out the window. And when he woke up, he didn't say a word on the subject.

One morning, a conductor shook them awake—all of a sudden this old conductor appeared—and he signaled that this was it, they'd arrived, it was the end of the line. The train had come to a standstill, resting on its belly on a beach. The track simply stopped up ahead, and the rails were rusty at their terminus because of the lapping water. The exiles didn't know where they were. Still, the sun shone pleasantly, and they disembarked after two weeks inside one railroad car. Esther felt dizzy, but Hilkiah held her. They left their suitcases on the train; the conductor brought them out and ran after them to hand them their luggage. A jetty poked warily into the water, and they walked on it like two veteran acrobats treading a tightrope, only for a few paces, but they wouldn't fall—they acted as each other's handrails. Suddenly a strong wind rose, and Hilkiah's yarmulke flew into the water and drifted for a bit. He didn't bend over. He had a phial filled with blood in his pocket. Later he will empty it into the sea. When it gets dark. When he's left alone.

Behind them, the train was being taken apart for salvage;

there was nothing else to do with it after its overlong journey: the return trip was canceled. And Hilkiah asked his wife, staring at the water, Esther, what is this place? The conductor who had brought them their suitcases had also taken down the white sheet from the window, and now he spread it out on the shoreline, on the wet seashells—over there, where the jetty extended into the sea.

35

ELIAZAR GREW FROM YEAR TO YEAR, and he soon turned four and then five, but Zedekiah was busy from morning to night—touring the city with his pair of industrious Babylonian inspectors, applying himself to the study of the Babylonian language at every available moment, and firming up his muscles as though fortifying a city—so his son's education he left for the most part to Tukulti and Noa. But sometimes he'd read to the little boy out of various poetry collections, lightly revising the poems. For example, the lines:

> I always always wanted Eliazar
> To tell you many words of love

And once he went up to Eliazar when the boy was brushing his teeth in front of the mirror and told him, in the mirror,

> You're a shining mint plant, Eliazar,
> Engrossed with mild thoughts

But the child didn't understand the strange language of poetry, not least because Mattaniah would pop up out of nowhere with these poems, waving his arms all of a sudden, without warning, like a magician with a clown's nose who waylays you in the street and starts yanking scarves from his sleeve. Eliazar felt the anguish in his father's voice when he stood on a stool in the middle of Eliazar's fifth-birthday party and, facing his little friends, declaimed,

> I know I'll die soon, Eliazar,
> Lo every tree beams already and shines,
> Eliazar

Once, Zedekiah took him to visit the graves of his forefathers Kings David and Solomon. The graves were in a sort of cellar. Zedekiah insisted that they go down there alone, just the two of them, without any security guards, and so it was. They held long, flickering tapers in their hands. The wax melted and scorched the boy's hand. His father kneeled before David's tomb, held on to the stone, and shouted, Save us, save us! Eliazar gazed at the shadows on the walls. Their tapers were placed on Solomon's tomb nearby. And suddenly they were snuffed out.

That same night, Noa found the boy sitting up in bed and looking into the dark from the high palace window. Eliazar, go to sleep, she told him. There's nothing there. But he replied, I saw the bat! and stared at his mother, his eyes shut tight.

And Zedekiah, on his way to bed on the ground floor, went around to see what all the shouting was about. When he found Noa standing there half naked, he said: Why are you walking around like that? You want the boy to have nightmares? And he noticed again how she'd gained weight since giving birth. What had first caught his eye about her, back when they met, was her slimness and her severe, sunburned Moabite look, but now nothing was left of any of that. Above all, he was repulsed by her tattoos, which in the past had been pretty and set firmly on her skin like drawings, but were now flaccid. Several weeks later, he hinted and then said outright that he expected her to do something about it, and she said that, yes, she'd lose weight, but it wasn't that simple. And she tried an array of diets. First she stopped eating wheat and wheat products, but this only made her ravenous, and she replaced wheat with fruits at best but, at worst and more commonly, with sweets. Looking through Mattaniah's eyes—she couldn't bring herself to call him Zedekiah, even though it was the law—she realized that none of it was working. He hadn't touched her much since she'd given birth, and though at first she was comfortable with that, after two, three months she understood that something had happened. Her close-cropped hair started growing back, and she didn't have it cut again, though he detested long hair: What, are you a lamb? he felt like telling her, but he stifled his gnawing resentments until he couldn't bear it anymore, and one day she caught him in one of the compound's many bedrooms screwing a minor that someone had procured for him.

He poured out the bitterness of his heart to Nebuzaradan, and the Babylonian listened attentively and then said in Akkadian: Look, it's a well-known predicament, in all the occupied kingdoms I come across the same problem. One thing is sure beyond all doubt, and this is that the queen needs an overhaul, and the king needs a few more women—no big deal! To make do in life with a single, solitary woman is for insignificant grocers, for postmen, for some puny poet . . . not for a king. And when Zedekiah wondered what Nebuzaradan meant by *overhaul*, the Babylonian said, Yeah, have her overhauled, why not? She'll only thank you. Zedekiah figured that Nebuzaradan maybe just meant that Noa should have her hair styled and said, Yes, why not?

A month later, a plastic surgeon arrived from Babylon along with a stylist, and men came and took Noa. They waited till she was asleep, then put an etherized mask over her eyes and mouth; still she tried to fight them, and Tukulti barked like crazy, but

Zedekiah held the leash tightly and said to Noa's masked eyes, Relax, it's only a beauty parlor. The annual ceremony marking his coronation was approaching; he couldn't ascend to the dais of honor accompanied by all her extra calories and that perm of hers, in which God only knew what was swarming, and those loose Moabite inscriptions etched on her shoulders and arms. And so they took Noa to Hadassah Mount Scopus, and the Babylonian plastic surgeon was already waiting for her there. When she woke from the anesthesia, they brought her a mirror; she looked at her hair, and it was short, as in the old days, and attractively colored with black, and all the surplus kilograms had been removed, to her astonishment and alarm, and they'd also given her breast implants, a gift from Nebuzaradan to the King of Judah. Everything was still bandaged, but in time the bandages would be removed, and she would return home like a bonbonnière. They'd removed all the tattoos from her Moab days when they lightened her skin tone *complet*, and they'd also injected permanent makeup as well as a monitored electrolysis facial and hair removal: We've given her a ten-thousand-mile overhaul! Nebuzaradan cracked. We changed her oil and replaced her carburetor and souped up her engine; she's like an eighteen-year-old right off the lot; you gave us a housewife and we delivered you a bimbo; you gave us a quiche and we've given you back a strawberry. Zedekiah gazed with bulging eyes at the amazing beauty who came home on high heels, though with her head lowered. And Eliazar looked at her and started hollering.

In those days, Zedekiah was still roaming the streets, largely with Nebushazban, who had big plans for the city. The closing of numerous local institutions did not escape the eyes of the Babylonian, and he told Zedekiah that it was high time to set right the monstrous redevelopment of Jerusalem that had taken place during Jehoiakim's reign and earlier, the product of worse than bad taste. Believe me, Zedekiah, he said, I've seen hideous buildings through the length and breadth of the empire—I've seen villas painted red and black in the cities on the coastal plain in Elam, and tenement blocks for one thousand families in Shushan, and waterfront high-rise hotels all along the Mediterranean—but the likes of this here I've never seen: all these buildings with fake fortifications, the new Bezalel building, and the Clal building, and the Hamashbir department store, and the new Central Bus Station. And that's not even close to the full list—just think of that horrific palace where you live. This doesn't do any honor to the king. And Zedekiah said, One can argue over taste in architecture, one can define all this as enlightened brutalism, as popular modernism for the masses, and I actually— Here Nebushazban cut him off and said: No, one *can't* argue; there's nothing to dispute on this point. And since there's no argument, we'll raze all these buildings to the ground, and if its brutalism you want, we'll apply brutalism against brutalism, we'll undertake a de-brutalization. And Zedekiah agreed and said, as he always did, Come to think of it, why not? And the Babylonian said: We'll demolish them; we'll carry out a material deconstruction of the urban architecture in the heart of your metropolis. (Nebushazban liked to talk critical theory.) We'll bring Jerusalem back to the days when it was a city of human dimensions, he went on, we'll conduct a reflexive de-territorialization of the local architecture. In other words, a double-recursive ironization of the master plan, a retroactive palimpsestization of the a-grammatological elements in the architectural complex.

And so began the years of rebuilding the city from scratch. Nebushazban declared that he would knead the city beneath his hands, he would mold her and prepare her for her glorious future. He didn't intend to waste his time in this city drinking wine, like his friend the glutton; he intended to leave his mark on the city. And the first stage in his plan was this: within two days, he scheduled the demolition of every building in Jerusalem that he considered *improper.* Until we cut the skyline back so it doesn't block out the hills, this won't be a proper city, Nebushazban said, and Zedekiah again agreed. How could he not agree? After all, he was a vassal king, though no one ever mentioned this, and in particular not the Babylonians.

Bulldozers were ordered to raze and level. Streets were widened, broadened into avenues. In a single day, the entire neighborhood of Nahlaot was removed from the map, and work began to replace it with an overpass in order to divert some traffic from the infuriatingly gridlocked city center. Then they turned Gaza Street into a six-lane thoroughfare, and next on the itinerary was to pave a *ruler road*, utterly straight and flat, from the Babylonian military encampment in Ramat Rachel straight into the Old City. Nebushazban did actually place a ruler on the map, drawing a line and then another line, telling the local king, whose name he'd forget every now and then, Tomorrow get this tarred for me, Mr. King. And, as an example to the masses, before the ruler road was put in, Nebushazban's urban-renewal project was officially inaugurated with the demolition of the entire Holyland complex. They dynamited all the buildings at the same time, regardless of size, and they filled in the Venetian canals because of their awful kitschiness, in Nebushazban's word. Jeremiah, who'd ascended to the roof of his parents' home in Anatot with his father's radio, listened to the news reports in a kind of serene despair, calm and devoid of bitterness—at this stage, nothing shocked him anymore. A few days later, he saw the Bezalel Academy of Arts and Design on Mount Scopus turned into a heap of white dust in less than an hour. Bezalel, really one for the books, Nebushazban lectured at the festive wrecking ceremony at the Mount Scopus amphitheater: Imagine having erected such an eyesore here, facing the desert. The eye refuses to open on such a sight; its lashes gum up out of sheer disgust. And to think that *art* was taught there, he said, horrified. What sort of art could one possibly learn inside a space that's utterly repellent? From a safe distance, his gloved hands lowered the plunger attached to the munitions charge, but maybe there was a faulty connection—nothing seemed to have happened. Then he raised his head and saw the devastation: his headphones were just so good that he hadn't heard the detonation.

And so they moved from one neighborhood to another, carefully excising everything expendable, like a copyeditor who's drained her sweet black morning coffee and, razor-sharp and focused, takes up her red pen with relish to strike out every egregious and excessive word from a text. In this way, however slowly, the city was copyedited and reduced to more humane dimensions: Oh, the laborious polish of the copyedit! Oh, the erasure that lets a little air back into these clumps of text and so shortens the urban novel, which was always a bit too bulky, and in any case unreadable! And many residents were impressed: Yes, he's finally done what we've always hoped for in our hearts. You can call it destruction, but destruction is in the nature of a city, demolition makes room for renewal, and our city really couldn't bear all those dreadful buildings for much longer, those monstrosities towering higher than two floors, even three—all that weight on the shoulders of such a small city.

Almost every night, the king would return home, coated in dust and lime wash, to his small child and his young wife; each act of demolition was accompanied by a royal ceremony, and he smashed bottle after bottle on the walls of towers and other doomed architectural atrocities. Even the Chords Bridge was blown up, but it only collapsed in part; its remnants were allowed to stay and become a memorial of sorts to the renewal of the city at the hands of Babylon.

After the destruction of Bezalel and the Holyland (the historic palace in the Old City reverted to being the only royal palace, and Zedekiah was forced to uproot himself and resettle in the old palace, which had been his childhood home) came the turn of the Clal building and the New Central Bus Station and the Wolfson Towers and the student dorms and the tenement blocks facing the pretty valleys of Kiryat Yovel and Kiryat Menachem; and on and on and on. After several months, it was necessary to stop, because their supply of dynamite had been exhausted and they had to put in an order for a fresh supply from Babylon. There was so much to destroy in Jerusalem—the more food one is served, the greater one's appetite grows. And on one of those nights when Zedekiah came home covered with dust, Noa stepped into the shower while he was rinsing himself off, and she removed her robe and stood before him naked. And he looked at her and said, You're amazing, Noa, but it's . . . I have to . . . it's a bit too much for me. And he pointed at her body. And he realized he was afraid of her. He drew his eyes away, and didn't turn back around until she was gone.

36

THE DAYS OF THE NEW KINGDOM had come. Once again, the currency in Judah was all replaced, banknotes as well as coins, and the king's vehicles were fueled up, and life returned to normal. And Mattaniah started zealously making a note of everything that needed to be fixed in his kingdom, so he could draw such matters to the attention of his ministers at their meetings. First, it was necessary to cancel parking fees for residents of the city. They pay a municipal property tax—why take an additional bite for parking? It's scandalous; this is *their* city, after all. And, in the same flutter of activity, he said: We should close off the city center from all private car traffic and restore the city to its residents, so they can walk about freely. And once a week we'll ban *all* vehicles, as on the Day of Atonement. Everyone loves it, so why not? What else? Chicks. He'd heard that thousands of male chicks were ground up every day in machines, and he immediately wrote an injunction and decreed that, beginning tomorrow, there would be no more grinding! And he also banned battery cages, while he was at it. Fowl that were created to walk upon the earth are cooped up their entire lives in what is essentially solitary confinement—you don't have to be a vegan in order to be revolted by such cruelty. And he forbade loud parties after ten o'clock at night. Just because she's celebrating her birthday, does that mean I have to go to work the next day half asleep? And he legalized the lighter drugs. After all, it's clear to everyone that alcohol is more dangerous than weed—by all means, light up, and take a breather from all your scheming. Let the people rest, let them get high, let them look around—just not straight ahead. What else? The chickens put him in mind of the morning when he'd heard that cattle were being shipped by sea and through the canal to and from Jerusalem, with thousands dying on the way from suffocation and hunger. Not that this bothered anyone, or kept them from eating these wretched refugees, who were slaughtered upon arrival. And so the king said: It stops as of tomorrow. No one in my kingdom will load a cow or a lamb on a boat or ship. After all, there's a limit even to cruelty. What else? Oh yes, real-estate agencies. What's all that about? Let the people work it out among themselves; let them advertise on bulletin boards and sell and buy houses and apartments on their own. Why should a third party reap the benefits? It fouls up the market. And he set a fixed price for all books: I mean, you aren't paying for the number of pages but for the content. It's ridiculous that a thick book should cost more than a slim one. A book's a book. And he decreed that no one person or corporation was allowed to own more than one bookstore at a time. Everyone's sick and tired of all these takeovers and mergers; the book trade should remain small-scale, one small bookstore and then another and another. No big-box bookstores, no huge hangars full of books—it's a debasement of literature.

Over the following days, he made more and more proclamations, seeking the counsel of his ministers and advisers and wife and poet friends. Everyone had to tell him what they thought needed fixing, and he wrote it down, and signed decree after decree. He prohibited housecleaning performed by anyone not living in the house in question: It's unacceptable that someone else should come and scrub the inside of your toilet seat for a few piasters! And he prohibited prostitution, intending to put a stop to the practice entirely, instituting the death penalty for pimps in the process: I don't understand how anyone can live in peace with this sort of thing going on. Just imagine for a moment that one of these women was your own daughter; would you be so sanguine about it then? After all, they've all got fathers, the girls! Or—what?—do you think they don't? He slapped the table in front of the minister of police, who tried explaining to the king that this had been the way of the world since time immemorial, lending support to his words by citing various texts. And close down all those casinos, the king added. Where do those whores hang around, he shouted, if not in our casinos? It's one form of immorality encouraging another. People come to gamble, and some whore sits beside them at the table, and then they lose everything and go up to their room with the whore so the night shouldn't be a total waste, and they fuck the whore, but it's usually all over within two minutes, and then they go back downstairs to the casino to try and compensate for the shame of having failed in bed, and they pawn a gold watch or a wedding ring in order to get a couple more chips, and again they gamble and again they lose, and again the whore watches them lose, and there's no end to it. The world's far too precious to be wasted on casinos and prostitution, and if people can't grasp this by simply looking around at the world, then they'll get the message soon enough by virtue of the king's new laws. There's no point having a king if a king can't educate his people, he thought.

Anyone who publishes a book of poetry deserves to receive a monthly allowance, he decreed. And the minister of culture said, alarmed, There aren't that many poets left; most of them have been relocated to Babylon. All the more reason, Zedekiah said. Every published poet who's managed to stick around will receive a stipend. Bring me the list of poets, and mark down the ones who've remained, he said. And the minister left and later returned with the list in his hand, and it transpired that fewer than ten poets out of ten thousand had somehow evaded deportation. Zedekiah went over each name, and next to some of them he drew an X, because in his eyes these particular poets weren't worthy of a stipend—one X and then another X and another—and then next to a few names he put a V. He saw his own name there, his old name, and hesitated for a moment as to whether he deserved an X or a V. He finally decided to award himself a V, and then felt ashamed and got out a black felt-tip pen and crossed off the poet that he had been, Mattaniah, before he continued down the list and saw Jeremiah. At this name, his heart stopped for an instant, before his hand unreservedly gave his old acquaintance a V.

He called in all his ministers and advisers, most of whom he knew only from the newspapers—Jehoiakim's people, the living incarnations of innumerable intrigues and conspiracies. A nest of vipers hisses in the palace, Noa, he told her later. How can anyone deal with people about whom the only thing you can know for certain, and I mean *for certain*, is that they're lying to you, telling you only what they think you want to hear? And I, Mattaniah said, a poet who has been crowned king against his will, must speak to them, and answer them, and consult with them. What sort of advice can they give me—the viper, and the adder, and my minister of finance the anaconda?

I should have fired all of you and appointed Jeremiah the prophet as my deputy king, he told his ministers at the opening of their weekly Cabinet meeting—deputy king, or at least a consultant. The serpents raised their heads and nodded, and then one snake laughed and laughed until you could see the venomous glands roiling in his throat. Cut it out, Zedekiah said, and he tried to remind his serpents of the children they'd been, of their humanity, before their arms and legs fell off, before they became covered with scales, before their tongues became so swift, and their eyes and whispers. And he recalled a line from one of Jeremiah's poems: *See, I am letting snakes loose among you, adders that cannot be charmed, and they shall bite you.*

Ladies and gentlemen, my distinguished ministers, he said. If anything is clear to me, it is this, and it's on the basis of this observation that we will conduct all of the kingdom's affairs: the world, as it stands, is insufferable. It's unbearable from moment to moment—that's my axiom. And if we haven't committed suicide yet, well, the least we can do is take every possible step to remedy the situation. We must live our lives, he said, in a completely different way. Any ideas? And there was a black racer who raised his head and hissed, We'll give all poets a monthly stipend of thirty shekels. But from the other side of the table an adder rose and said: Friends, you're draining the royal coffers. Where are we going to get thirty shekels a month for each poet? Thirty? Maybe thirty a *year*, but monthly? Twenty-five, tops! Not a shekel more! And an anaconda shook her head, and all the other serpents found themselves having the same thought: She'll swallow us like a whale scooping up a school of sardines. The adder asked, hesitantly: Twenty? Fifteen? And the king said: Friends, what are you talking about? There are fewer than ten poets left in Judah. And a cobra looked at a printout of their CVs and said, Six, to be more precise, and my king is the first among them. Zedekiah wondered where the other poets on his list had disappeared to, but held his tongue and then said, Okay, so I can see there's no point in passing special legislation for six people . . . And the cobra replied: Anyway, out of the six, there's a prophet who's in hiding—no one knows where he is—and offering him a stipend would be like putting guns into the hands of our enemies. As for the other four, look, we'll sell them into slavery, so in the end all we'll have left is one poet in the entire kingdom, only one poet. That simplifies things, and since the literature budget is grosso modo half a million, I propose we vote to allot that half a million a month to our last remaining poet, who'll serve as a trustee with unlimited right of action to the funds earmarked for the poets of Judah until further notice, and we'll act as the directorate. Zedekiah said: Are you nuts? I don't need it and don't want it. I wasn't talking about myself at all. Knock it off. I'm removing the proposal from the table. Now I want to prohibit experiments on animals. Just thinking about all those labs drives me nuts—the experiments they perform on cats in order to test some damn perfume or dandruff shampoo or even real medicine, sawing off the heads of monkeys, and other night-mares I can't even bring myself to speak about out loud. And we've got to stop parents from abusing their children; we've got to initiate a new parental educational program. I want all pro-spective parents to sign a contract before the child's birth, detail-ing their commitment to the future citizen, what they will and won't do for and to the kid. After all, everything in this world has a contract attached—you buy a pack of cigarettes and it's a con-tract between you and the store—but between you and your child there's no contract to speak of, no protocol. Anything goes in families; you don't have to commit yourself to anything; you can ignore your kid, you can raise your voice to your kid in anger. I'm going to put a stop to it, I'll teach the moms and the dads the basics; I'll give them a good foundation for parenthood. And while I'm on the subject, I also want to put a complete stop to all forms of pornography. It just makes no sense, no sense at all, that girls who happened to have turned into women ... The anaconda wiped a tear from her lidless eye and said: A momentous act of reform! What a reform, praise the Lord! Yes, exactly, Zedekiah said, and rebuked the racer: What's this business with the poets? It hasn't been put on the table at all ... And the anaconda drew out a black attaché case and placed it on the tabletop without saying a word. Write this down, the king said, and everyone cop-ied down diligently: No trees in Judah will be uprooted, cut down, or otherwise removed; every tree is the product of tens, hundreds of years' worth of labor. It's out of the question that they should be killed just so someone can make a stool or some-thing. And the emptying of waste into our riverbeds will be stopped immediately. Water is sacred, water is the very essence of life; henceforth, we will not pollute what is sacred, Zedekiah dictated. I also want to forbid the tearing of or disposal of cobwebs, he said. Such a marvelous phenomenon, and yet people are always taking out their brooms and pulling down these little wonders from the corners of their rooms. And I don't want any bad books to be published anymore. Only good books. The bad ones we can pulp. What, I'm being unrealistic? Look, I want there to be a decent selection in the bookstores. It makes no sense for any average Joe to pay to have his nonsense printed and consequently take up a deserving book's place. Tell me if my logic is faulty!

The discussion went on, with all of Zedekiah's proposals being passed. There wasn't a single nay. The ministers ratified everything: the bill that outlawed caging animals; the bill that outlawed child labor; the bill that imposed the Sabbath as a day of rest on man and beast alike; the bill setting up free medical care for man and beast alike; the bill immediately doubling the salary of all physicians while cutting their office hours in half; the bill prohibiting and canceling all literary prizes, of whatever stripe (It's a bitter disgrace, the king said, to receive a monetary prize for the work of one's mind!); the bill enforcing tolerance for all the gods of the region and the prohibition of smashing effigies and statues; the bill forbidding child sacrifice to Moloch; the bill banning war—this last ban being the gravest of all bans. And so on and so forth, more and more bills that he thought up at length in his office at the palace and all through the long nights.

Legislation progressed at a fast clip, almost as fast as the shredder they kept running one flight down, into whose maw the Cabinet secretary, a young and promising eel, carefully fed all the proposed bills after the conclusion of this and every meeting. And Zedekiah began to feel that the fabric of the world was finally being repaired, that the world's bruised skin and broken bones were slowly healing, that a first generation of chicks was being born without the clatter of grinding machines overhead, that all the furnaces of Moloch in the city were being extinguished and growing cold, that all men were laying down their arms, and every woman in bondage was at last free to fix her hair in the good light of day. Give me half a year—he told the serpents, and then the multitudes of his subjects during his rallies, and the media, too—a year at most, and I'll fix things up! This is where it all begins, he said, and after we set an example to the world, the rest of the nations will see that our way is best and will do as we have done. Give me five years and the world will be cured of most of its terminal diseases! We'll stop the glaciers from melting, we'll forbid the maddening use of plastic bags! he confidently told the microphones, and he heard his own voice resounding back to him when he rehearsed his speech from the top of the palace's highest tower, at whose base half a million people were expected to gather in a few hours.

As he stood there giving his speech to the empty, open expanse, he remembered, for some reason, that he'd taken a book out of the library some time ago that he'd neglected to return, and that undoubtedly he'd have to pay a heavy fine for it, and this vexed him, and he cut short his speech. He returned to his room, having decided to look for the library book, but he was distracted and glanced again at the black attaché case that the anaconda had forgotten, as it were, on the ministerial table. What's she got in there, he wondered, alarmed, maybe snake eggs? Maybe her black offspring have already emerged, and they're curled one inside another in the dark, and they'll lash out and bite me? But all that was in there, of course, was cash. And the king forgot all about his library book.

37

A YEAR WENT BY, two years went by, and the proposed bills were slowly but exhaustively processed by the appropriate committees—or so the king was told, at least. In the meantime, a number of rebel cells were uncovered on the margins of the kingdom. And the minister of defense arrived with the official figures, substantiated by reliable data. And there was no choice: the king had to strap on a bandolier, had to wage war. Zedekiah's battles were no more than local policing sallies, but his minister of defense understood the mentality of kings, so he made sure to let the king kill a few agitators personally. And Zedekiah, who thought he'd be repulsed by it all, was—all of a sudden—no longer repulsed. He mowed down the rebels from inside a hovering chopper, while the minister of defense hollered: Clean them out, Your Majesty, clean them right out. Soon the rot will reach the root—over there, behind those boulders—so shove your tooth-pick in all the way, let the gums bleed! Baalgezer, who had also served as minister of defense for Zedekiah's brother Jehoiakim, as well as for his father, Josiah, and was related to the sons of the Zeruiah dynasty, and had his white hair and his beard dyed a blazing red, sat next to him and held the cartridge belt for him, feeding him ammo, while Zedekiah, his eyes shielded by protective glasses and his ears securely plugged, aimed down into the alleyways and polished off the human tartar like dental floss dipped in wax and lead. And he told the minister of defense, I saw some of them dashing into that building over there, and the minister of defense said: You're an ace strategist, my king— nothing escapes your probing eyes. Even I, with all my defense experience, didn't notice that. If I have found favor in your eyes, my king, we'll replace your light arms with something that has a bit more weight. And he gestured toward a red button. Zedekiah asked, What's that? And the minister said, Let's have it be a surprise for Your Majesty. Aim here . . . a bit to the right . . . no, no, not in that direction . . . Now lock the sights . . . yes . . . Now push . . . Push hard, don't be scared . . . And when Zedekiah raised his eyes, the building was already a cloud of dust billowing up and sinking down again.

And so they'd set out, on the Sabbath, after the public morning-prayer, the minister and deputy minister and the King of Judah, to restore order. After all, a king who doesn't set his house in order only increases the mess; a king who doesn't clean only defiles; a king who doesn't hover above his citizens from time to time with a machine gun is a goner. Your citizens can only see you when you're high up in the air, no? And these gangs terrorizing the law-abiding Judeans have to be eliminated, yes? It's tough to see how anybody might think differently. Of course, I'd like nothing better than to ignore them and let them go on organizing and arming themselves, Zedekiah told Noa, but then, by the time they show up at the palace gates to slit Eliazar's throat, it'll be too late to do anything about it. It's easy for you to criticize, but I'm not hearing you give me any other practical solutions. I mean, it's not as though I'm raiding entire cities like the Egyptians and Assyrians, and I'm hardly impaling children on poles, am I? And I've never once burned a village. Come out with me on the chopper, just once, he told her. See for yourself.

I'll even let you gun down a few people, he shouted as the helicopter hatch slammed behind him.

NOW IT CAME TO PASS, after all these things, in the fourth year of Zedekiah's reign, that Broch set forth from his home in Beit Hakerem to the old-new palace in the Old City. He had disguised himself as a prophet and given himself the name Hanania ben Azur, and printed himself a calling card. He wished to counsel the king, and bowed down before the king. And he said, Thus says the Lord of Hosts, the God of Israel: I have broken the yoke of the King of Babylon. Within two years I will bring back to this place all the vessels of the Lord's house, which King Nebuchadnezzar of Babylon took away from this place and carried to Babylon. And Jeconiah, your brother's son, and all the exiles from Judah who went to Babylon I'll bring back to this place, says the Lord, on the light rail. For I will break the yoke of the King of Babylon.

And Zedekiah didn't recognize him, because Broch had grown a thick beard and pitched his hair up on his head like a tent, and he was wearing a loud checkered suit, and wraparound shades, like Ray Charles; also like Ray Charles, he swayed from side to side as he performed. And Zedekiah said, Look, Ray Charles, I'm not going to say I don't like what you're telling me, but it must be clear to you, Mr. Charles, that I'm taking a huge risk even listening to this stuff. Everything's been going pretty smoothly in my kingdom, or haven't you noticed? All I need to do is keep my two Babylonians in food and drink, demolish a couple of unnecessary buildings from time to time, and pay taxes. And the prophet said, Allow me, Your Majesty, if I have found favor in your eyes, to remind the king of Pharaoh Psammetichus's latest conquests . . . And Zedekiah said, Psammetichus? And the prophet said, Psammetichus, Psammetichus. Two years ago, a new king ascended to the throne in Egypt. He slid on down to Cush and gamboled on up to Sidon; he crept up on her and knocked on her bolted doors. And my noble lord certainly remembers that it wasn't too long ago that Egypt ruled over the Euphrates, and what was will be again, and there is nothing new under the sun. I have prophesied in your ear, lo, the days are coming when Pharaoh will return to drink from the waters of the Euphrates, and he'll drink from the waters of the Tigris, too, and therein he will wash away the blood of Babylon. You'll do as you please, of course, the prophet said, but when Pharaoh goes back home to Egypt, he won't be happy to hear that some of his protectorates have pledged allegiance to that little Satan Nebuchadnezzar—that some of his vassals have been plying Babylonian officials with the choicest wines and delicacies their lands have to offer. That corpulent captain of the guard has already become a byword for gluttony and a cautionary tale among the rabbinate; he's been pillaging every refrigerator and oven in Judah, emptying them like a human vacuum cleaner. Or, okay, let's talk economics, Broch-Hanania said. The king has invested all his money in a single stock, a single company, and its name is Nebuchadnezzar, Inc. Don't you think it's time to diversify your portfolio a bit? Wouldn't that be the wisest course of action? Leaving aside the question of risk, isn't it true that different investments tend to prosper in different market conditions? It's not too different from nature—are you following me? Some trees thrive in dry and cold conditions but shrivel up in a tropical climate. Other trees flourish in heat and humidity but wouldn't last a minute on the summit of a windswept mountain—and then there are trees that are best adapted to living in deserts, the prophet said. Can bananas grow at the North Pole? he asked. And Zedekiah answered, flustered, No, bananas can't grow there. So has the king understood? asked the prophet. And Zedekiah, who hadn't the faintest idea what Broch was talking about, said, Sure, at least as much as a person sitting in front of an investment consultant who's ashamed to show his ignorance regarding his own money, he said. To that extent, it makes complete sense. So what do you suggest? And the prophet said: I'll put it as simply as possible. The advice of this consultant is that, if someone doesn't believe in the Babylonian shekel, he isn't obliged to buy exclusively Babylonian bonds. It wouldn't be a disaster if he were to open a little sideline and invest in some Egyptian bonds, too, and even trade a few piasters for a bit of solid Egyptian gold . . . I don't see any problem there. It isn't that Your Majesty is rebelling against the King of Babylon; it isn't written anywhere that it's forbidden for my king to throw a little capital in Egypt's direction as well . . . Ever since your great brother died, the payments to Egypt have ceased, have they not? It'd be a pity if you repeated your brother's mistake. Let's try to learn something from history. You don't want to end up like him, in a bowl of hummus, do you? And Zedekiah shuddered and said, So what you're telling me here is that this is a free market, that there's no reason for an investor like me not to back some safe secondary stocks, just as a form of insurance, right? Like shoving a couple of dollars under the carpet—there's no law against carpets . . . And the prophet said, Right, exactly, carpets.

You'll see, Hanania-Broch told King Zedekiah, in another two years the Babylonian yoke will be broken, and then, at the right moment, you'll be able to show your portfolio to Pharaoh's ambassador. And, believe me, he'll show up—Pharaoh always comes back in the end—always, always. Babylon, Assyria, Media, Elam, Sumer, Akkad—kingdoms come and kingdoms go, but Egypt is eternal, like Jerusalem, as it is written, Egypt and Jerusalem for ever and ever. We're not like those fly-by-night kingdoms up north, okay? Be nice to Pharaoh and Pharaoh will be nice to you—that's only common sense, am I wrong?

So, like, what are the action items here, what practical steps do we take? asked King Zedekiah. And the prophet said, First of all, you can be sure that you're not alone, that other kingdoms also know what you now know—the kingdoms of Tyre and Sidon, for example, and Moab and Ammon and Edom. If I have found favor in your eyes, my king, you might invite these kingdoms around for a modest buffet lunch, and also make sure to invite an Egyptian observer. I think Koniyahu ben Elnathan, His Majesty's minister of the armed forces, has a pretty good command of Egyptian—no surprise, since his wife is . . . Well, maybe my king could put a helicopter at his disposal, so that he could head over to Egypt by the end of the day? Anyway, over lunch, we can all conduct a wholly academic-philosophical discussion about what might happen on the day after Babylonian rule ends in one of her satellite kingdoms. Did you know, the Babylonians call all our cities and kingdoms Hatti? It sounds like someone spitting, which is apropos, since from their point of view we're all inferiors, nobodies whose sole purpose is to pay them taxes and provide them with olive oil. But we're a bit more than that—isn't that so, my king? And Zedekiah chuckled: Yes, a bit.

Several days later, in the rabbinate, the King of Edom and the King of Moab and the King of Ammon and the King of Tyre and the King of Sidon and the King of Judah sat and ate sandwiches and drank wine and waited for the interpreter to arrive. The King of Tyre talked with the King of Sidon, but didn't understand a word spoken by the rest of the kings, while the King of Moab just about managed to make himself understood to the King of Judah, and the King of Ammon spoke to the King of Judah with practically no difficulty at all, and the King of Edom communicated mainly via gestures with the Kings of Tyre and Sidon, and only the Moabite was able to speak fluently with the Ammonite, or would have done so if not for the deep enmity between the two. Anyway, everyone somehow spoke to everyone, having to restrain their laughter, since all their languages were just cognate enough to sound on the verge of correctness without quite being *right*, which meant that everyone sounded a bit stupid to everyone else, and it would have been better, needless to say, given the matter at hand, to have sought out the assistance of an experienced interpreter who could have taken in the various Canaanite dialects and translated them into a form conducive to a serious political discussion.

What's with the interpreter? the King of Tyre asked the King of Sidon. They were relatives, in effect, shackled one to the other by numerous hubristic and incestuous ties, cousins who split their spheres of influence along the Phoenician shoreline. *We don't need any translator*, the Sidonite answered, *but these guys here . . .* and he pointed his chin at the Ammonite and Moabite, sitting on opposite sides of the table, and it seemed that at any given moment one would leap on the other with a drawn dagger in hand. Zedekiah glanced at his old Assyrian watch. The watch had been ticking a lot of late; that is, it was always ticking, of course, as watches do, but all of a sudden Zedekiah had become painfully aware of this ticking, and it was driving him nuts, particularly in the middle of the night, when things were at their most silent. He had gone to the palace's watchmaker and told him, *Fix it up, it's ticking.* And the watchmaker, feeling his oats on that day, said, *Sure, a watch ticks; it's not broken, Sire; it's just how watches are made, they're made to tick.* And Zedekiah shouted, *So cancel its ticking, watchmaker!* And the watchmaker said, *That's impossible.* And Zedekiah roared: *I'll cut you into pieces! Don't be fresh with me!* And, brazen, the watchmaker peered up at the king through his loupe and said, *It would be like extinguishing the sun; you can't separate a watch from its tick.* And Zedekiah said, *I couldn't care less, I couldn't care less.* And the watchmaker at last removed the lens from his eye with a shaking hand.

Zedekiah's greatest fear was, of course, that the Babylonians would hear of the summit, for such a gathering in itself would smell of sedition even before the first word was voiced. Half hidden in the shadows, on a bench, poking at a fruit salad with a toothpick, sat the Egyptian observer, holding in one hand an unofficial proposal from Pharaoh. Beside him sat his personal interpreter, who translated only into Egyptian.

And soon there ensued a discussion on the division of the spoils—meaning the division of the entire Middle East—on the day after Babylon fell. The Tyrians and the Sidonites opened with their humble demand to receive the entire coastal belt up to Gaza, including Gaza itself. We'll manage between ourselves, they said, but the sea needs to be ours, it's obvious. And the Moabite rose to his feet and slammed his fist down on the table and said: With all due respect, the two of them are already sitting on some nice beachfront property up there in the north; it's about time the Moabites got access to the sea, too. We're shut away in a hole beyond the river while you guys get to bathe every morning and surf the waves. No way, it's not going to happen. Moab will march to the sea, he shouted. Otherwise, I have no reason to take part in this revolt and sacrifice any of my mighty men. And the King of Ammon, Balis, who'd never dreamed of reaching the distant sea, who would never in a million years have thought of making such a demand, said: You took the words out of my mouth, Moab. After all, we Ammonites have been demanding as much since time immemorial—yes, *a corridor to the sea*, a seaport for the sons of Ammon. We demand that Judah scale down its borders a bit. If it's a pact, then let it be a pact all the way, or at least all the way to the shore. It's out of the question that only some members of the pact should hit the jackpot and not others. Likewise, the Moabite cut in, we demand the territory that we're entitled to in the south—namely, in Edom, which was unlawfully taken from us. Wadi Zered should be Moabite on both banks. Without that concession there's nothing to talk about—I'm getting up and leaving. And the Edomite took out a map and a wooden ruler and drew a straight red line between the cities of Zoar, Arad, Eshtamoa, Dvir, and Lachish. This is what I'd like to get, he said. It's really not much—it's the least we could possibly ask for.

And Zedekiah's eyes darted around the room as he said, Lots of demands, lots of claims. In fact, he himself wanted to lay claim to the Sea of Galilee, but he wasn't sure who was in control there these days. Okay, let's sit at the negotiating table and see what we can do. We'll see to it that everyone leaves happy, that everyone will both get a little something and give up a little something, as is only fair. Let's spread the map open, let's all get out our rulers and pencils. All things considered, it's a big region, and there's room for everyone, right? Everyone wants a little elbow room, and everyone wants sea, too. I understand perfectly—why should our partners beyond the Jordan be disadvantaged, why should their portion be diminished, why shouldn't they have a bit of open sea, to sail on and watch the sun set over? And someone said, And what about the Amalekites? And Zedekiah rose and said, Leave the Amalekites to me! Everyone politely applauded.

Then there was a loud noise from outside, as though a carriage was rattling by, and a man dressed in black entered the rabbinate restaurant. Finally, the interpreter! everyone thought. And they would have jumped right back into their negotiations if it weren't for the fact that the man was wearing on his shoulders and his neck the harness and poles of a plowing bull or horse. Are you the interpreter? Zedekiah asked. If so, what's with the getup? Are you here to plow or to translate? Because, look, if you've come to plow, this isn't the right field, okay? Everything's already pretty deeply plowed in here, he said. Then the King of Judah recognized the man in black, though he was greatly changed. He was considerably thinner, and had grown a long beard, and looked to have aged some twenty years, and his head was shaved, and the inside of his right forearm was tattooed with three words, Zedekiah noticed, to his utter astonishment: LAND, LAND, LAND. The man stepped into the center of the room, dragging noisily after him the shaft and wooden poles of a beast of the fields. The Sidonian asked, What's *this*? And the King of Tyre took in the display and said, cannily, I reckon he wants to say something about the enslavement of animals, or maybe about slavery in general, and maybe he wants to tell us that it's high time we free ourselves from the yoke of Babylon . . . ?

But Jeremiah answered him in his own language, On the contrary, and then added another *On the contrary* in every dialect being spoken in the room. He turned to each attendee and addressed him in his own language—including the Egyptian, who was watching all this with gloomy curiosity. And Jeremiah said, You must not listen to your prophets, your diviners, your dreamers, your soothsayers, or your sorcerers, who are saying to you, You shall not serve the King of Babylon. For they are prophesying a lie to you, with the result that you will be removed far from your land, I will drive you out, and you will perish. But any nation that will bring its neck under the yoke of the King of Babylon and serve him, I will leave on its own land, says the Lord, to till it and live there. Bring your necks, bring your necks under the yoke of the King of Babylon, and serve him and his people, and live, Jeremiah said, and as rapidly translated for every member of his audience, though he was staring fixedly at Zedekiah all along: Serve the King of Babylon and live. Why should this city become a desolation?

Next to the Egyptian emissary sat his personal interpreter, and this man explained at great length what had been said. The Egyptian interpreter then stood up, the Egyptian emissary nodding in approval, and approached Jeremiah, removing the pole shafts from his neck, and, without saying a word, raised them up and broke them in half on his bent knee. In such a manner will I break the yoke of Nebuchadnezzar the King of Babylon in two years' time, the translator said. Enough, now, this story's over and done with. No more theatrics, Jeremiah—we know you of old.

Jeremiah looked at the broken shafts. And Zedekiah, too, looked on, amazed, for it now became clear that this Egyptian interpreter was none other than Hanania the prophet, who'd visited him recently. And Jeremiah asked the Egyptian interpreter, Who are you? And the interpreter, instead of answering, spread out two enormous wings, and the wings filled the entire hall, and all the kings fell on their faces, saying, He's got an angel, he's got an angel. And the angel gathered its wings and sat down to sip the foam from his beer. And more food and beer were served, and Zedekiah said, Bravo, we finally have a clear sign; the strength of the yoke, which was of hard wood, was tested. And the king's dog was waiting under the table the whole while.

Jeremiah left the restaurant. He felt as if the bones of his hands and the bones of his feet had just been crushed. Ah, the shame of it. He walked down the street, sat on the iron bars of the safety railings at the bottom of Agron Street, and buried his face in his hands. He realized that his part in events had just ended, that not only the yoke had been broken but his prophecy as well. But isn't that only right and proper? It's the updated prophecy, Jeremiah, he told himself; a new prophet has risen, and you didn't even know. You've been fired without notice. Yes, it happens sometimes in large companies. They sent you a clear sign; an old man breaks the same wooden poles that you were commanded to prepare. All in all, it's about as impressive as water from a rock. And he thought, The ways are hidden, and who knows whether the golden calf wasn't the true God for Israel? Maybe the whole story should have begun with the calf. How can we know? There's always some uncertainty when you're talking to God; one can always be mistaken in interpreting divine speech. God's words have to be translated into the language of human beings, and who knows what gets lost in translation. Even if you hear the prophecy clearly and directly from the mouth of God, you're only human, and misunderstanding is a daily occurrence among our kind. As you are well aware.

A woman sat down next to him, and he recognized her as the complainant, who hadn't been taken into exile, like all the rest of the indigent crazies. And she told him: It doesn't matter. The wooden poles were broken only to forge iron bars in place of them! For thus says the Lord of Hosts, the God of Israel: I have put an iron yoke on the neck of all these nations so that they may serve King Nebuchadnezzar of Babylon, and they shall indeed serve him. Jeremiah pretended he hadn't heard her and got up to make a break for it, but she was already taking the iron safety railings apart, somehow, and he stopped and watched her until she approached him and fixed the bars on his shoulders as a weighty harness. And she told him: We're only dray horses, Jeremiah. We can't just run away from the carriages we pull behind us. And he started walking up the street with difficulty, accompanied by the clanging of the poles he was dragging over the asphalt—for the second time that day—back to the head of Agron Street, where he again entered the rabbinate restaurant, covered in sweat, shuddering.

The international conference was in full swing: maps were spread out, and the Egyptian was speaking, and the angel translating, talking of Nebuchadnezzar's surrender. When Jeremiah again entered the room, an hour after his first yoke had been broken, now bearing the iron poles on his neck, hors d'oeuvres were being served, before the main course. From the doorway, Jeremiah suddenly recognized Broch, and heard that they were calling him Hanania for some reason. He told him, Listen, Hanania, and Broch rose to his feet and stared at him in disbelief. Jeremiah continued: The Lord has not sent you, and you made these people trust in a lie. Therefore, thus says the Lord: I am going to send you off the face of the earth. Within this year you will be dead. And Hanania looked apologetically at all the kings and went up to Jeremiah a second time in anger and made to break the iron shafts; he took with him the broken wooden pole from Jeremiah's first round, wielding it like a club, and he spread his wings. And the kings screamed: Ahh, the wrath of Hanania! Ahh, the wrath of the angel of loathing! But Jeremiah slipped behind Broch's back and, thrusting his hand out, yanked off the contraption to which the wings were attached, and he bent the wings and tore the white paper feathers. You can buy this sort of junk in a costume store, you morons! he screamed at the kings. And the Egyptian emissary looked at his translator and rushed out to send a fax to his superiors, and Jeremiah stooped under the black-and-white striped iron poles on his shoulders and patted the head of Tukulti, who was still sitting under the table.

That very day, Broch faxed a letter to Nebuchadnezzar, via a Babylonian colleague, a fellow critic, saying that a revolt against Babylon was brewing in Judah, adding: By the way, the King of

Judah has a dog, a talking canine. Keep an eye on the large dog, Broch said, not only on the small dog of the House of David. And the King of Babylon certainly took notice. Jeremiah, too, sent a fax to Babylon, the following day, to the remaining elders among the exiles, and to the priests, the prophets, and all the people whom Nebuchadnezzar had taken into exile. He thought of his parents, from whom he hadn't heard a word, and he said, It doesn't matter; they'll understand that the letter is directed to them as well. And Jeremiah wrote to the exiled in Babylon: Build houses and live in them; plant gardens and eat what they produce. Take wives and have sons and daughters; take wives for your sons, and give your daughters in marriage, that they may bear sons and daughters; multiply there, and do not decrease. But seek the welfare of the city where I have sent you into exile, and pray to the Lord on its behalf, for in its welfare you will find your welfare. For thus says the Lord of Hosts, the God of Israel: Do not let the prophets and the diviners who are among you deceive you, and do not listen to the dreams that they dream, for it is a lie that they are prophesying to you in my name; I did not send them, says the Lord. For thus says the Lord: Only when Babylon's seventy years are completed will I visit you, and I will fulfill to you my promise and bring you back to this place. For surely I know the plans I have for you, says the Lord, plans for your welfare and not for harm, to give you a future with hope.

Jeremiah faxed his letter from the post office in Givat Ram and then walked up the almost completely deserted university campus path and sat at a computer in the National Library—which was also almost completely empty of students and teachers—to take a look at the news sites in Babylon. Truth be told, the King of Babylon had been informed of the plot to rebel against him even before Broch's fax, because a number of the rebels had taken out a little bilateral insurance, so to speak, reporting to him *from the start* of their trips to Judah, so that they wouldn't be suspected of belonging to the underground cell, heaven forbid. Whatever the case, this is what was written in the news: that

339

the king was going to celebrate the eighteenth year of his reign by setting out on a fresh expedition to the Land of the Hatti, and this time, it was promised, there would be no mercy, and he would also strike out against the Egyptian army in a two-pronged attack. You look at those pyramid things and your eyes sting, Nebushazban told Nebuchadnezzar over the phone from Jerusalem. What crime have the skies committed to deserve getting stabbed in the pupils by these big pointy tombs? Hasn't the time come, Nebushazban said, to file down those arrogant points, and, most important, to smash that big gaudy woman-lion sculpture thing of theirs? We've got to go down to Egypt and hack off her nose with a power shovel. And Nebuchadnezzar asked, So it's female, the Sphinx? And Nebushazban said, Of course. And then: It's snowing in Jerusalem, Nebushazban said into the black telephone. You can actually see it falling this very minute from the window. Is snow falling in Babylon, too? And Nebuchadnezzar replied, Yes.

38

ONCE AGAIN THEY SET OUT to the west and south. It was customary among my ancestors to ride out on military expeditions in iron vehicles and on horses, whereas I can launch a missile without budging from my chair and blot out the enemies of Babylon even before breakfast, the King of Babylon said, but what sort of impression would *that* make? How will I be remembered? They'll say, *This big king of yours, all he did was sit around and push buttons?* No, no, a military expedition must be long and difficult. Conquering a city is like conquering a woman. Imagine every woman you see just throwing herself at you because she knows you're the king—how dreadful! Or, anyway, that's what his father, Nabopolassar, had told him: What matters is not only the occupation and destruction, but also how you go about it all. There's a certain way of going about these things, and each king innovates his own personal variation on this process. It begins with finding a good pretext for the expedition— you can't simply march out for no reason. You need a revolt, a broken pledge, a personal insult, a lit match, you see? And you also need to take your sweet time in assembling your troops. No need to hurry. Let the match lighter sit and wait and quake in his palace. You've got to set out slowly, in good weather, in spring, and enjoy the journey. Sure, you could take a helicopter and arrive in a few hours, but any military expedition undertaken in haste will be as hastily erased from memory. You want, Nebuchadnezzar's father told him, to prolong the march in order to etch it into the memory. At least into your own memory. And once you're ready to set out, get the horses going early in the morning, as early as possible, even though the journey will be long, will last a month or two at least. Once you get under way, leave early, don't waste a minute. Ride out, and make sure to glance back at the infantry treading behind you. And try to think about everything they're leaving behind. And then fix your gaze on what's ahead of you, and know—or at least try to believe—that your men will be behind you for the entire journey, and on the way back, too. They might hate you, but it'll be the enmity of a son toward his father. And remember that the question can creep up on you at any moment—Nebuchadnezzar's father had once told him, when they were riding north, to the land of Ararat—the question can creep up on you: Why is any of this worthwhile? What's the point? I've got a big enough country already, and I've freed it from the yoke of Assyria. Now's the time to rest, to reap the reward, to taste the fruits of a successful rebellion, to take root, to plant vineyards. The world is far too big to conquer; even the greatest kings of Assyria stopped in eastern Egypt. Even they halted in their tracks once they saw how vast was the land stretching out in front of their noses, how long was the river from which they drank.

If so, why not stop mid-journey—no, even before the first step is taken—why not set the horses free, and send your troops home, and go back to bed? It's four in the morning, and you've got your iron helmet on, and you're slumping forward on your horse . . . The answer's simple, Nabopolassar told him, placing his hand on his son's shorn head. The answer is that everyone wants to conquer the world. Everyone wants to lord over a world empire. Every shoemaker in every country town is liable to rise at any moment and assemble an army of shoemakers and attack a neighboring town, and take hostages, and set out to execute, say, all the carpenters, and assemble an even bigger army, and two years later rule over all of Persia, after which he proceeds with his fellow shoemakers to conquer Hattusa, and to turn Suppiluliumas—or whoever might be king there now—into his bond slave. These Hittite names, Nabopolassar suddenly said, in a rare moment of humor, are like a coiled spring that's been twisted inside itself. And again his father asked him, Tell me, tell me, the names of the Hittite kings, and he shut his eyes as though he were listening to a child playing on a violin, and the fifteen-year-old Nebuchadnezzar said, for the hundredth time: Arnuwanda. Tudhaliya. Lavranash. Tahurwaili. Hattusili. Huzziya . . . And Nabopolassar couldn't help laughing: Hee-hee-hee. Huzziya, oh my, Huzziya—what an odd name. What sort of parents would name their child *Huzziya*? And Nebuchadnezzar said, Maybe in their language the name means something nice; maybe it sounds like a fine name to them. But Nabopolassar said, No, no, Huzziya is, objectively speaking, ridiculous.

Remember who we were only a few years back. Worse than shoemakers, poorer and weaker than shoemakers, which is why we walked around in our bare feet—we, the Chaldeans! Our entire empire is only a buffer zone, so that at home in Babylon the Babylonians can sleep late, and raise their sheep, and copy out ancient poems. When you get right down to it, wars will always be waged; the only question is where. That's why it's best that it take place far from home, and that those fires burn a long way away from where we live, lest anyone hear all that annoying screaming in our city. Because there'll be plenty of screaming. It's the way of the world. People scream, okay? Our business is to push back the screams, to keep them out of our house—like when you catch a mouse in your kitchen and bring it outside to a field where you can release it. Nebuchadnezzar said, But we kill the mouse. And his father told him: Yes, you're right. Maybe that wasn't the best example. But remember how we turned the trap upside down that one time, and he got away?

At first, Nebuchadnezzar would set out on the military expeditions, like his father, with horses and iron chariots, doing without most of the technological advances that were available to him. But after one of his enemies ambushed him—pinning down his convoy under heavy machine-gun fire, riddling his antique iron vehicles until they looked like colanders, and mowing down a great many of his men—Nebuchadnezzar understood that it takes two to tango, and that if the enemy wasn't going to stick to the old chivalrous ways, why, he, too, would have to make a few accommodations to modernity. And this was why the Babylonian army introduced a number of new weapons into its materiel, though for the most part the king's policy was still to avoid using heavy artillery to blow up the walls of a city but, rather, to insist on raising a good old-fashioned siege by following the standard operating procedure of his forefathers—siege engines and battering ram—after which he'd enter the city mounted on his horse, and with a two-thousand-year-old iron pike he'd dispatch the local king with a single thrust, etc. There were those who ridiculed Nebuchadnezzar for his conservative ways, but his father's precepts had a strong hold on him (his father, who, in the meantime, had died one day; one day he simply didn't wake up). But several years later, Nebuchadnezzar's back pain got so bad that he gave up expeditions on horseback and rode instead in a black Mercedes whose back seat could fold out into a sort of bed; it even contained a mini-fridge for water and champagne. And sometimes Nebuchadnezzar fell asleep while his mighty army was setting forth in the morning, and would be woken only by the irritating sound of the hammers of the builders of his siege engines circling this or that doomed town. Later, the rest of the troops would arrive with the horses. And sometimes he'd send his army ahead of him, and they'd make all the necessary preparations, and Nebuchadnezzar would be the last to arrive, together with his ministers. His car would stop next to this or that besieged wall, and he'd step out of his car, and with a tiny hammer—the sort used by doctors to test your reflexes by tapping your knee—he'd test the stones to locate an echo, and would then carefully mark this spot with an X, in pencil, though you had to get really close to make out the mark. And he would signal for a battering ram to be brought forward and aimed at this X.

39

As in a recurring nightmare, Jerusalem woke up one arid morning in the month of Tevet to find itself under siege. As for the racket of the construction workers building the siege engines around the city, it seemed as if they'd been at it for an eternity . . . while for Zedekiah it seemed that it was only a matter of minutes between his coronation eleven years ago and this siege. And he told his ministers and scribes: Hey, we got through Pharaoh; we'll get through this, too, no? Back then, too, they showed up and grabbed what they could and left the next day, right? And one of the scribes wondered, We got *through* Pharaoh? And Zedekiah said, It's only an expression.

Zedekiah ordered Baalgezer to attend to the siege and slammed the door in his face. Jehoiachin's childhood piano was still in the room, and Zedekiah ran his hands over the keys—as he'd done ever since the second Babylonian incursion had been announced. He recalled the serious music Jehoiachin had played in the stadium and decided that he, too, would learn how to play it. There were plenty of music teachers in the palace, and, one after another, they came and tried to teach Zedekiah the basics:

the black keys and the white, middle C, octaves, scales. The king
had little patience, however, and told them: No, no, I only want
to learn to play this one piece. Don't go teaching me the entire
rule book—I want to know only this one composition. And the
teachers looked at the score his nephew Jehoiachin had left
behind—Jehoiachin, of whom Zedekiah hadn't heard a word or
even half a word since he'd gone into exile a decade ago—and
they played the piece for him. The king would close his eyes and
listen to the notes wheeling about and then slowly wheeling
about again, and if no one had been there to see him do it, he'd
have shed a weighty tear.

One time, he lost his temper: Did I ask you to play that? I
asked you to teach *me*—if I wanted to go to a recital, I'd buy a
ticket. Why do you always have to show me up? Do you think
teaching means humiliating your student? He'd have murdered
this piano teacher on the spot, eradicating those blissfully shut
eyelids and those spindly fingers, if some eunuch hadn't entered
at that moment bearing a telegram. Zedekiah ripped the envelope open between his twin rows of strong teeth, which had been
whitened on a weekly basis, ever since he'd ascended to the
throne, by the royal dental hygienist—it is of paramount importance for a king to have good, straight white teeth. And the telegram said: Everything's okay, it's just two or three Babylonians
snooping around, sniffing the place out. We'll let them have
their fun and then we'll kick ass. No reason to worry. Zedekiah
didn't know who was sending him telegrams—Baalgezer, maybe,
or one of the deputies? Up in the palace, it was difficult to measure time; everything seemed to have happened yesterday or the
day before. So, even though it had been weeks since Zedekiah
went out on one of those happy Saturday-morning peacekeep-
ing jaunts, it hardly seemed possible that anything could have
changed in the meantime—after all, if something was going
on, he'd know about it . . . right? Wasn't the palace a part of the
Old City, and the Old City part of the city entire, and the city

part of Judah? Surely what happened to one would happen to all. Besides, if they hadn't gone out to shoot at insurgents lately, well, so what? There must have been a good reason for it. No doubt the last pockets of resistance had been flushed out, no doubt those gangs of troublemakers were off licking their wounds somewhere. There was no point in blowing up neighborhoods that had already been pacified—no point in brushing the brushed, he reflected, as he brushed his teeth.

And not far from there, the thorn of hunger sprouted in the city, and the thistles of thirst poked out of the cracks in the rocks. After two weeks of siege, because they were deprived of the supplies coming in from the villages in Moab and greater Judah, food started disappearing from the shelves, as though at the command of a cruel wizard's wand. At first, luxury items like ice cream and chocolate disappeared, and then other products started going, too, one after another, stuff you'd never expect to become scarce, like liquid soap, or moisturizing cream for your feet, or cumin. One day, for example, the city was all out of toothpaste—the last paste had been brushed off the last toothbrush—and that was that; it was no longer possible to brush, and every mouth reeked. The supply in the palace was secure, needless to say, but then the city ran out of toilet paper, and every home where anyone so much as *suspected* that there might be some stockpiled toothpaste and toilet paper was burglarized; even hospitals were ransacked of their emergency supplies. After several weeks, even the thieves and hoarders were all out.

And then vegetables became scarce. Everything that was stored was either eaten or had gone bad—how long does a cucumber last, even in the fridge? And the refrigerators of the land became filled with black carrots, and bruised bananas, and things went moldy and were beset by worms. And the emergency-supply granaries were opened, and bread was baked, and also bagels and cakes. There was plenty of flour in the city, but there were also plenty of people living in the city, and they started to hoard flour, and within two weeks the flour monopoly made as much profit as they'd normally make in a decade. But bread and flour also steadily grew scarcer, as month followed month. Since all the vegetables and fruits had already vanished from shelves, people started eating bread and pita around the clock in order to assuage their hunger, bread and pita and beans and other legumes—the hummus joints were among the last to shut down, so the nation was now slathering pitas with hummus morning, noon, and night: people would tear off a hunk of bread and scoop up some hummus and so gain another day, and another. But after a month, the hummus, too, was about gone, so they switched to broad beans, and they ate only broad beans. This was at the end of the month of Tevet, and in Adar they would be celebrating Purim, but instead of disguising themselves as clowns and cowboys and demons and walking mailboxes, the children of Jerusalem dressed up—under duress—as mice and rats, and they chased after every living thing they could get their hands on: cockroaches and cats and every sort of songbird. And the grilled-chicken shops started selling pigeons and ravens, and by then every alley had been cleared of its cats, and people were snatching dogs from their owners, from both homes and kennels, and off the streets as well. Everything changed so rapidly; sugar and running water and detergent and aspirin all turned into luxuries. But up in the palace, the birds still sang as they had for generations, including a parrot whose name was Joseph, and whose forefather had been King David's parrot. David's parrot had taught his son, and his son had taught *his* son, and so on down the generations, a single song from the Psalms—a psalm of David's from when he fled from his son Absalom—and Joseph, Zedekiah's parrot, which he'd inherited from his brother, which *he'd* received from his father, and so on and so forth, turned to the king and told him, as it did every time that he walked by the bird's big cage: I lie down and sleep, and I wake . . . But Zedekiah interrupted him: Cut it out, Joseph—enough. One more word and I turn you into a grilled shawarma parrot. Stop fucking with me.

As Passover drew near, the poor were invited by the rich into their homes, as usual, but whenever poor people accepted this invitation—a tenth of the population was poor or indigent by then—they'd be knocked unconscious with a wooden plank, or else they'd be shot on the spot, because it was generally assumed that if a pauper was invited in and discovered a supply of matzoth or fruit, within minutes, as though the news were being broadcast telepathically, the household that had been so wise as to amass supplies for a rainy day would be inundated by dozens of the poor scrambling for the sugar bowl. The rats of poverty have been hit hard, the king broadcast on his festive radio program in the month of Nisan. Sometimes a strange delivery would arrive in the city—it was unclear whether these were miracles from the heavens, or from the exiled Jews in Babylon or off in another diaspora—and a helicopter would drop down a crate of bananas or of avocados and the like, leftovers from somewhere else. And the hearts of the citizens would be filled with hope, but every such surprise delivery would result, apart from the few who were sated, in a few people getting trampled, and more than a few getting disappointed, since by the time most of them arrived, all that was left was a mound of pits and dark, tough peels. And so people started to cook their leather belts and sandals, and to scratch off and eat the wallpaper glue from the walls of their homes, because there was a rumor going around that this adhesive had been made from potatoes. And children started disappearing, and soon no pets were left in the city apart from the dogs in the palace.

A little less than a year slipped by this way, and the Babylonians didn't show any signs of giving up. The water in the city reservoirs began to dry up, and it was no longer possible to prevent the king from noticing what was going on. The minister of water knocked on his door and said: My king, happy holidays. I'll begin with some news of little consequence, really nothing to concern yourself with, but, um . . . there's a bit of a siege going on. And Zedekiah said, How simple it would be if you'd just come in and told me, There's *no siege*. The minister of water didn't know what to say, and the conversation ended right there, and so the minister bowed and left. The next morning, he tried again: My king, my king, there's a siege out there. And Zedekiah stared at him as though he'd never laid eyes on him before and cordially corrected him, saying, *There's no siege*. And the minister of water bowed and left, and the following day he knocked again and said, Your Majesty, I'm afraid we're in something of a siege situation, and Zedekiah stared at him as if seeing him for the first time and said, There's no siege, and the minister left without a word. And the next day he returned and said, My king, there's no siege, and the king felt trapped, since the minister had stolen his line, so he opened the window and beheld the green and peaceful prospect of Jerusalem, and he said to the minister of water: See? See? Everything's fine! And the minister of water came over and grabbed the switchblade on the king's table and sliced down the length of the skies and the mountains, which were nothing more than a pretty painting, and with his own hands tore down the view from every window. And Zedekiah passed from window to window, saying: Why are the cactuses dying? Couldn't someone sprinkle them with a few drops of water?! And the minister of water said: My king, there's scarcely any water left. People are dying, winter is dying, summer is approaching, and the cisterns are empty—the Chaldeans clogged our pipes. And Zedekiah drew near the honorable minister and roared: That's an outright lie, an outright lie. I took a bath today, didn't I? So where did all that nice hot water come from, Mr. Smarty-Pants? And the minister was suddenly filled with pity for this strapping young creature, and told him, Ah, well, undoubtedly the king witnessed a miracle when his bath was filled with nice hot water. And the minister saw how clean the king was, though Zedekiah didn't notice that the minister of water's shoes were torn at their toecaps.

THAT SAME NIGHT, it started to rain in Jerusalem. It was now the month of Adar, so a full calendar year had elapsed under siege, and the cisterns filled up, and many basins and household receptacles were set under the skies like gaping mouths. And Zedekiah, who by then had decided to surrender and head out alone to whoever might be out on the other side of the siege— figuring that whatever would happen would happen—hardened his heart. One doesn't argue with an obvious miracle, he said, surprised, and in the morning he beheld all his people drinking, and he was encouraged. It was the last rain of the season, but he didn't know that.

40

JEREMIAH KEPT OUT OF SIGHT in his parents' home in Anatot
during the siege. He'd been living there ever since Esther and
Hilkiah went into Babylonian exile a decade ago. He ate vegetables from his mother's patch and harvested olives from the tree
and sometimes opened a can of preserves. When he saw the reports on the latest siege, it was as though he were reading about
the defeat of some soccer team or another, in, say, Australia, and
it touched him about as much as seeing a scrap of paper being
swept down the street by a gust of wind. The last year went by
for him in complete silence. He'd fall asleep early and wake at
sunrise; he kept to a strict daily routine, mornings writing in a
notebook without paying any attention to what he was writing
and without reviewing what he'd jotted down, after which he'd
cook the most meager of meals and sit for hours in silence facing
the hillside, and maybe read a bit from the first prophets, merely
living and drawing breath.

One night, more than a year after the siege began, when to his
delight it abruptly started raining on the vegetable patch and olive tree, four policemen arrived and took hold of the four legs of
his bed while he was in a deep, blank sleep, and sneaked him into

the city in a Red Cross van (the Babylonians still allowed these to cross the siege line, for propaganda purposes). And they led Jeremiah to the court of the guards within the king's palatial residence, an ancient and fine home inside the walls of the palace, surrounded by fruit trees, adjacent to a pond, close by the Cotton Merchants Gate. Zedekiah stood before the sleeping Jeremiah, holding half a glass of water, and Jeremiah, who hadn't woken once while being transported, at last opened his eyes, still lying on his bed, albeit far from home. The stars above the king's palace came into view, the teeming Milky Way—but at this stage in his life, nothing could surprise him anymore. And he stared keenly at Zedekiah and at the stars that seemed to crown his head. Ever since the disastrous summit with the regional kings at the rabbinate, the King of Judah covered his body in long black garments in order not to flaunt his cuneiform tattoos in public, for in his heart he'd already pinned his hopes on the Egyptians—he had a feeling, no question about it, he had a feeling that the days of Babylon were over, and he'd also dreamed a dream in which a large river that emptied into the sea ran out of all its water, and someone in the dream told him, The Euphrates has dried up.

From his place standing over Jeremiah, Zedekiah asked him, So why did you prophesy and say, Thus says the Lord: I will give this city into the hand of the King of Babylon, and he shall take it? And Jeremiah closed his eyes and said: Mattaniah, that isn't a prophecy, just a description of reality; can't you see what's going on? The siege is already in full swing. The common people have no bread; the dogs you keep in the palace are better fed than your subjects. And the king looked at Jeremiah's rolled-back eyeballs, which he remembered from their childhood and from the club: they'd both close one eye and look through the telescope, and their eyelids quivered at the sight of the slender moon, which now, too, hung above the ramparts. And Jeremiah told Zedekiah, as he gazed up at the white light, as though talking to someone else, in the third person, all the things he'd already said in the city, and in articles that no paper would publish, and in letters he'd sent to all sorts of people holding positions of power: that the King of Judah would not escape out of the hands of the Chaldeans, but would surely be given into the hands of the King of Babylon, and speak with him face-to-face and see him eye to eye. And Zedekiah stooped over Jeremiah's bed and shouted: No, we'll fight. This is a war for our home; for them, it's just another town on the way to Egypt! And Jeremiah replied: Mattaniah, listen . . . Though you fight against the Chaldeans, you shall not succeed. And Zedekiah said: You have no mandate. What sort of prophet are you, instilling mistrust? And Jeremiah said, Let it be, Mattaniah, let it be. And Zedekiah leaned down close and grabbed the prophet by the collar of his pajamas and screamed: You'll call me Zedekiah, you hear? *Ze-de-kiah.* This envy of yours is driving you crazy; instead of helping, you're wreaking havoc. And he jerked Jeremiah back and forth, and the prophet made no effort to resist. There's a new pharaoh in Egypt; I've received a couple of tip-offs from him. You have no idea about any of this—you don't have the figures—and still you go on talking. You don't even know that a new pharaoh has come to power, a new and good pharaoh, and he likes me, and he'll come to our assistance. I'm already paying him. We've made a pact, and I've made other pacts, too, but you have no idea! And Jeremiah fell back on the bed and said, Thus says the Lord, I am going to give Pharaoh, King of Egypt, into the hands of his enemies, those who seek his life— And he wanted to say something else, but fell silent. His eyes shut and filled with tears. And the king stomped out of the court of the guards in a fury, and the prophet tried to go back to sleep.

The moon sank and vanished behind the walls of the city. From the direction of Sultan's Pool, Jeremiah caught sight of a thin plume of smoke before dozing off under the vault of the sky. A row of stars trailed along in their regular circuit, dragged along their ancient path, without stops and without tickets and without even a locomotive. And Jeremiah glanced around and saw the court dogs appear and leap onto his bed with him, by his side and at his feet, curling up their tails and lowering their ears, and so Jeremiah also lowered his ears and bent his knees— as the king saw from afar—in order to make room for them on the bed.

Zedekiah trudged up the stairs. After several minutes, he was sound asleep; after several minutes more, he started snoring, and Noa was shouting *Shhh!* from the adjoining room, but he didn't hear. Tukulti stood by the large window and stared for hours on end at the new star, which was still burning. In his huge and cold room at the end of the corridor, Eliazar read his picture book in the dark.

41

THAT NIGHT, A GUEST VISITED JEREMIAH'S BED in the court of the guards, located on the palace grounds. It was his uncle, the lawyer Hananel, who had a slight speech impediment and consequently pronounced his own name Hanamel, which is what everyone called him.

The dogs were startled awake and barked, and Hanamel, whom Jeremiah hadn't seen since the death of his sister, entered the courtyard and offered the dogs snacks drawn out of nowhere or from behind their ears, like a magician, just as he did years ago, when he'd return from some deal he had completed in Assyria, loaded down with gifts and promises of future treats. Once, Hanamel concealed Jeremiah's sister in a cardboard box and then drew her out laughing from the laundry basket, and another time he bore Jeremiah on his shoulders as they walked the length of the walls of Jerusalem, his uncle telling him about the city and its gates and for that matter why a city needs to have a wall. At the time, all the words he was using seemed so strange and distant— Assyria, siege, destruction, ramparts—as though it were all a sort of children's fable.

Hanamel sat on the edge of the bed where Jeremiah was

sleeping in the courtyard, and said, Jeremiah, Jeremiah, get up, it's urgent. And Jeremiah said, What, what's going on, who is it? And Hanamel said, It's me, Uncle Hanamel, you don't know me anymore? Jeremiah, barely opening his eyes, said: What? What are you doing here? How'd you get in? And the uncle said, I told them I'm defending you in court, I showed them my notary certificate—they bought it hook, line, and sinker. I need to talk to you. And Jeremiah said: What? Another trial? Again? Go ahead, talk, but I'm keeping my eyes shut, I'm beat, and his uncle was close to boiling over by now and said, But how will I know that you're listening, that you haven't dozed off? And Jeremiah didn't answer. Having no other choice, the uncle continued: You remember my field, next to your parents' place in Anatot, Jeremiah? I'm off to Babylon tomorrow. See, I've reached an understanding with them. I dropped in on them, as the saying goes . . . So, listen, I want . . . I need to sell you my field. You remember what a nice field it is? Right next to your folks' place. You can plant okra, corn—what do you say? And Jeremiah said: What? Are you nuts? That's why you've come here in the middle of the night? I thought you were bringing me . . . I don't know what I thought . . . Let me sleep, I'm so tired. And Hanamel said: No, my dear Jeremiah, we've got to make the deal. I'm leaving tomorrow morning on the first train to Babylon; I can't leave the field abandoned. I've brought the deed . . . And Jeremiah said, Uncle, go, go, can't you see that I'm confined here? And yet you're talking to me about corn . . . And Hanamel said: No, no, there's got to be a deed of purchase; after all, I'm a jurist. Too bad you didn't study law, Jeremiah. I always told Esther that you could've been . . . Well, look, the field, it's a dunam of arable land, and I've got building rights. You can farm there or build—it's good land—and I'll let you have it for seven and ten silver shekels. What do you say? That's a great deal, a great deal, way below the market value: a field like that should cost you at least twenty-five! That's what I'd call an opportunity, Jeremiah, and the only reason I'm letting you have it for that little is because you're family! And Jeremiah, still without opening his eyes, said: You know what? Whatever you say, I don't have that much money. To tell you the truth, I don't have any money, not even a piaster. And Hanamel said: No problem—here, take the money. I'm lending it to you without interest, and you'll give it back when you've got some. And Jeremiah was confused: So why make me pay anything, if the money's coming from you? And Hanamel said, There's got to be an exchange; otherwise the deal won't be registered at the land registry bureau as a business transaction. And the uncle took out a scale and weighed the money that Jeremiah gave him—that is, the money he himself gave Jeremiah so that he could officially pay for the field. A dog and its trainer were watching, and Hanamel said, There, you're witnesses that the deal was signed; everything's kosher, everything's on the level. When you get out of here, Jeremiah, the uncle whispered, go and harvest and eat the olives in your new field, and press oil from them, and at night light a candle with the oil. And Jeremiah stared at his uncle as though he were some sort of lunatic who'd leaped onstage in the middle of a play and started reciting the lines assigned to a king in an altogether different play. But he signed a copy of the deed, and Hanamel took the signed deed of purchase and told Jeremiah, You'll see, homes and fields and vineyards will be bought and sold again in this land. He got up, and Jeremiah told him, Don't worry, Uncle Hanamel, I'll water your olive tree, I'll send you olives. His uncle licked and glued the appropriate revenue stamps.

Dirt ramps were steadily rising against the walls of the city, to make room for battering rams and allow soldiers to ascend. It was possible to hear every drop of sweat dripping from the foreign construction workers outside as they set up the siege, and to smell their breath as they toiled and sang strange songs. Buckets and more buckets of dirt, and every now and then they'd find and pocket an ancient coin or a shell buried in the earth; if they ever made it home to Babylon, they'd give these to their children. Jeremiah, from his place in the sunken courtyard, couldn't see any of this, but there were moments when it seemed to him that he was hovering beyond the palace and observing everything from above. He heard the trucks unloading earth, and the soldiers on the ramps looking at the walls in boredom and casting dice on backgammon boards, and the tanks and cannons maneuvering before opening fire, and the Aramean and Edomite mercenaries calculating their earnings in advance by estimating the number of people they'd kill, and, back inside the city, the ever-increasing hunger, the growling bellies of children, the lips of women gummed over with thirst, the diseases that were starting to break out—a case here and a case there, the first sparks appearing at the tip of a huge heap of straw—and then the flies catching on that the city was about to be theirs, and the first diseased dogs, and then the first dog that sunk his teeth into human flesh. And Jeremiah stared at the walls like someone staring at a movie screen, and he saw and heard and smelled everything, and in his pocket was the copy of the deed of purchase. He saw his sister projected there on the wall as if she were entangled in the dense growth of olive branches, and when he drew up close to her, her eyes themselves were big black olives. Lying on his back, he spoke to the Milky Way: See, the ramps have been cast up against the city to take it, and the city, faced with sword, famine, and pestilence, has been given into the hands of the Chaldeans, who are fighting against it . . . The heavens opened above him, scores of lights without end, and they listened closely to him, patiently, as he went on: And you told me, *Buy the field for money and get witnesses*, though the city has been given into the hands of the Chaldeans, Jeremiah said. What's the point, what's the point, what's the point of all these charades? The theater is empty, no one is watching; it doesn't interest anyone apart from me, and no one gives a damn what I have or don't have to say. The field I bought I'll never see, and the olive tree will wither, and the property will be occupied, and squatters will take over the house. This city is already lost, Jeremiah said to the open expanse of the nocturnal sky. And the voice, to his astonishment, answered him, that ancient voice that had been revealed to him nearly twenty years before, and even earlier in his youth, which had shown him the swollen pot and the almond, and Jeremiah was amazed that it had really and truly answered him—it took his breath away. And what the voice said was: This city has aroused my anger and wrath, from the day it was built until this day, so that I will remove it from my sight. And Jeremiah drew his cotton blanket over his head and curled up.

A SHORT WHILE LATER, powerful hands shook him vigorously, and he was surprised to see Pashhur standing next to his bed— the one named Terror-All-Around—as well as the priest Zephaniah. Pashhur was silent, but Zephaniah said, The king sent us to you. Jeremiah didn't answer, and Pashhur looked in the direction of the palace behind them and said, King Zedekiah . . . And Jeremiah couldn't bring himself to look at Pashhur, so he looked at Zephaniah, who said, The king said to us: Inquire . . . Please inquire of the Lord for us, for Nebuchadrezzar King of Babylon is waging war against us . . . Perhaps the Lord will deal with us according to all his wondrous works . . . that he may go up from us . . . that is to say, Nebuchadrezzar . . . And Pashhur wanted to say something, make some sort of apology, but he really couldn't find the words, so instead he said, The army is assembled, armed with all weapons of war—as though Jeremiah were his commanding officer. And Jeremiah shut his eyes and said: Thus says the Lord, the God of Israel, I am going to turn back the weapons of war that are in your hands and with which you are fighting against the King of Babylon and against the Chaldeans who are besieging you outside the walls, and I will bring them together into the center of the city. I myself will fight with you with outstretched hand and mighty arm, in anger, in fury, and in great wrath. And Pashhur was relieved and said, Thank you, thank you, and Zephaniah the priest whispered,

Thank you. And Jeremiah realized that there must have been some misunderstanding, and then he realized what had been misunderstood, and he said, No, you're not getting it, it's "I will fight *with* you," not "with you" . . . that is, he's saying, "I will fight *against* you," I will strike down the inhabitants of this city, both man and beasts . . . they will die of a great pestilence . . .

Jeremiah spoke rapidly; he had a feeling that he was about to lose his voice. And he rose from the bed in the court of the guards and went up to Pashhur, in spite of the revulsion he felt toward him—it was like walking toward a large white scorpion—and said, Terror . . . terror . . . But Pashhur averted his eyes—he couldn't look at the prophet—and Jeremiah, who was two heads shorter than the priest, walked around him like a beggar hounding the people coming out of a restaurant, spitting words into Pashhur's scornful ear, saying, Thus says the Lord, see, I am setting before you the way of life—and the way of death. And Pashhur leaped aside in disgust, but Jeremiah stuck to him like a boxer and said: Those who stay in this city shall die by the sword, by famine, and by pestilence, but those who go out and surrender to the Chaldeans who are besieging you—they shall live and shall have their lives as a prize of war. For I have set my face against this city for evil and not for good. Pashhur tried to get away, climbing on Jeremiah's bed as though fleeing a stubborn rat. Thus says the Lord! Jeremiah added. And now, Terror-All-Around, if I've found favor in your eyes, get off, get off of my bed; I want to go back to sleep. He had still plenty to say to them: Act with justice and righteousness, and deliver the spoiled out of the hand of the oppressor, and do no wrong or violence to the stranger, the fatherless, nor the widow, nor shed innocent blood in this place, and so on and so forth. But he didn't see the point. No, enough. It's too late.

FROM THE KING OF JUDAH'S RESIDENCE resounded the notes of the étude for piano that Jehoiachin had played a decade ago in the stadium. Now the king himself was trying his hand, and he was even making some progress from one lesson to the next. Jeremiah lent his ear to the efforts of the person seated on David's throne in front of a piano. And he got out of his bed in the courtyard and moved the bed against the wall and climbed on it and jumped and clung to some cracks in the bulging stone wall of the courtyard of the guards, and he pulled himself up on a ledge, from which position he beheld for the first time, with his own eyes, spread before him panoramically, the massive edifice of the siege, and its thousands of soldiers, and he realized that the Babylonians had built an actual city around the Old City, a city ringing a city, a thin cow around a fat cow, and the thin would swallow the fat. Above the Babylonian city burned the new star, and the Babylonian astronomers who'd arrived with the troops stood there and gazed at it through their polished telescopes, and Jeremiah observed that, although it was shining over the Babylonian encampment, it wasn't shining over the city itself. This greatly alarmed him, and he stood up and ran to the king's residence, but the king wasn't there; in fact, the place was almost completely deserted, apart from a handful of servants who were running hither and thither. They kept telling him that the king had gone to fight against the Chaldeans at the head of a great army: The king has gone to welcome Pharaoh, who's come up from Egypt to his aid and has joined forces with the army of Judah, haven't you heard? The Babylonian army has retreated, sucked away by the Egyptians like dust into a new vacuum cleaner—surely the bitterness of death is past! And Jeremiah climbed up to his perch again and looked and saw that there were no tanks, that the very place where he'd imagined seeing fortifications a moment ago now seemed deserted, and an eerie silence prevailed over everything. He shook himself in disbelief at what he was seeing; he stood there and jerked his body as if he were shaking something off, but what? The Babylonian army had suddenly retreated, and the siege ramps and engines and battlements had been left behind unmanned, an empty shell of a siege without the bitter core. Zedekiah, the servants told him, had set free all the bondsmen and bondswomen and the animals from their tasks as a sort of enormous peace-sacrifice to appease God, and all masters of bondsmen and bondswomen and anyone who owned an animal obeyed and set free their slaves and their animals, be they fish in an aquarium or an old Canaanite slave. And, indeed, it was reported that the Egyptians were coming to Judah's aid; the good that was done in the land was immediately recompensed from the heavens, as the Babylonians released their grip on the siege and marched off to the coast to repulse the Egyptian blow. An enormous sigh of relief rose from the city, and the headlines in the papers announced WE'VE BEEN SAVED in letters covering half the front page.

After several days, during which not one Babylonian was seen, trucks with provisions began arriving from Moab and unloading food and medicine and soap and toothpaste and cans of dog food. And so all the masters bought back their former slaves for a pittance, and other animals were obtained to serve in the place of those that had been set free, and all of these were made into bondsmen and bondswomen, and they lapped up the canned dog food. And Jeremiah, who didn't know about any of this but sensed it all nonetheless, ran around in a panic, sweating profusely, from one room of the palace to another. He didn't know what was happening. Were the Egyptians indeed fighting with us—that is, *with* us? Had a vacuum cleaner indeed come up from the Nile? Contradictory verses burst out of his mouth—on the one hand, *Behold I proclaim for you a liberty,* but then, immediately, *Behold I proclaim for you a liberty to the sword, to pestilence, and to famine*—and he didn't know whether to speak the verse to its end or not. His brain throbbed with verses and scraps of verses, and his skull seemed to have split open and was awash in warmongers bent on destruction, and he didn't know what was going on, he just didn't know.

Tukulti stood in the corner of one of the palace rooms, looking gaunt, his ribs showing, staring out the window. Jeremiah asked him where the king was, and Tukulti didn't answer but trotted across the room and opened a secret door and entered, and Jeremiah followed him. They fled down a hidden corridor and descended some steps, and Jeremiah told Tukulti, I've got to get out of here, I can't sit in the jailhouse anymore. Tukulti barked, and an exit sprung into view. Jeremiah climbed a ladder through a round opening; he had a feeling that he'd been there before. And when he stuck his head out and looked into the light, he saw the door with three locks belonging to the rotator cell. His heart stopped, but he scrambled out anyway, and, as in an unending circular nightmare, one of the Temple clerks immediately seized him and screamed: Here's another one! So you think you're sneaking out to join the Chaldeans? A Babylonian siege can last five, ten years—everyone knows that. You've just got to settle in and see it through! And Jeremiah shouted back, That's a lie, I'm not joining the Chaldeans, and the clerk said, That's precisely what we're going to establish, and dragged him toward a number of officials who were there in the room eating lukewarm meatballs made of dog food along with stir-fried beans, passing the salt from hand to hand. And Jeremiah said, You've got to let me go, I've got to talk with the King of Babylon. And they made fun of him and said: Yeah, sure, maybe you want to talk to the King of Egypt, too? Are there any other kings you'd be interested in talking to? Hey, we can arrange whatever you want. And what exactly are you going to tell him, Jeremiah? That you want to hand the keys to the city over to him so that he can come and destroy the Temple? We're done, Jeremiah; the Babylonians have gone, haven't you heard? It's finished. Pharaoh is pushing the Babylonians toward the sea, crushing them like Babylonian garlic, and frying them up till they get all brown and bitter. The siege has been lifted. You're like someone flooring the gas pedal while the car is in neutral; you no longer have any meaning; you're a walking lie, prattling on and on, and we've got to stop the prattling once and for all, because there's only one thing to do with a poisoned well—it needs to be sealed. And Jeremiah said confidently—even though he wasn't sure about anything—confidently and forcibly: Do not deceive yourselves, saying, The Chaldeans will surely go away from us, for they will not go away. They will return, they will return, *they will return, they will return, they will return,* he shouted. It's only a short break—Pharaoh sent two hundred soldiers, it's only symbolic. It's only so he comes out looking nice in the papers. Babylon will trample over them within two minutes; *they're already dying, all of Pharaoh's soldiers are dying,* Jeremiah screamed. And though he had no idea what he was saying, he was describing the situation quite accurately. Pharaoh had indeed sent only a few troops who'd been condemned to death anyhow, and whom he'd released from prison in order to give them a chance to redeem themselves, but Babylonian arrows and bullets had already cleaved their heads, eagles were already hovering over the corpses, and the Babylonians were only resting from their long march. Tomorrow morning they'd be back on their siege ramps and manning their well-secured tanks and cannons. And one of the Temple scribes grabbed a baseball bat and whacked Jeremiah on the back as if he were striking a big gong, and Jeremiah said, Listen, listen all of you, stop beating me. And the scribe said: Beating? Who's beating? We're only having a little fun here on the Temple baseball team. And then he struck Jeremiah in the stomach, which doubled him up real good.

And Jeremiah realized that he'd been mistaken to leave the court of the guards. It would have been far better to remain in the compound with the dogs and their trainer—an Ethiopian, a refugee from one of Pharaoh Neco's wars in southern Egypt who'd drifted from one place to another and somehow ended up in Jerusalem, and who for some reason was afraid of people but calmed down in the company of dogs. He walked around the court of the guards on all fours, barking and yowling, and slept with the dogs in their kennel, and licked their faces and ears, and the King of Judah had put him in charge of the royal dogs; the king attended to his daily welfare and called him Ebed-Melech the Ethiopian—Servant of the King.

The Temple scribe again raised his bat, and told the officer next to him, Let this man be put to death, because he causes the soldiers who are left in this city to lose heart, and all the people, by speaking such words to them, for this man is not seeking the welfare of this people, but their harm. And the officer called up a senior officer, and the senior officer called the minister of defense, until the red phone rang in Zedekiah's room. Zedekiah was busy shoving his wife toward the king-size bed in near-total darkness—ever since her plastic surgery, he couldn't stand looking at her in the light. But the minister called and disturbed him right in the middle, stiff and lubricated, and Zedekiah cried out in exasperation and got dressed and rushed out. He went down to Benjamin Gate and grabbed Jeremiah and led him aside and bawled: Out of my sight, all of you! Let me interrogate him myself! And they were left alone, both of them dressed in black. Zedekiah asked, Has there been any word from the Lord? And Jeremiah whispered into his ear—on which he noticed for the first time a minuscule cuneiform tattoo (yes, here too)—and told him, *There was.* And Zedekiah asked, What? And Jeremiah said, into his ear, You will be handed over to the King of Babylon. And Zedekiah suddenly felt like telling Jeremiah, Look, I know by now that every word you've spoken is true, and that you speak with the true voice of God, but even though you speak nothing but evil words to me, know this, my dear childhood friend, it's been a huge privilege for me to see you and listen to you; I know I'll never again be so close to God. But different words altogether came out of his mouth. He opened the door and called out to his officers and to the scribes who were waiting a short distance away, and who all fixed their eyes upon their king: Enough, I'm fed up. The interrogation failed. Here he is, he's in your hands, for the king cannot do a thing against him. Take him back to the house of the guards. And he added abruptly, Give him a loaf of bread daily. Until such time as the city runs out of bread.

And the officers took him away, and one of them, who was called Malchiah the King's Son, for he professed to be in the line of succession, said on their way to the court: But the city ran out of bread a long time ago. The king is clearly suggesting something to us . . . Yes, I've got a better idea. Let's take him to my place for a bit. And Jeremiah said, But the king spoke, and Malchiah the King's Son said, But I'm Malchiah the King's Son, and I, too, have a say in this city—or maybe you think I don't have a say? And Jeremiah said, Fine, whatever, let's go, then. And Malchiah the King's Son said, What? And Jeremiah said, Okay, I agree, let's go to your place for a bit, and Malchiah the King's Son said, What? And Jeremiah said, Look, it's fine, I'm not arguing with you. For at that moment Jeremiah had decided that he was abandoning his hopeless task; he was renouncing this life growing more corrupt by the day, retiring from all his shouting with his parched, inflamed throat at deaf ears in the hopes of a redemption that wasn't going to happen for another seventy or seven hundred or seven thousand years at best, and all he now wished for himself was a swift death, so that his eyes wouldn't behold the horrors of the siege and the destruction of Jerusalem. For a moment, he felt happy that his sister had died a long time ago, that she hadn't been exposed to this coarseness, this avalanche of flesh, the awful defeat of humanity, and happy, too, that his parents were in exile. Though he hadn't heard from them in ages, he felt—that is, he *hoped*—they were alive and well, and that soon, perhaps—forgetting he was probably about to be killed—he'd be able to send them the letter he'd written: tomorrow he'd go to the post office and he'd send them the letter by registered mail. And then he started to laugh quietly, his head bent low. A registered letter, he chuckled, a registered letter! He took a quick peek at the view of Jerusalem from the upper floor of the Temple—he'd been led up there in an elevator to shorten the way to Malchiah's place—and it looked to him as though everything outside had been burned to the ground, like the aftermath of a forest fire, when everything is scorched black apart from a couple of greenish stains and some smoldering embers. But this vision lasted only a moment, and Jeremiah heard Malchiah saying, That's how I like my prophets, quiet and obedient!

As they entered the court of the guards, Jeremiah said, But you said that you had a better idea, I thought we were going somewhere else . . . Were you bluffing about wielding the scepter, Malchiah? And Malchiah the King's Son said, Lower him down into the pit, and Jeremiah said, Yes, a pit fit for the end! And Malchiah instructed four of the ministers who were accompanying them (or were they, in fact, the ministers' young sons, who were learning their fathers' trade, and who simply bore the same names? for they suddenly seemed awfully young to Jeremiah)— Baalzecher and Baalmelech and Baalgezer and Cohen-Mastemah— to tie the prophet up. And Malchiah said, Lower him down slowly, as though he were made of porcelain, lest people say we killed him: I want him alive, if barely, when he touches bottom; I want to sleep soundly tonight. And Jeremiah told the officers, It's just like with Joseph and his brothers, and you, too, are my good brothers, I understand you—you've got to wipe out all the dreams I dreamed, all the fears I woke in you. Thank you, thank you, for all the mercy you've shown me. But they didn't pay any attention to his words, and the four officers let Jeremiah down into the steep cesspool that stood in a corner of the court of the guards, behind the kennels, and they peered down from above and saw that there was no water in the pit, only muck.

And Jeremiah sank in the muck. Ever so slowly, he was lowered to the bottom, which was filled with sewage—sticky, slurping, putrid. He felt that he was being sucked into it inch by inch. And he felt a deep tranquillity washing over him, because he knew that in another quarter of an hour, half an hour tops, everything would come to an end: what mattered most was that they would leave him alone, what mattered most was to be alone. It was perfectly quiet there, as in a cave, but without any echo, and Jeremiah knew now that he was undefeated, that none of this was important—the pit wasn't important and the muck wasn't important. He had never been defeated; even though he'd been battered and bruised, he'd stood up to his trials. What exactly the point was of his having suffered through them all, he couldn't quite say, but, then, nobody was demanding an answer from him, either. By now it was very hot in the city—summer was here—but in the pit it was cool. Jeremiah already knew that the Babylonians would soon batter down the city walls and set Jerusalem to the torch, and that the flames would consume the court of the guards, and the palace, and the Temple, and the desiccated fruit trees in their enclosures, whose shadows his eyes had registered a short while before, on the way over from the Temple. But none of this concerned him, not at all, for he was deep in the pit, in this pit that would protect him and shield him the way a shell shields its pearl in the depths of the sea even as a whale glides overhead; even when Jeremiah died, this shell would still watch over him. For he knew that he would soon die there, floundering, that the pit would be both his executioner and his grave, and that the foul-smelling muck in which he would drown would harden over him after the destruction of the city in the heat of this dry summer, after all the city's sewage stopped oozing through the pipes, the way the piss and shit in a corpse likewise dry up and cease to flow. Though the city and its ramparts swam above his head, he was no longer in the world but under the world; the pit nourished Jeremiah deep in its bosom. And he called his sister to mind—she, too, had had a pit, her illness, and she, too, had been slowly sucked into the muck. And his parents, too, for that matter, had sunk in their Babylonian pit, he reflected: Why, the world's nothing more than an ocean of muck! Okay, the end. And he shut his eyes and relaxed, just as someone who's been clinging to the edge of a cliff might finally slacken his grip.

42

Nebuzaradan stepped stiffly out of his helicopter, an enormous handkerchief protecting his nose and mouth from the dust. He had eliminated the Egyptian nuisance with a single machine gun, mowing down the outlaws matter-of-factly from above, with his own two hands, reaping his crop. It was more like pest control than a massacre. There were some two or three hundred Egyptian troops, merely a symbolic annoyance sent by Pharaoh. In effect, the Babylonians executed a bunch of Egyptian criminals who would have had to be killed anyway, and in so doing probably even saved Pharaoh a little money.

And all the ministers and officials of the King of Babylon came and sat at the Middle Gate to judge the defectors who were now trickling out of the breach in the walls. And Nebushazban, too, returned after a short absence, promoted to the rank of Rab-mag, chief of the magi; he hovered in his own helicopter over the Holyland complex, whose demolition he'd overseen personally during his previous stay in Jerusalem, and he was astonished to see that the compound he'd razed to the ground with his own dynamite had been completely rebuilt. The city in which he'd re-sided for some three years, along with his comrade Nebuzaradan, and which had practically become a second home for him—he'd even considered settling there for good, having himself appointed as a local pasha—seemed to him, perhaps because of the stifling summer heat, a completely different place. The atmosphere in a city just prior to its being sacked and burned was heavy and oppressive and all too familiar to him. State policies had to be implemented—that was clear. It was awful, but also just. He knew that the Babylonians would be despised and fought, but, as the king said, the Judeans had asked for it.

Nebuchadnezzar offered food and drinks to the defectors, and the next day he sent them to demolish the walls of their own city, each and every man receiving a brand-new five-kilo sledgehammer. He instructed the defectors to work diligently, even as stones were cast down from above by the erstwhile relatives and friends of the defectors. I was fond of their king—his tax was barely two-thirds of what Moab and Sidon paid—and despite all that, what did he do? He ran off to Pharaoh. I gave him a discount, and he insulted me and rebelled against me! No, I don't get it. We had a personal contract between us, an oath, and he broke the contract, Nebuchadnezzar said. I'm obliged to act in accordance with what was stipulated in the contract—if I don't, I'll be going against my word, and all the other contracts I made with the kings of these lands will immediately become null and void. I act for the sake of our children and the women of Babylon, and in all my other kingdoms as well, he said. So—what else can we do? We'll raze their temples and their city, we'll cause as much damage as possible, we'll remove that ridiculous king of theirs with all his tattoos, we'll put him in handcuffs and whisk away that human obelisk to where he deserves to be—here, between the rivers. We'll plant him here like a tree. We'll plant him at my place in the garden like a Persian orange tree, he said. And a distant memory came to mind, from a time back who knew when: he's riding behind his father on a black horse, and a hand stretches back and offers him one orange slice after another, and the scent of citrus sweeps over the King of Babylon.

After you're done with the buildings, send them into exile. This time I mean all of them—maybe leave only a few hundred, to clear the rubble and bury the dead. We'll send a fresh shipment home; they'll be nicely received by the earlier exiles. We've shown enough understanding—there's a limit to my benevolence. A city without a river, the king said to Nebuzaradan and Nergal-Sharezer and the rest of the ministers, why, that's ridiculous! This city in summer is a furnace surrounded by a wall, Nebushazban said. It's as hot there as a pot of slow-cooking jam. It's going to be a nightmare for you, Sire, but I guess we can't always choose which city to sack. Shall we go, Sire? he asked. But Nebuchadnezzar said, I'm staying here, in Riblah. I'm already an old man, he said, even though he was barely fifty. You're all grown up now; you know what to do. So—enough, that's it, the king abruptly told his ministers. Strike up the band.

AND ALL THE MINISTERS OF BABYLON descended upon Jerusalem, this time not in smart service cars but in helicopters. And Nebuzaradan told his adjutant, Pass me a box of matches and some red wine. I mean a box of those big kitchen matches, okay? And in the meantime, why not aim a cannonball at the wall over there? Soften it up for me, so the battering rams will have an easier time—punch some holes in the breach for me. I want them to start getting an idea of what they're up against, okay? We'll release them from their suffering. And all the ministers of Babylon plugged their ears with their fingers.

All over the city, sirens were heard, as well as a ringing like a giant alarm clock. There were detectors on the walls that were sensitive to the slightest movement, and, like a motorcycle alarm that starts beeping whenever a cat passes by, the walls shouted at every hammer blow, at every patrol, at every direct hit, every head butt from the battering ram. A wall is a skin, Nergal-Sharezer told his troops, and, as with human flesh, there are hard and soft spots in it, spots that allow for entry and spots that don't. For example, good luck getting in through the heel. It's hard, it's dried out, it's too thick. You've got to find a soft spot, like the flesh behind the ear, or maybe sneak into the ear itself! A city under siege is like someone who's shut his eyes, stopped up his ears and nostrils, tightened his asshole, and is grinding his teeth. If you want to get in, you need to start by wrenching his jaw open and then tapping through his mouth, tooth by tooth. There will be some strong teeth, undoubtedly, but there's always at least one cavity, maybe filled in and maybe not. That's the master plan: we enter through the rot. And there's always something rotten, always. We take advantage of plaque, of apathy and negligence. And we've got to slip in carefully, stealthily. If the patient feels us burrowing in, he's naturally going to pull out his toothbrush—we need to make sure that, by the time that occurs to him, we're already in the city, Nergal-Sharezer summarized. We don't have much time—it'll be very hot here soon: you know what you've got to do. We've been in this sort of situation many times over. Don't expect a pep talk; we all want to get back home as soon as possible. And someone asked, So where's the hole in the rotten tooth? And Nergal-Sharezer pointed and said: There. Over there, there's a breach in the wall. Eight hundred inhabitants of the city have already trickled through to us, most of them relatives of the exiled from last time. We'll give them hammers to break down the wall for us, and whoever is up to the task will receive a one-way ticket to Babylon on the light rail. We've also received information about a prophet still being sheltered inside Jerusalem, he said, rising to his feet: The city's in the palm of his hand, apparently, and they say he's actually on our side. Here's a photo; try to take him alive and bring him back in one piece, okay? He could be useful later on. Does he have a price on his head? the master of archers asked, and Nergal-Sharezer stared at him and said, Sure, there's a small reward, and it's your head, Mr. Archer. Look how lucky you are, you got your prize in advance!

43

EBED-MELECH THE ETHIOPIAN raced on all fours in the oppressive dry heat, his tongue lolling out. A large white angel spread its wings out over the city, and he caught sight of it, though only its backside. He left the king's house and sprinted to Benjamin Gate; there, he knew, Zedekiah was sitting and observing the tightening siege, together with Tukulti and the Judean ministers. From their place up high, they watched the defeated dribbling toward the Chaldeans—two at a time, or four or six or seven. The entire city is clearing out, Baalgezer said anxiously. Let them, let them dribble away, Zedekiah fumed: *The animals that are not clean*, he quoted mockingly—well, don't worry, after the Babylonians serve them up grilled, no one will want to flee anymore.

Through his binoculars, Zedekiah saw a Babylonian helicopter making its descent, and he had the feeling that the person who'd step out of the chopper would be none other than the legendary wine drinker Nebuzaradan. The Babylonian cannons were arrayed equidistant from one another. They'd already breached the large outer wall that encircled greater Jerusalem—from Ramot to Gilo and from Givat Shaul to Abu Tor—using the bulldozers they'd requisitioned, the same bulldozers that had been used to build the wall in the first place and were still in use. Now the siege had gripped the walls of the Old City itself. Zedekiah suddenly had a good feeling, a sense that what he feared most wouldn't happen, that this was the high-water mark of the Babylonian invasion, but that the tide would soon turn and surely things would work out for the best: Jerusalem would be saved, as it had been saved from the Assyrians. He imagined the ensuing elation, all the high spirits in the wake of such high tension, when peace would be declared and people would rush into the streets, jumping for joy. And he told his ministers: Don't worry about it; this is as far as they'll get. God will fight for us, he will send us a sign, you'll see. And Zedekiah remembered how he had once dreamed that he won the lottery, he'd guessed all the numbers, and celebrated his good fortune for the rest of the night. Now he went on standing on a rock there and quoting fitting verses from the book of Kings; truly he felt the power of prophecy swelling within him, and his voice rose and spread in all directions, truly without limits: No, Zedekiah said, the invader shall not come into this city or shoot an arrow there, he will not come before it with a shield or cast up a siege ramp against it. By the way that he came, by the same he shall return, he shall not come into this city, says the Lord. For I will defend this city to save it, for my own sake and for the sake of my servant David. That night, Zedekiah said persuasively, Then the angel of the Lord set out and struck down one hundred and eighty-five thousand in the camp of the Babylonians; when morning dawned, they were all dead. And just after his prophecy, when his eyes were glued to his royal binoculars, Ebed-Melech leaped on him, wailing and lightly scratching the king's arms through his long, tattoo-hiding sleeves.

Down! Zedekiah shouted. But Tukulti understood Ebed's wails. And the "dog" and the dog both raced off in the direction of the court of the guard. Ebed-Melech led Tukulti, while Zedekiah lumbered behind them. The new crown that had been cast for him after Jehoiachin was sent into exile slid off his head, forcing him to wear it on his arm. And on their way they bumped into Eliazar and Noa, who were being taken to the palace at Zedekiah's command, even though Noa didn't want to go and insisted that they be brought back to their old home in Abu Tor. Her heart told her that the destruction would be particularly harsh inside the walls of the Old City, the walls that appeared on maps like a big bull's-eye beckoning an arrow to come and embed itself there, tearing Jerusalem apart.

Eleven-year-old Eliazar clung to his father's sleeve, and Zedekiah knelt for a moment beside him. Eliazar said, I heard what you said, Dad, I was standing up there and I heard you say an angel would come and deliver us, and I saw the angel in the sky, covering the city from one hill to another—but Zedekiah wasn't listening. And Eliazar said, Dad, I've got a question: Where's Babylon? And Zedekiah said, Babylon? Babylon is far, far away, and then he corrected himself and said, No, there is no Babylon, actually, there's no such place. And Noa couldn't stand the sight of him anymore, and started to walk away. Zedekiah thought mistakenly that she intended to abandon Eliazar with him, and he got up and followed her; she went on walking, and he stuck behind her, though he kept his pace leisurely, since he didn't want to give anyone the impression that he was chasing after a woman. And all of a sudden Eliazar was beside her, so Zedekiah turned away and continued on his way to the court of the guard. He didn't notice that his crown had slipped off onto the pavement.

DOWN BELOW, IN THE COURT OF THE GUARD, Jeremiah's mouth was by this point just beneath the surface of muck, emitting bubbles now and then, though his nose and both of his eyes (shut tight) and his brow were still in the air, and the locket around his neck with the wrinkled almond inside was floating on the muck and glittering in the dark. Tukulti saw the glitter and barked to Ebed-Melech and said, Take thirty dogs with you from the kennels and pull the prophet Jeremiah up from the pit before he dies. And the dogs threw a looped rope into the pit, which they knotted together out of rags and worn-out clothes that were scattered in the court of the guard. Ebed-Melech, who hadn't uttered a word of human speech for years, called down into the pit in a slightly florid Hebrew, Ho, good sir, put now these worn garments and rags under thine armholes! But Jeremiah couldn't hear him, and stared at the rope made of rags, wondering whether this was some sort of joke. All the same, he worked his arms free from the muck—it was like lifting weights, he thought—and fixed the loop of rags under his armpits, and thirty dogs mustered their strength and slowly pulled and raised and drew the prophet out. And they let him lie there and catch his breath in the court of the guard, next to the mouth of the pit. He looked more like a big turd than a human being: his body was entirely sheathed in muck and bundled in a coat of mud save for his eyes, which kept blinking, but they, too, were filthy. As he lay there in the corner by the rim of the pit, the dogs stared at him and cautiously wagged their tails. Zedekiah came and saw Jeremiah's state and gave orders that he be hosed down. Jeremiah didn't respond to the steady stream of water that struck him and rolled him over in the yard; in his mind, he was somewhere else entirely, far away, protected, surrounded by a wall and another wall and another wall and another wall. And then someone came up to him and removed his clothing and wiped away the remains of the muck with the same rags that had made up his life rope. And then they clothed him, also with the tatters that had served as his rope. But he paid no attention. He was little more than a corpse, wet, cast aside, spiritless, Godless, without angels, without prophecy, without thoughts, without memories, fatherless, motherless, sisterless, homeless, without relatives, without friends, without words, with no willpower of his own. He'd been in the pit and had been drawn out of the pit, but the pit remained within him; a pit had been drawn out of a pit, and muck was rising from inside the pit. Now there's no Jeremiah but only muck, now there is only muck.

An hour later, they brought Jeremiah—who still lay there at the foot of the palace, not far from the yawning pit—black coffee and half a pita, and he drank and ate a bit, and the waiter from the palace restaurant who'd brought him the food whispered in his ear, His Majesty Zedekiah wants to see you, it's urgent. And Jeremiah said, No, no one asks for me anymore, but the waiter insisted, It's urgent, the fate of the entire city is in the balance. And Jeremiah, who couldn't quite stand on his own feet, was placed on a large trolley used to distribute food and wine in restaurants, which the waiter brought from the royal store-room. Thus was the prophet wheeled across the palace's fore-court and brought into the third entrance and taken up in the service elevator. In a room within a room within a room was Zedekiah, naked apart from boxer shorts. He was soaked in sweat, and all of his clothes were scattered about the room, and one of his fingers was stuck between the covers of some book like a mouse caught in a trap. There were some yellowish snacks strewn over the floor. And the king turned to Jeremiah and asked, Have you found me, O my enemy? And Jeremiah said, I haven't found anything. And the king said: Jeremiah, Jeremiah, listen to me. They're very close, they've all come back; all the Babylonian officials and Rab-mag are sitting at the gate and sorting through my citizens, and they've started ramming the Old City wall. And as Jeremiah's gaze lingered over the king's burly body, he told him in a voice that could hardly be heard, My heart is shattered within me. And the king shouted: What? What's that? And Jeremiah said, Mattaniah, I myself no longer know what I think, but I remember what I've told you in the past. Every time I open my mouth, someone pounces on me and wants to kill me. And Zedekiah swore an oath to Jeremiah, saying, Okay, okay, on the name of the Lord, the Almighty who forged our souls, I will not put you to death or hand you over to the men who seek your life. And Jeremiah said: It doesn't matter, I'm already of no consequence. Don't bother swearing anything, Mattaniah. Listen to me, just listen, please. It's very simple: if you go out to the King of Babylon's men and surrender, your life will be spared and the city won't be burned down—you and your household will be allowed to live. But if you don't go out to the Babylonians, then this city will fall into the hands of the Chaldeans, and they will burn it with fire, and you . . . you won't escape.

Jeremiah peeked for a moment at the book that held the king's finger, but he was unable to identify the author. Zedekiah said: I get it, I get it, you're right, but what, but what can I do? I'm in a bind, you understand? I'm afraid of the Jews who have deserted to the Chaldeans' side—I might be handed over to them, and they would abuse me. How am I to go outside the walls? The Jewish deserters will grab me, and then who knows what'll happen. I smell a lynch mob, okay? They're armed with heavy hammers, they've been starved, you know how cruel they are—they'll eat me alive, they'll tear me to pieces . . . They'll chew off my head! he screamed, and Jeremiah said, with a confidence that he no longer possessed: No, don't worry; no, don't worry. The Babylonians won't hand you over to the mob. And even if they do, he added, *it doesn't matter*. Don't you get it? It doesn't matter anymore. You don't matter, I don't matter. Our clutching at life at any cost—it's all finished. You're clinging to a match while a tidal wave is advancing toward you. Let go of the match, Mattaniah. Enough—everything all around you is soaked through and through, the entire area is doomed to flood, the Babylonians aren't going to leave, they won't leave. And Jeremiah grasped the king's free hand and pressed his forehead against Zedekiah's, saying, You've got to get dressed and go out and give yourself up, and he started gathering the king's scattered black clothes and tried to get him into them.

Zedekiah seemed convinced, but he told Jeremiah, who was buttoning up the royal shirt: You keep this conversation to yourself or I'll have you killed. And if anyone sees you leaving here and asks you what we were talking about, tell them that you came to beg me not to lower you back into the pit. In the meantime, I'll think about what you said. It's not a decision one can make in a hurry, you understand. But, you know, thanks for everything, okay? And Jeremiah looked at the king for a long time, and noticed a missing button. All of a sudden, he was filled with the certainty that nothing would help now, absolutely nothing; he knew that he'd never see his old friend again—Zedekiah, who had once been the boy Mattaniah—and he looked into the king's eyes and said: Maybe none of it was meant to work. Maybe we're only actors, and everyone has his role, and your role was to be king, *the last king*, and my role was to see what was happening and shout about it and be ignored and so be able to tell the whole sad story. And Zedekiah told him, Jeremiah, if the worst happens— and I said *if!*—you can send Noa to Babylon, to your parents . . . Eliazar will stay here to fight by my side, and then I'll anoint him King of Judah in my place.

The book slipped from his fingers and dropped, and Jeremiah looked at it and read the title and shut his eyes tightly. He wanted to bend over and pick up the book of poems, but instead he made to leave, then stopped by the door and turned around, his hand on the mezuzah, and told Zedekiah: Ah . . . it's . . . it's not that bad, it's not that bad, Zedekiah. At least you got to be king . . . and a good king, all in all. With that, Jeremiah ran off and made his way to the wall. And all the dogs were there peering through the arrow slits. And Zedekiah came out of the third entrance to the palace and stood on a high turret above the dogs. Through his binoculars, he spied Nergal-Sharezer, who'd grown a trim little beard, and Nebuzaradan, too, who must have weighed more than three hundred pounds, and the crippled chief eunuch, Nebusarsechim, whose reputation as the *torturer of kings* had spread far and wide—Zedekiah was well aware of what he'd done to the King of Ashkelon. And at the sight of Chief Eunuch Nebusarsechim, he let go of the royal binoculars, which bumped against his chest as he ran to the Benjamin Gate, and he saw that he was all alone.

He met up with his few remaining valiant warriors at the Benjamin Gate, and Eliazar was among them, grasping a shield and sword. The king was glad to see them but held back from showing his feelings, for he knew that doing so would be interpreted as a sign of weakness. And evening descended. They got themselves into uniform, dressing the king up as a simple soldier, and they fled the city under cover of night through the king's garden at the gate, between the two walls. Before leaving, Zedekiah told Tukulti, Stay in the city, take care of the dogs; they won't shoot you because of our sins. And he then noticed that Tukulti was still wearing his old collar, and he bent over and removed the collar and stroked the dog's back. And Tukulti, flustered, wanted to say something to him, but he didn't say a word, nor did he howl.

And Zedekiah set forth from Jerusalem in a jeep, turning onto the road leading to the Arabah, their headlights off, with his son, Eliazar, by his side. We'll get to Moab, he muttered, we'll find refuge there, and there I'll anoint you King of Judah. We'll get a bit of oil and I'll anoint you, and a fresh shoot will spring up from the House of David. I'll explain everything about ruling the kingdom to you—it isn't that hard. They slipped through the southeastern purlieus of the city—drove through a tunnel under the Temple, he, his eleven-year-old son, and a company of his soldiers, all of them from the ordnance corps—mighty warriors to a man. The enemy was in the west, ignorant of his departure, or so he thought, but of course they'd seen him. They were lying in wait for him, or, rather, hovering—they'd called in a chopper rigged with a heavy machine gun to track him down. Chief Eunuch Nebusarsechim sat next to the pilot and said, Hold it, don't swoop down quite yet; let's enjoy the show, give him a chance to panic a bit, get a load of his troopers running for cover. And the chopper mowed them down left and right with a businesslike *rat-tat-tat*.

Zedekiah drove in serpentine zigzags in his Mercedes jeep, covered with dust from the road, strengthened by the presence behind him of his son, who made him feel more focused. I'll save him, he thought; the bridge to Moab is close, and we'll find refuge there. He looked at Eliazar and suddenly saw that two of the boy's right-hand fingers had been pulverized; the boy didn't cry, however—he didn't say a word, didn't complain, actually laughed—and Zedekiah felt nauseated. All of a sudden, he couldn't remember where the boy had been all these years. He remembered him at age three, but now here he was, big, as though it had happened all at once. There were some strange gaps in his memory; he couldn't see through the haze in his mind. But never mind that now, he thought, now it's only me and him, as the chopper dipped down behind them over the plains of Jericho, before it overtook them and nosed around and landed. It took its time landing, and more sand and dust filled Zedekiah's eyes, even though he had the roof up and all the windows firmly closed and the A/C blowing. Chief Eunuch Nebusarsechim stepped out of the chopper, leaning on a walking stick and holding in his other hand an enormous sword sated with the blood of kings and princes. He limped over to the King of Judah as though to cut off his head and the head of his son, who got out of the car after his father and held on to him without speaking a word. But then another car pulled up, and a large dog leaped out, all skin and bones, and the torturer of kings turned to face the dog, readying his sword, but the dog didn't attack him, only latched on to him with his two eyes. And, staring all the while, the dog went up to the king and his son, who were crouching together in the dust amid a chaos of tire tracks, and he, too, crouched with them, to protect them with his own body, and he howled, and Eliazar howled, and Zedekiah howled into both of their howling. And the three of them were seized and taken to the King of Babylon in Riblah.

In Riblah, Zedekiah and Tukulti stood on either side of Eliazar. Tukulti licked the boy's minced hand. And the prince raised his eyes for a moment, looking at his father's ear, and then collapsed by his side, and Tukulti's coat was spattered with the boy's blood. And Nebuchadnezzar entered and saw what was happening and suddenly felt a deep revulsion, as though he were in the middle of a book that he wanted, *this very minute*, to shut and stop reading. And he nodded his head at Chief Eunuch Nebusarsechim, who approached from behind, and before Zedekiah's eyes the eunuch shot the unconscious boy in the head, and he shot Tukulti in the head as well, and he hung their corpses on a hook. A moment later, with a thrust of his enormous sword, he sliced out both of the king's eyes in one stroke, and darkness descended on Mattaniah; the light of his eyes and his soul were snuffed out as though a lightbulb had popped inside him, and all its slivers pierced him in a million places. Since he had no eyes to cry with, the crying filled his insides and overflowed within him, and he died outright at that moment, even though his heart was still beating and his blood was still coursing through his kidneys and through both his legs and arms; even though he was still breathing, he was, literally, the walking dead, the blind walking dead, and they bound him in fetters to take him to Babylon.

AND IN THE FIFTH MONTH, which is the month of Av, on the seventh of the month, Nebuzaradan, captain of the guard, arrived in Jerusalem, and in his right hand he held a matchbox and in his left a bottle of red wine. Inside the box were one hundred long kitchen matches, and on the box was a picture of the city. He burned down the king's residence, and then he went from house to house and burned down every building, and soon the wine bottle in his hand was the empty. And in the purlieus of the city, soldiers were tearing and crushing and sweeping suburbs off the map, and mopping up the last fugitive Judeans on every mountaintop and every hilltop, and from the cracks in every boulder. Eventually, they reached the stadium where the upside-down observatory dome still stood, and they clambered up to the rim of the bowl, where weeds and tall thorns had begun to grow and densely covered its perimeter, and they set the whole thing alight.

IT WAS A HOT SUMMER, as it always is in the month of Av in Jerusalem and environs, and the air was dry, and the winds fanned the flames, and the brush fires ran wild through the city for the entire month, and it was forbidden to put them out. The Babylonians even made sure to line up the city's remaining firemen in a cistern beforehand and mow them down. Now fire will be king, said Nebuzaradan, and with one last match he lit up the wine bar where he'd been in the habit of drinking, and then filliped the empty matchbox into the fire.

So, when the Babylonian troops at last breached the inner walls of Jerusalem, the city was already destroyed from within. Nebuzaradan motored down the lanes of the Old City in his white Mercedes, with a giant bulldozer as well as the army's engineering corps and a fleet of tanks clearing the way ahead of him and crushing any cars that had been left parked where the streets were too narrow for him to pass. And the Jews who fell into his hands spoke to Military Intelligence about a prophet who was still in the Old City, locked up with the king's dogs, and who had implored the nation to surrender and pay obeisance to the Babylonians. And when the captain of the guard entered the court of the guards, he saw that very prophet, he saw all the hungry dogs, and he saw the black man-dog stooped over and drinking from a dripping fire hose, and he saw the prophet standing and looking around at the fire and the debris and the destruction and still talking, talking, talking, and talking. Nebuzaradan went up to him, and in his middling Hebrew, which he'd learned during his earlier years in the city, he told him, So, behold, I loose thee this day from the chains which are upon thy hands; if it seem good unto thee to come with me into Babylon, then come, and I will look well unto thee, but if it seem ill unto thee to come with me to Babylon, forbear. The giant Babylonian's words were so grandiose and incoherent that Jeremiah, dumbfounded, could only look away. And Nebuzaradan fetched a small tray from his car, which was already hot inside from the fierce summer heat and from the sporadic bursts of fire in the city, and on the tray was a meal and several small gold coins. But Jeremiah threw the coins on the ground. Ebed-Melech came and snatched some food for the ravenous dogs, and he lay hold of the coins, too, while he was at it, and Nebuzaradan took heed and brought out more food from the trunk of the car, and the dogs ate warily, and Ebed-Melech ate with them. Jeremiah's eyes were glazed over, and he didn't notice that the captain of the guard was staring at him again, and didn't notice Nebuzaradan's departure; for it was at that moment, seeing a Babylonian officer standing in front of him, with thick clouds of smoke rising on all sides, that he knew, really knew, for the first time, that he was truly a prophet—and yet he didn't care anymore. And he muttered: Arise, cry out in the night, at the beginning of the watches pour out your heart like water, before the presence of the Lord; lift your hands to Him, for the lives of your children who faint for hunger at the head of every street. Look, O Lord, to whom you have done this: women eat their offspring, the children they have borne, priest and prophet are killed in the sanctuary of the Lord. The young and the old are lying on the ground in the streets, my young women and my young men have fallen by the sword; on the day of your anger you have killed them, slaughtering without mercy. And Nebuzaradan looked from his car at what the siege had accomplished over the last months, the children that had been eaten and the scattered remains of their corpses, the beheaded priests, and he saw a shriveled bull that was being dragged to the slaughter as a scapegoat. The bull knew precisely where they were dragging it, and kicked and scraped its hooves against the earth and lowed, but someone took out a bunch of dill, and the hungry beast wasn't able to resist the strong smell and advanced toward the dill, and then again it stopped in its tracks, and again it was lured, and Nebuzaradan saw this and shook his head in revulsion, and then watched as someone crouched down by the bull as it crossed her path, and she poked at its hooves and drew out bits of barley, which she ate in a mad frenzy of hunger. Someone else was nibbling at the tiny thorns that were growing out of an abandoned camel trough, and a falafel vendor was walking around with a pita filled with salad and what might have been falafel balls in his outstretched hand, but the stench that rose from the pita was so nauseating that no one dared approach him, and soon he tripped over a corpse and fell. And there was a man there dressed in the attire of a high priest, and he stood in the midst of a demolished house and prayed to the new star burning above. And six women ascended the ruined wall, intending to jump, for the unavoidable defilements were by now well under way. Women were being violated in the streets and in their homes and on the roofs of their homes, and they fled to those parts of the city wall that were still largely intact, some having already been raped, others fearing being raped, and there they started to leap silently from the wall. But no one paid any attention, and they leaped and leaped.

And their bodies were shattered on the boulders inside Jeremiah the prophet's head, together with all the other incidents in the city, and this panorama of destruction was broadcast directly into Jeremiah's brain there in the court of the guards, as though he'd swallowed all the news channels. The dam of prophecy burst open, and the river was a mighty current, and he saw everything, and he heard everything. But this time his prophecy was of events occurring in the present moment rather than the future, and he was inundated by every ache and pain of the destruction of this city as though he were the ocean and affliction were the rivers feeding into him. Everything streamed into him, every widowed mother, every child devoured by its parents, every elderly person who died for lack of medicine and water, every parched lip, every home blown up with its inhabitants trapped under the rubble, every bird that had been left in its cage when its owners died and hadn't received its feed and water in the summer heat wave, and all the city cats, to the very last one, who died in the heat of Tammuz and Av and were immediately consumed by crows as well as human beings, and all the pigeons and crows and alley cats that were snatched and whose necks were wrung and who got eaten after the first two weeks of the siege, and all the dogs that were asphyxiated in order to fill the mouths of the hungry, all the vegetation that was burned by the fires begun by the kitchen matches—flowers, seedlings, and trees—all the amputated hands, all the unhinged doors, all the buildings that had turned into heaps of dust. They all seemed to be hollering in Jeremiah's ears, and they screamed, Stop this, hold it back, rise up and stop it at once! Everything that he'd prophesied had indeed occurred, this catastrophe was second to none, and Jeremiah saw now that it had always been unavoidable. Suddenly he grasped the whole of the Bible, from the beginning of creation to the present moment, as a book whose end could never have been other than utter destruction—from the moment the heavens were separated from the earth, and man from animal, and Adam from Eve, and the drowned from the saved, it was only a question of time until a nation would be set apart and chosen, and only a question of time until that choice would lead to aloofness and arrogance and rebellion, for the demands upon them were too difficult, they never could handle it, beginning with Adam and Eve and ending with Zedekiah. Hence exile and ruin were inevitable. It was already planted in the story of the Garden of Eden for everyone to behold, but no one, no one had beheld. And all of a sudden, Jeremiah understood that his fate, his abandonment were never matters of chance, they were the whole point, so that people would be able to see from then on that a prophet had been sent to warn them but to no avail—he was forced to operate on his own, alone, cast out.

And there was nothing left for him to do now, apart from sitting there in the court of the guards that had been broken into by bulldozers and dynamited to clear the way for the captain of the guard—who kept drinking from his bottle, the wine seemingly never running out—as he pushed on in the direction of the Temple and the palace. Jeremiah didn't glance back or up in order not to see the flames: He has made my flesh and my skin waste away, and broken my bones. He has besieged and enveloped me with bitterness and anguish. He has made me sit in darkness like the forever dead. He has walled me about so that I cannot escape; he has put heavy chains on me. Though I call and cry for help—he shuts out my prayer. Jeremiah didn't understand what he was saying; he didn't know if he was speaking about himself or whether the city was speaking through his throat about itself. He merged with the city, and its lament was his own voice, and his mutterings its thoughts, but no one heard him anyhow, only Ebed-Melech the Ethiopian, and the dogs all in a frenzy— Ebed-Melech howling and running in circles there in the court of the guards.

And Jeremiah turned to Ebed-Melech and grabbed him, and from deep within the shambles of his own mind he said, Don't worry, calm down, calm down—you won't be delivered to the people that you fear. And he added, Your name will no longer be Ebed-Melech but Baruch ben Neriah, My Candle Is the Lord, for the candle of the Lord has been lit in you. And they held each other tightly until they both stopped shaking, and Ebed-Melech stood upright on his feet and told Jeremiah: Jeremiah, come, let us go to Mizpah. There's nothing left for us to do here. And Jeremiah looked at him and said, A bear lies in wait for me, a lion in hiding. And Ebed-Melech, which is to say Baruch, didn't understand, so Jeremiah added: He comes from everywhere. He comes from everywhere. Here, too. There, too. And Baruch asked him: Who? Who? Nebuzaradan? And Jeremiah said, The bear, the bear and the lion.

Nebuzaradan entered the Temple, half of which was already in flames. And he drained the last drops of wine from what turned out not to have been an inexhaustible bottle after all, and broke the empty vessel against the altar, and he took the pillars of bronze and their socles and the brazen sea and smashed them into pieces, and the pots and the shovels and the snuffers and the censers and the ladles, and all the vessels of brass used in the

Temple service were taken away by his soldiers, and the fire pans and the basins, that which was of gold, in gold, and that which was of silver, in silver, the captain of the guard took away. And there was also a charity box for the poor, and he pried the lid open with his keychain screwdriver; there was nothing in the box. And a truck arrived, beeping as it pulled up in reverse, and on it they loaded everything, the bronze, the silver, and the gold—whatever remained from last time. The arsonists had to grab whatever they could lay their hands on before they got burned by the fire they'd set. And in one of the rooms whose doors had been forced, and which seemed to Nebuzaradan like a cave, he saw a sort of altar with large green leaves emerging from within that covered nearly the entire hall. As he strode into the thicket in order to find out what was going on in there, he got stuck as in a rain forest. His comrades-in-arms called out to him, Oh, master, where are you? And he drew his sword and tried to blaze a trail to the interior, but he still couldn't find the center out of which all the greenery was growing. He pulled out a flashlight and peered this way and that, and saw that there were millions of ants on the branches and leaf stalks and on the white-and-violet flowers. On one of the flowers he thought he saw an ant praying and asking for mercy for its nest, and the ant looked him straight in the eye, and this was too much for him. He got scared and retreated back along on the trail he'd blazed, and when he found his comrades waiting there with flame-throwers, Nebuzaradan said, We've got to burn it all up, absolutely everything, and left.

And several warriors entered the Holy of Holies, which they'd almost missed, since to them it looked like nothing so much as a tiny broom closet. They thought there was nothing there, but in the end they found two frightened cherubim hiding behind a curtain. And they took them and put them in a cage, and loaded them along with the rest of the loot onto the truck.

———

AND NEBUZARADAN HAD THE CHIEF PRIEST, Seriah, forced into a train car, and the second priest, Zephaniah, and the three guardians of the threshold, and Pashhur the priest, otherwise known as Terror-All-Around. The other senior leaders and officials were first rounded up and crammed into a holding cell, where they approached the Babylonian with ready money to obtain their release. But the captain of the guard was in no need of hard cash at this time, so he politely rejected these remittances. The scribe who was so free with his baseball bat was taken and gently relieved of his weapon. The so-called King's Son, Malchiah, didn't escape, either, nor did the honorable ministers, including Baalgezer and Baalmelech and Cohen-Mastemah and all the others—unless these were their sons, now bearing their fathers' names and positions? Soon they were all taken in an orderly fashion to Riblah, where their captors told them that these measures were preparatory to their eventual resettlement on an oasis where they would build the House of God in Jerusalem anew: You will be the leaders of the restored city and you will build a new temple for yourselves, and you'll levy a nice little tax, to dispose of entirely as you see fit. And they understood that, after all, things could certainly be worse, so of course they all boarded the light rail without a struggle, and as cold and carbonated drinks were offered to them, they were already starting to plan the new regime and the new division of power. And the light rail glided on, indifferent to their squabbling. When they reached the good place they'd been promised, they were lined up with their faces against a wall at the rail stop and were cut down by several rounds of machine-gun fire, and the station workers buried them between the railroad tracks, lengthwise, legs drawn up to their heads, and they were covered with the dirt and gravel from the track, the trench having been prepared before they left Jerusalem. And the light rail headed back south without delay to collect another delegation. And so Judah went into exile out of its land.

44

FROM HER ROOM, Noa caught sight of Eliazar climbing into Mattaniah's armored jeep, and she shouted, No, no, but no one in the car could hear her behind its darkly tinted and double-glazed windows. She knew that Mattaniah was fleeing to Ammon or Moab—he'd talked about it time and again—except that, in the general panic of the retreat, she realized that he'd forgotten her. Unless he intended to order her a taxi or something. Unless the idea was that he'd send for her as soon as he reached a safe haven beyond the river. From the window, she watched Mattaniah slam the passenger door, stride over and climb into the driver's seat, and start the engine. She lingered there for a moment, fancying that she saw him leave the car again and seek out her staring eyes. But when she blinked he wasn't there any longer, the cars had vanished, and all that remained on the asphalt were the words PRIVATE PARKING FOR THE KING'S USE ONLY. And nearby stood the king's hulking new motorcycle.

She descended to the ground floor and walked down the royal corridors. The old palace was practically empty—the able-bodied had long since fled—and as she paced around she thought, This can't be, this can't be. She didn't care about the destruction, only about this, that her husband had kidnapped her son. Though she didn't say it outright, not even in a whisper. Only *This can't be*. And from one of the windows she caught a glimpse of Jeremiah, though she didn't realize it was the same Jeremiah she'd once known. No one could have recognized him by then; old age had pounced on him all at once, and he looked at least sixty years old, whereas *her* Jeremiah would have to be about the same age as Noa, she estimated: forty. And he was lying there in the courtyard surrounded by stray dogs and seemingly talking to the clouds. She knew that she was standing on the brink, that if she didn't hold fast she'd certainly fall, and her hands shook so badly that her words fell away like a shower of autumn leaves. She didn't know exactly what was going on, she didn't realize the extent of the devastation, she only saw the rooms, the corridor, the chaos. And then she stepped out to the open parking lot, and she raised her eyes and saw that the roof of the palace was ablaze. Someone had abandoned a home-delivery scooter right by the entrance, leaving its engine running, so she mounted the scooter and shifted into first gear. The scooter whistled shrilly. She accelerated.

Noa drove, the sun on her right, down the Jerusalem-Jericho road. In the near distance she saw a cluster of habitations she wasn't familiar with, and, seeing a sign, she sounded out the words MAHYAM—LAJAEEN—SHUAFAT in Arabic script, with some effort, though she didn't know exactly what it meant. But then she saw a sign in English and understood that this was a refugee camp. Funny, she'd never heard of such a thing, certainly not here. So many shoddy buildings so close to home. And it wasn't clear whether anyone was living there or if they, too, had been exiled with the rest of the population during Jehoiakim's big deportation, which by now had been long forgotten. She drove along the length of the camp's wall and realized she'd been mistaken: it wasn't a single wall but a maze of crumbled walls, like mangled pages in a book, sprawling out in all directions, useless barriers of pulverized concrete. The Chaldeans had destroyed everything;

the overriding order had been to smash the walls, every wall. She entered the camp by mistake and drove right up into the shadow of the half-demolished high wall, where there was some kind of low-slung building still standing. And she parked for a moment and peeked inside, and saw children there, maybe two hundred children and young boys, stooped over in rows, sewing athletic socks. Then she sped away again and drove past Anatot, linked back up with the main road, and started to drive eastward, toward Jericho. She soon ran out of gas, and kept on coasting downhill until the road leveled off. But she hadn't reached the Jordan yet, as she'd hoped. The scooter emitted an ear-piercing screech, and she dismounted. She continued on foot, reaching out her hand to Eliazar, but Eliazar didn't give her his hand. She sat down on three steps near the road, leading nowhere, and rested for a bit, covering her mouth with four fingers while her other hand was held with her palm up and slack in front of her. There were some dry leaves on the steps, but she couldn't see a single tree. It was terribly hot, and there was no shade. She walked on, maybe half an hour, maybe an hour more. And no one crossed her path. When she looked behind her, she couldn't see Jerusalem any longer, only rising columns of smoke. It felt hotter and hotter, and she took off her clothes, at first her pants and then her shirt, and she wrapped the shirt around her head to protect herself from sunstroke. Her silicone implants weighed her down. Her beauty was unbearable, but there was no one around to see her. The sun blazed on toward three o'clock. From a good distance away, Noa saw a faucet at a rest stop on the route to the Dead Sea, and she walked in her bare feet, swaying along the length of the yellow line on the shoulder of the road, and turned in toward the bay. She stooped and opened the faucet, but no water came out, only a screech. It was an old faucet, and its pipes hadn't been connected to the water main for a long time. The sun moved in the sky and covered for a little while the new star that had trespassed on its circuit. And Noa turned off the dry faucet, though there was no need for her to do so.

45

A LL THE MONTH OF AV, the fires went on burning, and the winds fanned the flames, and no one had the strength to try to beat them back with a battered fire extinguisher in hand, or even a blanket. One woman wore a scarf on which were printed images of various cities and countries; she walked around the city day and night, and in her mouth were only six words, words she'd utter to whomever she saw, if in different intonations: How the gold has grown dim. How the gold has grown dim? How the gold has grown dim . . . How the gold has grown dim! How the gold has grown dim?! How the gold has grown dim!! How the gold has grown dim. And to Jeremiah and Baruch ben Neriah, too, she said, How the gold has grown dim, when she ran into them on their way north into the hills, and Jeremiah looked at her and answered, King Nebuchadrezzar of Babylon has devoured me, he has crushed me, he has made me an empty vessel, he has swallowed me up like a sea monster, he has filled his belly. How the gold has grown dim, the woman said to the black man who walked beside Jeremiah, and he looked her over and answered, like an echo, How the gold has grown dim, and she said, Thank you, thanks a lot, you, you're the only thing that hasn't.

And Jeremiah and Baruch continued on foot to Mizpah, which is in the neighboring district of Benjamin. On the way, Jeremiah stopped in his tracks for something by the side of the path that caught his eye, and when he bent over to get a better look he saw that it was fingers and thumbs that had been cut off the hands of Jews. And he picked up one of the fingers, looked at it from close up, and said to the finger, Now darkness has fallen on the Torah, now darkness has fallen on prophecy. And he picked some of the dirt out from under its fingernail and he slipped the finger into his shirt pocket. And he suddenly remembered how his father had spoken at his sister's grave, turning to the mourners to say, Dear friends, know that I decided to ascend the tower on Mount Scopus and jump, to go there straight after the funeral and jump, but I thought about you and the grief I would cause you if I did so, and that's the only reason that I've decided not to do it, and will instead return home, and sit. And Esther, Jeremiah's mother, who held on to Hilkiah's shoulders until her knuckles turned white, only said, Yes—since it was she, in effect, who'd had the idea of the tower, the idea of jumping, she who suggested this to his father: Let's go together and jump. We'll send Jeremiah to Hanamel—he'll adopt him.

Mizpah had become the seat for those charged with reorganizing Judah on behalf of the Babylonians; they had even appointed a reliable and loyal governor. As expected, Gedaliah the son of Ahikam the son of Shaphan was authorized to govern Judah, and with him they posted a small Chaldean garrison, twenty or thirty swordsmen, as well as some (largely administrative) officials in order to help prepare for the aftermath. Jews far and wide heard of the new seat of power and started trickling into Mizpah, seeking refuge under Gedaliah's wing, refuge and some peace and quiet, some peace and quiet, a little space in which to breathe again. And a refugee camp was set up there, and blankets and medicine and water were delivered from far and near. Jeremiah, who saw that things were being organized efficiently, set out without announcing his arrival or his departure, and Baruch left with him, walking a few paces behind him. And they walked this way for hours in the oppressive heat, and Jeremiah didn't say a word. He stopped only once, spinning around to tell Baruch, who was following close behind, Let him put his mouth in the dust—there may yet be hope. And Jeremiah crouched down and scooped up a handful of dry earth and shoved it into his own mouth. And Baruch said, Get it out, get it out, and he tried to clean the prophet's teeth and tongue with his fingers. On their way, they ran into some pilgrims, who gave them both a little water. These pilgrims hadn't heard of the destruction; they came from villages in the Galilee, and they bore in their bags wheat and barley and semolina and oil and honey. They freely offered Jeremiah and Baruch bread and honey, and the two of them soaked the dark bread in oil and ate, and then they soaked it in honey and ate. The pilgrims asked, Is Jerusalem far? And Jeremiah stared at them as though he were stark staring mad, and only pointed with his hand in the right direction. After some time, the two parties resumed walking, one toward the shattered east, and the other away from there.

And when the sun was about to set, Baruch beheld a hill, and on it there were a few homes. He didn't know the name of the place, and he clutched Jeremiah's shirttails and drew him up toward these buildings. And at the edge of the village, there was a house beside an empty field, and in the field was a crooked olive tree. Jeremiah went up to the tree, and Baruch tried to crush out some oil for them, even though it wasn't the oil-harvesting season. They chewed the bitter, hard olives, and then they leaned against the tree and slept there that hot night. The following morning, Baruch said, Let's try to get inside the house—for it was clear that the place had been abandoned, like all the other homes in this small village. And Jeremiah didn't say anything; he only recalled the words he'd heard as they left the city: How the gold has grown dim. And he knew that the gold in this verse didn't just mean the precious metal—this gold hinted at something else—but he was far too exhausted to be able to think clearly and understand what. Then he remembered how his uncle had once told him that producing olives, and in particular the oil inside the olives, called for a great effort on the part of the olive tree, and consequently olive trees bore fruit only every other year; the year following the harvest, the tree had to recover from this effort. And Jeremiah leaned against the tree and then turned around and hugged it tightly and kissed it and told it, You've got to rest, tree; you've got to sleep for a year. A black-hooded bird stood above him, on a branch of the crooked olive tree; it piped a short song, and vanished into the deserted house across from them. And it sang from indoors a bit longer. Baruch went inside the house and brought out some clothes, black garments—there were only black garments in there, in one of the closets—for Jeremiah and himself. The clothes fit them both, even though they were a woman's shirt and pants. And they took their old clothes from the court of the guards and bundled them up and burned them in a barrel. And Jeremiah cocked an ear toward the house and asked Baruch, Do you hear? They're still playing. But Baruch didn't hear a thing.

46

THE REST OF THAT SUMMER, they lived without blankets under the olive tree, and they ate the olives that remained on the tree and the edible weeds that grew there and the carob pods and figs that Baruch found and gathered from the trees in the little village, and some canned food as well that the fugitives and the exiled had left in their homes and which had escaped the notice of the looters. Foxes and wild boars and hedgehogs prowled between the homes, and in the myrtle beds grew nettles, from which Baruch brewed tea. And Baruch and Jeremiah learned to identify the wild animals, and watched over them, and stroked their fur and their quills when they dared come up close. No one passed on the road to Jerusalem, and tall thorn bushes shot up on byways. Jeremiah and Baruch lived there as on a desert island and never strayed far from their tree. Sometimes Baruch would enter one of the houses nearby to hunt for any provisions that had been left behind, and he'd fall asleep there at night, lying on someone's bed, and he'd find all sorts of stuff, like photos of a boy and girl—usually together, usually standing close to each other and embracing—and diaries written in the local language. Though he couldn't read them, it was clear that these diaries belonged to a young girl who'd obviously been sent into exile, and Baruch would examine the remnants like an archaeologist. Then, in the morning, he'd tidy up and wash, ready to go. But Jeremiah, without saying as much, refused to leave the plot of land, refused to leave the tree, as though he were chained to it by his neck.

And one day, two months after they had set out, at the beginning of the seventh month—which is to say, Tishrei—all sorts of high-ranking officials, civil and military, appeared before the tree, as well as some ordinary soldiers and civilians. There were maybe thirty or forty souls, a mixture of simple Jews and warriors and fugitives from the sword. And they approached Jeremiah and begged of him, Be good enough to listen to our pleas, and pray to the Lord your God for us, for all this remnant, for there are only a few of us left out of many, as your eyes can see. Let the Lord your God show us where we should go and what we should do. And Jeremiah recalled someone who had said something apposite, a hundred years ago, maybe a thousand years ago, and he wanted to quote this verse: Stand at the crossroads . . . where the good way lies . . . and find . . . fiiiind . . . rest . . . ahh . . . for yo-ur-so-uls . . . But not a sound came out of his mouth, no, not a word, and Baruch came out of the house and asked what was going on, and the crowd told him, in so many words, that Gedaliah had been murdered, as well as the Jews who'd been with him in Mizpah, and the officials and the Chaldean soldiers that the King of Babylon had assigned—all were slaughtered and thrown into a large pit by a man of the House of David, whom Baalis, the King of Ammon, had sent to take the life of the governor and restore the glory of the House of David. Now the remnant of Judah has perished, a fugitive said. And Jeremiah offered him an olive from the tree.

Jeremiah listened to all of this and remained silent, and the people, who assumed that the black man coming out of the house was the prophet that they'd been looking for this last week in the hills north of Jerusalem, turned to Baruch. He stole a quick look at Jeremiah and told them, I will pray to the Lord your God according to your words. And they waited at the edge of the field. Ten minutes later, Baruch stepped out again and told them, Be not afraid of the King of Babylon, of whom you are afraid, be not afraid of him, says the Lord, for I am with you to save you, and to deliver you from his hand. And I will grant you mercy that he may have mercy on you. And someone shouted, We've seen his mercy, and he pointed at the university campus on Mount Scopus and at the Bezalel building on the facing hill, which by now had blended into the landscape like little more than mute extensions of the rocky sediment. We're waiting here for nothing; the Ammonite will send his assassins again; we've got to flee to Egypt. And Jeremiah, who had been leaning all along against the tree and listening to the conversation, started to laugh quietly, at first to himself and then out loud, and he beat his fist against the tree as he doubled over with laughter, and the people stared at him in pity mixed with revulsion. And then they turned back to the black prophet, and Baruch said, If you are determined to enter Egypt and go to settle there, then the sword that you fear shall overtake you there, in the land of Egypt, and the famine that you dread shall follow close after you into Egypt—and there you shall die.

And Jeremiah listened and laughed—truly, he roared with laughter—and he climbed up the tree and waved his hands and shouted: Egypt! Babylon! Egypt! Babylon! And Baruch went up to him and hugged his feet and calmed him down and told the assembled, Don't go to Egypt; remember what I told you. And one of the newcomers, a senior officer who introduced himself as Azariah son of Hoshaiah, told Baruch: You're lying. The Lord our God did not send you to say, Do not go to Egypt to settle there, for Baruch son of Neriah—and here he pointed mistakenly at Jeremiah, perched on a branch and hunched over like a monkey, eating an olive—is inciting against us to hand us over to the Chaldeans, that they may kill us or take us into exile in Babylon. And again Jeremiah broke into laughter and clapped his hands, and they all rose to their feet and gathered their scant belongings and the little they'd stealthily looted from the homes in the village, and they got under way, plodding up the hill on the side of the deserted hospital, and Jeremiah stood up and to Baruch's surprise joined the end of the procession, and Baruch followed him. And they all crowded into the abandoned bus number 9 that they came across parked at an angle in the bus tunnel on Mount Scopus, and they drove all night with their headlights off, heading southwest, tanking up at the deserted gas stations, and they drove in complete silence; only the sound of the engine could be heard. The next day, they arrived in Tahpanhes, which is in Egypt. Stretched out on the rear seat of the bus, Jeremiah wondered what had happened to Zedekiah and Noa and their infant—how old would he be by now?—but only for a moment, no more, and again he sank into a confused, troubled sleep. Slivers of prophecy rose within him on the way to Egypt, about all the neighboring countries, far and near—about Elam and about Edom and about Egypt and about Babylon and about Moab and about Aram and about Ammon and about Kedar and about Hazor and about the Philistines and about whomever—and in his prophecies he warned the entire world against various disasters and grave errors. He walked among the kings in his visions, and in his hand was a wineglass filled with red wine. When he offered them to drink, they refused. And he said: You'll drink this whether you like it or not; you'll drink it under duress; you'll drink, you'll drink and drink, and throw up, and fall down, and you won't get up ever again. Make ready your buckler and shield and draw near to battle, for the sword will devour those around you. Have no fear, my servant Jacob. See, waters are rising out of the north and will become an overflowing torrent. Ah, sword of the Lord, how long until you are quiet, and Chemosh will go out into exile, leave the towns and abide in the rock, you who dwell in Moab, and be like the dove that nests on the sides of the pit's mouth, for I have broken Moab like a vessel that no one wants, terror and the pit and the trap are before you O inhabitants of Moab, and the blood of man in Edom will be boiled.

Words and puns and golden phrases surged from within like fireworks. All of a sudden, his idiom and style turned brilliant and polished. If only there were someone who would listen, he'd happily detonate all these colorful concoctions for them, flaunting them shamelessly, but neither Moab nor Edom nor Baalis, King of Ammon (who waited in his palace for the return of Ishmael, son of Nethaniah, his faithful and handsome assassin), nor Aram nor Hazor could hear Jeremiah's words—neither the prophecies of wrath nor those of consolation, saying: I will bring back the captivity of the children of Ammon, for I have made Esau bare, I have uncovered his hiding places, your terror has deceived you, although you make your nest as high as the eagle, from there I will bring you down. No one heard a word of any of it.

And Jeremiah, sound asleep, was tossed from side to side there in the bus, which was driven by a young boy. Baruch sat next to him, and every so often translated into his own tongue and jotted down in his notebook what Jeremiah was muttering in his sleep, completing any incomplete sentences. When Jeremiah woke from his troubled sleep, he felt that he could almost speak coherently now, and all of a sudden he was tempted to tell someone, anyone, saying Babylon is taken, Bel is put to shame, Merodach is dismayed, for out of the north a nation has come up against her. And he beheld a clear picture in which God clasped a golden cup filled with wine. He remembered the swollen pot, but by now there was nothing he could do with such pictures and words, and he spoke a few more words to the rear window, prophesying about Babylon: And with you I smash nations, and with you I destroy kingdoms, with you I smash the horse and his rider; with you I smash the chariot and the charioteer, and with you I smash man and woman, and with you I smash the old man and the boy; and with you I smash the young man and the girl, and with you I smash the shepherd and his flock, and with you I smash the farmer and his oxen, and with you I smash governors and deputies, and I will repay Babylon and all the inhabitants of Chaldea all the wrong they have done in Zion before your eyes, and I will smash and I will smash and I will smash and I will smash and I will smash. And he remembered the old jug, and realized that the jug was still speaking. He told Baruch, Babylon is suddenly fallen and shattered. And he took the red emergency hammer and thought of smashing the jug that wasn't really there, or the pane of glass that was, but desisted— all of a sudden he felt like comforting all the passengers in the bus, the long line of wretched refugees, all sorts of former senior officers and citizens who'd become powerless. But all they heard was Jeremiah repeating the words *And I smashed*, and someone told his friend, Come on, enough already, knock it off. And he then turned to Jeremiah and said, *We're not listening to you*, get it? Two of the passengers whispered to each other briefly, and they went up to the monkey, and they stopped the bus, and they forced Jeremiah out of the bus. But before leaving the bus, he managed to stop for a moment alongside Baruch, who remained in the bus and wasn't allowed to accompany his friend. Jeremiah took out a notepad, and he told him, Read this when you have a chance, dear Baruch, and when you finish reading, tie a stone to the pad—here Jeremiah handed him a stone that was exactly the size of the pad, but heavier—and cast them into the Euphrates, saying, Thus will Babylon sink, and it will not rise again because of the disasters that I will bring upon her, and they will be—

Jeremiah wanted only to complete this last sentence, just one more word, but they shoved him out of the bus, and one of the officers going down to Egypt took the stone that Jeremiah had given to Baruch and examined it up close. They left Jeremiah in the sand in the middle of nowhere on the highway leading to North Sinai. It was possible to make out the great sea from there, which neither Jeremiah nor the other Judeans had ever seen, and he turned to the sea, his heart swelling, and understood that the sand was the sea's border, and that the sand kept the waves back. This came to him like a staggering discovery, even though it was a known fact to all, and he beheld with wonder a fleet of ships making its way south to Egypt, and he stretched his hand out as if to caress them. Then he bent down and dug a shallow hole in the sand and buried the almond from his locket in the hole and covered it back up with sand, using his foot. And he thought, The tide will flow up to here, the water will come up to here. And he shut his eyes under the desert sun and took one or two steps in the direction of the sea, thinking, I'll wash myself in the sea, and then I'll shave off this tangled beard—it'll be such a relief. A desert wind rose, sweeping everything along in its path, and Jeremiah saw a straw drifting off in midair.

IT WAS FIVE-THIRTY IN THE MORNING, and someone from behind threw the stone he'd left with Baruch at Jeremiah. It was just a joke, but the stone hit the back of Jeremiah's head, and though he tried to open his eyes to the light, it was dark now, for in one stroke he'd lost his sight. Only the new star still shone there in his eyes, except that its light was now as bright as the light of the sun. He took one step forward in the direction of the starlight, his arms flung out wide like a tightrope walker balancing himself. Baruch sat on the bus and stared down at the notepad Jeremiah had left him; he couldn't bring himself to look out the window, so he buried his eyes in the pad and jotted down from memory on the empty pages at the end of the pad what he'd just heard from his friend. And someone outside picked up a second stone, and another, and after they'd finished pelting Jeremiah with stones, they strode down to the sea to take a piss before returning to the bus. Baruch glanced at them as they boarded and sat or stood in the aisle. At first he didn't understand what was going on, and then he realized, and he rushed out and ran and stumbled in the sand toward the heap of stones, some small and others large, from which a pair of bare feet poked out, their ankles exposed. And he circled around in distress, but he didn't remove the stones; all he did was stand there and wail.

He collapsed in a heap in the sand, but two short, sharp honks came from the bus, and he got up and shook the sand off his face and went back, his feet sinking in the sand. But the driver, following the order of one of the officers, wouldn't let the black bastard back aboard, and they all laughed at this. And Baruch looked up at the driver and knocked at the bus's door as it started on its way. The officer, who'd had his fun, now ordered the driver to stop and open the door after all, and Baruch boarded and found a seat, and they went down to Egypt. And after some time, they stopped by the Nile, and Baruch trudged in the mud with the other passengers along the banks of the river, and they stooped over the water to drink, and Baruch, too, stooped. He left the notepad on a stone and drank, and then he plunged into the river and was gone.

A Note About the Author

Dror Burstein was born in 1970 in Netanya, Israel. After practicing as a lawyer for a mere twenty-four hours, he devoted himself to literature, producing fourteen books of poetry and prose since 1999, including the novels *Kin* and *Netanya*. Among numerous other honors, he received the Bernstein Prize for his debut novel, *Avner Brenner*, and the Isaac Leib and Rachel Goldberg Prize for his 2014 novel, *Sun's Sister*. He lives in Tel Aviv.

A Note About the Translator

Gabriel Levin is the author of six collections of poetry, numerous translations, and a collection of essays, *The Dune's Twisted Edge: Journeys in the Levant*. He lives in Jerusalem.